ACROSS THE GREAT DIVIDE

Book 1 The Clouds of War

Michael L. Ross

ELM HILL

A Division of
HarperCollins Christian Publishing

www.elmhillbooks.com

Across The Great Divide

Book 1 The Clouds of War

Published in Nashville, Tennessee, by Elm Hill, an imprint of Thomas Nelson. Elm Hill and Thomas Nelson are registered trademarks of HarperCollins Christian Publishing, Inc.

Elm Hill titles may be purchased in bulk for educational, business, fund-raising, or sales promotional use. For information, please e-mail SpecialMarkets@ ThomasNelson.com.

Library of Congress Cataloging-in-Publication Data

Library Congress Control Number: 2018958218

ISBN 978-1-595559340 (Paperback)
ISBN 978-1-595559272 (Hardbound)
ISBN 978-1-595559500 (eBook)

DEDICATION

For my wife, Marti, without whose support this would never have happened.

CONTENTS

BOOK 1

THE CLOUDS OF WAR

"I worked night and day for twelve years to prevent the war, but I could not. The North was mad and blind, would not let us govern ourselves, and so the war came."

—JEFFERSON DAVIS

WILL ON HIS OWN

April 1859

Lexington, Kentucky

Trouble seemed to follow Will Crump. Today, his particular trouble was weeding, planting, and a straggling three-year-old sister. Any other day, he might have paused to take in the beautiful countryside. Will trudged toward the north field of his father's eighty-acre farm, determinedly dragging a burlap feed sack full of corn and carrying a hoe. A slingshot hung out of his back pocket, in hopes that he might see a rabbit.

His sister Lydia stumbled along behind, carrying her corncob doll and singing to it. Will fumed. He had no time to look after Lydia; she should be his older sisters' problem. He felt the weight of his responsibility as much as the heavy sack. Without his father, the work would take much longer. Without a plow animal, finishing the plowing was impossible.

The heat would soon blister the ground and his arms. The swimming hole beckoned and he longed to jump into its wet coolness. Will had no eyes for the kaleidoscope of wildflowers or the emerald grass. He had no ears for the symphony of birds in the Kentucky spring around him. He itched to get his work done before the coming heat, and glared back at Lydia.

"C'mon, Lydia, hurry up—don't fall behind! I got lotsa weedin' and plantin' to do before lunchtime."

Lydia scowled, flipped a strand of long brown hair back into place, and halfheartedly tried to move faster.

Will straightened his back and attempted to lift the seed bag. Muscles bulging, he strained with all the force his five-foot-five, fifteen-year-old frame could muster. Sweat ran down his forehead. It was no use. The bag fell to the ground with a thud. Will shook his head, picking up the hoe, and resumed dragging the bag. Lydia stopped, watching her big brother with her thumb firmly implanted in her mouth. As Will dragged the bag onward, Lydia solemnly resumed trudging along after him, her eyes blue and round, her bare feet, dusty from the road, peeking out from under her yellow calico dress. Their mother had entrusted her to his care for the morning.

A week ago, the family mule died. Will's father left, searching for a new plow animal that the family could afford or acquire by trading work. Will's oldest sister, Julia, was visiting their aunt's family in Nicholasville for a few days. Albinia, two years older than Will, often went to see her friend Lucy at the Clay plantation. The extra chores his mother took on with his sisters gone meant that she had little time to make sure Lydia stayed out of trouble.

They crossed a small bridge over a gurgling creek lined with bulrushes and cattails and soon arrived at the field.

"What's in the bag, Will?"

"Corn kernels for plantin', so's we got corn to eat come next fall and winter. Now sit down here in the corner of the field, play with your doll, and stay put. Don't go wandrin' off or bother me with fool questions. I'll be looking for you each time I come down the row," Will said irritably.

"All right. Me an' Sally will play here."

"Good girl. Now mind—stay put!"

With that brotherly admonition, Will set off with his hoe, first attacking any weeds that had gotten the jump on his planting. His father had told him before leaving, "I'm countin' on you to get that north field ready and planted while I'm gone. Ol' White Tail and me got it mostly plowed 'fore he died on us, so that shouldn't be a problem for you. But if we don't get it planted, next winter could be mighty lean for us. You be the man of the house, I know you can do it."

Will bent to the work, concentrating on every green sprig he could detect growing in the rows of brown earth. At the end of each row, he looked to find Lydia happily instructing her doll on the fine art of giving a tea party and giggling merrily. As the sun moved higher overhead, he became steadily hotter. He focused even more on his work until a shadow loomed overhead—a hawk, circling lazily in hope of any rodent the hoe might scare out. Will looked up at the hawk, suddenly realizing that he had not checked on Lydia lately. Had it been two rows or three? A quick glance confirmed that her corner was empty.

Just then, a piercing scream came from the direction of the creek. "Willeee!"

Will dropped the weed in his hand and sprinted toward where he thought the scream came from, carrying the hoe with him.

"Willeee!" Lydia screamed again. "It's a snake!"

He arrived just in time to see his sister at the creek's edge, a large water moccasin slithering through the water toward her. He thought of the slingshot, but the risk of a miss was too great. Could he get there in time? Will darted forward.

"Lydia, it will be all right. Don't move." He tried to sound calm and steady, which was difficult given he was out of breath. His own fear made him feel shaky. He quickly reached forward with the hoe and struck at the snake's triangular head. The snake dodged, struck the hoe with its fangs. Will tried again and missed. When the snake struck at the hoe a second time, Will took the opportunity to flip it several feet away and grabbed Lydia, running back to the field. He almost dumped her on the ground, nearly collapsing and out of breath. She began to cry, and Will rolled over. He hugged her close.

"There now, Lyddie girl, don't cry. You're all right. You're all right." He crooned to her softly, and soon the sobs ceased as she rested her head on his shoulder.

"C'mon now, let's go back to the house and get ya cleaned up. Maybe Mama has some lunch for us by now. What d'ya say to that?"

She looked up adoringly and nodded, seeming to forget her terror of a few minutes before.

"Where's Sally?" she asked.

"Ya prob'ly dropped her back there, near the creek," Will sighed.

Cautiously retracing the path to the water's edge, he found the beloved corncob doll and dusted her off, handing her back to Lydia. Hand in hand they walked slowly back to the rough wooden cabin they called home, passing the long split-rail fence along the dirt road marked with ruts from the heavy farm wagon. The road kept going on, but a small path turned up behind a grove of poplar trees. A clearing opened into a barnyard with chickens, ducks, and geese busily pecking the ground.

The cabin was a log-and-mud-chinked affair built by Will's father using trees cleared off their homestead. Its center stone chimney divided the two rooms, one where the family slept and the other the kitchen and living area. The only hint of luxury was one glass window that let sunshine into the kitchen, a product of one year's bountiful harvest. Off to the side was a small barn, providing shelter and safety for their meager livestock, and built into the hillside was an icehouse, where blocks of ice cut from the river could be stored packed in sawdust or hay. In front of the cabin, seemingly asleep, lay Rustler, their brown-and-white hound dog. He opened his eyes, tail flopping slowly at Will and Lydia's approach, and went back to sleep.

As they arrived at the cabin, Sara Crump brushed back chestnut hair that escaped the bun she wore pinned in back. She was just finishing laying the table for lunch.

"Well, there you two are—and probably hungry," she said. Glancing up and seeing Lydia's tear-stained face, she rushed over and scooped her up in her arms, her brown eyes full of concern. "What happened?" she asked Will.

"There was a big snake, an' I was scared, an' Willy saved me," said Lydia.

"Wasn't anything special," Will said. "She sorta wandered off, and I brought her back."

Setting Lydia down, Sara sighed. "Sounds like more than that. But thank the Lord you're safe. So what did you learn about moving away from where Willy told you to be?"

Hanging her head a little, Lydia mumbled, "It's not safe, and I might get in trouble."

"That's a good girl." Sara smiled. "Now get some cold water from the pump for Willy."

When Lydia was out of earshot, Sara asked, "What sort of snake was it?"

Will was embarrassed. "Water moccasin."

"That was a brave thing you did saving her like that, but next time make sure you keep a closer eye on her. Sometimes a little more care saves the need for heroics later."

"Yes, ma'am."

Sara smiled at him, softening. "I appreciate all that you're doing while your pa is gone. You're almost a man, and I hate to ask you to take care of Lyddie too. But I have to keep the fire going and be in and out of the cabin all the time—I just can't keep dragging her around. You can at least put her in one place and just keep an eye on her. But you've got to check on her often. Three-year-olds can disappear in a flash. I think you learned that today."

"Yes, ma'am," Will said with a guilty sigh. "She just seemed to be doin' so well, and I got working on plantin' and the weeds and plumb that I forgot to check after a while." He felt like slumping on the log bench by the table but instead busied himself with helping his mother lay out food, slicing the ham with sure, strong strokes.

Lydia came back, dragging her doll behind her and carrying a carved wooden cup filled with cold water, which she extended to her brother.

"Here, Willy."

He looked down and smiled at her, accepting the cup and gulping the water gratefully. Lydia walked over to the miniature rocking chair her father had made for her. She carefully seated her doll in it, wiping dirt off its face, and then began lecturing her sternly, "Now, Sally, you've got to keep more clean. You can't just get dirty an' messy; you got to act like a lady." Will suppressed a chuckle, listening to his sister echo the admonitions her mother had given her so many times.

When they sat, Sara nodded at him as they held hands around the rough table and he offered grace. The simple meal of ham, applesauce, and peas from the garden was over quickly. Will was about to leave for the field again when their dog began barking and baying, wagging his tail at the same time. Will hurried out into the yard, wondering if he should grab the Springfield musket that hung on pegs over the door. Hesitating, he decided against it.

He looked to the edge of the clearing and saw two yoked oxen coming down the road, driven by his father. Curiously, he also carried a shiny rifle slung over his shoulders. Will wondered how he'd managed to buy one. Rustler ran to greet him, startling the oxen, who eyed him warily.

"Hello, Son!" Robert called out cheerily.

"Hello, sir." Part of Will wanted to run out and hug his father as he used to when he was younger, but he stayed put, wanting to retain his "man of the house" image. Will watched as Robert took off his hat, freeing curly brown hair, and wiped the sweat from his forehead before he unyoked the oxen and led each one to a stall in the barn. As soon as he finished, Lydia, who had been impatiently hopping from one foot to the other, ran to her father, having no ladylike scruples whatsoever. Robert grinned and scooped her up in his arms, holding her high over his head. She squealed with laughter and then hugged him tightly when he brought her down. Extricating himself, he walked to where Sara waited in the doorway and gave her a quick hug, then made his way to the water trough and pumped a drink into the ladle that hung there, drinking long and deeply. He pumped some more to pour down his back.

Will was puzzled, since his father had planned to get another mule yet had come home with oxen. He would not have dreamed of mentioning it to him, however, and simply smiled, glad to have him home.

Robert entered the cabin and sat at the table. He glanced with affection at Sara as she got out bread, cheese, and a few vegetables from the garden. Will left and came back with the ladle full of water for his father and sat across from him. Lydia excitedly filled Robert in on the morning's events, with her father reacting in exaggerated surprise, giving Will a knowing look. Will felt proud at being treated like an adult.

"What news from the girls?" asked Robert. "I know Julia was anxious about yer sister's health. Any idea when she'll be comin' home?"

"No word from Julia yet," said Sara. "I spect she's goin' about with her cousins and makin' eyes at some of the boys. And Albinia is still over at the Clays' place visin' Lucy. I expect Albinia back within a few days. Prob'ly one of James Clay's boys will see her home."

"Hmm, with all the work around here, you'd think the girls would stick closer to home. It ain't like we got slaves and maids. Still, I s'pose if'n they are always here, they'll never find themselves a beau." Robert grinned. He didn't seem to really be upset about the girls being away.

"Well, I had me a couple of adventures." He smiled. "Came upon a fella on the Louisville road—a tree fell and trapped his legs underneath when he was choppin' it. I helped him get free and to the doctor in town— he was an elderly gent, and so grateful he wanted to bless me for helpin'. I couldn't refuse without offending him, so I used what he gave to help get the oxen and a new rifle."

"Robert, what a blessing!" said Sara. "Though I understand you didn't want to take charity, it will make such a difference for our family."

"Yep, I figger with this pair I might be able to farm some more land. We'll have to see how it works out, but the Lord always provides."

"You said 'a couple of adventures'—anything else?"

"Yeah, the second wasn't nearly so happy. I camped one night not far off the road. Just after I put my fire out and was about to go to sleep, I heard an awful commotion in the brush. I looked over to see, wonderin' if someone was trying to steal the new oxen. I heard hounds baying, and a group of men with torches come along. Seems they was huntin' a slave, run off from the Jameson place. I 'spect the noise I heard first was the slave himself, so they weren't far behind. They asked if I'd seen him, and I could truthfully say I hadn't."

"What if you had?" Will wanted to know.

"I don't rightly know, Son. You know I don't hold with slavery but it's legal, and the Bible tells us to obey the governin' authorities. I'm just glad I didn't have to make the choice—tellin' the truth is always the best way, but there's times when it seems like it's not."

Robert slapped his thigh and rose. "Time to go put these oxen to use. Will, you can come along, start learnin' to drive'em. I imagine your ma can manage Lyddie for a while. With two of us, we might get another whole field plowed before dark."

* * *

Julia stood in front of a mirror over a pine dresser brushing tangles out of her hair, the sunlight coming through the high bedroom window in her uncle's cabin catching the copper highlights. If not for the tangled mass, she might have appeared at least pretty. Her face wrinkled in concentration and disgust as she tugged with comb and brush, trying to tame her unruly mane. Usually, she gave up and wound the curls into a tight bun at the back of her head. Tonight, however, she wanted to look special, more grown-up, for her uncle's barn dance. Her cousins, Rose and Violet, had already spent hours primping and gossiping about which farm boys might come. Julia, being twenty-one, wanted to appear more mature than the younger girls. Nonetheless, she felt a flurry of barn swallows in her stomach. She only visited here a few times a year, when her mother visited her sister or a family member had time to travel with her. She knew that behind her back, her cousins talked about her short, slightly plump frame and despaired of her ever getting married. Julia herself sometimes worried that she would end up a spinster.

Finally victorious over the tangle, she began the arduous process of working with a curling iron she had heated on the stove. She made columns of curls around her head as she'd seen in a magazine, each one held in place by artfully hidden pins. She did not want to risk one coming loose as she whirled dancing the evening away.

An hour later, she called Rose to help her lace her stays and corset so she could actually dress for the evening. Rose, a willowy sixteen-year-old blond with a rather plain face, smirked.

"I'll tighten you up—but you tryin' to be awful fancy with them hair fixin's!" She dutifully yanked on the strings to compress her cousin's waist to socially acceptable limits.

Julia grimaced. "Not that tight, Rose! My ribs'll pop out!"

Rose sniffed. "If you want to look like a prize bull instead of a belle, it's nuthin to me! But most of them boys ain't gonna be lookin' at your hair, I can tell ya! Wish't we could trade some—you got paddin' where I could use it, and you could use to lose some of yours."

Julia sighed. "I have to admit you're right on that. Okay, go ahead. Pull harder. I'll breathe in."

Rose scolded, "And don't go eatin' like a farmhand, neither. Me'n Violet's gonna stash some of the food, 'specially the cakes, to eat later after the company's gone. You can join us if you want. But fellas like to think that the women eat like birds, even if you'd faint from starvation if it were true."

Violet appeared, her thick black hair and stouter frame a contrast to her sister. She joined the tugging and pushing. "Whatcha tryin' to do, be the talk of the ball?" she snickered. "Ain't nothing but farm boys comin', and most of 'em just as interested in your cookin' as your figure, and certainly not your hair."

Julia frowned. "Can't we just relax and have fun without worryin' about which boy'll pick who? I don't know most of 'em anyway, and I'm not interested in getting hitched to some plowboy, either. My mama did that, and look where she is! I want a man with prospects, one who's going somewhere in the world."

Violet looked at her slyly. "Well, I did hear a rumor that one of the Todd boys from Lexington might be out this way. Supposedly he's checking on some property and might come tonight. You know his daddy is a banker, Robert Todd. Word has it they're pretty rich. 'Course, it could be just talk," she said. "And why he'd bother with the likes of us, that'd be a wonder."

Julia straightened and sucked in her stomach extra hard. As the three left the room, she sniffed. "Any girl can try to better herself. I certainly intend to."

* * *

As Julia entered the barn, she scanned the chairs set around the walls and a makeshift stage of hay bales at the front. She watched the three Negro slaves hired to play for the event as they tuned up. Her uncle did not own any slaves but had hired these from nearby Waveland plantation. Julia had overheard him talking about them. Some slaves had privileges to play for money or do other skilled labor when their masters did not need them. Julia again felt a tightening in her throat and stomach, nervous with anticipation.

Guests began to arrive, one or two in carriages, but most in farm wagons or on horseback. Despite her intention to appear nonchalant, Julia watched eagerly as the young men arrived. She also watched the other girls to work out who her competition might be. She did not really expect that any of the men would be of suitable station to attract her interest, but she remained hopeful. She paid sharp attention while appearing distracted by the music, tapping her toe in time to the beat. One particularly handsome stranger, dressed in a well-cut expensive suit, caught Julia's attention. He arrived in a fancy carriage with driver, footman, and groom, and was accompanied by a young woman with tawny hair and blue eyes. Her slim figure and average height were enhanced by a burgundy velvet gown with flashing sequins. She looked like a princess among the country maids assembled there. She laughed and talked animatedly with the young man, who responded in kind. Julia felt a twinge of jealousy. Listening to the gossip around her, Julia discovered that the young man was Samuel Todd, of the banker Todd family. She kept an eye on him without being too obvious. Soon there were about twenty young people and another thirty to forty elders, including her aunt and uncle, who were busy greeting the guests as they entered.

The music started again, and the young men approached potential partners. No one came to ask Julia to dance, but she pretended not to notice as she made her way to the punch table and took some for herself. Then she strolled back to her seat next to the two other girls not chosen to form squares. Julia watched as the young woman in the burgundy gown, said by some to be Sam Todd's cousin, acquitted herself beyond Julia's skill. She knew the right movements and placement, as well as some of the fancier steps other girls neglected. Julia made her observation less obvious by use of the fan she had borrowed from her aunt.

As the music ended and couples took a short break, Julia turned back toward the punch table. She bumped into a blond young man, dropping the fan to the floor. Flustered with her clumsiness, she lost track of the handsome Sam Todd, but found the young man she'd bumped stooping to pick up the fan for her.

"Hallo, ma'am. Allow me."

The young man handed her the fan. He towered over her, at least six feet tall and built like an oak tree.

"I am Hiram Johannsen."

Julia saw country bumpkin written all over him but had no wish to be rude.

"Thank you, Mr. Johannsen. I'm Julia Crump, here visiting my aunt and uncle."

She curtsied and made to turn away.

Hiram quickly stammered, "M-m-may I have the next dance with you, Miss Crump, if you are not otherwise engaged?"

His Swedish accent made her name sound more like "Crimp" than "Crump." Julia anxiously scanned the crowd, hoping one of her cousins might be nearby, but saw no polite way of escape.

"Of course, Mr. Johannsen."

He offered his arm as the musicians struck up a Virginia reel. Relieved, she took her place opposite him, and the dance began. With a reel she could be part of the dance, but there would be no occasion for close contact or much conversation. Hiram proved a surprisingly capable and nimble dancer despite his size. It was somewhat comical as they made the bridge for the other couples to pass through at the end, as Hiram had to stoop and the other couples had to duck to accommodate Julia's short stature. She felt awkward and embarrassed, although Hiram smiled at her constantly and seemed taken with her. Julia had to admit he was handsome in an oxish sort of way, but she racked her brain for a way to escape. When the dance ended, she quickly thanked him and excused herself by telling him she must go and see if her aunt needed any help with her guests.

When she found her aunt, Julia encouraged her to sit and rest. Julia refilled the punch bowl while listening to the conversation going on around the table. The girl in the burgundy velvet was holding forth in a most unladylike way while her companion Sam Todd smiled indulgently.

"Slave owners are just stealing from the Lord and from the blacks they own," she intoned indignantly. "England has shown that slavery can be successfully abolished. Why, the Bible itself says that if a slave can be free, he should be, and that in Christ there is no slave or free, that all men are brothers."

Sam tugged at her elbow, attempting to steer her away from the group of collected listeners.

"You must excuse my cousin, gentlemen. Louise reads more than is good for her. Come, Louise, let's encourage the darkies to play, and we can dance to more of their excellent music," he encouraged.

Louise wasn't moving. One of the gentlemen at the table, wearing a rough-cut suit, said sneeringly, "And does not your own family own slaves, Miss Todd?"

"Indeed, Mr. Jameson, they do, and more's the shame of it."

"And who will tend the fields to grow the cotton and crops that keep you in silks and fine dresses if the slaves don't do it? Free the slaves and England would not have to use troops to win back the colonies, they'd win them back through economic collapse. The British would simply buy their raw goods from elsewhere in the empire, as our rising prices made us a laughing stock, if we could even provide them at all."

"Mark my words, Mr. Jameson," Louise replied. "Freedom is coming, and all across the South planters and others who fail to anticipate it shall suffer." With that, Sam was finally able to prevail upon her to join the set forming for the next dance.

Julia quietly moved away, pondering what she'd heard. Would freeing slaves really be so bad? Then again, what would they do? The slaves here did not seem particularly wretched. Jolted from her reverie by another of the farmers, she accepted his offer to dance and joined in a lively polka, contriving to steer them next to where Sam and Louise were dancing. Her partner, a clumsy yokel with three left feet, kept stepping on her toes and apologizing. As she dodged one of his careless stomps, she bumped into Sam Todd behind her. Julia lost her balance, twisted an ankle, and fell in a heap of petticoats. Her legs went shooting out, tripping Sam, and causing him to pull his partner down as well, while the yokel stood staring at them and Louise glared at her. Sam ignored Julia and solicitously helped his partner up, apologizing profusely. Julia flamed with embarrassment. The music had stopped, and everyone was looking at them. She wanted to sink through a crack in the floor. She would not impress Sam Todd now. She wanted to apologize to him, but found Hiram Johannsen offering her a hand up. By the time she was on her feet, Sam was nowhere to be seen.

"Thank you, Mr. Johannsen. Again, I am in your debt," she said, seeking where Sam might have gone.

"Not at all, Miss Crump. May I get you some punch? Or perhaps you'd like to get some air?" he said, offering his arm.

"Well, ah, Mr. Johannsen," she said, looking around somewhat frantically. Sam wasn't there. Perhaps he'd left after the embarrassment of their fall? Making up her mind, Julia brightened. "Yes, perhaps some air would be just thing," she said, noticing some people still staring at her.

As they walked to the barnyard, she saw that her cousins were pointing and laughing at her.

"Are you quite all right, Miss Crump?" asked Hiram, observing her slight wince as she walked.

"Oh yes, it's nothing. Just twisted my ankle. Thank you for rescuing me. Perhaps ... I should go to the house and lie down for a while."

"Let me help you."

Gratefully, she leaned on his arm for support.

"I hope we'll see one another again," he said at the door.

Later, when everyone had gone home, Violet came into Julia's room, and said "Looks like you found your plowboy after all."

"It was just a dance," Julia said defensively. To herself, she thought, *And he was handsome. On reflection, his courtly manners made him seem... less like a yokel.*

* * *

Will rose early and did his usual chores. Now that his father was home, he would be able to go back to school. After Sara packed him a lunch in a pail, he began the five-mile walk in good spirits. He enjoyed learning, and if he got into trouble with his parents, it was usually because he was poring over a borrowed book rather than attending to additional farmwork. He was well through most of the fifth reader and ahead in trigonometry as well, so if he missed a day or two of school, it was not a real problem. Today he strode merrily, enjoying a cool break in the weather and lifting his face to the clear blue sky as he took in the sound of the songbirds. He went the long way, using the bridge to cross the creek. Other times he waded right through it, arriving at school still dripping.

Arriving half an hour before the bell, he found most of the boys involved in a game of "Annie Over," tossing the ball and laughing. It would have been fun to join in, but, feeling his new, more grown-up status, Will decided against it.

Scanning the field, he saw two of the older boys, Jesse Davis and Ben Drake, were tossing a girl's violet bonnet back and forth between them. They were teasing the prettiest girl in the school, Jenny Morton.

Angrily, she shouted, "Give it back!" and leaped in such a manner as to expose her pantalets in an attempt to catch it. Jesse was a tall boy who'd gotten his growth early, nearing six feet, with curly black hair and mischief in his blue eyes. Jenny was fourteen, her blonde curls dancing in the air as she jumped fruitlessly after the bonnet.

"What'll you give for it, Jenny?" Ben teased. At sixteen, he was a solidly built farm boy, some inches shorter than Jesse and as frisky as a colt just turned loose for spring. His brown hair was shorter than most boys— to stay cool, he said. Muscles rippled in his arms as he tossed the bonnet back to Jesse.

Jenny's face was scarlet, and her blue eyes snapped like snake whips. She made a fist. "I'll give you a black eye if you don't give it back!" This just made the boys laugh. Jesse almost dropped the bonnet. The boys were so preoccupied with their quarry they didn't notice Will walk over.

"Give it back to her," Will said calmly. "No need to pick on a girl."

"Who asked you?" Jesse retorted. "Hey, maybe he wants to wear it! Latest fashion for bookworms, right Ben?" He tossed the bonnet back to Ben, high over Jenny's head and out of her reach.

Ben laughed and turned to toss the bonnet back to Jesse, but before it left his grasp, Will's head hit his gut at full charge. Ben dropped the bonnet and doubled over, gasping. Will snatched it up and returned it to Jenny, who fled toward the schoolhouse with a quick, grateful look back at him. Will faced his adversaries. He took a fighting stance, waiting for Jesse to attack, but Jesse walked over to Ben and gave him a hand up.

"Whadja go and do that for? We was just funnin' her." Ben was still bent over, trying to regain his breath.

"I don't think she thought it was fun. Picking on someone weaker is just mean."

"Aww, you're just sweet on her, that's what! You'd better watch your back!" Jesse fumed as he helped Ben toward the school.

In the schoolhouse, Will took his seat with the older boys. The room held two rows of wrought-iron desks with polished wooden tops. Girls sat on the right, boys on the left, with the youngest pupils at the front, owing to their tendency to cause mischief. The teacher's podium and bookcase sat on a raised wooden platform. A chalkboard, a picture of President Buchanan, and the American flag were at the very front of the classroom. A separate podium had a large Bible opened on it.

Mr. Powell called the boisterous students to order, asking the first reader group to come forward and recite. Though the schoolmaster was of average height, he towered over the little ones, who seemed in awe of him. His eyes moved constantly around the classroom, peering over the spectacles that gave him a owlish look. The young scholars took turns reading aloud the lesson and reciting their Bible memory verse for the week, with Mr. Powell occasionally coaxing and correcting.

Will attempted to open his desk lid to get his slate and copybook to work on his trigonometry. He tugged but found the desk tied shut with thin wire. He jerked, causing a banging noise and a disapproving glare from Mr. Powell. As soon as Will untwisted the wire and got the desk open, he felt a wet splat, as something hit the back of his head and dripped down his neck. Pulling a cloth handkerchief from his pocket, he wiped the back of his head and found a used plug of chewing tobacco stuck to his hair. As he quickly glanced backward, Ben smirked at him. Momentarily his temper flared, but he faced forward again. Jenny glanced over her shoulder and smiled at him empathetically. Will wondered if Ben and Jessie would be waiting for him after school along the road home. It nagged at his thoughts, but he tried to push it aside, concentrating instead on the math problems at hand.

He finished in an hour, and when called to recite, demonstrated mastery of the answers and explanations. Returning to his seat, he found no further evidence of devilment from the boys. He quickly lost himself in the description of the rebellion at the Massachusetts state prison in his reader. He wondered at the statement that death was better than the flogging and imprisonment suffered by the inmates, thinking how he might respond to such treatment. He thought perhaps it might be best to endure the treatment rather than risk death.

The remainder of the school day seemed to pass swiftly. Will barely noticed his surroundings, though occasionally he noted Jenny looking back at him when Mr. Powell was occupied helping another student. Her glances gave him a warm feeling in the pit of his stomach.

At four o'clock, Mr. Powell said the final prayer of the day and dismissed everyone. Will hung back, reading, until he was the last student left in the classroom. Apprehensively, he gathered his books and left the school building, unsure what might be waiting outside. As he emerged into the sunshine, he noticed Jenny off to the right side, apparently waiting for him.

"Will?" she called to him. "I wanted to wait for you and thank you properly for what you did today. I'm sorry those mean boys caused trouble for you. Would you mind walking home with me? I know it's a little out of your way, but if Ben and Jessie are waiting for you, they won't expect you to go this way. And, well, if they're waiting for *me*, I'd rather have you with me. Please?" Her blue eyes and dimples smiled at him. Will felt an unaccustomed flutter low in his belly.

"Sure, Jenny, if you want."

WILL'S GUN

Late April, 1859

Next Saturday, in the early morning light, Will drove to Lexington for supplies. Arriving at the dry goods store he presented his list to Mr. Hobson, the owner, who peered at it from behind his round-owl spectacles. He wore a clerk's visor over his receding hairline and a white pinstriped apron over a dark vest and white shirt. His rotund frame bent forward, and he smiled at Will.

"Good to see you, Will. Reckon it'll take time to get this order together. Why don't you park your rig over by the livery stable and walk around? Come back in, say, half an hour."

"Thank you, sir."

"Don't suppose you'd be interested in any of that penny candy, on the house like, you being so grown up and all?" Hobson grinned at him.

Will grinned back. "Well, sir, seeing as you're so kind to offer, guess it'd be rude to turn it down."

He drove the wagon over to the livery stable, parked, then wandered down the street. As he was passing the First Presbyterian Church, he stopped before the notice board in front. The bold lettering on the front cover of the group of pamphlets pinned there caught his eye: "Hints on Slavery." Glancing through one of them, Will saw the words "To emancipate the whole slave population gradually has been the uniform plan...." He remembered hearing and seeing other work from the minister that proclaimed slavery against the law of God. Will stuffed the pamphlet in his pocket to read later. He was turning to go when he bumped into a tall, lanky boy with curly black hair carelessly emerging in all directions from under his cap.

"Sorry, didn't see you there," said Will.

"S' okay. My pa, he can write something fierce, can't he?"

"You the parson's son? I'm Will Crump."

"Yep, that's my pa. I'm Joe Breckinridge. Good to meetcha. I got an older brother named Will."

"Haven't seen you at school."

"Oh, my pa, he's got his own ideas on education. He's got me goin' up to the university. He hopes I'll be a preacher, too, someday, but I'm plannin' to join the army. My pa says he thinks it will come to fightin' about slavery soon enough. Says the slaves all got to go free, maybe get sent to another country. "

Just then, a slave boy of about ten years old came and tried to get Joe's attention. "Massa Joe, your pa wants you right quick."

Joe made a face, then turned said, "All right, Josiah, I'll come. You live in town, Will?"

"No, we have a little farm a ways out of town. I came in for supplies."

"Well, come by the parsonage next time you're in town. We're new here, and I don't know too many of the fellas yet."

* * *

When Will returned from town loaded with the supplies he bought at the general store, his father had just finished feeding the stock. They unloaded the wagon together, with Will giving news of friends in town, including reports of the new minister for the First Presbyterian Church, Robert Breckinridge.

"Pa, the minister is publishing pamphlets saying it's against the law of God to hold slaves—that God will punish the South for it. Yet he seems to own slaves himself."

"That is a wonder. I would think honor and honesty would demand that he free his slaves. Slavery is wrong—I think a man ought to do his own work, and when he has too much land to farm himself and he can't afford to hire help, he has too much. They're already shootin' each other in Kansas over slaves. A man only needs enough to support his family. But I also don't hold with telling others how to live—that's between them and God. Especially some bunch of Pennsylvania lawyers and merchants that never tried to raise a crop, like President Buchanan. No man should be deprived of property by force."

Will thought this over. "But what about those born to slavery who never had a chance?"

Robert rested the feedbags he was lifting on the wagon gate and looked directly at his son. "S'pose you work hard, sell fifty bushels of corn, and then take the money and buy ten calves. Those calves grow up and have two calves each. Now suppose someone comes along and says your calves can't have more calves, and they will free all of your calves to roam if they do. Is that fair?"

Will shook his head. "Of course not!"

Robert hefted the bags, putting them in the feed closet in the barn. "No one's been allowed to bring in slaves from out of the country for nearly forty years. The slaves that are here are descendants of those brought here decades ago. There is no way to get new slaves, new workers, other than through the children of the slaves already here. So what right does some Northerner have to come and take them away from the people who bought their ancestors fair and square? Unless the Northerners want to suspend the Bill of Rights! That's why that law a few years back, the Fugitive Slave Act, was passed—to preserve the rights of Southern slave owners. Joseph in the Bible was a slave, and God blessed Egypt because of it. They weren't punished or cursed. But it ain't worth fightin' over 'less someone's threatening your home."

"I guess you're right about that, Pa," Will said slowly. "And it doesn't make much sense—a slave owner writing pamphlets against slavery."

They finished unloading the last items from the wagon.

"Come on in the house, Son. Got something to talk to you on." Robert led the way into the cabin, waiting and closing the door behind Will as he entered.

Robert reached into the corner behind the door and drew out the old Springfield musket; in its former place now hung the new Enfield.

"I been thinkin', you doing a man's work around here, 'bout time you had your own gun. Think you could put this one to good use?" He smiled.

Will tried to look dignified when he wanted to jump up and down. He took the gun from his father and, looking down at it, could not contain the huge grin that spread across his face. "For keeps, Pa? You bet I could! I'll be real safe with it, and I'll bring home a deer!"

* * *

The next day, dawn crept sleepily over the horizon, the sun slowly rolling back the clouds like covers on a bed. The morning warmth began to burn them away. Will saw the pink clouds and tendrils of light and paused a moment to drink in their beauty, before saying a silent prayer and then hurrying back to get stock fed and morning chores done—woodbox full, water carried, and all ready for the day ahead. He wanted to get out hunting before full light, before the deer retreated to their beds in the forest glens for the heat of the day. Will had been shooting the old Springfield 1812 family musket since he was nine years old, but even though he'd shot it many times with his father, he wanted to prove himself.

He was very proud of having his own gun. He determined to show his father that he was worthy of his trust by bringing home the family dinner. Will's sleepiness gave way to tense excitement. A slight breeze rustled the branches of the ash and beech trees, making the sun dapple and dance on the forest floor. Across the road to Versailles was a cleared field where deer occasionally ventured for whatever greenery the farmer may have planted. Will was hoping to find one bold enough to allow a clear shot. He jumped when a red squirrel scurried across the path just to the left, but he steadied himself and remained concealed. His father had taught him that an impatient hunter goes hungry.

The morning was cool, but the flies and other bugs buzzing about made concentration difficult. Scanning ahead, he saw no deer or movement. He cautiously crept forward to a fallen tree and crouched behind it. From here, through a break in the trees, he could see patches of the Versailles road about twenty-five yards ahead, and across it, the open field. The wind was coming from slightly to his right, blowing into the forest, away from the open field. Will slithered to the edge of the forest, just staying under cover of the bushes along the road, where he had a clear field of view. He had already primed the musket with powder, and now that he was in position, he slowly rolled to his back. He waited, withdrew the ramming rod, and then shoved home the patch and bullet. He set his powder within easy reach so that he could prime the pan and be ready to fire. He kept scanning the field, waiting. Half an hour passed with nothing to show for it but annoying mosquito bites.

Then Will looked north along the road, momentarily taking his eyes off the field. A movement in a birch tree about fifty yards away caught his attention. Two eyes peered back at him from the branches—a puma! At the same moment, he heard the sound of hooves coming from the south on the hard roadway. A rider wearing a black felt hat and a long black cape approached and passed. The cape fluttered and bounced in the wind as the bay horse moved along at a fast trot. Will saw the puma move, tensing as though to spring. No longer worried about concealment, he grabbed his powder, stood, primed the pan, aimed, and fired, all in the space of a few seconds. The puma dropped out of the tree, mid-snarl, at the feet of the astonished rider's horse, which reared and whirled madly, as the rider struggled to regain his seat and his control. He pointed the horse away from the puma, back toward Will, and managed a controlled lope, stopping the trembling bay a few feet away.

"Nice shootin', Son!" said the black-bearded stranger. "Guess that'll teach me to be in such a hurry I don't see the surroundings. What's your name, boy?"

"Will Crump, sir."

"I'm John Morgan," the rider said, extending a hand, which Will shook. "I do believe I owe you a debt, sir. When you are able, come around to my house in Lexington. It's across the street from my mother's, Henrietta Morgan—ask anyone, it is well known. Then I can thank you properly. At the moment I'm pressed for time, so I'll bid you good morning and wish you success on your hunt." He flashed a smile, tipped his hat to Will, and spurred off in the direction of Louisville.

Will did not know what to make of the invitation but decided he would tell his father and follow up on it if possible. He went back to stalking deer and, within an hour, found a small buck that succumbed to another crack from the musket, a head shot. He skinned the puma, pulled the carcass into the woods, and butchered the deer. Then he made a travois to transport his catches. By the time he dragged the plunder home, the sun was well overhead. He would be late for school today, but he did not suppose his parents would mind too much, given his gains of the morning.

ASHLAND

Late April, 1859

A few miles away, at Ashland, the Clay plantation, Albinia and Lucy faced each other across the breakfast table. The paneled walls, long shining table, and white marble fireplace were a stark contrast to the rude cabin of the Crumps. Albinia enjoyed her visits here, which provided a window into a world of the aristocracy that she longed to be part of but could only glimpse from the outside. Lucy sat, propped by pillows, in her new cane-backed chair with wheels. She was often in pain, due to a spinal injury as an infant, and unable to walk well. She enjoyed Albinia's friendship, for she had few visitors despite having a cheerful and agreeable disposition.

The contrast in their social station was obvious from their dresses. Albinia wore a sky-blue taffeta she had made herself with castoff materials, in the Levite style of some fifty years past, with a white lace collar. Albinia was scarcely over five feet tall, with a slim figure, but she looked taller next to Lucy, whose slight, sickly frame made her look as delicate as a china doll. Lucy wore the latest fashion: a beige gown—which complemented her light brown hair and cheery blue eyes—with lace-and-fur trim, a hoop skirt, voluminous petticoats, and open bell sleeves. Lucy's curls danced as she listened to Albinia and laughed, her small mouth showing perfect teeth. A slave boy hovered in the background, in case the two young women might desire anything. Lucy and Albinia took no notice of him.

"And did you just see that ridiculous hat Martha Binsley had? I mean really, it looked like a dinner platter with a bird's nest tied on top!" Albinia was saying.

"How it stayed on with her nose stuck so high in the air I'll never know," said Lucy. "I don't mean to be unkind, but she acted like some kind of princess." She began to cough, and when she recovered, she said, "Luther, fetch me some water." The slave boy moved quickly to comply. He was about five feet tall and looked about fourteen years old, dressed in homespun breeches and a rough cotton shirt two sizes too large that hung loosely on him like a flour sack. Luther poured the water, careful to keep his distance from Lucy and his eyes cast down as much as possible. Lucy took the crystal glass automatically, without any acknowledgement of where it came from.

Albinia looked at Luther, pausing while he poured. Though used to the plantation slaves, she wondered what he was thinking. She pitied him and thought, *I suppose we should just be grateful that the Lord has provided us with fine clothes and fathers that love us.*

Luther kept his eyes to the floor and retreated a discreet distance, the picture of respect and decorum. Albinia wondered what he thought of Lucy. She was kind enough, she supposed, as a slave owner. Lucy's father had purchased him from the Jameson plantation two years ago as a birthday present, along with Phoebe, who served as her lady's maid. Albinia supposed Luther might be thankful he was a house slave and not a field hand. She had heard rumors of the cruelty of Jameson and others. Surely, the boy must be grateful for the relatively benign treatment of the Clays.

Lucy commanded, "Luther, push me onto the veranda and bring Albinia a chair. Fetch my writing desk. Albinia will want to be going home in an hour or so. Tell the groom to have the chaise ready. I will write you a pass, and you will escort her home. And I'll want my sewing; tell Phoebe to fetch it."

Luther hustled to comply and, after returning, spent another hour standing on the veranda. Albinia helped Lucy learn some complicated embroidery stitches to adorn a new pillow sham. She visited Lucy regularly, both for friendship's sake and to teach her to sew. They had met when Lucy's father, James Clay, had commissioned a special dress for Lucy from the dressmaker's shop in town, where Albinia helped for wages. In the process of the fittings and alterations, the girls became fast friends, and Albinia had come to the plantation often due to Lucy's limited mobility. Lucy prevailed on her father to engage Albinia for sewing lessons. As an aristocratic young lady, Lucy should learn needlework, and Albinia delighted in an excuse to come visit.

At the end of Albinia's visit, Lucy wrote a pass for Luther, which he carefully put in his pocket. The pass would prevent someone thinking he was a runaway.

"Thanks for your company and the lesson. I so appreciate our times together. Perhaps next time you would like to try playing our pianoforte? I love music. I am not skilled like my mother, but I could teach you what I know. It is a small thing to help pay for all you teach me. Sometimes when I handle a needle, it feels like I'm all thumbs," Lucy said, laughing.

"The pleasure is all mine. I love to visit with you, and I would love to learn to play piano. I could only play when I come here, of course, but it never hurts to know such things. Coming here is restful, compared to taking care of Lydia and doing the chores at home. Will I see you at church? And then perhaps late next week we can get together again, if Ma can spare me. But I'd best get home now. Wouldn't want Luther out after dark," Albinia said, glancing at him.

She put her sewing into her reticule and took her leave through the ornate arched doorway of the dining room, past the spiral staircase, and out the front door of Ashland. A chaise was waiting, a two-wheeled light buggy meant for two people. Luther followed silently and mounted the carriage box, taking the reins from the groom. Albinia thought he enjoyed these brief times when allowed to drive, allowed to be with the horses and to see the world beyond Ashland's hundreds of acres of hemp and forest.

The six-mile drive from Ashland to the Crump homestead was a familiar respite from constantly attending Lucy's needs. Albinia knew the Clays trusted Luther, or they would not allow him to go so far from home.

She settled herself into the chaise. They were off at a slow trot, the bay horse's mane and tail flying in the wind, the reins gathered in Luther's right hand. The black chaise had a covering over their heads, the cloth adorned with the Clay family crest. The red wheels and spokes had iron tires that clattered over cobblestones as they jolted along out of Ashland and onto the country roads leading north and west toward Versailles and the Crump homestead.

"Getting hot today, isn't it, Luther?" asked Albinia, attempting to pass the time.

"Yes'm, likely gonna be unusual hot for April," Luther said, keeping his eyes on the road and skillfully maneuvering the bay around roots and potholes.

"Think the hemp will do well this year?"

"So I hear, ma'am. I only know what I hear from darkies in the fields."

Albinia remembered wondering what he was thinking earlier and now took a chance. Usually, she just sewed on the way home.

"Do you get bored working in the house?" she said, looking over at him.

Luther showed surprise, then said simply, "Not my place, ma'am. I just serve Miss Lucy and do as I'm told."

"Do you ever wonder what it would be like to be free?" asked Albinia.

She could see by the look in his eyes that he was frightened by such a question.

"No, ma'am. De good Lawd seen fit to make me a slave, an' brought me to Missy an' Massa Clay. Dey good to me, as massas go. Got no reason to question de good Lawd," he said, not looking at her.

"But why? I have often wondered why God made me a white woman, one who's poor and just waiting to be married. I wonder what it would be like to travel, to see the world, the things my brother talks about from books—like the ocean. Don't you have any dreams?"

"Miss Albinia, why talk like dat? You know well enough ain't no use for a slave to dream. I belong to Miss Lucy. Dangerous for any slave to dream beyond dat. One day, we all be free with Jesus. Dat be freedom, on the shores o'hebbin."

"Do you have family, Luther?"

His face looked pained and sad. "Yes'm. But not at Ashland. My mama Jemima, an' my sisters Olivia and Clara, over to Jameson's farm, where Massa Clay bought me from. Olivia, she just thirteen, I reckon, and Clara about ten."

"And your father?"

Anger and fear flickered over his face quickly.

"I don' know. You know ain't no real marriage for slaves. An' asking about yo pappy just askin' trouble. Now why don't I sing for ya rest the way? De horse, he likes it when I sing."

It seemed Luther was trying to divert her from her questioning. Albinia, sensing his discomfort, nodded and allowed it. His voice had already changed, and in a surprisingly melodic baritone, he sang hymns and songs about Jesus and "de debble." The horse's hooves trotted on the lane, the bump and creak of the wheels seeming to act as a percussion section, keeping time to the music.

After two hours, they drew into the dooryard of the Crump farm. The Crump men were not there, but Sara and Lydia greeted them. Luther set the brake and helped Albinia down from the chaise. Then he watered the horse at the trough and gave him a nosebag of oats, brushing him and checking his feet. He let horse and chaise stand resting in the shade of an enormous ash tree.

Turning to Sara, he said, "Missus Crump, could I get a drink from yer pump? I got my own cup." He produced a carved wooden cup.

"Of course, Luther, help yourself," said Sara. She hurried inside and emerged just as he had gotten a drink and doused his head. "And here are two johnny cakes for your trip home."

Albinia saw he was amazed by this simple kindness. "Thank you kindly, ma'am. Lawd bless you! I best be getting back. My pass is no good after dark, and Miss Lucy be worried."

Waving, Albinia, Sara, and Lydia went into the cabin as Luther mounted the chaise.

* * *

Luther set out at a fast trot. He knew he had to pace the horse, but he also had no desire to meet a patrol alone, especially as afternoon lengthened into evening.

Once or twice he stopped and pulled off the road, to let the horse rest, but also to listen for the sounds of approaching hooves that might mean a patrol. Still more, he feared the baying of hounds, signaling slave catchers chasing their prey.

More than once, he touched the precious pass in his pocket. He had no idea what it said and knew even this could be scant protection against some of the patrols, but he had to trust the fact that Lucy, a Clay, had signed it, and few would be willing to cross her father, James.

Luther guessed Lucy either did not know or did not care about these fears and dangers when she sent Luther to drive her friend home.

He turned onto Richmond Road leading to Ashland and stopped for what would be the final time. Suddenly, he heard hooves and drunken laughter coming up the road from behind. Fearing the worst, Luther urged the horse to just under a canter, not wanting to lose control or break a wheel on a rock, and dashed wildly up the road for the safety of his home plantation.

About one hundred yards from the turn onto Ashland's drive, three horsemen came out into the road in front of him. He pulled back hard on the reins to stop, so as not to run into them and injure Massa Clay's trotting horse, the chaise, or the horsemen themselves, any of which could spell his doom. He sat, gazing about wildly and gripped by terror, sweat dripping down his face and back as froth came off the horse's flanks, its sides heaving. The hoofbeats and hollering from behind came steadily closer until they surrounded him. There were four horsemen in back and three in front, all of them carrying pistols or clubs. One had a long black snake whip attached to his saddle.

Luther glanced from face to face in sheer horror, forgetting to lower his eyes. The men hooted and jeered. The one on the far left riding a common paint pony had a gray slouched hat with a feather sticking jauntily out of it, yellow teeth, and a stubbly black beard. His unkempt clothes showed him to be a poor "cracker" farmer, volunteering for slave patrol duty to show himself a man of power. His face pulled into a condescending sneer with a hungry look in his eyes that seemed to want to devour Luther. He shouted to the others, "Looky what we got here! Got us a black out for the evening, boys! Or maybe he done stole a horse and buggy, trying to run away."

The man next to him sat on a long-legged chestnut stallion that kept fidgeting and trying to get the bit between his teeth. "Naw, Frank, I think we got us a blackbird thinks he can fly away. But round here we put blackbirds in pies for supper, cook'em good." His red mustache and beard wrinkled in ugly laughter at his joke, his finer clothes denoting he must be one of the lesser planters. The gold stickpin in his red cravat glittered in the failing sunlight, the last rays glinting off the silver fittings on the pistol stuck in his waistband.

"Why, I recognize this black, boys!" said the last horseman in front. His terror mounting further, Luther recognized the voice of his old master, Jameson. "He used to be mine, but he got uppity and thought he was special. Clay offered me a good price for him, worth at least a couple of hunting dogs, so I let him go. Looks like he's still uppity, thinks he can just up and take a horse and buggy! What say we teach him some manners, boys?"

"Shore nuff, Jameson," said one of the riders from behind. "But if he's Clay's, we best find out his business first 'fore we have any fun. Wouldn't do to get the Clays down on us."

"All right, boy," said Jameson, fingering his black snake whip, "What's your business this evenin' that you're out on the roads? Running away?" Jameson laughed nastily.

Luther, remembering his role, made sure to keep his eyes down on the road. He wanted no reason for Jameson to hurt him—and hurt him he knew he would, given half an opportunity.

"Massa Jameson, I'm a good slave. You know dat. I been sent on business by Miss Lucy Clay to deliver her friend Miss Albinia home, 'bout six mile from here. I try my best to get home by dark. I gwine show you de pass Miss Lucy give me."

He carefully reached into his pocket with two fingers to give them no cause to think he might be pulling out a weapon and brought out the pass signed by Lucy. The man called Frank moved his horse over and examined it in the fading light.

"He's shore nuff got a pass—says here signed Lucy Clay. Reckon it's legitimate?"

Luther reached for the pass to retrieve it, but Frank held it just out of reach.

Jameson said, "Let me see that." Spurring his horse over, he took the pass from Frank, to Luther's alarm.

"Why, this ain't nothing! This is just a grocery list he probably stole. I don't see a pass; do you, boys?" he jeered, tearing the paper into small shreds. "I think we got us a runaway. Everybody knows a black off his plantation after sundown, regardless whose he is, gets nine lashes. Right, boys? We got to do our duty as patrollers. Get'im down!"

Three men behind dismounted, and Luther's terror knew no bounds. Wildly he looked for a way of escape, but the forest was thick on both sides of the road, and the ditch on each side was too deep to allow the chaise to pass without flipping over. Returning to Ashland without the chaise would earn him a whipping there.

"Please, Massa, please! Don't do this! Ya know it ain't dark yet, and I got a pass from Miss Lucy! The house is just up the road—go an' ask her if she done sent me out with her friend."

Rough hands pulled him down from the chaise. One of the men set the brake and tended the horse while the others tore off his shirt, tied his hands over his head, and bound him to a tree. Jameson dismounted with a wicked grin on his face, unfurled the black snake whip, and cracked it a few times in the air to test it. He broke a small branch near Luther's head and laughed.

"All right! Let's see how uppity you are now."

Jameson coiled the whip and prepared to lay on the lash, standing only about eight feet from Luther, helplessly tied to the tree. "I don't have to worry about damaging *my* property now, and the law is on my side." He struck viciously, with all his strength, drawing blood and leaving a long, angry cut across Luther's back.

Luther cried out in agony, "No, Massa, no! Please!"

Just as Jameson prepared to give a second stroke, the sound of hooves thundered on the road. A fine-looking sorrel stallion came to an abrupt halt. A burly man climbed down and, pitching the reins at the nearest man with an air of authority, bore down upon Jameson. The sun was just disappearing behind the ridge.

"And what do ye think ye're doing with Mr. Clay's property, eh?" came the Irish-accented voice, belonging to Sean Flanagan, overseer at Ashland. "I don't believe it's after sunset, and this young buck was sent to do a job by Miss Lucy herself. Ye'll kindly drop that whip, Jameson." Flanagan drew a pistol from his belt. "Else I'll blow a hole in ye the size of Georgia." The pistol was pointed at Jameson's head. "Did ye not see tha lad's pass?"

"Pass?" Jameson said innocently. "We saw no pass, right boys? Only a list of grocery supplies that he does not have. I could not see the use of that. I figured perhaps he'd been sent on an errand, tried to run away. We're just protecting Mr. Clay's property, as the law says."

"With that kind of protection, Mr. Clay would be bankrupt in a fortnight. Cut him down!" Flanagan cocked the pistol to add emphasis to his words.

Begrudgingly, Jameson signaled one of the other men, and they cut Luther down from the tree.

"Pick up your shirt, boy," Flanagan ordered, without taking his eyes or the pistol off Jameson. "Now you gentlemen stand aside, or me boys will be forced to give you reason for horsemanship."

Glancing over their shoulders, Luther's tormentors saw a number of Negroes with pitchforks standing behind them, menacing the horses. Reluctantly, they parted. "My boys will just follow us home. Luther!" Flanagan commanded. Luther slowly and painfully mounted to the driver's position, as Flanagan climbed in as passenger, tying the reins of his horse to the rear of the chaise. "Anyone who moves gets a ball in the head or Mr. Clay to deal with tomorrow," he said.

Recovering his evil joviality, Jameson called after them, "That's all right, boys, let'em go. Hey, Luther! Shall I pay a visit tonight to your mother, or your sister, do you think?"

Safely in the buggy, Luther glared at Jameson, but did not dare respond. He knew that any provocation would be taken out on his mother and sisters—Jameson's threat was not empty. Anger blazed in him, but outwardly he kept it in check, except for the burning in his eyes. He clicked to the horses, and the buggy began to roll, the other slaves serving as a rear guard, walking backward warily toward the plantation road.

Luther was still bleeding and in pain, but he dismounted from the chaise and gave it and the horse into the care of the groom, an elderly slave named Albert who had been born on the plantation in Henry Clay's time. Albert had white specks of hair and wizened features, a ready smile and a soft whisper for the horses he cared for. He stooped with age. Seeing Luther's pain, he clucked softly. "You got one dem patrols on you? Lawd a-mercy! Go see Auntie May. I'll take care all dis. Get cho sef fixed up 'fore you go to Miss Lucy. Ain't no sense upsettin' her wid it."

"Thanks, Albert. Believe I will."

Instead of going to the yellow-brick slave house near the great house that served as his quarters, Luther went down to the lower slave quarters nearer the fields. Night was falling rapidly; he knew he did not have long before quarters would be checked, and he still had to look in on Miss Lucy for any last-minute orders before she retired. A fire burned in front of Auntie May's cabin, who acted like his mother. She had a huge heart and looked after four motherless boys on the plantation. She was sitting on a stump by the fire, a wiry, middle-aged woman with premature gray streaks in her hair, wearing cotton homespun dress, and humming softly, staring at the fire just outside a whitewashed brick hut. The slave quarters were luxurious by most standards; they even had glass windows. Auntie May looked up at his approach.

"What'choo doin' down from de big house, Luther?"

"Ran me across patrollers, got cut." He turned, showing the blood that had seeped into his shirt.

"Oh, hon. Take dat shirt off and lemme see what I can do."

"Gotta be quick. I still got to see Miss Lucy before dey goes to bed."

Rising, May went to fetch a bucket of water and a rag. Luther took his shirt off, and she carefully washed away the dried blood from the angry welt on his back. He winced a few times but made no sound.

"At least dey only got you once. How'd you manage that?"

"Flanagan came and stopped 'em. Jameson was in de group. He'd a taken my hide off."

"Didn't Miss Lucy gib you a pass?"

"Yes'm, but Jameson, he just rip it to shreds, say it don't count. Nobody gonna take de word of blacks like us."

"Ain't dat de truth," she said, finishing up. She went into the hut and got a clean shirt. He tugged it on gingerly, trying not to break the wound open. "Get on up to de big house; don' want more trouble. I see you Sunday. Pump some mo' water over it if'n ya gets de chance," advised May. She gave him a brief hug, and Luther hurried off toward the mansion.

LEXINGTON RIFLES

May 1859

Will trudged from the one-room schoolhouse, heading to the corner of Second Street and Mill Street. The afternoon was already hot, mosquitoes buzzing and flies active. He thought about his encounter a few days before with the dashing young gentleman on the Versailles road. He had talked it over with his father and decided to follow up on whatever opportunity the young man might offer. His father had heard favorable things about John Hunt Morgan and decided it might be worth Will paying him a visit.

The town was bustling. A new batch of slaves milled about at the Cheapside auction block. Will puzzled over what Morgan would do—after all, he had already thanked him, hadn't he? Will had just done the decent thing, shooting the cat about to attack the unwary traveler. His brow furrowed and he felt nervous, sweat trickling down his back. He did not want to seem like some money-grubbing opportunist. Reaching the white arched door of the brick mansion, Will knocked. An elderly Negro dressed in a suit and white cotton shirt opened the door.

"Yes, sir? What may I do for you?" he asked.

"I've come to see Mr. Morgan. Is he at home?" said Will.

"Do you have an appointment, sir?"

"No, I don't. But Mr. Morgan said I should come and see him. I met him on the Versailles road the other day."

"Are you the boy with the fine shootin'?"

"I reckon so. Is Mr. Morgan in?"

"Wait here. I'll see if he's receiving visitors. You can sit here in the entryway if you like." The servant hurried off toward the back of the house while Will gazed about, afraid to sit on one of the rich dark wood chairs with bars in the back, taking in the yellow walls with white trim and a curved stairway to his right. Ahead, he could see a reception area and a pianoforte. After a few minutes, the young man he'd met on the road came striding in, his coal-black hair, long, straight nose, black beard, and expressive, close-set eyes just as Will remembered. The man's mouth curled up at the corners in a smile of recognition.

"Well, if it isn't my young marksman! I did want to thank you properly, Will."

Will gazed up at the six-foot-tall, trim figure. "Yes, sir."

"I appreciate quick thinking and good shooting. I asked around a bit about you. I understand you'd like to go to university?"

Not sure where this was leading, Will hesitated but then replied enthusiastically, "Yes, sir! I like to read and learn. I have just about finished what the local school has to offer. I want to be a lawyer, but I only know some Latin and no Greek."

John Morgan pursed his lips and chuckled. "I have a proposition for you. I am a businessman, and I hate to see talent wasted. However, *because* I am a businessman, I expect to get a return from my investment. I would like to invest in you. Suppose there were a spot open at Transylvania University here in Lexington for you, say for a year, to see how it goes. Also, I've started a local militia, the Lexington Rifles, to learn military procedure and some cavalry maneuvers. We mostly drill as infantry, however. Your fine shooting skills would get some use, maybe even improvement, if you were to join us. Interested?"

Will felt as if a whole new world had just opened at his feet. He could scarcely contain his excitement, but he did not want Mr. Morgan to think him young and silly. "Yes, sir!" He beamed. "Thank you, sir!"

"Excellent!" Reaching into his pocket, Morgan produced a letter bearing a red wax seal and handed it to Will. "You just take that letter round to Mr. Lewis Warner Green at the university. Tell him John Morgan sent you. And report to the little college lot at Transylvania Wednesday afternoon at five. Look for Corporal Thomas Logwood. He'll see that you get situated. It is across from Morrison. Don't be late!" he said with mock severity.

"Yes, sir! I mean, no, sir! I mean—I'll be there!" stammered Will.

"Good, good!" Morgan said, growing serious, fixing on Will with gray-blue eyes. "You know, discipline and honor are important to any man. It is how armies function, how battles are fought, both by soldiers and in our own lives. Knowing how to fight, how to act together as a unit—these can be valuable skills. A man needs to know he can depend upon his brothers in arms. One day not too far off, I fear our fair state may be at war, a war to preserve our state, our way of life. We may have to fight for what we believe. Could you do that?" asked Morgan.

Will was thoughtful and prayed quickly. Could he really fight? In a war? He decided that if it was to protect his home and family, he could. He nodded. "Yes, sir, I could. I believe that freedom means being able to do as we think right and best, with God as our guide, not just acting because someone far away told you to."

"As do I, Will." Morgan extended a hand, treating Will as an equal. "Until our next meeting."

The old servant showed Will out. He could scarcely believe it—in an afternoon, his life had been transformed, the door open to seemingly limitless possibilities—education, military training, and a new friendship at a social level previously beyond his reach.

* * *

The following Wednesday, Will showed up at the college lot as instructed. He looked at the young men milling about, searching for someone in charge. Most of them wore bright green uniforms with brass buttons, and several sported sabers hanging at their sides. There were stacks of muskets and squirrel guns about, no uniformity in weaponry. Will carried his Springfield musket and felt blessed to have it, seeing some of the other guns. He nervously scanned the group, conspicuous as a newcomer without a uniform. He noticed a tall, lean man, who looked to be in his early twenties, with a light brown mustache who seemed to be giving instructions and trying to get the men to come to order. His hazel eyes sparkled with mirth as he jovially tried to get a few to move into line. Will approached him.

"Excuse me, sir, but I'm looking for Thomas Logwood. Mr. Morgan sent me, said I was to be allowed to join."

"You have found him. You must be Will—Captain Morgan told me you'd be coming. Tells me you are quite a shot with that musket. Well, today you will mostly get measured for a uniform and watch what we do. See that stocky, brown-haired fellow there? He'll get you signed in and started."

Will jolted in surprise, recognizing Ben Drake from school, and just behind him, Jesse Davis. They looked quite different in their dashing uniforms, making Will suddenly feel apprehensive and a little inadequate. Ben turned in his direction and walked over with a sneer.

"Well, if it ain't the hero of the Battle of the Schoolhouse! Looky here, Jesse, what we got—come to find out how real fightin' is done!"

"He won't last," said Jesse. "He'll find out this here is work, and go home to mama."

"Mr. Morgan sent me. I'm proud to join," said Will.

"That's *Captain* Morgan to you!" Ben said. "The rules is simple—do as you're told. Lexington Rifles got one basic idea: '*Our laws, the commands of our captain.*' Captain Morgan is our commander and we follow him, no questions asked. And you may have that musket, you may think you know how to use it, but what you *don't* know fills this here book." He pulled out a copy of *Hardee's Rifle and Light Infantry Tactics* and handed it to Will. "This ain't just some social club. You gotta work, and you *earn* your spot." Ben walked over to a portable writing desk set up on the green and pulled out some papers. "You sign up here, and you learn the manual of arms before you can do much. Jesse, measure him for a uniform, and then get him outta the way for today. Next week, you can have fun drillin' him." He turned and left Will to Jesse, as though he were beneath further notice.

Jesse measured, took notes, and handed them to Will. "You either get your own uniform made or you pay fifty cents at the end of the first month. Next week, you drill in regular clothes. Today, you're just here to watch and see if you can keep up. There's a performance in two weeks. If you practice and Captain Morgan thinks you're good enough, he *might* let you be with us." Jesse smirked. "Miss two practices in a month and you're on report. Do that two months straight and you're out. Harvest and plantin' season no exception. We drill when it's hot and when it's cold, rain, snow, or heatwave. You can't take it, go to mama 'cause she ain't here. That over there," he said, pointing, "is the lieutenant, James West. And that feller," pointing back in the direction Will came from, "is Tom Logwood, the corporal. You'll get to know the sergeants and others in your company *if* you stick around. Now get off the field and watch how real men work!" Jesse walked off without a backward glance.

Will moved to stand under a tree and watched in some amazement as the seemingly motley group moved quickly into order at the loud command of the lieutenant.

"Assemble, company! Attention, company! Shoulder arms, company! Present arms, company!" The men and boys rapidly performed the series of rapid-fire commands as if they were but one person moving in unison. Some did not have uniforms, marking them as new recruits like Will. Others looked smart and polished, most likely sons of planters and merchants in town. After an hour of marching and arms drill, the Rifles dismissed. Tom Logwood came over to Will with a smile and offered a handshake.

"I have to have you take the oath," said Tom. "Read it over. Ben, Jesse, you serve as witnesses."

Will read and repeated the oath.

"I, Will Crump, promise to faithfully execute my duty to the Lexington

Rifles and the commands of our captain, John Hunt Morgan. I will loyally follow God and the Rifles, regardless of personal cost, and defend our state and our city from all threats."

"Sign the register, and welcome to the Rifles! You're fortunate you already have a musket—some of the fellows have to use broomsticks till they can afford one. You will want to save up for a bayonet, though, so you can learn those drills and a saber if you're going to be mounted. You'll also want a pistol. Have a horse?"

"No. Mr. Morgan said he'd let me come to his place and learn to ride, but my family only has oxen."

"Don't worry. If Captain Morgan said you'd get a chance to ride, you'll learn quickly enough. Now let me show you some of the basics."

For the next hour, Tom showed Will how to do most of the movements from the manual of arms, drilled him on them, and taught him to march, stand at attention, parade rest, and other commands. It was nearing dusk when he good-naturedly waved Will home, saying he'd see him next week.

* * *

It was nearly dark when Will finished trudging home from the university grounds. He was tired, a bit grimy, and not looking forward to homework. He hung his rifle on the pegs and then went to feed the oxen and complete his other evening chores. Coming back in, he found his mother and Albinia bustling about preparing the evening meal, with Lydia doing a little dance in the corner.

"Hello, Will." His mother gave him a quick smile and returned to stirring the soup in the kettle on the cast-iron stove. "How was your first day with the Rifles?"

"All right, I guess. I've got a lot to learn, and I found out that Ben Drake and Jesse Davis are in the group, so that won't make it easier. Funny they never said anything about it at school. But I met a fella, Tom Logwood, who showed me a lot of the drill. I think we might get to be friends. But

I've got a favor to ask—I'm supposed to come up with my own uniform. Binia, could you sew one for me?" Will dug out the paper where Jesse had scrawled the uniform measurements and handed it to her.

Albinia swiped at an errant strand of hair, set the measurements on the table, and continued slicing carrots for the soup. "I can sew it, but where are we going to get the material?"

"I asked about that—Hobson carries it in his store. I reckon I could do some odd jobs for him, maybe work off the cost that way. Jesse measured me," he said. She glanced at the measurements and stuffed them in an apron pocket.

Sara looked worried. "But, Will, how will you find time to do that? You've got the new drills on Wednesdays, practicing, all your farm chores, and schoolwork besides. And if you're really starting at university next week, the work will be more than the little school you're in now. Your father won't stand for school getting in the way of farm work, you know that."

"Just get up earlier, I guess," said Will.

"That's the spirit," said Robert, coming in the door. "No reason to be afraid of hard work. You're a smart boy, Will. Your mama's right, I need you here on the farm, but I 'spect you can work hard enough to manage. Least if you want to be in that university and doin' drills with them rifle boys. Morgan seems a fine man, and I've got nothin' against you tryin' to better yourself. When you see opportunity, you got to pray and then grab it by the throat, 'fore it runs off!"

Will looked imploringly at his mother, knowing she would be unable to resist his father's enthusiasm.

She set the bowls on the table and resignedly started dishing out the soup.

"All right. If your father says you can, you can. But mark my words: you'll end up sick or in trouble because of this. Why get involved in all this rifle stuff—what for? Do you really care all that much about what goes on in Washington?"

"I care about our neighbors. I care that each state consented to join a union of states, and should have the right to determine its own affairs. Besides, the Rifles is mostly just a way of payin' back Mr. Morgan for the opportunity to study, to learn law. Someday I'd like to be a lawyer, maybe even a judge. I want to help people in trouble. University is a way to do that. And I figure I could do worse than to learn from Mr. Morgan."

* * *

In church the following Sunday, Will shifted on the hard pew, uncomfortable in his starched collar. He stared up at the vaulted ceiling, attempting to focus on the words of the minister, Robert Breckinridge.

"Look yonder! What is it that I see? Is it not my agonizing Lord upon the cross? Hark, Hark! Do you not hear? O Father, if it be possible, let this cup pass from me, yet not my will but Thine be done!"

The minister's close-set eyebrows and long bushy salt-and-pepper beard gave him a severe appearance, as if he were an Old Testament prophet. He affected the rising and lowering tones of his idol, George Whitefield, who in the previous century had enthralled thousands with his theatrical sermons. Will secretly thought Breckinridge aimed at keeping anyone from going to sleep.

"Do you not see the Savior, hanging there for you upon the cross? Who can but be moved at His passion? That He died for all, yes, even the slave and the sinner, the evildoer and the righteous? Slaves, though subordinate beings, can yet claim salvation through the passion and generous love of our Lord! And for this magnanimous love, slaves owe Jesus a debt of gratitude, of obedience. In the epistle to the Colossians, the Bible tells you, 'Slaves, obey in all things your masters according to the flesh; not with eye service, as men pleasers; but in singleness of heart, fearing God.'"

Will often read the Bible on his own and wondered at this singling out of the slaves—did not all men owe obedience to Christ if they claimed Him as Savior?

"We must love our fellow man, as Christ loved on the cross! Yes, even our slaves, for in the letter to the Ephesians, the apostle Paul tells us, 'Knowing that whatsoever good thing any man doeth, the same shall he receive of the Lord, whether he be bond or free. And, ye masters, do the same things unto them, forbearing threatening: knowing that your Master also is in heaven; neither is there respect of persons with him.'"

Will saw that the congregation shifted uncomfortably at this, a few frowns displayed.

"Slavery has existed down through the ages, and yet it is to be hoped that one day it will cease. Some have gone so far as to say that our nation should be split, that our differences are so large as to be unresolvable, the great divide between North and South cannot be bridged. Some states talk of secession. In the North, in Massachusetts, some cities refuse to obey the law to return slaves to their place of origin, to their rightful masters. They say they are sanctuaries for the slaves. This is obviously against our Lord, who says in Romans 13 that all must obey the governing authorities. Some even threaten to take up arms in rebellion. Yet for what would we fight, on one side and on the other? What are the interests at stake, so immense and so opposite, that justify either party to embark upon a war that in its prosecution is bound to wreak terrible destruction to all? What are its probable effects, and how much of what each side wishes to fight for is really attainable? These are questions which every enlightened man, every free citizen, is bound to ask himself. The answer to them involves our lives and fortunes and liberties, nay, even more than these, our duty as citizens, as patriots, and as Christians."

In spite of himself, Will dozed. He missed the rest of the sermon, awakening with a start as his father stood for the closing hymn. After the service dismissed, Will wandered out into the churchyard, toward the stable, hoping to catch a glimpse of some of the fine horses. His riding lessons at the Morgan farm were progressing, and he had developed a keen interest in horses. A group of girls chatted, dressed in their Sunday finery, including Jenny, wearing an aquamarine dress with a high waist and white lace blouse. She glanced over, saw him, and started making her way toward him just as he reached a particularly fine Missouri Fox trotter, hitched to a doctor's black buggy. Will was absorbed in the horse, a dark bay with a white oval between the eyes, one white rear sock, mane, and tail so dark as to be almost black. He was admiring the legs and lines of the horse as Jenny approached.

"Good afternoon, Will. Haven't seen you much lately. Like the horse?"

"Oh hello, Jenny. You're looking fine today! Guess I've been pretty scarce, going to university, drilling with the Rifles, working at the store, keepin' up at the farm." Turning to the horse, Will said, "Isn't he a beauty? I'll probably never have a horse, but I'll bet this fella can really go!"

"Do you know how to drive one?"

"Well, I can drive our oxen, and I used to drive the mule. Don't figger it's that different."

"Perhaps not, but you might want a couple of driving lessons before my uncle would let you try him."

"Your uncle? You mean…?"

"Yes, he belongs to my uncle, my mother's brother, Dr. Simpson. I think I could persuade him to let you try him out if you want to learn. Especially if you took me along," she said, smiling. "In fact, here he comes now!"

Will was excited. "You mean it?" Already he imagined himself breezing down the lane out into the country, the horse effortlessly moving at a fast trot. Then he suddenly realized what Jenny was saying.

"Are you sure you'd want to go? Might be kinda fast…."

Will had been thinking only of the horse, the freedom to move quickly through the summer's day. He liked Jenny, but he did not want to raise any expectations. Yet what he would not give to drive that horse….

"Well, if you'd rather not," said Jenny, looking disappointed.

"Oh no! That'd be great! I just didn't want you to be scared."

"I don't scare easily, Will Crump," she said, gazing at him steadily. She turned and introduced him to her uncle.

"Uncle Tim, this is Will Crump. He seems to have an eye for fine horses."

"Well, it'd be hard to find a finer one," said Dr. Simpson, a tall man in a brown derby hat with black mutton-chop whiskers showing a touch of gray and silver-rimmed spectacles. Intelligent brown eyes seemed to take Will's measure and liked what they saw. "Ever driven a trotter?"

"No, sir, just our mule and some oxen. But Mr. Morgan's been teaching me to ride, and I'd sure love to learn!"

"Well, I've some calls to make out the Versailles road. You headed in that direction?"

"Yes, sir!" Will replied enthusiastically.

"If you don't mind waiting at the stops, you and my favorite niece could come along. You could learn, if you like." Dr. Simpson smiled generously.

"Thank you, sir! Let me just go and tell my parents."

When Will returned, they all climbed into the buggy, Dr. Simpson helping Jenny into the rear seat, Will seated beside the doctor, who drove. Dr. Simpson spoke animatedly as they drove through town, showing Will how to maneuver the horse through the city traffic. Once out in the country, he let Will take the reins, offering advice and correction.

In bed that evening, Will thought back on the events of the day and thanked God for one of the most enjoyable days of his life.

SISTERS

May 1859

Julia stared around impatiently, sitting on a bench in front of the Lexington stage depot, waiting for someone from her family to show up. She had sent a message with a neighbor for someone to pick her up. She was tired, having started at four in the morning from her uncle's house. Now she was hot and sweaty, and dirty. She felt unfit to be seen, the wind from her stage trip having pulled her hair into a rebellious flyaway frizzle. She dreaded bumping into someone she knew while sitting and waiting. She pretended to be poised and comfortable. At least she could bring news that her aunt's health was better. Julia stood, resolving to find a mirror at the dry goods store in order to fix her hair, when she heard an unfamiliar voice address her by name.

"Miss Crump?"

She turned to find Hiram Johannsen, the tall blond bumbling farmer from the barn dance standing behind her, hat in hand. With an effort and an embarrassed flush, she endeavored to smile politely and respond.

"Why, Mr. Johannsen, what a surprise seeing you here!"

"I was on my way to Louisville and had some time. My father owns several steam boats, so I come to Lexington often to supervise freight delivery from the river." He smiled. "I remembered you from the dance."

Julia took in this information and silently reevaluated him. Perhaps he was not as much the bumbler as he seemed. Maybe he was not a poor farmer, either.

"Why, yes, Mr. Johannsen. I remember our dance also." She looked at him with new eyes. He was handsome in a giant, oafish sort of way. He smiled not just with his face, but with his blue eyes as well. She noticed his well-cut suit. It fit him marvelously, in spite of his stocky, well-muscled frame. He looked as if he could just pick up a wagon and carry it, rather than riding in it. She would have to inquire about his family.

"Would you like to go over to the café, Miss Crump, for some tea?" Hiram asked politely

Julia was debating the wisdom of this, when a wagon with oxen turned the corner, with Will driving. "Perhaps another time, Mr. Johannsen. I look a fright after my trip. My brother is coming now, and I really must go home after such a long time away. My father is Robert Crump, and we live on a farm on the road to Versailles. If you come to Lexington often, perhaps we'll see one another again some time."

The wagon rumbled to a halt by the depot, and Julia saw Will looking at her with questioning eyes. He hopped down, and Julia made introductions. After he and Julia were safely away, he turned to her.

"So where did you meet him?" asked Will.

"At Uncle's barn dance," said Julia, flustered.

"Pa's going to want to know about him if he's spending time around you," opined Will.

"Well, I don't know whether he will or not. And I don't know much about him."

"Other than that he could substitute for one of these oxen," snickered Will.

"Now you mind your own business, Will Crump!" said Julia defensively. "He seems nice enough. It's just his accent that makes him seem awkward, I think."

* * *

Albinia glanced up from her work at the dressmaker's, surprised to see Will and Julia across the street at the stage depot. She had not known her sister was returning today. Her hands mechanically kept stitching the Jenny Lind collar on the blue-and-white gingham day dress she was making for the mayor's wife. Julia and Will were talking with a tall, stocky blond man and then quickly turned away and left in the wagon. Albinia wondered at this, since Julia usually did not talk to strangers.

The bell rang, and Albinia went to the front of the shop. She broke into a smile, seeing a slight dark-haired familiar woman.

"Katy! What brings you here? Did I leave something at your place last night?"

"No, no. I just wondered if you'd be staying with us tonight too. Ma wants to know how many for supper."

"You are so kind to give me a place to sleep at times, to prevent so many trips to town. I wouldn't want to impose. No, I'll be going home tonight. Will is taking me."

"Are you sure? Ma's having fried chicken."

"Stop tempting me!" Albinia laughed. "I really should go home. Ma gets worried when I'm out too many nights. Thanks, though."

Watching Katy leave, she noticed Luther, Lucy's slave from Ashland, entering the dry goods store, apparently on an errand. She wondered at Lucy sending him out alone, after the incident with Jameson, which she had heard about. Then the figure of Sean Flanagan drove down the street and she revised her opinion—Lucy must have sent Flanagan as insurance that Luther would not be harmed.

She turned her attention back to her stitching. The shop paid her by completion. It was up to her how long she worked each day. Tiring, she carefully folded the dress, extra material, and other supplies. She put them in her assigned cubbyhole. Mrs. Gordon, the owner of the store, was very strict with her girls about neatness and keeping track of supplies and orders.

As she emerged from the shop, locking up and carrying her reticule, she noticed a large poster on the signboard outside the shop advertising a meeting of concerned, God-fearing citizens, to discuss slavery, and featuring the famous journalist, William Lloyd Garrison. The meeting was set for this evening. She knew Will had drill for the Rifles, so she decided at once to attend and hear this great speaker. She could still ride home with Will if she left the meeting early. Though she had grown up seeing the great Lexington slave markets and pens all her life, for some reason, her contact with Luther tugged at her heart. She began to see the sadness and anger, as well as the mirth, behind the expressions of the slaves around her that she encountered in town. More than once recently she passed an auction, witnessing the hopeless, vacant look in a mother's eyes as her children were sold to different owners. Somehow, she had begun to see the slaves as people rather than as a means for white privileged folk to get what they wanted. In town, away from her father's scrutiny, she had begun to read discarded newspapers, even once seeing a copy of *The Liberator*, published by Garrison, as well as the opposing views of the *Journal*, denouncing him. Will might come looking for her after drill, but if she hurried, she could meet him at the drill field before he became suspicious. She knew without a second thought that her father would not approve of a young woman going to an abolitionist meeting, especially unescorted. She almost laughed at the look she could imagine on her mother Sara's face if she knew what her daughter had planned–scandalized would not begin to describe it.

Just then, Luther emerged from the dry goods store carrying some very large and apparently heavy boxes. Someone had discarded a cigar, still burning, on the board plank step leading to the street from the store, where Flanagan's wagon waited for the supplies. Luther could not see the ground, and his bare foot landed square on top of it. Grimacing in pain, he stumbled and dropped the top box. She heard a tinkling sound, as if from broken glass. Luther set the other boxes on the end of the wagon. Flanagan suddenly appeared, cursing the boy.

"Ye lummox! Now look what you've done! It's broken and ordered all the way from Philadelphia! An whose hide is it d'ye think the Clays will be seekin', eh? Mine, that's what! Because I came as yer nursemaid!"

A blackjack club appeared in his hand, and he beat Luther on the head and shoulders, drawing blood. Luther raised his arms to protect his head, and received a vicious kick in the ribs, rolling him into the street, where he lay moaning.

Albinia turned away, horrified, and walked to the corner hotel with a small café suitable for a lady. She sat at a table near the window and tried to think through what she had just seen. A boy, beaten for an innocent mistake. She had always been aware of slavery—you could not live in Lexington without seeing it firsthand. Fully one fifth of the population were slaves. However, rarely had she actually witnessed violence. She had heard stories, of course, but as a young lady, her parents shielded her from the ugly truth, the dehumanization of slavery. She shivered, suddenly adding up the things that had been at the edge of her consciousness. She remembered the sad look in the eyes of Luther and the other slaves at Ashland when they thought no one was looking. She envisioned the slave pens down by the docks, where slaves were crowded in like cattle. She remembered her father's preference that she not work on Fridays when the slave auction took place. Each piece fell into place, forming a horrifying reality. In her mind, again the blackjack fell, the blood spurted. Anger and resolve replaced revulsion. She would go to that meeting, and she would find a way to help.

She arrived at the hall, and found a small crowd milling outside. The doors were not open yet. Those gathered were overwhelmingly male, very few women, and none of the women was dressed even as well as she was. The men appeared to be tradesmen, though there were one or two gold-headed canes in the group, congregated together, and talking animatedly. A few police arrived in a wagon, looking to prevent trouble. Albina moved toward the door, trying to get out of the street. She was standing at the window of the assembly hall, next to an older gentleman in a dark gray broadcloth suit and top hat. He wore an expensive suit, she noticed, with a row of buttons down each side. Albinia heard a commotion toward the end of the street. A group of men with torches were shouting angrily and moving in her direction. The gentleman next to her looked at the ruffians, trying to see what they were doing. He spoke to one of the policemen, and the doors to the hall opened. Just at that moment, a rock arced through the air, smashing the window next to Albinia. There was a gunshot, then pandemonium. She ducked, bumping the man, and jostled forward on the human wave, pushed into the hall. Everyone was trying to escape at once. Police formed a barrier to keep the men with torches from entering. She could hear the mob shouting insults. Albinia turned to the gentleman.

"I beg your pardon, sir! I didn't mean to bump you!" She noticed with alarm that he had pistols strapped inside his coat.

He smiled, "Quite the ruckus, isn't it? No problem at all, Miss...?"

"Crump. Albinia Crump."

"Cassius Clay at your service. Have you attended one of these meetings before, or heard Mr. Garrison?"

"No. No, I never have. I've just witnessed violent cruelty to a slave. Are you related to the Ashland Clays?"

"Yes, cousins."

"You know Lucy, then?"

"No, I've not had the pleasure. Her father and I are ... not close. I heard Mr. Garrison speak when I was at college and came away convinced of the evils of slavery, though my family has owned slaves. I've worked ever since to defeat it, though it has not always won friends for me. You're not hurt?" he said, gesturing to the hole in the window.

"No, just shaken, I suppose," said Albinia.

"Understandable. Allow me," he said, offering his arm, and escorted her to a seat near the front of the hall.

"I ... ah ... may have to leave early, Mr. Clay. My father does not know that I am here, and my brother is drilling with the Lexington Rifles. He'll be my ride home."

"Ah, secrets, then? Safe with me. Allow me to have my valet escort you when you need to go. David?" said Mr. Clay, motioning to a man in the shadows. "Please see Miss Crump to the Academy grounds safely, whenever she wishes to go."

Albinia was surprised to see a tall young white man, in a waistcoat, rather than a Negro servant. His auburn hair curled untidily over one ear, and his copper-colored spectacles gave him a studious look on an otherwise handsome face, with intense green eyes spaced evenly, a long straight nose, and a high forehead. A watch fob peeked out of the waistcoat pocket, and he bowed politely to Albinia. "At your service, Miss," said David, retreating to the shadows at the edge of the hall. As he moved away, Albinia glimpsed a derringer in another pocket, but her heart involuntarily skipped a beat—such a handsome young man.

The hall began to fill, and the noise at the back died down, muffled by the buzz of voices as those seated conversed in muted tones. After a few minutes, a well-dressed man appeared on the stage and signaled for quiet.

"We thank you all for coming. The plight of the many enslaved in our nation, who only want to escape across the border to freedom and prosperity, is known to most of you. Born into a life of poverty, hard labor, and abuse, with no means of bettering themselves save risking their lives to escape, our black brethren have few to champion them. With the passage of the Fugitive Slave Act, even that escape may not be enough to save them from the cruel chains of slavery, excepting a few cities brave enough to stand up to the tyranny of the government and the minions of the South, giving sanctuary to runaway slaves and sending the slave catchers home, empty handed. Mr. Garrison, our speaker this evening, has risked life and fortune to bring them to the attention of Christian hearts everywhere. Without further ado, I give you William Lloyd Garrison!"

On the other side of the hall, a man stood and shouted, "Thieves! Traitors!" but the crowd largely ignored him. Their attention turned to the man stepping on stage. His black coat was of the best material, his bow tie neatly tied under a flaring white collar. He had a receding hairline that left the front of his head bald, but this only enhanced the intelligent looks of the brown eyes, spectacles, and thin mouth. Once Garrison began to speak, everyone quieted down, as his booming voice filled the hall.

"Let me define my positions, and at the same time challenge anyone to show wherein they are untenable. I am a believer in that portion of the

Declaration of American Independence in which it is set forth, as among self-evident truths, "that all men are created equal; that they are endowed by their Creator with certain inalienable rights; that among these are life, liberty, and the pursuit of happiness." Hence, I am an abolitionist. Hence, I cannot but regard oppression in every form—and most of all, that which turns a man into a thing—with indignation and abhorrence. Not to cherish these feelings would be recreancy to principle. They, who desire me to be dumb on the subject of slavery, unless I will open my mouth in its defense, ask me to give the lie to my professions, to degrade my manhood, and to stain my soul. I will not be a liar, a poltroon, or a hypocrite, to accommodate any party, to gratify any sect, to escape any odium or peril, to save any interest, to preserve any institution, or to promote any object. Convince me that one man may rightfully make another man his slave and I will no longer subscribe to the Declaration of Independence. Convince me that liberty is not the inalienable birthright of every human being, of whatever complexion or clime, and I will give that instrument to the consuming fire. I do not know how to espouse freedom and slavery together."

Garrison continued, linking Christianity and abolition, imploring for common sense. Albinia was spellbound, but noticed uncomfortable looks, whispers, and murmurings around her. Clay, next to her, seemed unperturbed, but many of the gentlemen with trappings of wealth shifted restlessly. A heckler near the back stood and shouted, "And you gonna feed 'em? S'pose you'll have 'em to Sunday dinner and marry your daughter!" He laughed nastily, getting a ripple of laughter from the crowd.

Garrison interrupted his discourse to look at the man and said, "Perhaps, one day, the color of a man's skin and the money in his pocket will not matter so much as the character in his heart. I pray that day comes quickly. In the meantime, sir, I have met many former slaves with better manners than yourself. Perhaps you could learn from them!"

This drew a howl of laughter from the crowd, and the man sat back down, glowering. Garrison continued his speech, winning at least grudging admiration from most of the crowd for his boldness in declaring the abolitionist manifesto. Before Albinia knew it, he was wrapping up, making his final remarks.

"What then is to be done? Friends of the slave, the question is not whether by our efforts we can abolish slavery, speedily or remotely—for duty is ours, the result is with God; but whether we will go with the multitude to do evil, sell our birthright for a mess of pottage, cease to cry aloud and spare not, and remain in Babylon when the command of God is 'Come out of her, my people, that ye be not partakers of her sins, and that ye receive not of her plagues.' Let us stand in our lot, 'and having done all, to stand.' At least, a remnant shall be saved. Living or dying, defeated or victorious, be it ours to exclaim, 'No compromise with slavery! Liberty for each, for all, forever! Man above all institutions! The supremacy of God over the whole earth!' "

Albinia stood, and looking to where David stood at the edge of the room, made her way toward him, after thanking Clay.

"Sir, there is really no need for you to accompany me. I am used to going about the city streets. I must go and meet my brother quickly or stay in town all night."

"Miss Crump, you may be used to the streets, but the hour is late. Please let me take you in Mr. Clay's buggy. It will be swifter and safer. You may not realize it, but just being at this meeting makes you a target. Mr. Clay has received death threats for his views. Standing for liberty has a definite price. There might be those who would take advantage of your position to harm you. Let me entreat you to accept my services," said David sincerely.

Albinia looked at him, searching the green eyes, and, seeing softness and sincerity, decided to accept.

"Well, it would help to arrive quickly. I'm not in the habit of accepting rides from unknown gentlemen, but perhaps in this case, Mr. ...?"

"Horner. David Horner. I have been in Mr. Clay's service for some years. Let's go then, since you are in a hurry."

David parted the crowd before her, and escorted her out a back way, conferring briefly with his employer, who agreed to await his return. He assisted her into the light buggy, looking into her eyes, holding her arm a fraction longer than necessary, she noticed. The buggy had two matched bays in harness. As they emerged from the side street, Albinia was glad she accepted the ride, seeing that the mob assembled prior to the speech was still there, and pelting those emerging from the hall with refuse and epithets. She heard cries of "Lynch him! Let's get him, boys!" A few noticed their departure and broke off to give chase. A rock shattered the lantern on Albinia's side of the buggy. She crouched in fear, but the pursuers swiftly fell behind as David urged the horses forward at breakneck speed.

"Is it always like this?" Albinia asked as they drove.

"Often, and sometimes worse. In New York a quarter century ago, they had some intense riots. The depth of feeling on the issue of slavery stirs the passions of many people, both ways. Mr. Clay and I have been committed to working for freedom in the political arena for some time. Men have attacked Mr. Clay on the streets. Any abolitionist risks censure, social disapproval, and sometimes his own safety. If you'll forgive me, I find it amazing that as a woman you would expose yourself to that kind of risk—perhaps you were unaware?"

"I was, but that doesn't change anything. After hearing Mr. Garrison, it simply increases my resolve to try to be of some help. After all, belief without action is dead, is it not? That's what the Bible teaches."

"Yes, but do you know what you're risking? Truly being involved in abolition goes beyond meetings and speeches. Your status as a woman would not be protection enough. There are those who would try to sully your reputation, hurt your family, perhaps even harm you physically," he said delicately.

"Is not God our protector? What can I do?" Albinia wanted to know.

"If you're really sincere about wanting to help, I can put you in contact with abolitionists helping slaves. However, I urge you to consider carefully and talk to your family. It is not something to do lightly. You could be put in prison for helping. It's probably best to just pray and leave the actual work to those better able to defend themselves, and with less to lose."

"Mr. Horner, do not mistake me for one of your drawing room lilies that chases first this fancy, and then that, nor yet some flighty flibbergibbet that impulsively jumps over cliffs without looking. I admit I did not know the intensity and violence of the opposition, but that does not deter me. What I've seen today, and what I've heard from others, convinces me of the justice of fighting for freedom. If God has a role for me in that fight, then shall I shirk to take it up?"

David pulled the horse up at the parade ground, seeing the Rifles milling about having finished their drill. He gazed at her a moment then said, "You are remarkable, then." Gesturing toward the soldiers, he said, "But have you thought about your family? You say your brother is in the Rifles. Clearly, he must not share your zeal for slaves' freedom. And your father? What will he say? I presume you are unmarried. And your friends? Did you not say you were friendly with Lucy Clay?"

Flushing a little, Albinia drew herself up. "Yes, I am unmarried. As for my family and friends, I do not know. But I know what God will think of me if I shrink back, and that in the end is all that matters."

David helped her down from the buggy, pressing a card into her hand. "I can be found at the address on the card in the evenings. Please think and pray carefully. If you are still determined to be involved, you can send word and I will contact you. For your own safety, do not speak of this openly. I cannot really encourage you, but if you will persist, then there are those who would use your help. Until then, I bid you adieu." He held her hand longer than necessary, and her eyes with a fond gaze, then turned and climbed back into the buggy.

Albinia put the card in her reticule and spotted Will, sitting on the ground with his back to her, cleaning his rifle. He was concentrating and did not notice Albinia's approach.

* * *

"Hey, Crump! Wake up! Your mama come to get you!" snickered Ben Drake.

Will looked up with a grimace to see Albinia standing there. "At least I don't need spectacles to tell a pretty young lady when I see one," he said. "This is my sister, Miss Albinia Crump, and I'd appreciate it if you'd treat her with respect," Will said. "I'd hate to have to teach *another* lesson about how to treat a lady." Finishing reassembling the rifle, Will stood and turned to his sister. "Let's go, Albinia, and let these *gentlemen* get on with their evening. I got chores still to do when we get home."

Ben and Jesse watched him go with suppressed mirth.

"You might want to take a moment to remove that sign from your back," said Albinia, smiling.

"What?" Will said, feeling his shoulder. Someone had pinned a sign saying "Dunce" to his back. "Drake again. I wonder if he'll ever let it go."

Just as they were leaving, Tom Logwood came toward him.

"Crump! Before you go, Captain Morgan says I am to tell you that you are doing well enough to be in the performance. Be half an hour early. And congratulations!"

"Yes, sir! I'll be there," said Will excitedly.

He led the way over to the wagon where the oxen waited. He took their grain bags off and stowed them in the bed of the wagon, then helped Albinia up to the rough, high wagon seat.

"You were late this evening," Will stated, as the oxen plodded through the darkening streets. "Good thing I brought this," he said, gesturing to the swaying lantern his father had rigged up to a post on the wagon. "We may need it before we get home." In the soft twilight, stars were beginning to be visible.

"I'm sorry. I just lost track of time," Albinia said truthfully. "Will, what do you think of slavery?"

Startled, he looked at her, but could not read her face in the dimness. "What do you mean? Slavery just is, that's all. Always has been, back to Biblical times."

"Yes, but *should* it be? I have heard you say that England got rid of it. Why not America?"

"That kind of talk will get you in trouble. What would Father say?"

"You know Father is conflicted on slavery. Father would follow the Bible."

"And the Bible tells slaves to submit to their masters, both kind and harsh," said Will.

"But it also says if they get a chance to be free, they should take it," argued Albinia.

"And do what?" said Will. "Maybe you didn't hear about it, though I think you sneak some newspapers sometimes," Will smirked at her. "But there's a Senator Hammond who spoke a few months ago. He talked about how there's more beggars on the streets of New York City, freed slaves, than any city in the South. I don't hold with cruelty, you know that. But where would all the slaves go? How would they support themselves? And here in the South, how would the plantations operate? You know how hard Father and I work just to take care of our eighty acres. The plantations have hundreds of acres—they can't support them without slaves to work the land. Paying them wages would just drive prices up and put farmers into ruin. Out in Kansas, you got pro-slavers murdering abolitionists, if you didn't know. Both sides got problems. Freeing slaves would just create another lower class, like the thousands of Irish coming in. Where do they get jobs?"

"So you think it's impossible to free the slaves?" pressed Albinia.

"I don't know," said Will honestly. "But it sure ain't gonna happen soon, and not without a fight. Too many people depend on it."

Albinia rode in silence for a few minutes. Then she turned to Will. "Would you fight for it?"

Will had moved on in his thoughts, thinking his sister must have had some strange conversation in town that provoked this line of thought.

"Fight for what?"

"Abolition, getting rid of slavery."

"I don't think I would. Each man has to decide that sort of thing for himself, I think. I would not own a slave, but I don't think I can tell others not to. And like Father says, I don't hold with depriving a man of his property without paying him for it. Nobody 'cept God should tell him how he's got to live. It's his choice before God. The rest of it is more than I can figure out."

"And what choice does the slave have?"

"About as much choice as I have to be born a poor farmer in Kentucky. God put me here, and I figger He knows what He's doing. It's His job to order things, not mine. I got enough on my hands with trying to study, drilling with the Rifles, keeping up on the farm, and just getting through the day being dog tired, without takin' on things I can't change."

"Can't, or won't?" Albinia persisted.

"Blazes, Binia! Can't you leave it alone? There ain't anything you can do either! Ain't you got enough to do making dresses and helping Mama without taking on the troubles of the world? Leave it be."

They rode in silence the rest of the way home.

Escape from the Jameson Plantation

June 1859

The knock came at the door, just as Luther's mother, Jemima, and his sisters, Olivia and Clara, sat at their rickety table for their evening meal of potato porridge and moldy bread. The sound struck terror into Jemima. No slave would knock or be out of quarters at this hour. It had to be either the overseer Barmer or Jameson himself.

"Quick, girls! Ya hide back in dem blankets. I'll see what dey want, try to get 'em to go away. Jump now! Can't make'em wait."

The girls hurried to obey, leaving the dinner where it was. Jemima's mind whirled. There could only be one thing wanted at this hour. Trembling, she went to the door and opened it. Jameson greeted her with a scowl, reeking of the whiskey he was holding.

"Come to pay a visit, 'Mima," he said, grinning nastily. "Or leastways, your girls. Where could they be? Not out after hours, surely." He peered into the cabin.

"No, suh," said Jemima hastily, not daring to look up. "Dey gone to bed, tired out after workin' today."

Jameson pushed her roughly aside, forcing his way into the cabin. He stood, looking her up and down, glassy eyed in his drunkenness for a moment. His hair appeared disheveled, his black and gray stubbly beard showing neglect, his eyes bloodshot. Though only about thirty years old, Jemima had smooth coal black hair with streaks of premature gray, and had a slim muscled figure from hours of fieldwork, callused bare feet showing from beneath a patched, worn muslin dress. She stood a head shorter than Jameson, her eyes fixed on the floor, as she tried to think of a way of escape. She never saw the fist coming that smacked the side of her face, knocking her to the floor. She cried out and raised her arm to protect her head as a boot kicked her stomach, hard. Jameson's eyes flared slightly at the dinner on the table, three earthenware plates and wooden forks. He swept them all aside, making the plates crash to the floor.

"You're lyin'! And you sayin' those girls have to work too hard? They're lucky they have food and a roof over their heads. Or maybe you'd like to live outside this winter, eh? Leaves startin' to turn, you could make'em a pretty blanket, hey? What you say to that, you black wench?" Looking in the corner at the blankets, Jameson saw a slight movement.

"Come on out here, you two pickaninnys! No use hidin' in those dirty rags!" He stalked over and grabbed the blankets, pulling them off and throwing them to the opposite side of the cabin.

Jemima stood quickly, fearful but enraged. She wanted to shield her girls, but pleaded, "Please, suh! Take me! Let my girls go! They can go next door! I'll be nice, I promise! I do whatever you want! Just let my girls go!"

Jameson turned on her and shoved her hard to the floor, so her head hit it with an audible thud. The door was still standing wide open.

"Barmer!" he roared, calling for the overseer.

A hulking shape filled the door, a powerful man well over six feet tall, carrying a whip in his hand. His brown bushy beard and full eyebrows over small, close-set eyes and a small forehead, combined with his tremendous size, gave him a gorilla-like appearance.

"Yes, sir?" he said.

Jameson took a long swig from the bottle of whiskey. "Take her to the block house for the night, teach her some respect. If she gives you any trouble, give her nine lashes in front of all of them in the morning, and you can have her. If she behaves well, let her out tomorrow. No food. Either way, make sure she does a full day's work tomorrow."

"Yes, sir!" said Barmer. He motioned towards the door with his whip, eyeing Jemima with a hard glare as she hastily got to her feet. "Go on! You heard Massa Jameson!"

Jemima was quick to obey, but glanced back over her shoulder at her girls cowering in the corner on the mat. She took a few steps outside the cabin, and she heard a cry of pain. Her youngest, Clara, came sprinting out the door, holding her face, headed for the cabin next door. Jemima wanted to run to her, to hold her, to protect her. Barmer prodded her once in the back with the butt of the whip. She knew what would follow if she did not obey. She could not save them, either of them, her precious babies. The conflicting storm raged in her heart. She walked, forlorn. Her eyes stared straight ahead to the icehouse also known as the blockhouse, modified to be a slave punishment cell. The door opened into a yawning black hole, steps leading down to a bench. Moonlight glinted on the chains and shackles. She knelt on the bench, as required, and silently let Barmer put the shackles around her wrists and ankles, stretching her arms and legs out in different directions. She prayed in her mind, hoping this would be all, but Barmer went to the wall and began cranking the block and tackle that lifted her painfully, dangling in the air, rusted shackles cutting into her flesh. She would be at the mercy of the rats and bugs, no water, no way to scratch, and no possibility of sleep or comfort—all the while her mind torturing her with what must be happening to Olivia. Barmer gave the tackle a last jerk, leering at Jemima, and laughing.

"I'll be back in the morning for you ... or maybe sooner, if I get a mind," he said suggestively. "The massa ain't going to want to be bothered."

* * *

In the morning, Jemima bent over the slave cot, comforting Olivia. She crooned softly as the girl sobbed, stroking her hair, gently rubbing a cool wet cloth over the bruise on her cheek. Her own back, legs, and wrists hurt, but she did not mind that. She was thankful that Barmer had only come back this morning and let her out, only that, with no other damage. She would have to go to the fields soon, and dared not delay, since she was confident that Jameson would be watching.

"Where he hurt you, baby? Don' be afraid, you can show yo mama."

Olivia moaned, pointing to her cheek, a gash below her left breast, her hips, and between her legs. "Mama, it hurt so bad. Why he hurt me so? What'd I do?"

"Hush, now. Don' worry. You didn' do nothun. He just a mean man, and he hurts us because he know someday all this gonna be gone, and he stan' before his Maker with no excuse and no power over us or anyone else. He just cain't stan' the thought that black folks like you an' me might be in hebbin. He like de debbil—he know his time is short. He does misery to others while he got the power to do it. It make him feel big and impawtant. But in de end, he just a man."

She washed and cleaned her child's wounds, poulticing and bandaging the best she could. She spoke and prayed gently while she did it, but in the back of her mind she raged, prayed revenge, and cast about for a solution. The crisis had finally come. Jameson would no longer just abuse and rape her, but her daughters as well. She might even be sold, since he had tired of her, and then she would have no way to help or soothe her babies. She might never see them again.

* * *

Luther crept to his slave bed that evening aching in every part of his body, but particularly his gashed head. He had again gone to Auntie May and obtained a bandage made from ripped petticoats. He felt like he was moving in slow motion, slightly dizzy, with a throbbing headache. The cuts were not very visible, but the pain came from inside. He had stumbled through the rest of his duties for the day, provoking more than one annoyed remark from Miss Lucy about his clumsiness. When she asked him what was wrong, he answered honestly that he had stumbled and

Flanagan had "disciplined" him for it. Privately, later, he had overheard Lucy berating the hapless overseer about his treatment of a valuable slave. That had not stopped her from telling him not to be so careless, though. She sent him to bed early, telling him not to bother with his usual evening duties; she would get Phoebe to fill in for him. He sank down on his pallet, relieved not to have to move.

He had almost dropped into the blessed oblivion of sleep, when he felt himself roughly shaken. Opening his eyes, he saw double for a moment; he found one of the other slaves, Jackson, leaning over him, looking very worried.

"Luther! Luther! You gots ta come quick!"

"Says who?" Luther shot back sleepily. "Miz Lucy done give me de night off."

"Yore mama, that's who! She done come all de way from Jameson's plantation. She say she risk her life to come, and you best come now!" said Jackson sharply.

Groggy and still in pain, Luther roused himself, worried and afraid. His mother had run away! Luther was sure that she did not have a pass. He stumbled and followed Jackson in the dark, his questions flared into sheer terror.

They did not dare take a torch or a lamp. Ashland might not be as severe as the Jameson farm, but a slave out wandering near the boundaries of the property and the wood late at night was bound to attract suspicion and questions. Twice Luther fell, and Jackson had to help him up. It occurred to Luther that Jackson was taking risk on himself that he did not have to. The clouds parted and came together again; the half-moon a help and a danger at the same time, as the light showed the way but exposed them to potential discovery. They stayed close to buildings, in the shadows, listening intently to the night sounds, every twig, every chirp, a cause for renewed terror. Once, as they started to move from building to tree, they heard the crunching of boots as a white groomsman came by. They froze, and waited until he passed a good distance away.

Finally they reached the edge of the wood, near the road. Crouching behind a huge catalpa tree, Jackson slowly looked around and listened. When all seemed clear, Jackson whistled four quick chirps, paused, and then repeated them, sounding exactly like a cardinal. After a brief pause, he tapped loudly on the tree, like a woodpecker. Again, a brief pause, and three hooded shapes emerged from the underbrush near the road. Jackson poked his head around the tree and motioned them over. The moon chose that moment to emerge, and Luther saw the faces of his mother and two sisters. They came to him, embraced him briefly, and moved quietly to the cover of a small grove of ash trees.

"Mama! What you doin' here? Dey catch you, dey kill you! And Livia and Clara, they get sold South—or worse!"

"I just couldn' stand it no mo'! It's one thing he come after me—I can take it. But last night, he come after Livia. An' pass me to Barmer. You know what'll happen next—he come for Clara. My soul just die! We headin' nawth. I knowed we ain't likely to make it, but I gots ta try. I die either way."

Jackson just shook his head.

"Most folks they gonna run, they got plans, and help, months, mebbe years ahead—the fools just run, and get deyselves caught. You all best get walkin' back, fast as you kin, and hope you don' get caught or noticed you was gone. I don' know how you even knew to get here, but soon as dey know, dey gonna set de dawgs after you. An' you cain't run dat fast. Not wid dese chillin," finished Jackson.

"He right, Mama! Dey catch you, dey whip you till you cain't stan'. A hundred lashes, then dey brand you. You live thru dat, dey find other ways to debble you. An den you get sold. Or dey sell de chillin. If de dawgs don' chew 'em up!"

Clara began to sob quietly in fear. Jemima, wavering, looked over to her.

Olivia spoke, "No. I don' care. I'd rather die, slow or fast, than go back. Dat debbil, he come agin, I kill him. Then they hang me sho'. An' Clara here, it be de same."

"You could come wid us!" said Clara pleadingly. "You our brudder. We needs a man along. I'll keep up—or you leave me. Livia tol' me about las' night. I ain't lettin' it happen to me," she said, suddenly resolute.

"You all crazy," said Jackson. "The patrols get you before you get two miles."

"We pass three patrols on de way here," said Jemima proudly. "Got directions from free blacks, cabin in de clearing a few miles back."

Jackson said, "You lucky—did you know some blacks own other blacks? I'm leavin'. De ketch me wid you, I get de same as you. Ain't nobody gonna believe me. But since you crazy, I be crazy too. Dey prob'ly beat it outta you an' I done fer. But I cain't just watch dese chillin go to death widout hep. So listen close. Look at de sky! See ober dere? De stars dey look like a water dipper in de sky, de cup facin' up. Den see ober yonder, anudder smaller dipper, upside down. Look in a line from de top corner of de big dipper cup to to de last star in de handle of de small dipper. See de bright star in between? Dat de nawth star, de freedom star. Travel toward it, you goin' nawth. You got to go nawth till you get to de big ribber, de O-hi-o. And you got to cross it. I hear de patrols be fierce on de ribber. Dey keep de boats locked up. But you got to cross it, you want to be free."

"O thank you!" said Jemima fervently, clasping his hands.

"Don' thank me none—I prob'ly just signed you to death. You nebber heard it from me, and I nebber saw you. One more thing—hide in de day, go in ribbers and criks whenever you kin, and each day, when de sun going down, travel away from de sun awhile. Don' trust anyone, white or black. Look for towns called Paris and across de ribber, Ripley. I knowed 'cause I went on a trip wi' Massa Clay once. I heered from some other darkies that the Methodist minister, Tom Painter, in Maysville, nawth o' Paris on de ribber can be trusted—but I don' know. Thas all I know, and you nebber saw me, hear? Y'all go on back home!" Jackson turned and crawled away, not looking back.

Left with his family, Luther felt torn in two. How could he leave them? Yet, how could he go and risk capture and death? Did Jackson know what he was talking about, or just repeating vague rumors he'd heard? How would they eat? How would they elude the patrols?

The sound of Irish shouting shattered his indecision.

Flanagen roared, "What're ye creepin' about? Ye black imp of hell! I should flay you alive and use the skin for bootblack! On yer feet! We'll get to the bottom of this!"

Luther knew he had minutes before the dogs would be on them. Flanagan's wrath would seek a new direction. If Flanagan caught him, he would be out for revenge. Urging his mother and sisters, they crawled on all fours swiftly toward the bushes at the road's edge. Then, looking both ways, they sprinted across the road and into the forest. Luther's head was spinning from the effort.

THE CLOUDS THICKEN

June 1859

Will's stomach tightened. He had not been feeling well the last few days. He had survived his first two exhibitions with the Rifles, but today was special. Jenny would be watching, and had invited him to her uncle's after the show. Will had gone buggy riding with her twice, and started meeting her after university classes ended for the day. He enjoyed her wit and sense of humor. He tried not to show it, but he could feel himself attracted to her. She showed a surprising knowledge of horses for a girl. Today he was supposed to lead his squad in the load and fire drill. His uniform itched. He feared soiling it by throwing up. He was determined not to miss today's exhibition. Their captain, John Morgan, would also be there to review the troops. As he turned the corner, carrying his rifle and walking toward the university grounds, he almost bumped into Joe Breckenridge.

"Hey, Will! Good to see you," said Joe, extending a hand. "Haven't run into you much since our last hunting expedition."

"Oh, hello, Joe! I guess since we don't have school together in the summer, I just haven't run into you. I'm still working at the store and the farm."

"And the uniform tells me you're doing something else as well."

"Yes, Captain Morgan asked me to join the Lexington Rifles. I'm going to the university grounds to put on a show now. Why don't you come?"

Joe thought hard. "All right, I'll come and watch—but as far as I know, Morgan's group is pro-slavery. You might want to think about what you're getting involved in there."

"Captain Morgan is for Kentucky and believes each state has the right to determine its own destiny. Anyway, this is mostly for show."

The boys fell into step together and in just a few minutes arrived at the parade ground, where people were already gathering, and there were twenty or thirty other green uniforms. Will was cursing himself for inviting Joe now, since there would be one more familiar person to witness if he failed. He excused himself and quickly found the privy at the edge of the field. Emerging, he felt queasy but slightly more solid on his feet. As he walked over to take his place, he spied Jenny standing by the rail and waved at her, receiving a smile and wave in return. His heart fluttered, but he told himself to concentrate on the task ahead. He reached his squad.

Lieutenant West bellowed, "Company, attention!"

Will fell into his spot along with all the others, making a perfect line.

"Order arms! Shoulder arms! Company, march!"

Will marched with the others, but again his stomach lurched, and he tried not to stumble, to keep in step. The commands came faster, and some of the moves became more complicated. Morgan often told them that cavalry sometimes had to function as infantry, and they should know how to do it. They might not look crisp and smart on the battlefield, but they had learned to obey quickly and without question. As his squad wheeled and passed Ben Drake's, he almost did not notice a foot stuck out to trip him. At the last second he gave a decidedly unmilitary jump to avoid the foot, earning a rebuke from the sergeant, but not loud enough for everyone to hear. After what seemed an eternity, he heard the commands, "Halt! Present arms! Parade rest!" Now was his moment.

"Company C! Support arms! Shoulder arms! March!"

Will led his group forward, four abreast. Morgan chose his group because they now all had muskets or rifles.

"Halt! Prepare to load!"

As the commands came, Will was to be the first in his line to load, ram, and prime his rifle. The others would follow his lead within a fraction of a second. It would appear simultaneous to those watching, if done correctly. They loaded patch and powder but no actual bullet, to avoid shooting spectators. Will's hand shook a little while pouring the powder, spilled some, but managed it in the required time. He knelt to fire as the line behind him started their loading process. He felt his stomach wobble and barely avoided vomiting and dropping the rifle as it fired.

After the exhibition concluded, and his company dismissed, he shakily walked toward the sidelines. He could feel the heat of fever. Jenny came over with her uncle, Dr. Simpson. Joe Breckenridge and Archie Moodie, a member of Will's company, approached from the other side.

Archie spoke first. "Good recovery there, Crump! I saw what Drake was trying to do. You outsmarted him. You're a credit to the Rifles!" He clapped Will on the shoulder, making him stumble a little. "Say, Crump—are you not well?"

"J—j –just a little queasy, I guess."

Jenny reached out and touched his forehead. "Why, Uncle Tim, he's burning with fever!"

Dr. Simpson examined him briefly. "Joe, Archie, please help me get him to the buggy. Archie, will you take his rifle?"

"Sure, Dr. Simpson. Let's go, Joe."

Each put one of Will's arms over his shoulders and guided him to the buggy, with Dr. Simpson and Jenny following. Once he was in, Will suddenly sat up and said, "Albinia! I'm supposed to pick up Albinia!"

"Shh! Lie back. We'll see to your sister," said Dr. Simpson. "Can either of you boys go over to the livery, get his ox team, and pick up his sister at the dress shop?"

"I'd surely like to help, but I got to get home to help my pa," said Archie.

"I'll go," said Joe. "It's not that far from the church, I can let my pa know."

"Good," said Dr. Simpson. "I'll come out and pick you up in the morning."

"And I'll come too, if Uncle will let me?" said Jenny imploringly.

"Of course, my dear," said Dr. Simpson.

* * *

Albinia locked the dress shop and dropped the key into her reticule. She turned and scanned the street, and saw in the distance a wagon with oxen approaching. She assumed it might be Will, amid the bustling horse and foot traffic. As the wagon drew closer, she recognized with a start that her brother was not driving.

"Miss Crump, your brother sends his apologies, but he is not well. Dr. Simpson has seen to him, and if you accept, I am to escort you home," said Joe, climbing down from the wagon.

"Mr. Breckinridge, isn't it? The parson's son?" asked Albinia.

"Yes, ma'am. At your service."

"Under the circumstances, I appreciate your assistance. What's wrong with Will?" she asked worriedly.

"I'm not entirely sure, ma'am. He was at the exhibition with the Rifles. Afterwards, he just suddenly took ill, fever and all. Doctor took him home."

"Then please take me there as well, as soon as may be."

Albinia accepted his help into the wagon, noticing his curly hair and courtly manners. She had seen him at church, of course, but never had any occasion to converse. She could not help comparing him with David Horner. David was so intense, but this young man seemed reserved and polite, with just a hint of humor and mischief in his gray eyes. She knew he was Will's friend but little else about him. She settled herself in the wagon and watched as Joe expertly guided the oxen through the busy streets. In the gathering twilight, people hurried home to their suppers. Joe took a route she usually avoided, past the Cheapside slave auction block, deserted this time of day. There was a stench from the nearby slave pens, where men, women, and children sat in shackles, staring vacantly into the evening. As they turned onto Broadway, moving toward the Versailles Road, Albinia saw a movement in the alley. Three or four Negroes walked into the alley from the road. The last one nervously turned and looked back, eyes growing wide as he recognized Albinia. It was Luther.

Albinia hesitated and then told Joe, "Stop the wagon!"

Without waiting for help, she jumped down and headed toward the alley. She heard Luther tell the others to run, as he turned back to face her.

"Luther! What are you doing here? You'll be picked up as a runaway!"

"Please, Miss Albinia, just get back on that wagon! Don't draw attention to us! They after us, and we got to get away!" pleaded Luther.

"You'll never make it! Don't you know you're right near the slave market now? Any one of those drivers could see you and pick you up! You're in great danger!"

"I know it, Miss Albinia. But the dawgs won't find us among all these other slaves. But my momma just cain't go back to that man! I got no time to explain, and I got to try! Please, just leave me be! Pretend you never saw me!"

Albinia was frightened, and torn. Suddenly, she made up her mind.

"Come get in the back of the wagon, under the hay and the tarps. I know someone who can help you. If there are dogs tracking, they'll never find your scent if you're riding in the wagon. Bring the others. Hurry!"

Fear, anger, mistrust, and hesitation crossed Luther's face and eyes. Luther quickly decided.

"Momma! Livia! Bring Clara and come. I know dis lady, she gwine to help us," said Luther.

"But Luther, you heard Jackson, not to trust...," said Jemima.

"Ain't no time to argue. Those dogs, we ain't got rid of 'em yet, I reckon. Come!" urged Luther.

And with that, they all came. Joe's eyes got big as they emerged from the shadows, and he started to protest. Albinia shushed him, abandoning propriety.

"Joe, I know Luther. He wouldn't do this without a good reason. You don't have to be part of it. Luther can drive the oxen, and if he's with me, we won't be questioned. I wouldn't ask you to risk yourself. Thank you for what you've done and being a good friend to Will. But now you need to go," she said firmly.

"No. I'll stay. Get them in the wagon and tell me where to go."

Albinia was frustrated and afraid, but there was no time to argue. She helped Luther and the others into the back of the wagon with the hay and covered them with canvas, working quickly. Albinia got David's card out of her reticule, and by lamplight read the address to Joe.

"Don't hurry the oxen, Joe. We want to look normal, just heading home after picking up supplies. When we get there, put the wagon in the back in the alley. I'll go find David, and he'll tell us what to do next."

Darkness fell over them like a heavy cloak. Joe's hand shook as he lit the lantern on the front of the wagon, and remounted. Albinia knew he was afraid but he had decided to stay, against her urging. The streets were clearing out. People were in the homes. The slave patrols might come through, but wouldn't check a wagon with two white people in town before curfew. Her heart pounded, her throat was dry. What if David wasn't home? What if a patrol came by as Luther got out of the wagon? What if David didn't want them, or didn't know a place for them to go? If caught, she and Joe would go to jail. She didn't want to think about what would happen to Luther and his family. Under her breath, she started praying, praying for God to shield them from prying eyes. The oxen seemed to move in slow motion, and any moment she expected to hear the harsh laughter and challenge of a patrol.

After what seemed an eternity, but was really only about fifteen minutes, Joe pulled the wagon into an alley. Albinia whispered to Luther to keep still and be quiet. Joe helped her down and waited with the oxen. She went up the back stairs of the building and saw the light of an oil lamp through the window. She knocked on the door, tentatively, then louder. At length she heard footsteps, and the door opened to reveal David, looking sleepy and haggard.

"Miss Crump?" David looked confused and surprised. "What brings you here? And at this hour?"

"Mr. Horner, I apologize. I didn't know who else to turn to. I ... I ... have some friends, with me. Negro friends. Runaways, I think. I need help," she stammered. "B ... But if you won't help me, I'll take them anyway. Will you help?"

David looked first surprised, then grimly amused. "You've taken a great risk coming here. For all of us."

Disappointed, she said, "All right then. If you won't help, sorry to bother you. I thought that after the other night...." She turned to go.

"Just a moment, Miss Crump. I did not say I wouldn't help you. This is not the ordinary way of doing things. Anyone might see you here. Come in quickly, while I make ready."

Too frightened to protest about impropriety, she let herself be ushered into a small parlor, simply but elegantly furnished. A small Chippendale slant desk and chair were against the wall, with the single oil lamp on it. Papers were strewn across it, as though she had interrupted him in the midst of correspondence. A red trimmed rug, slightly threadbare, was in the center of the floor, and two side chairs in the corners.

David disappeared without a word into a room, and she waited nervously. When he emerged, she barely recognized him. He wore a battered straw hat, overalls, and a flannel shirt. A gray wig poked out from the straw hat, and smoke curled up from a corncob pipe. The glasses were gone. His green eyes sparkled with laughter at her astonishment. She noticed he wore a holster with a cartridge belt. The holster had a long barreled revolver in it, and he carried a double-barreled shotgun, and a jug.

"Evnin' ma'am! Allow me to introduce meself. Edwin Stoddard at your service," he said in an Irish brogue with a mock bow. Then seriously, he continued in his normal voice, "If you're going to do this, learn to disguise yourself. Never be someone recognizable. Come, we haven't much time."

She followed him obediently back to the wagon below, still too astounded to say much. She finally spoke up and wanted to introduce Joe, but David stopped her.

"I don't mean to be rude, but it's best I don't know your name, sir. You've obviously been assisting Miss Albinia, as any gentleman would do. However, I strongly suggest that you leave. Walk or if you must, take the bay horse from that shed just over there," David said pointing. "Go a different way than you came, and Godspeed. There's no need for you to take further risks. Quite frankly, where we are going is not a place that you should know about."

Joe looked conflicted. "I've come this far. What do you think, Albinia?"

She flashed him a special smile. "Joe, I think you've already done far more than could be expected. This was not just a simple ride home you've given me. Please, do as our farmer friend here says," she said, glancing sideways at David. "I've already endangered you enough. Please."

Joe helped her into the wagon and then said, "All right then. May I come and see you and Will soon?"

Albinia was in a hurry to be off, and her head muddled. She wasn't thinking about the import of these words. "Of course. Come soon. I know Will would want to see you. And thank you!"

Joe walked off into the gloom, further down the alley. Albinia watched David mount the wagon and lay the shotgun across his lap, barrels pointed away from her. As the oxen started off, he quietly asked Albinia, "How many do we have?"

"Just Luther, his mother, and two sisters. The mother and sisters belong to Jameson. Luther is Miss Lucy Clay's personal slave."

David groaned softly, then said, "Lord have mercy. The Clays have some of the finest dogs, and the money to hire slave catchers." When they were passing buildings on the street with no one about, he quietly addressed Luther.

"Luther, you've started something very dangerous. Not only your life but mine, Albinia's, and everyone you meet is at risk. If you hope to reach freedom, you must be as silent as a grave back there. Don't move. Don't talk. Breathe quietly. No matter what happens you must be silent, and you must follow my orders. I mean you no harm, and I will do my best to save you."

The oxen moved along, their shoes clopping along the hard earth of the street. Albinia saw that David turned northeast, along the Paris road. When they were nearing the outskirts of town, he spoke again.

"Can you act drunk?" he said.

"What! No, I never had a drink in my life!" said Albinia indignantly.

"Well, this may be the time to start," said David, handing her the jug. "If we're stopped by a patrol, you should act as ridiculous as possible without dragging it out. Drink some of this, just to give your breath the smell. Then follow my lead and let acting do the rest. I won't let anyone hurt you, but it's best if you're not anything like yourself. In the dark, they may take you for a trollop—let them. Just don't get down from the wagon for any reason if they stop us. If I have to start shooting, get down as low as you can and stay there."

Frightened, Albinia took a few sips from the jug. The unaccustomed liquor burned her throat and she coughed, handing it back to him. The moon began to rise above the trees. Stars began to be visible. The wagon jarred and bumped along the Paris road. Albinia tried to see in the dark, glancing nervously along each side of the road, expecting at any moment for a patrol to pop out from the bushes. Her nerves stretched tight.

After some time, David turned off into a small clearing. He began to get down. "Stay here," he said, handing her the revolver. "I hope you don't have to use it, but don't hesitate if there's trouble. Run toward town, staying off the road. Don't wait or think about anyone else. Otherwise, I'll be back in a few minutes."

He took the lantern. She clutched the revolver in fear, not really knowing what to do with it. She watched as the lantern grew further away, and then appeared to climb a small hill. The clouds passed in front of the moon. Around her, it was utterly dark. In the distance, she heard the baying of hounds briefly. Then it stopped. She heard the boards in the wagon creak as one of Luther's family shifted position. She jumped at every cricket, every owl hooting. After a few minutes, she heard a night-ingale. Then the lantern waved back and forth at the top of the hill. A few more minutes passed and she heard the call of a whippoorwill, followed by crunching feet as David emerged from the gloom with the lantern.

"It's clear ahead, tonight," he said. He clambered into the wagon, took the reins and the revolver, and again put the shotgun on his lap. Urging the oxen forward, in a few minutes they came to a stone church off the road to the right, just as the moon came out from behind the clouds. A small sign proclaimed it was Hopewell Presbyterian. David drove the oxen around to the rear of the church and dismounted. He knocked in a pattern she couldn't figure out on the bulkhead doors of the church base-ment. The doors quickly opened.

"Get them in quickly!" said a gray-haired, bespectacled figure. "I don't know how long we have. Any pursuit?"

"None that I know about now. But one of these belongs to the Clays, so they'll be looking."

David walked to the rear of the wagon, lowered the tailgate, and pulled out the tarp.

"Quickly, in the church! Don't ask questions, just do it," said David.

Luther and Olivia looked at each other doubtfully, but Jemima urged them. "We here now. Do as dey say. We got to trust de Lawd."

They passed into the church basement. The bulkhead doors shut. Albinia felt uneasy. Did she really trust the man at the church? David seemed to, so she supposed she had to as well.

David and Albinia drove back to town without incident. She asked him to drop the wagon at the livery and her at the dress shop. She would change and go to Katy's house for the night. In the morning, she would find Jenny and Dr. Simpson.

* * *

Albinia located Dr. Simpson and told him that an ox had thrown a shoe. She explained that this made Joe obliged to turn around, and she spent the night in town. They took Dr. Simpson's buggy to pick up Joe from the church, and the wagon from the livery. Albinia would ride with Dr. Simpson and Jenny, with Joe following behind in the wagon. Albinia still felt shaken from the previous night's adventure, and bone achingly tired. She knew, however, that she must show none of how she was feeling at home. She briefly got a chance to let Joe know what had happened, and entreated him to say nothing to anyone. He reluctantly agreed. Albinia felt guilty for not rushing home to see her sick brother. She also felt cautiously exultant that perhaps she had helped Luther to escape to freedom.

Arriving at the Crump homestead, she found her parents so concerned about Will that they barely asked her questions about her absence. Aside from a thoughtful glance from her father when she mentioned the ox shoe, no one seemed to question her story. Lying to her parents also bothered her. She could not possibly tell them the truth. As long as Joe was here, she could barely breathe, thinking about what he might say or let slip. And what was happening to Luther?

* * *

It was already early afternoon when Will awoke. He had no memory of how he had gotten to his bed. He was in the back room of the cabin, which the whole family shared as a sleeping room, divided by blankets as curtains. Will had a straw tick on the floor in a corner. The blanket pulled back and he woke to see his mother looking in on him.

"How do you feel?" she said softly.

"I'm not sure, Ma. I'm not feelin' hot anymore, but weak."

"Your father said to stay in bed today. He'll handle chores. You have visitors, if you're up to it. Dr. Simpson and Jenny are here, and Joe Breckinridge."

"Jenny? Here?"

"Yes, she and her uncle have been waiting for an hour. They didn't want to wake you."

Jenny appeared at the gap in the blankets with a steaming mug in her hand.

"I have some dogwood bark tea for you. My uncle says you should drink it all, slowly, if you can keep it down, and some soda crackers."

She came in and set the mug on the small low table near the straw tick, Sara still looking on. Jenny sat on a crude stool, watching him. Will pulled his head up on an elbow and smiled weakly. Jenny hesitated, looked lovingly back at him, and rose to leave. Will wanted her to stay but knew it was not proper, and he did not have the presence of mind to ask. Suddenly Jenny turned back, bent over the bed, and kissed his forehead. Then she rushed from the room, leaving Will and Sara astonished.

* * *

Albinia took the time while Jenny was with Will to put away her things, and begin to get the noon meal ready.

Her father had come from the fields to see about the buggy and the doctor. Albinia was startled to see Jenny rush out of the back room, and wondered. Joe went in to see Will. So far, Albinia had avoided being alone with Joe except for a few seconds in town. Even though in her own musings she compared him to David, she felt uncomfortable with Joe. He was her brother's friend, and he had honored that friendship with his service to her. Yet she thought she detected a spark of interest from him that had nothing to do with Will and everything to do with her as a woman. As she stirred the stew, she thought of ways to discourage this interest.

* * *

The night Luther escaped, Albinia was afraid. Now, a week later, it actually seemed exciting. She wondered about Luther and wanted to see David. As she sewed in the shop in the afternoon, she thought about how she could see him again. She was mindful that she shouldn't go around to his apartment over the store again—she didn't want to attract notice. Besides, it wasn't proper for a young woman to openly pursue a young man. Surely he attended church? She didn't know which one. Perhaps she could send a note to Cassius Clay and inquire after him. He must frequent White Hall, being in Mr. Clay's employ. Her needle kept moving as these thoughts spun in her brain, and she heard the bell, signifying a customer in the front of the shop. She set her work aside and went out to see who was there.

She found a little girl who looked to be about ten years old, in a finely made play dress, and David Horner. Albinia could hardly believe her good fortune. David was here!

"Yes, may I help you?" she said, giving no indication that she knew him, lest it give something away.

"Yes. I hear that you make fine dresses here. This is Miss Laura Clay," he said, indicating the little girl, who curtsied, "daughter of my employer, Cassius Clay. The Clays have a summer party in three weeks. Mrs. Clay desires her daughter to have a new dress, as well as one for herself. Mrs. Clay was unable to come today, but sent measurements from her last gown. She thought that might suffice until she could come herself for a fitting."

He handed her a paper. Albinia looked down at it and struggled to conceal her surprise. The paper did have measurements, but also a note that read,

Meet me tonight at the Charbonneau restaurant, 7 sharp. If you cannot come, tell me the dress won't be ready for a month. If you don't wish to come, tell me you are too busy to make the dress. It concerns our package.

Albinia smiled and turned to Laura.

"Well, Miss Clay! Let's get you measured—if we are to have you a suitable dress in three weeks, and one for your mother as well, we must start immediately!" Albinia caught David's eye, and he acknowledged her communication with a smile.

"If you'll follow me, Miss Clay," said Albinia, taking her into the rear of the shop out of public view. Laura chatted gaily about her family. She found it interesting that Albinia knew Lucy, whom she'd only met once. Albinia expertly used the measuring tape and scribbled notes while talking. She was quite used to this with her customers. However, she did have a little trouble concentrating on what Laura was saying, because of her excitement about the prospect of meeting David at the restaurant. How thrilling, and very improper!

Albinia guided Laura back to the front and showed her some patterns to choose from, along with pictures of what the completed gown might look like.

"I shall come round in a week to see how the dresses are progressing, then, Miss…?" inquired David.

"Miss Crump. Albinia Crump. Thank you. Give my regards to Mr. and Mrs. Clay."

David and Laura left the shop. Two complicated dresses in just three weeks! She would have to work hard—but she would see David!

* * *

Promptly at seven, as David requested, Albinia entered the restaurant. She arranged with Katy to spend the night, and sent a message by a neighbor for her father not to come and pick her up. She had told her father there was too much work in the shop to come home, which was only the truth. She didn't know what to expect, but in her heart she hoped for a quiet, romantic dinner where she could get to know David better. The Charbonneau was one of the best restaurants in town, usually beyond her means.

Her heart sank as she saw another couple seated at the table with David, near the back of the restaurant. She'd been hoping for a dinner alone with him. She indicated to the waiter that she was to join that party. She consoled herself that at least she might find out about Luther. He'd said it concerned their package.

"Ah, Miss Crump! How kind of you to join us! May I present Mr. Franklin and Mabel Johnson?"

Franklin was a sturdily built white-haired man, medium height. He wore a decently tailored suit, but looked like one familiar with manual labor. Mabel was stout, with a smile that made her whole countenance beam, wreathed in wrinkles. Her hair had once been chestnut, now streaked with gray.

Albinia was confused. She couldn't understand why they were here, but didn't wish to be rude. She greeted them warmly and seated herself, looking inquiringly at David.

After the waiter came and they ordered, David spoke.

"I'm sure you all may wonder why I've brought you here. Let me explain. There are certain delicate packages, which occasionally need personal attention and careful delivery. I'm sure you take my meaning. Mr. and Mrs. Johnson here have helped for some time in taking these packages and keeping them for me, until it becomes possible to take time to deliver them to their ultimate destinations. There may be times in the future when I am unavailable, due to my travel with Mr. Clay, as he speaks frequently in the cause of abolition. I handle many duties for him, including his personal security. During those times when I am gone, I wish you to know that Miss Crump here, and Mr. and Mrs. Johnson, are to be trusted. In addition, Miss Crump, you will find that Mr. and Mrs. Johnson know a great deal about this package delivery business that you do not. You would be wise to learn from them. I will undertake to teach you to drive a team of horses myself, a necessary skill in matters that concern us. For propriety, Mrs. Johnson may accompany us at times on such ventures, or both of them together. Usually, the different links in our chain do not know each other, for safety. However, in this case, it seems best to acquaint you, so that no packages are lost in the event of my absence. Mrs. Johnson, you may contact Mrs. Crump through the dressmaking shop over at High Street and Broadway. Miss Crump, should you need to, you can contact Mrs. Johnson through a worker at the freight office named Lewis. It's best if you contact one another as little as possible, only at need.

Mr. Johnson is a cooper, and a fair hand at fixing almost anything. Mrs. Johnson is a cook for the Bryant family of Waveland."

Through all this, Albinia listened with amazement. She would never have guessed these people to be involved in the Underground Railroad. She supposed, that was, after all, the point—no one would suspect them.

"But what about the package we delivered a week ago?" wondered Albinia.

David hesitated, as if unsure whether to answer in this setting. He lowered his voice. "Once a package moves down the line, we don't usually attempt to follow it. However, in this case I can tell you the package is where we left it. The size of that package makes it difficult to move. Even single packages sometimes have to wait weeks or months at a time, until the right means of moving them is found."

Albinia was surprised. She assumed David would have found a means of moving Luther into freedom by now.

"Miss Crump, I can see that you have a good heart, and from what Mr. Horner has told us, some spirit and gumption as well," said Franklin. "If I may, a bit of advice. Patience. Always patience. Rash moves lead to trouble. And much is at stake."

Albinia felt patronized, but had to admit to herself she had no real experience—just the one night. Apparently they'd been doing this for a while. All right then—she would learn.

"I assure you, Mr. Johnson, I am a ready and willing learner."

"Good, because we've work to do this night," replied Franklin.

They finished the excellent meal speaking of other things.

* * *

Albinia went with Mabel to a house outside of town, near Winchester and Cleveland roads. She marveled at how well Mabel controlled the team of horses and carriage that they drove. Entering the house, they went upstairs. There was a room filled with women's clothing, all different sizes and descriptions.

"Find something that fits," said Mabel. "From what David says, you could probably make yourself costumes, but there isn't time tonight. Pick something that's nothing like what you'd usually wear, either fancier or dowdier. Think of it as putting on a show for the patrols—if one of them passed you on the street the next day, they shouldn't know it was you they saw the night before. Of course, your costume needs to fit the mission. It won't do to be dressed as a floozy if your only companion is black; no one would believe you an owner, for example. Try to vary your outfits and your story—no telling when you might encounter the same patroller twice."

Albinia chose three outfits—a poor farmer's wife, fatter than herself, with a wig, a saloon girl outfit, and the dress of a fine lady, worthy of one she might make for the Clays. She could alter them for better fit later.

Mabel took a small pistol out of a drawer and stuffed it in her reticule.

"You'll want to get something to shoot. No need tonight, with the three of us along. But soon you'll want something, and learn to use it. Surely your father or brother will have no objection to teaching you to defend yourself, where you are in town at night on occasion. Tonight you're along to learn. No doubt Mr. Horner will take you some other times, day or night. We mostly operate at night, even though that's when the patrols are out, because there are also fewer people to encounter. Many nights it's just a peaceful drive in the starlight. You'll need to learn to drive, not only in the daytime but at night as well. I often use the ruse of a sick relative in need, or a baby needs deliverin'."

Mabel turned to her seriously. "This is no lark, Miss Crump. If you're not willing to risk jail for these people, I'll take you home now. The slaves have been in jail all their lives, as it were. We give'em a chance at what we take for granted. We call it the Underground Railroad—but it's really just people helping people. Some 'conductors' on the road are black themselves, free men. Not so many women, due to the danger." She laughed. "Myself—I'm old, nobody would bother with me. But patrollers are a sorry lot, with the law on their side. Some wouldn't think twice about taking liberties with a young pretty woman."

Albinia was disconcerted, and a little afraid. Could something … like that … really happen? Then in her mind she saw Luther, fear and hope in his eyes, and little Clara, afraid but determined. How could she do less than a little ten-year-old slave girl who risked everything? Didn't God say to give what you have the power to give?

"I … I hadn't thought of it. I suppose those are things I should have thought about after my experience with David, uh, Mr. Horner."

Mabel smiled at the slip. "Like him, do you? Well, he's handsome enough. But that's a poor reason to be involved in this," she said grimly.

Albinia protested, "No, no, that's not it. I … I saw a slave of a friend mistreated. It made me realize how hard life is for them. When he tried to escape, I helped him, took him to Mr. Horner. I didn't know anyone else. Where do they come from?"

"The slaves? Everywhere. Some from around here, some from as far away as Alabama and Mississippi. You'll get a message to pick up a 'package' at such and such place on a particular evening. If something goes wrong you send word, usually through a message to me or Lewis, and we try again."

They got into the carriage again—no one would have recognized them from the restaurant. Albinia had a blonde wig, and appeared almost fat. Her makeup made her look ten years older, and Mabel helped her paste on fake blonde eyebrows. The costume and makeup might not have passed inspection in the daylight, but in the dark, no one would know them.

David and Franklin were waiting for them. They concealed the carriage on a side road, and all piled into a two-seater open wagon. The June night was warm, the moon just rising.

After a mile, they turned down a dirt track, went about a hundred yards, and stopped. Albinia was puzzled. It looked like the middle of nowhere. Fields of tall hemp were on both sides of the little road, with forest at the edges. The dark of the dim starlight made the night feel spooky, as if someone were watching. She watched as David dismounted, with Franklin on guard, holding a shotgun.

David walked toward a small shack, back in the trees that she hadn't noticed before, singing softly the song, "*Steal away to Jesus.*" Franklin kept looking around on all sides. Mabel got down and went back up the dirt track with the lantern, keeping watch on the rear. After a few minutes, David returned with a tall black man. David quickly removed a false bottom from the wagon, and the Negro scrunched himself into the cavity. Albinia judged he must have been well over six feet tall. David replaced the cover, and then moved a few boxes on top of it.

"All right," said David. "We've been to a party. Franklin and Mabel here have to catch a steamboat, and we've come all the way from Red River. That's our story if we're stopped. Anthony?" David addressed the man in hiding, "you must stay hidden, and quiet. All our lives depend on it. Whatever you do, don't panic."

The wagon reversed, going north toward Paris. The horses moved at a surprisingly fast trot for nighttime. They moved through the pleasant summer night, seeing no one on the road until just before Paris. A lone horseman came out from the shadows, holding up a lantern, and bid them to halt.

David repeated their story. Franklin said something about pressing business from the Red River ironworks. The horseman looked curiously at the ladies but seemed almost bored, waving them on.

After a few minutes, they stopped at the back of the Methodist Church. Mabel and Franklin got down and stood guard. David moved boxes and extracted their passenger, ushering him into the church. Albinia didn't see who received him.

On the way back to Lexington, David told her that the man Anthony had come all the way from Louisiana on his own, had been hiding out in the fields for months trying to make contact with the Railroad to cross over north.

They dropped her off with her costumes at the dress shop. Albinia found an empty trunk to stow the clothes in, changed back to her normal appearance, and walked to Katy's house, letting herself in the back door. She would tell them she'd worked until nearly dawn, which was not far from the truth. She sank into bed, excited but bone weary.

* * *

Julia got Will to drive her to town the next morning. She wanted to visit a church friend and do a little shopping. She was also curious about Albinia. Why was her sister staying in town so much? Goodness knows there was enough work to do on the farm.

She went to the dress shop, but the door was locked. Albinia was not there yet. She thought that odd. She went round to Katy's house and found Albinia at table, just finishing breakfast.

"Julia! What brings you here?"

"And I might ask why you weren't home, and nor at the shop, at nine in the morning?"

"I wasn't aware I needed to report to you," Albinia said crossly.

"Ma was expecting you. You really should send word if your plans change."

"And you really shouldn't be so bossy, meddling in everyone's business. If Ma needs me, she knows how to tell me. Besides, the shop is flooded with work right now. I simply don't have time to go back and forth every day. You know my wages help keep the farm afloat," she said pointedly.

Julia sniffed. "All the same, you should let people know. I'll be in town until noon, then Will is driving me home. His teacher is sick today, so no school. You'd be welcome to ride home with us."

"Thanks, but I think I'll stay in town again tonight," she said, with a glance at Katy. "Assuming that's all right."

"Always welcome here," said Katy. "It's so nice to have another girl to talk to. Unless you'll be out late again."

"Out late?" inquired Julia.

"Oh, just working at the shop late. I told you—there's so much work right now."

Julia eyed her sister suspiciously but said nothing.

* * *

Julia looked around town, mostly window shopping. She bought a few grocery items for her mother and walked past the freight office toward the livery to meet Will. She almost bumped into Hiram Johannsen, who was leaving the freight office.

"Miss Crump! How delightful to see you again! May I carry those for you?" said Hiram, referring to the groceries in her arms.

Julia felt flustered but intrigued. Why did this gentle giant keep noticing her?

"Why, thank you, Mr. Johannsen. That would be most helpful. I'm just going to the livery to meet my brother."

"If I may say so, your outfit is very becoming. Do you come to town often, Miss Crump?"

"Oh, usually once a week or so."

"Then perhaps I will see you again. I'm in town for business. I often have to go up to the river, but our offices here in Lexington need frequent attention."

He put her parcels in the wagon, tipped his hat, and left her to wait for Will. Julia felt flattered, but could not account for his attention. What could he see in a poor farm girl like her?

JOHN BROWN'S BODY

October 1859

Julia was on her hands and knees in the garden, harvesting pole beans and beets. She was wearing a patched slightly ragged work dress. Her hair flew in wisps in all directions as she worked. Her hands were muddy, caked with dirt. She heard Rustler barking, and assumed he was after a squirrel. As she worked, she mused about Hiram. Lately, he seemed to be everywhere when she went to town. He was at church, the general store, the livery. She wondered if this was coincidence or design. Was he really trying to see her?

Looking up, her father approached on the wagon. That must be what made Rustler bark. When he got down from the wagon, he walked toward her.

"Julia, I was in town, and this big fella came up to me, said he was a friend of yours. Some kinda foreigner, I reckon. Told me he'd met you at the Dorsey's barn dance last spring. He handed me a letter for you. Anything I should know about?" Robert asked quizzically.

Julia was startled. She stood, absently wiping the mud from her hands onto the work dress. "No, Pa, I don't think so. It must have been Hiram Johannsen. I've bumped into him a lot lately, in town. We did meet at the barn dance. His family is apparently a rich shipping family on the river, steamboats. He seems nice enough."

"Guess you'd better take the letter, see what he says."

Julia accepted the envelope and saw the formal address to Miss Julia Crump. She turned it over and broke the seal. Hands trembling a little, she opened it. Why would Hiram write to her, unless…. She began to read.

October 20, 1859

Dear Miss Crump,

I hope we have advanced far enough in our friendship that I may presume to write to you. I want you to know how fondly I think of you, and look forward to our meetings. Dare I hope that you feel the same? Your beauty and refined behavior have captured me. I often struggle to find words—English is still difficult for me. I very much want to spend more time with you. If you approve, I would like to speak to you and your father about calling on you. I apologize for this being so sudden, but I fear that the recent events in Harper's Ferry will bring our country closer to war. I will join the home guard formed by the governor, and fight for the United States if need be. I love this country. I wish to be more certain of your affections, before war comes, and let you know of mine. I will speak to your father, and await your answer at church on Sunday. I hope to become the happiest of men.

Your servant and dear friend,
Hiram Johannsen

Julia was speechless. She turned pale, then red. What would her father think? What was he talking about, Harper's Ferry? For that matter, what did she think herself?

"Well?" said Robert.

"I … I … Here—you read it."

Robert scanned the unfamiliar hand, but had no trouble making out the text. "Looks like you got yerself a beau. If'n you want him, that is. Do you?"

"Yes. No—I don't know! He's a nice fellow, but I don't know that much about him. What's he talking about, events in Harper's Ferry?"

"I'm surprised you didn't hear—whole town's talking about it. Got some folks pretty riled up. This fella John Brown, he tried to start a slave revolt up in Harper's Ferry, Virginia. He tried to capture a federal arsenal. Problem was, for him leastways, hardly any slaves joined the revolt. He got captured, gonna be on trial soon. Lotsa folks fearing the slaves will all revolt, kill them in their beds. Got the slavers and abolitionists at each other's throats, more'n usual."

"I'm sorry that happened, but I don't see how that affects us."

"Thing is, lotsa folks saying the Yankees gonna come free the slaves, by force. The governor wants to be neutral. He's forming a Home Guard, a militia, to defend the state. Sounds like Hiram aims to join. I plan to. Not gonna let a bunch of outsiders come in and have a war on my farm."

"So you'd fight with the slavers?"

"Didn't say that. I'm hoping no fighting comes at all. I agree with the governor, stay neutral. Hiram, he's going with the Union. If it comes to it, likely I will too."

"But Pa…."

"Don't worry your head about it. Now, what about this beau?"

"He's a gentleman. He's rich. I always wanted to marry off the farm, you know that."

"More to a husband than how much money he's got. Sounds like he might be goin' off to war. Can you handle that? And more important, do you think you could love him?"

"I don't know. I just don't know."

"Well, then, I guess the question is, do you want to find out? I can ask around, find out about his family. That's always important. Only you can decide if you want to spend time with him. Maybe even the rest of your life."

Julia wrinkled her forehead in thought and prayer. "Yes, Pa, I believe I should try. I am twenty-one. Most girls are married by my age. I am no great beauty. We aren't rich. If I turn down such a nice young man, I may not get another chance. In another few years, I will be a confirmed old maid. This way, I may yet have a chance at love and my dreams. Though I can't say I understand why Hiram would be interested in me. There must be other girls of his social class prettier and more polished than me."

Robert smiled. "Don't sell yourself short, Julia. I've always thought you were destined for better things. You may just find love and a whole new life open in front of you."

"But how can I possibly wait until Sunday? I'll be a nervous wreck!"

* * *

The following Sunday was rainy and windy. Julia fretted about getting her shoes muddy, or her dress. She agonized over fixing her hair—how should it look? What if Hiram did not come? What if he changed his mind?! Now that Julia had made up her mind to allow the courtship, she was deathly afraid of losing it. She looked in the tiny cracked hand mirror, trying to see more of herself in it. She was too fat, and too tan, she thought. She didn't look like a refined lady. What should she do? What should she say? She'd never seen a play, and didn't know a thing about acting. Maybe now was the time to try, though. Perhaps she could make Hiram believe she knew more of the refined social circles than she actually did. Now she wished she had accepted Lucy Clay's invitation to attend their ball last year with her sister, instead of declining for lack of a decent dress.

Wrapped in a rain slicker, her shoes wrapped in feedbags, she sat on a wooden box in the back of the wagon with Albinia. Her pa sat in front, driving, with her mother beside him. Even after a few months, Will still had bouts of stomach flu. Today he was too ill to attend church. During these spells, Jenny came twice each week with Dr. Simpson. Seems she wasn't the only one with beau prospects. Who would have thought it? Her little brother! As they jounced down the road to town, Julia tried to take her mind off the upcoming meeting with Hiram by analyzing her sister. Albinia was strange lately, detached. When Julia tried to talk to her about Hiram's letter, Binia had just smiled and congratulated her. She exhibited no curiosity, and acted almost disinterested, far away. Julia wondered if *she* were disguising some secret beau. Albinia just sat there, almost limp, staring into the rain. Julia noticed that she looked tired and worn. They used to talk and laugh on the way to church. Perhaps she was imagining it. Maybe it was just the dreary weather. Drat the rain! Why did it have to be so awful on such an important day?

Julia sat in the pew with her parents and scanned the church for Hiram. He had to be there! Finally she spied him, up front on the left. He was too big to miss! But who was the woman with him? It was too far away to tell—Julia could only see the bonnet and the back of a dress. Uncertainty clawed at her. Surely he could not be sitting with another girl, on a day like today!

Julia went through the hymns, responses from the liturgy, and prayers with mechanical distraction. She just could not really pay attention to Reverend Breckinridge's hour-long sermon. She strained so much to gain a glimpse of the woman seated next to Hiram that it earned her a reproving glance from her mother. She usually enjoyed the hymns, but today could not wait for the final amen. After it came, she was impatient with her mother, wanting her to wrap up her conversations so they could move out to the churchyard, where Hiram was sure to find her. The rain stopped.

Once outside, Julia tried to politely greet people, yet not engage anyone in conversation, lest Hiram fear approaching her. Finally, he was coming. Julia managed to signal her father to come over as well. At first, she was too short to see the person with Hiram, only that she too was coming. When they got closer, relief flooded her as she realized the woman with him must be an older relative. Julia sized her up, noticing her gray and blonde hair, blue eyes, and a few wrinkles, with a white bonnet. Her long gray dress with white collar seemed old-fashioned. She walked steadily, as though with hidden strength.

Hiram spoke first. "Good afternoon, Miss Crump. I trust you are well?"

Julia hesitated, getting herself under control, then said, "Yes, yes, Mr. Johannsen. I am quite well."

"May I present my mother, Mrs. Kirsten Johannsen?"

Julia curtsied and offered her hand. "I'm delighted to meet you, Mrs. Johannsen. I did not know Mr. Johannsen had family here."

"Pleased to meet you also," offered Kirsten. "I have heard Hiram talk of nothing else lately. I'm just visiting, from Cincinnati."

Hiram cleared his throat nervously. "Did ... did you receive my letter from earlier this week, Miss Crump?"

Robert chuckled as Julia blushed. "Indeed she did," he answered for her.

Julia was flustered but managed, "Yes, Mr. Johannsen. I did. I must say it was a pleasant surprise. I've discussed it with my father."

Hiram shuffled his feet and looked at Robert inquiringly.

Robert said, "I hope you won't mind, Mrs. Johannsen, but I checked on your family. Seems you Johannsens have a solid reputation on the river. You've been in the country about twenty years?"

"Yes, that is right, Mr. Crump. We sailed to Philadelphia from Stockholm, after leaving our home in Uppsala, Sweden, in 1839. My husband could not come today due to business concerns. We have been fortunate to start a steamboat company, and have some modest success. My husband thinks the country will grow westward, and his company will grow with it. He sees a great future in steam."

"Well, that's mighty smart, ma'am. Your son here's asked to keep company with my daughter. I see no reason why not. Though this trouble with the slaves may cause some problems. I hear Hiram is planning to join the militia?"

Hiram spoke up. "Yes, Mr. Crump. I love this country. In Sweden, we could barely hope to have a farm. But here, we have many opportunities. If there is war, I want to defend my country."

Robert nodded. "I respect that, Mr. Johannsen. I plan to join the militia myself."

Hiram beamed. "Then we are agreed?"

Robert chuckled. "Well, you just might want to take Julia into account. But as far as I'm concerned, yes, you two can keep company if you want."

Hiram turned to Julia. "Miss Crump, I would be honored if you would consent to my courting you."

Julia smiled. "And I would be honored to know you better, sir. I hope that we may spend many happy hours together."

Kirsten added, "I shall be glad to know you better also, Miss Crump. Perhaps you will consider spending some part of the Christmas holidays with us in Cincinnati?"

Inwardly excited, Julia calmly responded, "With pleasure, Mrs. Johannsen."

Julia thought Hiram looked as giddy as she was.

"Would you and your family join us at the hotel restaurant for lunch, Mr. Crump? It would be our pleasure to treat you, as a celebration."

"Don't see why not," said Robert. "I'll see if I can round up the other ladies."

* * *

Will recovered strength slowly after his bouts of stomach flu. In two weeks, he felt able to stand, walk, and drive the oxen again. His stomach stabilized. He ate constantly, voraciously. He dug into his schoolwork with renewed fervor, determined to catch up, particularly on the Greek grammar. He drove into town feeling the fall chill and beckoning winter as November began. He stopped at the livery and unhitched the oxen for the day. He spied the livery owner, who was also the blacksmith.

"Hey, George! Good to see you."

"Will, good to see you up and around. I hear you've been poorly."

"Ah, just a stomach thing. Doing well now. Heard you helped out my sister awhile back."

"Sister? Which one?"

"Albinia of course. Julia hates riding with these oxen. Heard you fixed a shoe awhile back."

"You musta heard wrong. But it's been awhile ... let me see ... Albinia was here, sure enough. But she just dropped off the oxen and picked 'em up next morning. She and that feller she was with."

"Joe Breckinridge?"

"Naw, wasn't Joe. He picked 'em up for her. But seems I recollect a different feller was with her the night before. Can't remember everything. Too long ago. Whole town's in an uproar over the John Brown revolt in Virginia. I hear they sent troops to put it down. Trial just finished, John Brown gonna get hisself hung."

"Hmm. Well, anyway, thanks for lookin' out for the oxen. I got to get to class. See you tonight."

Will walked from the livery to class. He tried to conjugate his Greek verbs, but the conversation with the blacksmith kept intruding in his thoughts. The oxen had not thrown a shoe. He hadn't been well enough to pursue it. But why would Albinia lie? Who was the other fellow?

Pa will have her hide if she's sneaking around, thought Will. *I best warn her and see what's she's up to.*

He kept walking, faster now to make time, and rounding a corner, almost bumped into his friend Joe, heading to a different part of the college.

"Joe! Where you headed?"

"Supposed to be mathematics—but I'm going over to sign up."

"Sign up? For what?"

"Haven't you heard? After John Brown's slave revolt, the governor is raising a militia, a home guard. To defend the state in case of trouble, white or slave. I figger to join."

"I could speak to Captain Morgan, if you'd be interested in the Rifles."

"No, thanks. I think the militia will support the state, neutral for now—but be antislavery. I know my pa has slaves, but even he doesn't believe keeping them is right. He is giving Josiah his freedom papers this week. I don't hope to fight, but if it comes to that, I want to be fighting for our homes, our families, and not for rich planters. I know not everyone thinks that way. Did you know my cousin? He's actually vice president of the United States. He thinks more like you."

"Whatever you say. Just thought I'd offer. Got time to go hunting this weekend? Before we get snow?"

Joe smiled, "Sure, Will. One last time before Christmas. Meet out on the Paris road, where we saw that big buck?"

"I'll be there," said Will, and hurried off to class. After school, Will went over to his job at Hobson's store. He waited on customers, swept, and unloaded crates in the back to stock shelves. As he finished for the day, Hobson came over. He looked like he had something on his mind.

"Will, I need to talk to you."

"Sure, Mr. Hobson. Anything wrong?"

"Well, yes. And no. You've done a good job here, Will. You work hard. No one can complain about that. It's just that, well, your drilling with Morgan and the Rifles ... some customers stopped coming in. They say they won't give their business to slavery sympathizers. They figure if you are with Morgan, and you work here ... well, it reflects badly on the store. It cost me business, frankly more than you're worth. I like you, Will. Times are changing. With this Harper's Ferry business, things are more divided every day. I have heard rumors about the Presbyterian Church splitting over it. It's getting so you have to pick a side and if you don't, people will assume what side you're on, anyway."

Will was stunned. He had no idea people would even take notice of him, or whether he was with the Rifles. He just viewed it as a fun learning experience, and a way to pay back Captain Morgan for his generosity.

"So what are you saying, sir?"

"I'm saying I'm going to have to let you go, unless you're willing to drop the Rifles. I know you have been sick and it seems like a rotten time to tell you, when you're just getting back on your feet. But while you were out, some customers came back. They weren't shy about sharing the reason they hadn't been coming in."

"But what about my debt, for the uniform materials, the bayonet, the other things? You've known all along I was doing this to be with the Rifles."

"I know, and I feel bad about it. I will just write off the debts—you do not need to pay on them anymore. Consider it a last gift, either way. But I can't lose more business because of a slavery sympathizer."

Will felt the bottom drop out of his stomach. A slavery sympathizer? He thought of himself as just a hardworking, ambitious young man. Slowly, Will nodded.

"I understand, sir. Thank you, but I will find a way to pay what I owe. I am sorry to have troubled you, or your business. I made a promise of loyalty to Captain Morgan. He has paid for my school. He's taught me to ride. That is the greater debt, both in money and in honor. I appreciate the opportunity that you have given me. But I will honor my commitment to Captain Morgan."

Will hung up his storekeeper apron on its hook and left. It was almost sunset. He walked toward the livery to get the oxen. He felt confused, dejected, and angry, all at the same time. His emotions buzzed like a nest of hornets in his head. What should slavery have to do with him? He did not own slaves, or desire to own one. He was not entirely sure what he thought of the whole issue. Of course he had seen the slave markets, and seen slaves in chains. He had heard stories about cruel treatment. He had heard about the debates between Lincoln and Douglas in Illinois. That was none of his affair. He had all he could do to keep up with his studies, the Rifles, and home life. And now, there was Jenny. He was hitching the oxen and turning his thoughts to that much more pleasant prospect, when a coach went by with a woman in it. She turned her face toward him in the dim light for just an instant, not seeing him. It was Albinia.

* * *

Luther sat in the darkness and waited. Jemima and the girls lay on pallets, sleeping fitfully. He did not know how long they had been here. All he knew was that periodically the false wall that hid their compartment in the church basement slid aside, admitting the parson with food. He also exchanged their chamber pot. Once or twice, early in their time, his wife came and tended Luther's head wound with poultices. It had healed. He kept telling them to be patient. Luther was getting nervous, wondering if the man was just waiting for the slave catchers to come. He wondered if they should break out. The dogs would not have their scent now. He got up and began pacing.

He heard sounds outside the door. They had just eaten. It was not time for more food. He grabbed the little stool as a weapon and hid to the left side of the door. If there were slave catchers, he would fight.

The fake wall slid to one side. There was darkness, no light. Luther could barely make out a shape in the doorway. Jemima woke and called out, "Who dere?"

The figure only responded with a shushing noise, moving into the room. Luther hesitated and was almost ready to strike when he heard Albinia speak.

"It's Albinia. Do not be afraid. I have come to move you. Friends are outside waiting. It's midnight. You must be absolutely silent. Move normally, do not rush. Attract no attention to yourselves. You must trust me and the others. Ask no questions."

Luther relaxed, but wanted to protest. A million questions filled his mind as Albinia turned and motioned them to follow. Luther made sure Jemima went last, himself first, in case of any kind of trouble. Jackson warned them not to trust anyone. Yet how could they not follow Albinia, having come this far?

As they stepped out into the starlight, the freezing wind tore through their thin clothing. A large dark buggy with small windows waited, hitched to two Belgian draft horses. Luther heard Albinia urge them inside. "Quickly! There are blankets inside, and I'll be with you."

He could see two dark shapes up on the driver's seat outside the buggy compartment. There was no moon. He could tell nothing about those to whom he was about to entrust their fate. As Luther stepped into the buggy compartment, his foot struck something that rattled and felt like a chain. He almost jumped out again.

"What you do, Miss Albinia? They be chains in here!"

Jemima and the girls shrunk back. Albinia impatiently whispered, "I know! I am not betraying you! I'll explain, but just get in!"

Luther was terrified but saw no options. He got in the buggy and helped the ladies, including finally Albinia, into the compartment. As they settled in the seats, Albinia shut the door and rapped on the outside. The horses began to pull.

"Stay low. Pull the blinds over the windows," Albinia said. "The chains will only be used if we're stopped by a patrol. They will chain me, too, saying I was helping you escape. If it looks like you're already caught, they'll leave us alone."

Jemima trembled and asked, "Where dey takin' us? Who dat drivin'?"

"It's better you don't know who it is. If you get caught, they'll beat you to make you tell who helped you. I'm willing to take the risk, since you already know me. But there's no point in putting others in danger. We're going further north."

Clara whimpered, but Olivia declared, "If we caught, I fight till dey kill me."

"I understand," said Albinia. "But let's hope it doesn't come to that. Whatever you do, do not panic. Now let's be quiet. Try to sleep if you can. Your next stop may not be as comfortable as the last. After this, I won't be able to be with you, but I won't lead you to anyone who can't be trusted. You must believe that. I wouldn't risk jail and worse myself if that weren't true."

Luther spoke once more. "Why you do dis, Miss Albinia? Why you hep us?"

"Because I believe that God wants me to. That He thinks no man has the right to enslave and harm another. Because I think that Jesus loves you as much as He does me."

Luther shook his head. "I hear white folks say dat, like de parson. But ain't any ever risk dey neck for me before. You different."

They sat in silence, listening to the creaking of the coach, the horses hooves, and the irregular bouncing along the road. Luther saw Jemima and the girls lulled back to sleep, but he was determined to stay alert.

He still could not understand why Albinia would risk anything for him. Wasn't she Lucy's friend?

After what seemed like forever, the coach pulled to a halt. There was a tense silence, and Luther was about to open the door when the coachman tapped three times fast in succession, and then two slow taps. The coach began to move, turning around. Luther wanted to jump, but Albinia grabbed his arm. "Stay put!" she commanded. "It means there's a patrol. Put these shackles on the girls and your mother, and then yourself. I'll do my own. Act like you're terrified, that you've been captured. And take this...," she handed him a knife. "Put it under you, and don't use it or let it show unless you absolutely must."

The coach moved slowly back towards the church. In the dark, no one would be able to see the tracks of their turn. In a minute or so, Luther heard voices outside.

"Halt! What's a coach doin' sneakin' around in the night?" asked a rider.

The Irish driver responded, "Sure 'an we caught ourselves a few blackbirds, tryin' ta fly north for the winter. We've just saved ye' some trouble. Begorra, an' we caught their helper as well—white, can ye believe it? We're headin' back to Lexington, to the sheriff."

Another rider laughed. "Well, it's a fine birdcage, I'll give you that! But you won't mind then if we just take a look?"

The coach door opened. Torches illuminated the interior. Luther saw a man with a floppy hat, a scraggly beard, and a pistol in his belt. The man poked his head and torch inside. Clara set up a piteous wail. "Please, massa, please! Dey done caught us, we jus' vistin' kin. We ain't seen our daddy almos' a year! Mercy!"

Jemima and Olivia took it up, "Mercy, massa!" Luther just gave a terrified glance, and dropped his eyes to the floor, one hand fingering the knife. Olivia buried her head in her arms, showing the shackles on her wrists to the rider outside.

The rider turned his attention to Albinia. "A white woman! In with those slaves! Y'all ought to be ashamed! Don't you know where you belong?"

Albinia sounded defiant. "I belong in Heaven, with my Savior." She raised her arms, showing she was chained. "These chains will fall away, by God's grace."

"Oho! One of those religious ones. Well, we'll see if you sing the same tune to the judge. Common, thief!"

The rider on the ground turned back to the coachmen. One of the other riders had never let a shotgun barrel drift away from the driver. "I suppose you're all right then. Too bad, would have been fun to roast these blackbirds in a pie! Maybe even sample this white little missy!" He leered at Albinia, laughing. Then with a sigh, he shut the coach door.

"All right, on with you then. Don't think I won't check the sheriff." The riders followed the coach for a distance. Luther heard Albinia whisper, "Don't make a sound. Hopefully they'll just leave."

They heard the sound of receding hoofbeats. The coach moved slowly for few minutes, then stopped. Luther heard the coachman thump twice slowly, then three times rapidly.

"All clear," said Albinia. "We'll wait just a minute, like we're resting the horses. Then move on. We won't make Paris tonight. We'll have to put you in the emergency place. Whatever you do, stay there. Someone will come for you when it's safe. Keep the knife, just in case."

Albinia passed a key to Luther. He unlocked her chains. Then she freed everyone else.

Luther saw resoluteness in Jemima. "Now I know, de good Lawd give us you for an angel," she said to Albinia. "You could of given us to dem patrollers."

After half an hour, the coach stopped again. The coachman pounded on the side five times rapidly.

"Time to get out!" said Albinia. "Here is where I leave you. Follow the directions of the coachman. Do not try to find out who they are. You can trust them as you trust me. They will take you to a place of safety. Stay put! Only come out if you hear someone singing, "*Steal Away to Jesus*," and five rapid thumps on the door. I know you know that song, Luther. We're near a creek, the south fork of the Licking River. If your water runs out before someone comes, you can try to refill it, but only if it is night. I'm sorry not to leave you in a safer place, but with the time the patrol took, there's no choice. You can't be out in daylight. Now go, and God go with you!"

One by one, Luther and his family got out of the coach. Light was beginning to touch the horizon in the east. They could just make out a creek about forty yards from the road.

A black hooded figure motioned them to follow, and they did. He led them down to the creek, across a big log used as a bridge. Coming to the other side, he seemed to plunge into the underbrush. Clara stumbled, and Luther picked her up. Still speaking not a word, the man motioned them to stop. He stooped and felt around in the mud, coming up with a cleverly hidden rope. Holding up a hand to tell them to stay in place, he walked toward a large oak tree with low branches. He looped the rope around one of the branches, then pulled. Seemingly out of nowhere, a large square platform overgrown with brush lifted, revealing a dry hole, reinforced with timbers, and steps leading down into it. By the growing light, they could barely see rough cots, a bucket of water with a dipper, and a little table with bread and dried meat on it. After they were all in, the man at the top waved, as in farewell. The platform began to close over them, like the lid to a coffin. They were alone, in the dark again.

* * *

Curious about his invitation did not begin to describe Will's feelings as he drove the oxen toward Dr. Simpson's place. He had gotten used to the doctor and Jenny stopping by while he was ill, but now that he was better, those visits had ceased. Then one day after school, he stopped at the post office for the family mail and found a formal invitation. The invitation was for dinner, the following Friday evening, at the Simpson house, North Broadway and Fourth Street. His interest in Jenny, not just her uncle's horses, had grown greatly in the last few months. Will thought himself far too young to be involved in a serious relationship. The threat of war was changing things, however. He'd heard of young men seventeen and eighteen years old getting married recently. What did Jenny and Dr. Simpson have in mind?

Knocking on the door, Will was admitted by a young white servant maid. Will had never been to the house before and was surprised, since most servants were Negroes. He followed the servant into a drawing room and sat to wait. The surroundings were ornate, reminding him of Captain Morgan's house. Blue and silver wallpaper surrounded a marble fireplace, with dark mahogany Empire chairs and settee scattered around the room. After a few moments, the white swinging door opened. Dr. and Mrs. Simpson entered, followed by Jenny, looking her best. Dr. Simpson undertook introductions. Mrs. Mary Simpson was a slight woman, with dark blonde hair, small smiling mouth, and brown kind eyes, dressed in a deep green velvet gown with brown side skirts. After brief small talk, the servant announced dinner, and they proceeded to a parlor off the main dining room. A small round table was set for four, with Dr. and Mrs. Simpson seated across from each other. Jenny and Will were across from each other also. Dr. Simpson said grace, and the courses began.

"Will," said Dr. Simpson. "I've heard of your desire to study law. Is that still your intention?"

"Yes, sir," said Will. "I hope to. I have always thought it a fine way to help people. That is why I wanted to go to Transylvania University."

"An admirable ambition. And I understand from my friend the provost that you are doing well."

"I try, sir. I believe I will make honor roll this term. Captain Morgan has been kind enough to pay my way. My parents could never afford it. I was working at Hobson's to help out until just recently."

"Oh? Nothing to do with your illness, I hope? I could have a word with him again."

"No, sir. Mr. Hobson said that my participation in the Lexington Rifles was losing him business. People wouldn't shop there because they thought I must be pro-slavery, and Mr. Hobson too."

"And are you?"

"No, sir, not exactly anyway. I've taken an oath to Captain Morgan, for his help and sponsorship."

Will saw Jenny looking over at him. Her eyes pleaded, her head tilted, her brow furrowed, entreating him to listen and agree. It was obvious she wanted to speak—she seemed to be holding back a torrent of words.

"Suppose I told you that a friend of mine, a judge, needs a clerk. Someone to look up cases for him, learn to read the law. In time, it could lead to a full position as a lawyer. The position has a salary, of course, enough to cover your studies at the university. You could earn the law degree as well. You might have to live in town. I don't know that there would be time for farm work, but perhaps enough wages to help your family hire some help. There also would probably not be enough time to participate in the Rifles. What would you say to that?"

Will sat in disbelief. What could he say? "That's mighty generous, sir. I don't know what to say."

Jenny burst in. "Will! Please! This is your chance! You know the Bible says a house divided against itself cannot stand! Abraham Lincoln up in Illinois made a speech about that. He said the country has to become all slave or all free. Everyone says war is coming. That the states are going to split. The country is deeply divided. Will, you don't want to be on the wrong side!"

"Now, Jenny, dear," Mrs. Simpson reproved. "Will must do as he thinks best. It's not for us to say. And certainly not fitting for young ladies to speak of such matters." Turning to the waiting servant, she said, "Susan, you may serve dessert."

"Yes, ma'am."

Jenny was silent, but her face again looked like she was holding back a flood of thought.

Dr. Simpson said, "You must excuse Jenny. She is impetuous and too informal. Still, what she says has some merit, even if said out of turn. The time approaches when all men will have to choose whether to support their state or the United States. It is not an easy question. Your loyalty to Mr. Morgan is understandable. Yet your loyalty may be misplaced. Mr.

Morgan has many admirable qualities—but he is also a gambler, a philanderer, and a slave owner. In fact, there are rumors that he is the father of one of his slaves, while his wife lies ill. I say this not to gossip, but to have you fully consider the character of the man you follow, perhaps into peril. I might add that I have seen your growing affection for my niece. While you are both yet too young, eventually I could look with favor on a suit by a young man of your quality, provided he chose his course wisely. Will you consider my offer?"

Will felt torn in two. His affection for Jenny, the obvious potential of the opportunity warred with his loyalty to Morgan. "Sir, I should give this some thought and prayer, talk with my parents and Captain Morgan. I don't feel I can answer right away."

Jenny's head dropped with a large sigh, her mouth drooping in a frown, holding back tears. When she looked up, the hurt in her eyes cut him to the heart.

"Of course, I understand," said the doctor. "Take what time you need. Let us hope that events do not move too quickly for that decision."

Will rose, and Susan escorted him out. Just as he was closing the garden gate on the street, he turned and saw Jenny.

"Will. I know I'm not always the proper young lady. I'm headstrong and speak my mind. I don't always wait on others. I'm trying to learn. I shouldn't be out here, I know. It's not proper. Uncle and Auntie have been good to me and tried to teach me. I know I'm too young. But I just can't stand it anymore. I have to know, Will. Do you care for me? Really care?"

Will looked in her eyes and clasped her outstretched hands. "Yes, Jenny, I do. But you must understand I honor my word. I cannot promise without thought and prayer. I have my family to think of. How will my father manage without me on the farm? There's more to this than just you and me."

"But if you stay with the Rifles, then we'll never be together. My uncle is joining the home guard, as a doctor. He expects to side with the Union."

"I … I just don't know, Jenny."

Jenny turned, and ran crying into the house.

* * *

The next few weeks passed slowly for Will. He continued his school-work and drilled with the Rifles. He considered talking to Captain Morgan, but knew he needed to talk to his father. He didn't see Jenny or Dr. Simpson. He felt stuck and wanted to avoid the problems, yet knew they would not go away. He saw two men shouting and shoving on the street, arguing over slavery. Southern states threatened to secede if a Republican candidate won the next year's presidential election. More people were taking sides. Will knew his father still thought neutrality was best. Will just wanted life the way it had always been.

As drill was finishing with the Rifles one day, Captain Morgan came to address them.

"Men, you should be proud. I know some would call those among you yet boys, but you are drilling and behaving like men. I am proud to lead such a force. The time is coming when we will be tested. We've put on exhibitions and learned the tools of fighting. Soon, we may have to use those tools in battle to defend our homes, our families, and our state. The Yankees want to destroy our economy. They want to impose tyranny, to deprive us of the things our forefathers fought for less than a hundred years ago in the Revolutionary War against Britain. They want to tell us that the Negro is the equal of a white man, though their own Constitution says otherwise. We know they bear the mark of Cain. The state of Kentucky willingly joined a union of states, but not to have the will of Washington imposed upon us. We should have the right to chart our own destiny, even to leave the United States if we so vote. We will fight for our homes. We will not let them take our guns, our slaves, or our land. Your loyalty will be tested. Even families may split on these issues. Are you with me?"

Cheers and shouts of "Yes!" resounded all over the field. Will was caught up in the enthusiasm and yelled his assent. He walked to the livery, got the wagon and the oxen, and drove to the dress shop to pick up Albinia. As he pulled up to the door and set the brake, a young man left the shop. That seemed odd to Will. He made up his mind to talk to Albinia about the strange way she had been behaving. She came out of the shop, locked the door.

"Evening, Will," she said, allowing him to help her into the wagon.

"Evening, Binia. Who was that?"

"Who?"

"The young man that just left the shop. Not too many men customers, I imagine."

"Oh, him. Just wants a party dress for his wife. Thinks I can make it from his hand measurements." She held her hands out to show the size of a waist. "I told him to send his wife's maid with an old dress of hers that fits, if it is supposed to be a surprise."

"Hmm," said Will, accepting it. "Been meaning to talk to you. But you haven't been coming home in the evening too much lately."

"The shop has been very busy," said Albinia evasively.

"Maybe. But some things don't add up, and I wanted to talk to you before mentioning them to Pa."

Albinia looked fearful and defensive. "Such as?"

"Such as I talked to the livery man about that time when I first got sick a while back. He says he never changed a shoe on the oxen. So why did you say he had? And another thing, a while back I saw you riding in a coach, headed out of town. You've been acting strange—distracted, forgetful, like you're in another world. Julia's seen it too. I would not be surprised if Ma starts on it with you soon. You got a secret beau or something? You know Pa won't like that."

"I would appreciate it if you didn't mention it to Pa. Yes, all right, if you must know, I do have beau. However, I do not know where the relationship is going. I am not ready for Pa to pass judgement. I will be seventeen in just a couple of weeks. Some girls are already married at my age. I think I should have the right to make up my own mind before getting Pa into it."

"Is he respectable?"

"Of course he is!"

"Do I know him?"

"I'd rather not say. Please, Will, just trust me on this. It is important. I ... I'll try to be more helpful and present when I'm home. But there are going to be times I need to stay in town. More than in the past. I may be visiting Lucy more too. My wages from the shop help keep the family afloat, you know. Like when there's a poor harvest. I'm not a child."

"All right, Binia. I won't say anything yet. But if this beau of yours is around by Christmas, you'd best talk to Pa about him."

She smiled at Will warmly and gave him a half arm hug on the wagon seat. "Thank you! You have no idea how much that means to me. I promise if he's still around at Christmas, I'll talk to Pa."

* * *

Darkness. Seemingly unending. Luther knew they had been here in this hole far too long. He had risked sneaking out at night, with Jemima's help, refilling their water bucket, dumping their chamber pot, and even setting a few snares for rabbits. Albinia had told them to wait. They must move soon or starve. What had happened? The moon would be a thin sliver.

Jemima motioned for Luther to listen. They were all silent. Faintly they heard a voice, singing. Then a tramping sound like boots penetrated the earth. Then more singing, clearer now.

Steal away, steal away, steal away to Jesus

Steal away, steal away home I ain't got long to stay here....

The man's voice rang out in the night. Then Luther heard five thumps overhead. Luther whispered to Jemima, "Let's see." He clutched the knife. They climbed the steps and slowly pushed upward on the platform. Peeking out, the dim beam of a hurricane lamp shined where the voice came from. Gathering courage, he and Jemima pushed hard up on the platform to open it fully.

"Over here," he said softly.

The light came closer, revealing the form of a young black man not much older than Luther.

"Come on," said the voice. "We ain't got much time."

Luther, Olivia, Jemima, and Clara all followed the young man. When they had gone a short way, still covered by trees, they saw another man in the shadows. In front of him were four new wooden coffins, lids open, empty.

"Get in," said the voice.

"What? You cain't expect us to…," protested Luther.

"Get in!" interrupted the voice. "Get in or run, your choice. The patrol will be along in about fifteen minutes. You might just end up in them anyway."

Trembling, each of them lay down in the coffin that was their size. The two men acted quickly, closing the lids, nailing them shut. He tried to control the claustrophobic panic. Then Luther felt himself lifted, carried, jolting along a path, and set on some solid surface. He guessed it was a wagon. Then he heard what sounded like the other coffins loaded into the wagon and Clara crying softly. He heard Jemima speak, "Hush, child! We need to be quiet, like we're dead."

"That's right," said the voice. "Don't be afraid. You're gonna steal away, north to freedom. If we're stopped, you must be dead. If they open the coffins, don't breathe. Do not move or talk, or make any noise at all. Keep your eyes shut. We'll tell you when it's safe."

Luther heard the driver cluck to the horses, and then the wagon began to move, jolting and bumping down the road.

CHRISTMAS ROMANCE

December 1859

Albinia worked on a wedding dress with a difficult chiffon overlay. She just could not seem to get the gather in the back right, ripping it out for the third time. She heard the bell at the front of the shop and sighed in frustration at the interruption. She put on her pleasant face for dealing with customers, and came to the front counter. She was surprised to see not a woman but Joe Breckinridge. He was dressed unusually fine for a weekday, carrying a bouquet of pink Christmas roses. She could not imagine what he was doing or why he had come. She smiled inwardly at his seeming discomfort. Nevertheless, she went forward and greeted him warmly.

"Hello, Mr. Breckinridge. What a surprise! What brings you here? A dress for your mother?"

"No, no. And please call me Joe, as you did before. These are for you," he said, thrusting the flowers at her. "I haven't seen you much at church lately, so I thought I'd come to the shop. I ... I ... well, there's the box social at the assembly hall on Sunday, and I wondered if you'd be there. I saw your pa at church. He laughed and said it seemed like all his ladies were in bloom, but he said it would be all right if I asked you."

Stalling, as she tried to think what to say, Albinia took the flowers. "How very pretty! Wherever did you find them this time of year? Let me get them in some water. I'll be right back." Albinia went back to the rear of the building to get a glass and some water from a bucket in the corner. As she walked, her brain went in a whirl. What should she tell him? Yet she had told Will she had a secret beau, and would tell her father by Christmas. She needed a cover for her slave activities. Joe was her age. Could he be the excuse she needed? It was just a social. Saving lives was important, too. She walked back to the front where Joe was waiting, smiling at him.

"There! They will do nicely in this. It was very sweet of you to bring them. I do not see how I could turn down such a gentlemanly gesture. Of course, I must speak to my father about anything further. However, I am beholden to you in that … that other matter a few weeks back. It would be fun to get to know you better, Joe."

Joe's relieved and excited grin made her feel guilty. "Thanks—Albinia! May I call you that? I'll be counting the days until Sunday!"

* * *

Julia fussed and primped at the mirror.

"May I help?" Sara asked.

"Would you? I want to look nice for Hiram as much as I can."

"Gladly—let me! Your dress is lovely. We just need to fix your hair, and maybe a little homemade blush I made last summer, with the hibiscus and beets."

A few minutes later, Hiram's carriage drew up. Julia pinched her cheeks, almost ruining the effect of the blush, and hurried out to meet him. She was so nervous her brain went in five directions at once. This was to be their first real outing together, as a courting couple.

"Julia!" Hiram beamed. "I've been counting the hours, looking forward to our outing." He quickly hugged her, then lifted her as if she were a feather into the carriage. It was about fifty degrees, and sunny, so he had the carriage top down. The matched Morgan horses stood quietly. Hiram situated Julia with a lap robe and a foot-warming stove, and they were off!

"Hiram?" Julia hesitated … she was getting used to using his first name, but it still seemed strange. "I … I just want you to know—I'm going to try my best to be a good wife and companion for you. But I'm really nervous! I don't feel like I know you that well, and I'm so afraid of doing or saying the wrong thing. I'm flattered, but I still don't understand why you chose me."

Hiram chuckled, then grew serious. "Don't you know? That's one of the things I love about you—you're beautiful and don't even know it. And I see a lot of strength in you, but not, how do you say... selfish?"

"Strength? How?"

"Like that time last week I saw you in town—the butcher tried to cheat you and gave you a bad cut of meat—but you spoke up, politely, and let him know you were no one's fool. And that time at the dance...."

"Don't remind me!"

"All right—but you showed strength and dignity—you didn't let a little embarrassment overcome you. Some women would have made it worse crying, screaming, blaming someone else. You didn't. And even though you were in pain, you didn't complain."

They drove on in silence for a while, stopping occasionally to admire the scenery. Hiram began singing comical Swedish folk songs, acting them out while at their stops. Even though Julia didn't understand the words, his antics left her holding her sides in laughter. About two miles later, Hiram turned off the main Versailles road onto a side road.

"I'm sorry this is bumpy, but there's something I want you to see."

They stopped, but Julia couldn't see anything remarkable, only trees. Hiram got down, coming around to her side of the carriage.

"What is it, Hiram? I only see forest."

"Just come, you'll see," he said, helping her down.

When she was down, he took a thin strip of cloth and tied it around her head over her eyes.

"Now I can't see anything!" she protested. "What's going on?"

He took her hand and led her forward. "Just come ... trust me."

Julia felt uncomfortable but very curious. She followed, stumbling, but Hiram's strong arm was always there. He guided her with his hand,

and the other hand in the small of her back, occasionally telling her to look out for a rock or a branch. It seemed they were walking on a path.

After a few minutes, Hiram brought her to a stop and turned her to the left. He removed the blindfold and Julia gasped. In front of them was the most beautiful sunset she had ever seen, over a small lake. Pinks, golds, purples flaming everywhere in the sky, clouds like soft feathers spread out across the expanse of blue, with the water quietly lapping at the pebbled shoreline. Ducks bobbed on the lake nearby, and as she watched, a fish jumped above the water after an insect. Just down the shoreline was a little cabin, but not the rude sort that she and her family lived in—this was handsomely built, with all glass windows and sawn lumber. In front of the cabin was a table, all laid out with food, candles, and a roaring campfire for warmth. She turned back to Hiram.

"How did you...?" she started to say, and then saw he was down on one knee.

"I want to do this right, after the way of your country," he said. "Miss Julia Crump, will you marry me?" he said, holding out a gold ring with a large blue sapphire and diamonds on each side. "I want it to be because you want, not because our parents say. I will always love and protect you. If God allows, I will always come back to you."

Julia was stunned. They had already promised to court, but this was beyond her wildest dreams. "Yes ... yes, Hiram, I will."

He put the ring on her finger and gave her his arm, escorting her to the log table, helping her into her seat. They had wine, fish, and duck, everything prepared to perfection. She couldn't imagine how he could have arranged it all. They talked and laughed. Hiram told her of his boyhood, his father, and his family in Sweden. He told her about starting as a cabin boy, mopping decks and cleaning staterooms, in his father's steamboat business. Julia told him about her dreams of traveling, and her sorrow at the loss of her brother, the one between Will and Lydia.

The stars began to come out. Hiram took a whistle from his pocket and blew on it. Two white servants came from the cabin and began to clear everything away. So that's how he'd done it!

Hiram helped her back to the carriage and lit the lanterns. The servants drove another small wagon—Julia noticed they were armed. Hiram began singing hymns on the way home in the moonlight, English hymns like "Rock of Ages" that she knew, and she joined in. It was late when they arrived back at the Crump homestead. Her father was standing in the dooryard with a lantern, as though trying to decide whether to come after her—but Julia saw him relax at the sight of her smiles.

Hiram helped her down, and gave her forehead a quick kiss. She wished her father had been in bed—she was twenty-one, after all!

"Until tomorrow, my beloved?" asked Hiram.

"Until then."

* * *

Will continued to drill with the Rifles. He supposed he was stubborn, but he did not like manipulation. Dr. Simpson's offer felt like he and Jenny were trying to run Will's life, tempting him to break his word. His father had encouraged him to join the Rifles, and even with the present tensions, had not yet told him to quit. He occasionally saw the Home Guard, with Joe and his father, drilling on another field. This gave him an odd feeling, but he knew others in the Home Guard with pro-slavery sentiments. He heard that the commander Simon Buckner was for Kentucky rather than the Union. He paid more attention to news and politics, particularly this Lincoln fellow everyone was discussing. Lincoln's wife was one of the Todds, but she had not been back to Lexington recently.

Will knew he was stalling, avoiding making a decision. He had not answered Dr. Simpson yet but would have to soon, to avoid being rude. After supper, Will saw his chance to talk to his father. Julia was off with Hiram. Albinia had not come home. Will suspected she was with her beau. Robert settled into a chair in the corner, mending a harness by lamplight. Will pulled up a stool next to him.

"Pa, I got something on my mind."

Looking up, Robert said, "All right, Son. What is it?"

"You remember I was invited to the Simpsons a while back?"

"Yes, Son. Seems like Jenny's sweet on you. Fine family, the Simpsons."

"Yes, sir. I like Jenny a lot too. That's just the problem. You know I lost my job at Hobbs over the Rifles. Dr. Simpson seems favorable to a match between Jenny and me when we're older. But he's dead set against the Rifles. He doesn't seem to hold a good opinion of our captain."

"Well, times are changing. I still hope for peace. But there may be war. People are taking sides. It may be that both of us will have to choose."

"But you encouraged me to join the Rifles. I have given my word of honor, my oath to the Rifles, and Captain Morgan. He's paid for my school and been ever so kind to me. Dr. Simpson is offering me a job with a friend, learning about the law, and will still help me go to school. That might mean Jenny and I could be together. I don't know what to do. I must decide, and soon."

Robert paused, brow furrowed. He shifted forward, then back, uncomfortably. "I've been thinkin' and prayin' on just that, Will. It troubles me. It isn't just fancy drills with some guys on a field anymore—we're training for war. Will, I really think you should quit the Rifles. Not because of Jenny—young girls can be fickle—you don't know that you two would end up together. You do know the Rifles will not follow the Union, if it comes to war. Dr. Simpson is making you a fair offer. I based my encouragement to enter the Rifles on opportunity, the chance to live your dreams. I never had much of a head for books, or the chance to be anything but a farmer. I wanted something different for you. Things have changed. No one could predict things would get this bad. You're young. When you joined the Rifles, you weren't yet a man. The Bible says not to make rash promises. It's time to be a man and make a man's decision, looking to God. I trust He will guide you. But I don't want to face you across a battlefield. And I'm afraid that's where this is headed."

Will grew angry. He threw up his hands, stood, and glared at his father. "But haven't you taught me to obey? Haven't you taught me the importance of a man's word? About following God no matter what? And now, because it's inconvenient, and something better is offered, I'm supposed to say I didn't mean it?" he shouted.

"It's dangerous to promise something to God too quickly. After you've thought about it, it may be too late. Is your honor worth getting killed over? Is it worth fighting your neighbors? Your friends? Your family? Proverbs 6 says if you're snared by your mouth, ask your neighbor to free you. You could go to Morgan." Robert's voice held a pleading note. Will knew he didn't have to depend on his father for a living, not with two sponsors vying for him.

Will paced the room. "And how would that repay him? Would you not pay a debt?"

Will got his coat and walked out into the darkness. He needed the chill to distill his thoughts. Was his father right? Was it that simple—ask and walk free? Yet did he want to be free of the Rifles? And what about honor—keeping your word. The Bible had things to say about not keeping oaths, too. He prayed. He wrestled and thought. Finally, he decided.

* * *

Albinia was exhausted. It was exciting helping slaves to freedom. However, late nights, the need to keep up at the dress shop, and the stress of maintaining secrecy were taking their toll. Tonight she again stayed in town. She wondered how long she could keep her family from finding out what she was doing. She knew Will was already suspicious. Katy, who provided her a bed, had gotten curious too, so that some nights she simply slept a few hours on a cot at the back of the dress shop. She let her friend think she had gone home, and her family think she had stayed with her friend in town. Her conscience pricked as she deceived people, but it was for a good cause.

She locked the front of the shop. The owner liked to come in midmorning, so she needed not worry about that. In the rear of the shop, she cleared off an old trunk and opened the lid. Inside were costumes. She selected a patched and worn housedress, to look like a poor farm wife. She changed quickly, putting her own clothes in the trunk. Then she donned a black wig, pinning it carefully, and did her makeup to look a decade older, as David taught her. She was nearly unrecognizable. Last of all, she took a double derringer from a drawer and checked to see that it was loaded. Satisfied, she dropped it in her reticule. Making the wedding gown got her eight dollars to buy the gun. She never expected to use it, but David encouraged it.

She exited the store by the back way. Walking out to the alley, a bearded unkempt man in a battered hat accosted her. She informed him she was not that type of woman and moved quickly away, meeting David at a saloon. According to plan, she walked in and approached a table where David, in his Irishman costume, was playing cards and drinking.

He looked up and saw Albinia. "Ah, there ye are, mah darling! I can see me luck is changing," said David.

"Please, come home, David!" she said pleadingly.

Pushing away from the table, he said, "Gentlemen, I fold. I can see there are other ways to win tonight." He put an arm around Albinia and gently propelled her back to the street. Once there, he took her hand and led her around back to a wagon. There were two draft horses hitched to the wagon. A padlocked wooden box sat in the rear, large enough to hold two men. He helped her into the wagon, mounted, and began to drive.

"Where to this night?" she asked.

"A rather long trek, I'm afraid. A farm on Harrodsburg Road out almost to Centerville. We may not be back in town before dawn. And much more risk of patrols. Our story is that I'm getting pumpkins, delivering you and them to my cousin. His wife is having a baby, and you're going to help her."

"All right. How many people?"

"Just one tonight, I'm told. I apologize for the familiarity back there, it just seemed necessary to avoid suspicion."

"You don't have to apologize. I don't mind."

"You don't?"

"No. I enjoy our excursions, and spending time with you, besides helping the slaves."

"I do too. I was hoping you might feel that way, but did not want to assume. I ... I have some bad news. I must go away soon. I've been offered an opportunity to help Mr. Garrison up north. Mr. Clay is releasing me. When I go, you would be on your own. I understand if you would rather not. A woman alone at night with the patrols would be too dangerous. You would have to find a way to do it in the daytime. With your job at the shop, I do not know how you would manage. Mabel and Franklin may be able to help, but...."

Albinia bit her lip, missing him already, but still determined to help. "No! I can manage. I will just sew and sleep at night, go home more. It would actually relieve some pressure. I think my siblings are getting suspicious. I told Will I have a secret beau."

"And do you?" He seemed to stop, as if he wanted to take her hand. She could tell there was more than casual interest in the question. His eyes held hers intensely.

"Well, sort of. I mean, we've spent a lot of time alone together, more than usual for a couple not formally courting." There, she had said it. She was frightened of what he might think, yet she longed to hear that he felt the same.

"Given what you've told me of your father, I hardly think he would approve."

Albinia laughed, breaking the tension. "You are absolutely right there."

He held the reins one handed, and reached for her hand.

"I've never met a woman like you. Sometimes I cannot decide if you are reckless or brave. I admire you all the same."

Her heart thrilled to his touch, and she felt the heat in her face. Changing the subject, she said, "How ... how long will you be gone?"

He snapped the reins to move the horses faster. "I honestly don't know. Mr. Garrison is much under attack here, and in the North. He is speaking in many cities. If war breaks out, I could be stuck there, to be candid."

"Oh," she said, greatly disappointed, withdrawing her hand. "Then I suppose there's no point...."

"Don't say that! Let me ask you this—if I were to send you a train ticket, would you come?"

"You mean...?"

"Yes, exactly. If I'm not able to come back, I want you to know—I want to marry you. I've tried to be proper, but, well—the situation just doesn't follow the usual rules."

She grabbed his arm and put her head on his shoulder. "Oh, yes! Yes, David, with all my heart. I hope my father will understand someday, but whether he does or not, I want to be with you."

They pulled up to a barn. David stopped the horses and turned to Albinia. She looked up at him adoringly. She thought he was going to kiss her. He leaned toward her, their lips almost touching.

She jumped as the lights went on in the house and a dog charged the wagon, barking. David turned and leaped down, waiting tensely to see who was coming. A lantern moved out from the house. Albinia heard a cranky voice saying, "Who in tarnation come visiting this time of night?" A man came toward them with a shotgun in one hand and lantern in the other.

David immediately slipped into his Irish brogue. "Ah, well, an' it's just a poor wee Irishman and his lady come to collect midnight pumpkins and squash. Verra delicate, these pumpkins. Don't like the sun."

"All right, then," said the man, lowering the shotgun. "I think you'll find what you're looking for in the barn, third stall on the left, under the hay. Knock on the stall three times if you don't want a pumpkin to fall on your head."

David and Albinia opened the barn. David drove the team and wagon inside, shutting the door. He went and knocked on the stall, then lit a lamp. Out came the "pumpkins"—a Negro man about forty years of age, with some grizzled gray hair, and a Negro woman, with light yellow brown skin, almost white, about thirty years old.

David climbed up into the wagon and unlocked the padlock on the box, opening it. "Come," he said. "I'm afraid you'll both have to squeeze in."

Albinia saw the man flash a smile, but the woman looked more doubtful. She moved toward her. "Don't worry," said Albinia. "It will be all right. We've done this before."

The man chuckled and climbed into the bottom of the box. "Lawd have mercy! We done worse dan dis on de plantation just for not getting' Massa his supper fast enough. We be fine."

The woman gingerly climbed in after him. Albinia heard her mutter something about escaping being as bad as punishment. When they settled, David relocked the box and quickly loaded pumpkins and squash from the stall into the wagon, some on top of the box. He climbed back into the driver's seat, motioned Albinia to open the door, and put out the lamp. Once outside, he jumped down and helped Albinia into the wagon, holding her hand, and giving her cheek a quick peck as she got in. She thought it held a promise of more for later.

Soon they were off down the road. The moon was setting, and soon it would be pitch dark, as they intended. She observed that he kept the big Belgians moving at a trot, since the load was light for them, and speed was important. Albinia pulled the blanket and muffler around her as the cold night breeze hit them. She snuggled closer to David as well, who looked at her with a quick smile. She noticed he did not head on a route directly through Lexington, but circled west some to avoid the center of town. If they kept this pace, they would make it back to Lexington before dawn. When they were north of town on the road toward Russell Cave, they heard hoofbeats off to the right and then ahead, just as they crossed a bridge.

"A patrol," David said tensely. "Remember, on this side of town, we're delivering pumpkins and squash. I'll be a drunk farmer. But be ready for anything."

Six horsemen came out of the night, one bearing a torch. They spread across the road in front of the wagon.

"What are you two doing? Early for market, isn't it?" asked the lead horseman roughly. The torch showed a black scruffy beard and long coat, a pistol glinting in the light on his belt.

"Aye, if to market we were going. I've a cousin up Centerville way. He's in need of our pumpkins and squash. His wife is delivering a bairn, and needs the midwife, if it's any business of yours," said David in his Irish brogue.

"When we're on patrol, everything is our business," laughed one nastily. He dismounted, handing the reins to a companion, and moved toward the wagon. David and Albinia turned to watch him. He lowered the gate on the back of the wagon and started to climb in.

"And what might ye be doin'?" David inquired. "We're not taking passengers."

"That's what I'd like to make sure of. Seems you're carrying more than squash back here. What's in the box?"

"Just a few family heirlooms I'm takin' to my cousin. Now if ye'll get out of me wagon, I'll be on me way!"

"I think we'll have a look inside the box, if you don't mind," said the one with the torch.

"By all the saints, I do mind! Ye ruffians and scoundrels! For all I know, ye're a pack o' thieves, out to steal me grandsire's silver. Now get down, I say!"

"Ruffians and thieves are we, eh?" said the one in the wagon. "If you take that tone, maybe we'll just have a little fun with the woman here." He reached for Albinia.

Flashing in the torchlight, David pulled a Bowie knife and slashed at the hand reaching for her. She was terrified and fumbled for the derringer. The man howled in pain from a gash across his palm. Another leaped down and grabbed the lines to the Belgians. Albinia saw David try to urge the horses forward, but the torch waved in front of them terrified them. A man approached from David's side to drag him off the driver's box, but

David reached under the box and brought out a Navy Colt, firing and hitting the man in the shoulder. Albinia harnessed her fear and determinedly took aim at the one with the torch. Her shot hit his leg, then the horse. The horse spun in terror, and the torch dropped, making the other horses rear and spin. Another man reached from the side for Albinia, swinging a fist at her. She heard a shot, and something hit the side of her head. She knew nothing more.

* * *

When Albinia woke, she felt a dull throb on the side of her head. She felt disoriented, not knowing where she was. Slowly, she focused. David's anxious face was above her. She was lying on her cot, in the rear of the dress shop. She tried to sit up, but David gently pressed her shoulder down.

"Don't try too much yet. You've had a nasty bump on the head. I'll tell Dr. Simpson you slipped and fell on the ice. I've let your shop owner know. When you're up to it, Dr. Simpson will take you home. I must go soon, to avoid suspicion."

"Did they...?"

"Our passengers are fine. Thanks to you. Your quick thinking and using the derringer made possible our escape. But this points out why you must never try this at night on your own. Once I leave to go north, you must only work in daytime, and only when it's really safe. Mabel and Franklin can help some, but they are far south enough that making all the deliveries may not work."

"No! I can do it. I want to do it."

"There's my brave girl!" David bent and kissed her forehead, and she winced. "Oh, sorry. Didn't mean to hurt you."

She managed a smile, "No, it's all right. And I'll be fine. Go ahead, go, before someone comes in. I'll just rest a little, then get up and take customers until Dr. Simpson comes. And David ... I love you!"

* * *

Will sat down to write. His heart was heavy. He had waited so long to respond to Dr. Simpson's offer, he felt they might be insulted. He'd barely spoken to Jenny for almost two weeks, and she had not approached him. Christmas was only two weeks away.

December 11, 1859

Dear Miss Morton,

He crumpled the paper and began again—Jenny wasn't concerned about being proper with him, and it didn't convey what he felt.

Dear Jenny,

I have been meaning to talk to you for some time now. I hope you will not think me a coward for writing rather than speaking to you in person. My intent is for both of us to think carefully before speaking things that cannot be unsaid.

I have considered carefully your uncle's generous offer, and I will speak to him directly today at church. As much as I admire your uncle, and am thankful he would even consider sponsoring me in such a manner, I cannot accept. This has been a difficult decision for me. I know in my soul that this must be the decision. I cannot go back on my word to Captain Morgan. If I were to do that, I would not be the man to whom you have generously given your affections. I think that if I am not honest, for the sake of gain, then I am not a man at all.

Please do not assume from this that I have no feelings for you. I am deeply touched by your affection and hope to yet advance in your regard. Whatever happens, please know how much I care for you, and pray for you. If God permits, someday I hope to properly court you, as you deserve, if your uncle will still permit it.

I hope you will do me the honor of accompanying me to Captain Morgan's Christmas party at the Mill Street house across from his mother's, Friday December 23, at six o'clock in the evening. Please feel free to bring your aunt and uncle as an escort. If you will come, please meet me after school this Tuesday at the park in front of Morrison. I will count the hours until then.

Yours affectionately,
Will

He read it over three times, deciding it struck the right tone. He was not officially courting Jenny, did not have permission to do so. Technically he should not use her first name, but he knew Jenny would care little for that. He wanted her to know that he did have feelings for her, yet he did not wish to make a promise for love and marriage that neither of them might be able to keep. He wanted to soften the blow of refusing her uncle's proposal, yet be clear that he could not compromise, even for her. Breaking his oath wouldn't let him sleep at night—he'd feel ashamed and compromised in everything he did. He folded the letter and sealed it with some candle wax.

* * *

Will hurried to finish his calculus exam, his mind distracted from integrals by his meeting with Jenny. Would she be there? Or would her uncle prevent her? Will spoke to Dr. Simpson as promised and he politely but stiffly received the refusal. Will was unclear what his attitude might be regarding further contact with Jenny, but he hoped that Jenny's impetuous determined nature would persuade her uncle to let them continue meeting. After all, Dr. Simpson knew it was a point of honor.

Will finished the last problem and handed the paper to the professor, hurrying down the steps of Morrison to the park. Soldiers in unfamiliar uniforms drilled in the same area the Rifles used. Getting closer and crossing the street, both his father and Joe Breckinridge were among the soldiers. Will felt uneasy in the pit of his stomach. What if war actually came?

He waited anxiously at the edge of the park, scanning the streets and the park itself for any sign of Jenny. Her school should have let out half an hour ago. He stamped his feet and moved about to ward off the cold. His mind filled with foreboding, yet inventing a hundred excuses for why she might not come, but still care for him.

After what he judged to be another long half an hour, a doctor's buggy with a familiar horse approached. As it stopped at the edge of the park, Will saw Jenny and her aunt, driven by a servant. The servant helped first her aunt, then Jenny down, and attended the horses. Jenny did not wait for her aunt but rushed over to Will.

"Will! I knew you'd wait!"

"You got my letter? You're not angry?"

"Yes, I got it. I am of course disappointed, but I understand. At least sort of."

Her aunt came over at a more sedate pace.

"I'm not so sure Uncle Tim does, though," Jenny continued.

"Yes, I'm afraid he can be stubborn, especially where Jenny is concerned," said her aunt. "But he'll likely come around. In the meantime, we wanted you to know that Jenny and I will accept your invitation to the Christmas party. I'm afraid my husband will not attend. He doesn't want his patients thinking that he supports Mr. Morgan."

"I'm sorry he feels that way," said Will. "But I am delighted that you will come." Embarrassed, he flushed and said, "I'm afraid I can't offer to pick you up except in our farm wagon."

Jenny's eyes danced in amusement at his discomfort.

"Don't worry, Will. We'll meet you at the party," said Jenny. Her aunt politely withdrew back to the buggy, leaving Jenny and Will a small amount of privacy, yet she was still close by.

Jenny faced Will, with her back to her aunt. He seized the moment to take both her hands in his. "Jenny, I hope you know how much I care for you. I've thought of you night and day the past few weeks. Being with you, well, I feel like I'm skipping on the clouds. But I know that there's this business with slavery, and some say there will be war. I care for you, but I don't want to promise too much yet. I couldn't bear to break my word to you. It means more to me than even my promise to Captain Morgan."

Jenny's face glowed, then sobered. "I understand, Will. I care a great deal for you too; you know that. I'm afraid I haven't been very proper, hiding my feelings the way a young woman should. But I don't know how to not be myself, either. My heart sings when I'm with you. I don't know how not to show it. I do hope you'll consider the things my uncle has said. He's not a man given to hasty conclusions." Nodding toward the field, she said, "And your father and your friend Joe are on the other side. Please think carefully what you're doing, Will. For both our sakes."

He released her hands. "I will, Jenny. Pray for wisdom. But I know God wants us to honor our promises. And I think if you come to the party, you'll see that Captain Morgan and the fellows in the Rifles aren't so bad."

"Until then." She turned and went back to the buggy, leaving Will hopeful but concerned. How could he overcome her uncle's opposition?

* * *

Will nervously drove the buggy to Morgan's Mill Street house. The horse and buggy were a recent gift from Hiram. He'd explained to Captain Morgan about bringing guests to the party. Morgan smilingly agreed, and even advanced Will enough to buy a new suit for the occasion. Now Will was in his unaccustomed finery, uncomfortable in his starched collar and wondering what Jenny and her mother would think of it all. He took a deep breath and, exhaling, saw the cloud of steam from his breath in the frigid air.

A slave took the reins of the buggy as he dismounted. Will went just inside the fence to wait for Jenny. With Hiram's gift, he could have changed arrangements and picked them up. He wanted to surprise Jenny with the buggy and his new suit, hoping her aunt would allow them to drive the few blocks back to the Simpsons' alone after the party.

After about ten minutes, Will saw the Simpson buggy arrive, with a servant driving. Mrs. Simpson and Jenny were in the rear seat. Will stepped forward, brushing the servant aside, to help them. Jenny wore a bright blue gown with a pink rose pattern and lace at the neck. Her pink wrap matched the roses in the dress. She smiled at Will and blushed as he held her hand getting off the carriage. Mrs. Simpson smiled politely, but her pursed lips and wrinkled forehead held a slight indication of disapproval. Will could not tell if it was directed at him or Jenny. The servant looked at him haughtily, as though annoyed at having to be lumped with the slaves as he tended to the horses.

"Good evening, Mrs. Simpson and Miss Morton," said Will formally. "I'm delighted that you could come." He bowed, and Jenny seemed to suppress a giggle. They each gave a slight curtsey, and accepted his arms to usher them into the house.

Captain Morgan himself greeted them at the door, all charm. "Good evening, Will! And who are these beautiful ladies?"

"May I present Mrs. Simpson and Miss Jenny Morton? Mrs. Simpson is the wife of Dr. Tim Simpson, with whom I believe you are acquainted. The doctor was otherwise engaged this evening."

"I understand. My wife is indisposed at present. Welcome! I hope you enjoy the evening. Christmas is always an occasion to rejoice. Sid!" he motioned to a light-skinned Negro slave. "Take their coats, and show them to the parlor where they can get warm. Until later, ladies?" Morgan tipped his hat and turned to the next arriving guests.

As they walked to the parlor in Sid's wake, Mrs. Simpson whispered, "That was uncommonly courteous of him. Not at all like the reports I've heard."

They joined the group around the fireplace, near the Christmas tree with candles lit. Will recognized James West, Tom Longwood, Archie Moodie, Ben Drake, and Jessie Davis, as well as others of his company. There was a round of introductions of the men and their ladies. One new man in particular caught Will's attention. Basil Duke was a handsome young man twenty-one years of age. He was talking and laughing with Captain Morgan's sister, Henrietta. He seemed to have an easy way with all the Rifles, joking and bantering. Will heard a rumor that he and Henrietta might become engaged.

Then someone proposed a Christmas song, and they all sang the new, "Hark, the Herald Angels Sing." The mood was cheerful, and even Ben Drake came over to shake Will's hand and meet Mrs. Simpson. Jenny gave Ben a polite but icy greeting, by Will's estimation. Someone struck up a chorus of another new song, "Dixie," enthusiastically sung by all of the Rifles. Mrs. Simpson and Jenny, unfamiliar with the song, stood quiet and slightly embarrassed at the unabashed Southern sentiment. Just then, Sid announced dinner. The fare was sumptuous, including turkey, oysters, sangaree, marmalade ice cream, baked beans, and potatoes. Much of the dinner conversation centered on the execution of John Brown in Virginia and his attempted slave rebellion. As the slaves served dessert, Captain Morgan opined, "John Brown got only what he deserved. He was a rabble-rouser in Kansas, with many deaths to his credit. It is God's mercy that he didn't get his hands on the Federal arsenal at Harper's Ferry. Indeed, he should have known that the slaves would not join him. Why should they? Their masters feed and care for them. They have few worries and concerns. When a man buys a slave, it is a covenant to care for him. How else should they survive, not having the wit and industry of the white race?"

Mrs. Simpson fidgeted and then spoke, "But what entitles one man to buy another at all? What of Abraham Lincoln's speech, where he said, 'I think slavery is wrong, morally and politically. I desire that it should be no further spread in these United States, and I should not object if it should gradually terminate in the whole Union.'"

There was a stressed silence around the table for a moment, and then Morgan said, "Perhaps the rail splitter wants to take up the labor of the slaves and provide their upkeep as well. I can just see him bending to pick cotton and harvest hemp. Actually, I've seen pictures where he'd make a great scarecrow!" This received general laughter around the table, and Mrs. Simpson said no more.

"And now, why don't we retire back to the parlor? There are some musicians who will help us to dance the remainder of the night away," said Morgan.

Couples paired off, and a waltz began. The evening passed in a whirl. Will danced several times with Jenny, and just enough with other girls to be polite. Mrs. Simpson sat in a corner and drank punch, nonalcoholic. She declined all invitations to dance, even Captain Morgan's gallant attempt. When at last couples began to leave, Will approached her with his proposal that he and Jenny be allowed to drive back to the Simpson's alone, with her buggy following.

"It's not quite proper. I doubt Dr. Simpson would approve."

Just then Jenny came over, and hearing Will's proposal, she added, "Auntie, please? It's Christmas. You'll be right behind us. It's only ten minutes to home and Will is driving, not a servant."

Seeing Jenny's pleading gaze, she relented. "Well, all right. No detours. Straight home."

"Thank you, Mrs. Simpson. Believe me, you have nothing to worry about," said Will.

They went out into the cold, and a slave brought Will's horse and buggy. Will helped Jenny into the seat, then mounted the driver's box, released the brake, and chirruped to the horse. He did not hurry, taking it at a slow walk. He smiled when Jenny slid over close by him.

"Will? I don't understand Captain Morgan. He seems every inch a gentleman. I know he's been generous and nice to you, kind of like Uncle Tim with me. Nevertheless, he owns the slaves. He seems to treat them all right, I guess, but kind of like young children, even the adults. And that Sid—did you see how light colored he was, and how much he looked like Captain Morgan? Your Captain Morgan is a confusing man. There's a lot to admire, and yet...."

"Jenny, you just don't know him. You should see the way he treats everyone in the Rifles. Like family. Everyone knows, if they have a problem, just go see Captain Morgan."

"Maybe so. But something about him just doesn't add up. I'm afraid, Will. I may be only fifteen, but I just sense something about him. For sure, he doesn't think much of the Negroes."

"But Jenny, he cares for all his Negroes. He takes care of them, just like he said."

"Owning slaves is evil! Oh, Will! I care so much for you! I don't want to see you swept away in a senseless war. Please! For me ... just think again about leaving the Rifles. Then at least if war comes, you'll have a choice."

"I have a choice, now. I've made that choice. We've been over this. I can't go back on my word. I can't let the fellows in the Rifles down. What if the Northerners make an army and invade Kentucky? Shouldn't I defend my family, my home? Shouldn't I defend you?"

"All this talk of Northerners and Southerners makes me crazy. Why can't we all just be Americans and Christians? The Bible says that there is neither Jew nor Greek, there is neither slave nor free, there is neither male nor female: for ye are all one in Christ Jesus. Why can't we all just be one people? I know you care about God."

"'Wherefore putting away lying, speak every man truth with his neighbor: for we are members one of another.' If I quit, then everything I've done is a lie. Is that what you want for me?"

"No, but..."

"There is no but. It's one or the other."

Jenny silently slid away, and they finished the drive in silence. She refused his help down, lifted her skirts, and jumped. A petticoat tore, but she ignored it. She almost just went in the house, but then turned. "At least pray, Will. Promise me you'll do that. There has to be a way. What if you asked Captain Morgan to relieve you of your promise? Have you thought of that? Anyway, I had something for you." Jenny reached into her reticule and pulled out a piece of needlework. She handed it to him, bound with a bow.

"I had something for you too." He handed her a small box, wrapped and bound with yarn. "Open it."

She opened it and found a silver pin, a Mary Luckenbooth pin from Scotland. "Oh, Will! It's beautiful. However did you…?"

"Not half as beautiful as you. Think of me when you wear it."

"I will. And think of me when you pray."

Her aunt's buggy drew up and she walked away, into the house.

* * *

Julia fussed and fumed. She packed and repacked her borrowed steamer trunk three times, trying to decide how to make the most of a meager wardrobe. She was traveling north with Hiram and his mother, to meet the rest of the family. Her father and Hiram met a week or so ago, under the eagle eye of Hiram's mother, to conclude a marriage contract, according to Swedish custom. The Swedes thought the actual marriage ceremony a formality that came later. They would not yet share a bed, bowing to American custom. Julia was uneasy. She had grown to appreciate Hiram, his gentleness, and humor. His mother was an altogether different matter. Julia did not know what to make of her, and constantly felt that she didn't measure up to some undefined standard.

Of course, Julia had no dowry, beyond a few blankets and other items Albinia was sewing for her. She could hardly match the economic status that a wealthy Swedish family would enjoy. It mattered little to Hiram. In fact, against custom, he gave her father a handsome Percheron draft horse and buggy. Hiram had been teaching her to drive a horse. He felt it silly for a woman not to know how. It was common in the old country, he said. He had given her a sum as well for clothes, but there was no time to have them made before the trip. They were to leave in three days.

Again she despaired of how to make scarves, stomachers, and accessories interchangeable enough to make her appear to have more than three outfits, which was all she owned. Finally she closed the trunk, latching it, and sat down on the bedstead, almost ready to cry. This was her chance, wasn't it? Her chance to break away from the humdrum and work of the farm. She could learn to move in society. She wouldn't have to worry about whether the harvest would be good, or what yokel might try for her hand with her father. This was what she wanted—to marry a rich man. Then why did she feel so unsure? That contract business made her feel like Hiram was buying a prize cow! However, that was ridiculous—she knew he cared for her. She treasured the memory of the evening by the lake. She knew she wasn't that pretty, like her sister. She still wondered at times about Hiram choosing her. What did he see in her that she didn't see herself? She wasn't silly enough to think a girl like her could choose and marry for love. It was a miracle someone wanted her at all. She shook her head, just as Pa called from the outer room, to see if she was ready yet. She pulled on a bonnet and set her jaw. This *was* her chance! She resolved to make it work and be the best wife to Hiram that she could.

"Ready, Pa!" she called, making her voice firm. She pushed aside the blanket divider to indicate her father was welcome to enter. He came in and stopped, just looking at her a moment.

"Well, look at you! Pretty as can be! I declare, Julia, I can't believe you're goin' off to be married. Seems to me you were only born yesterday. And here you are, lookin' like a fine lady!"

"Oh, Pa! Don't tease me! I can't bear it. You know it's not true."

Robert looked surprised, then amused. "You don't give yourself enough credit, Jule. You should take a better look in one of those mirrors the Johannsens likely have. And see yourself on the inside the way God sees you. You'd be surprised!"

He went over and picked up her trunk, taking it out to the buggy.

Sara, Lydia, Will, and Albinia crowded around, giving hugs and offering congratulations.

"Well, milady, if you're ready, your carriage awaits. Promise you'll write to us. And if you get bored with the ladies' teas and charity events, come see an old farmer sometime."

"I will, Pa. We will come back to visit when we can."

She and Robert went outside, and he loaded her trunk into the new buggy. The horse was hitched, standing and waiting. Robert began to climb into the driver's seat, when Julia said, "Oh, please, Pa! May I drive? Hiram's been teaching me. I suppose his mother will have servants to do it, and I may not get another chance soon."

Robert chuckled and scratched his head. "All right, if it makes your heart happy. One last drive with my little girl." He helped her up into the seat and handed her the reins before climbing in on the other side. She released the brake, clucked to the dappled gray horse, slapped the reins, and took off at a smart trot. Her father smiled approvingly. "Looks like you had a good teacher!"

On the way to town they talked and laughed, reminiscing about silly family things from years past. Julia began to realize how much she was going to miss the old farm, her family, even her gossipy church friends. She was going to an unknown place, to live with strangers. She didn't know how to play this game. She had no training. No one had told her the rules. She was leaving everything familiar behind. Once the ceremony took place, there would be no turning back. *Oh, dear God, help!* she thought.

They arrived at the train station. She was to meet Hiram. They would take the train to the Ohio River, then one of his family's steamboats to Cincinnati. Her father helped her out of the buggy, and a slave porter took her trunk when her father reached for it. Robert shrugged and let him. They saw Hiram waiting on the platform and waved. Turning to each other, Julia broke and wept. "Oh, Pa! I don't know how to leave you." She clung to him, hugging him as she had not since she was a little girl. He held her until she stopped crying, as he used to. He offered her his worn handkerchief, telling her to keep it. Then they turned and mounted the platform, going to Hiram.

"You take good care of her, Mr. Johannsen. I'm giving you a jewel."

"*Ja*, I will, Mr. Crump. I will take very good care of her. We hope you may come to Cincinnati sometime, and see."

"Well, this old farmer doesn't travel much. But if I can, I will."

They shook hands, and Julia watched her father turn and walk away. His shoulders slumped, as if from sadness, and he seemed somehow more frail and diminished than the man she had always admired. She turned to Hiram, smiling determinedly. He took her hand, and they boarded the train. She had never ridden on one, and within minutes, the fields were whizzing by at unbelievable speed. Each *clack* of the wheels was carrying her farther into the unknown. Farther away from home the train car sped, as the whistle blew mournfully.

* * *

Luther stretched and yawned. At times, it seemed he was still dreaming. He and his family were in Ripley, Ohio, sleeping in beds like white folk, in the house of one John Parker, a free black. He knew they were not altogether safe here, but free! On free soil! The coffins found their way to Reverend Elijah Green, a free black minister and former slave. He hid them, and switched real corpses in for inspection, then switched again before they crossed the river, driving over in a hearse in broad daylight. The Parkers were kindness itself. Today John was taking him and the women a little further north. There was a community of free blacks where they could find work and a place to live. Though somewhat dangerous due to slave catchers, they could choose to stay or move further north still. Unaccustomed to such choices, Luther did not yet know what to do. All he knew was he, Jemima, Olivia and Clara were free! They had full bellies, and soft beds. No one was cracking whips at them, or forcing them into the fields before dawn. He did not have to stand for hours waiting on Lucy's whim. True, he and Jemima would have to find jobs, maybe Olivia too. As for Clara—his sister could enjoy being a child. Maybe they could even attend school, learn to read. Mr. Parker said there was a place called Oberlin, up north, where black people could go to school too.

He shook Olivia and Clara gently to wake them. He heard a knock on the door and found Mrs. Parker had brought them tea and a light breakfast. They were still in hiding in the Parker house, but today ... today would be their first steps outside the protection of those who had helped them north. Jemima opened her eyes and smiled. It warmed him to see his mama happy. She rose and dressed quickly. They all gathered around a small table with real chairs.

"Lawd, we thank you for dis day! Dis day of freedom we thought would never come! Thank you Lawd also for dis food. Bless de Parkers, and protect them. Protect all those that helped us, even those we got no idea who they were. And Lawd, wherever she is, bless Miss Albinia! Amen!" prayed Jemima.

"Amen!" said the children. The meal was quickly consumed, and another rapping at the door was heard. Jemima opened it and, to her amazement, the little Parker children, Hortense and Horatio, came in, each carrying a dress and shoes, and a new pair of trousers and shirt for Luther. Self-consciously, the oldest said, "Mama says to give you these things, to celebrate freedom. Just like God gives us gifts when He sets us free."

"I ... I don' know what to say! Thank you, girls, and thank your mother! Glory be, we gone to hebbin!" said Jemima. The girls squealed over their new dresses, and Luther changed at once, rolling up his ragged traveling clothes he had worn for many weeks. Then he turned to his sisters.

"Hush, now! We got to get goin'. Won't do to keep Mr. Parker waitin'."

They gathered their few possessions and went out to the wagon in the carriage house. Slave catchers sometimes watched the house, so they would have to be smuggled out under bales of hay. The wagon had high sides, and a compartment in the bottom where they could squeeze in. Then the compartment closed, and several layers of hay bales were placed on top. It was cold, and the hay was scratchy, but they would soon be free! John warned them not to sign or make a mark on anything someone gave them, without getting him or another trusted person to read it. Some Negroes found themselves enslaved as indentured servants in the North, he said, by crafty people taking advantage of their illiteracy. He made the trip to the community once a week or so. They could always get a message to him. They bumped along the road in the suffocating confines of the compartment, but each clop of a hoof, each turn of a wheel seemed to sing "Freedom!" to Luther's ears. Just when he thought he was going to freeze solid, the wagon stopped. He heard Mr. Parker get down, then low voices, and the sound of the wagon tailgate lowering. Then there were steps above them as the hay was unloaded. Weeks of traveling in fear left him nervous and uneasy. *What if slave catchers stopped us?* he thought. Luther tensed and gripped the knife he still had.

Finally, someone lifted the last bale of hay out of the wagon, and the compartment opened. To Luther's relief, the smiling face of Mr. Parker greeted him, surrounded by a group of ten to fifteen other black smiling faces.

"Welcome to freedom!" one of them said. "I'm Ned Smith, the blacksmith for this town." He extended his hand, which Luther shook. "I hear you know a thing or two about horses. How about comin' to work for me? Not much, just room and board, plus two bits a week. Plenty of room for your family until you get your own place. What do you say?"

Luther could hardly believe his ears. "I say bless you! And thank you!"

Jemima burst out, "Lawd a mercy! We thank you from de bottom of our heart! I think we done found de promised lan'!"

They followed Ned to their accommodations at the back of the stable, really just a couple of empty stalls. There were straw ticks for beds, a rude table, and stumps for stools. He showed them the privy, and told them to come to the cabin next door for supper at sunset. Luther noticed the rest of the men disappeared. When they came to supper, Luther saw that Ned had a wife and three children.

"This is my wife, Katy. My children are Ruth, Mark, and Ben. And there," he said indicating a tall older boy," is Sam. He'll be working with you. He comes from the Nawth, up New York way."

Luther immediately noticed a hostile glare from Sam, who looked to be about nineteen, a lean muscled mulatto. He also noticed Ruth, about his age, slim, pretty, and shyly smiling at him. Mark looked to be about ten, and little Ben about eight. Their meal was simple and quickly concluded. Ned suggested they retire early, to be ready for work in the morning. As

Luther lay in the stall, breathing the air of freedom, he wondered where their road would take them.

* * *

Julia felt tired and excited all at once. She experienced so many new things. First, she rode on the train. Then she had her own hotel room in Maysville. She never stayed in a hotel in her life. Now some shopping, and then boarding an actual steamboat to Cincinnati. Everywhere there were new sights, unfamiliar places, and people. Hiram never seemed to falter. He was at home in this world. On the street they met people who knew him, treated him with deference and respect. She began to see him through new eyes yet again. She felt the wonder of a child who emerges from a cabin to her first snow, with everything utterly changed. She watched as Hiram shepherded their steamer trunks on board the ship. The captain deferentially bowed, and a crewman showed each to their staterooms, the best on the ship. She felt constantly as though she were in a play where she did not know the lines. Servants popped up everywhere, asking her wants and opinions. It made her head spin. She tried her best to mask her feelings of excitement and inadequacy. Going from country farm girl to wife of a wealthy steamboat owner in such a short time, she struggled to absorb it all.

As the boat cast off and began its journey on the river, she sat in a chaise lounge looking out the window as the beauty of the river went by. Hiram came in smiling.

"Are you comfortable, Julia? Is there anything you would like? Lunch will be served in an hour. But if you're hungry before then, I can have the steward bring something."

"No, no, Hiram. Everything is perfect. I … I'm just in a whirl. I had no idea you lived like this."

"This? Oh, it is nothing. Just a few comforts. Sometimes, with the stress of running the business, I wish I could just be a simple farmer like your father."

"And Pa would trade places with you in a moment, if he could. Farming is a hard life."

Hiram looked unusually serious for a moment. "All life is hard; money doesn't change that. It is up to us to choose joy and make the most of each situation. Once a person has the basic needs, the rest is just a matter of comfort. I know friends who have plantations and wealth—yet they are miserable." Brightening, he said, "But you need not worry about it. My only thought is to make you happy. There will be plenty of time after we are married to decide how you want to spend your time."

"I hadn't thought ... I'm so used to working on the farm."

"Mama will help you. She knows important people in Cincinnati, Louisville, and Lexington, all along the river, even in St. Louis. You can be a great help to me in the business by the connections you make with other wives at teas, balls, and charity events." He took a little silver bell from his pocket and set it on the table next to her. "I have some cargo orders to attend to. A shipment of slaves, I think. If you need anything, just ring the bell. Morris, the steward, will get whatever you need." He gave her forehead a quick kiss, then left the room.

The hour passed quickly. Julia alternately looked out the window and read a book. She had to admit, getting used to this life of ease wasn't too difficult. No pigs or chickens to feed, no butter to churn, and she didn't have to dig in the dirt for the garden. She supposed servants would also do laundry, mending, and cooking.

"Luncheon is served in the dining room," Morris informed her, and escorted her to her place. Every possible delicacy was present. It would have been delightful, but for Kirsten Johannsen sitting across from her, criticizing her every move. Julia supposed she meant to be helpful. In truth, she had no idea which fork or spoon to use for the different dishes. She had no idea lunch could be such a complicated affair. A woman screaming interrupted their peace and the chamber music. Julia was startled.

"That's no concern of ours," Kirsten said. "Just eat your lunch."

Ignoring her, Julia dropped her fork, pushed back from the table, and rushed through a doorway out onto the upper deck. On the main deck, a crowd of Negroes was gathered, in chains. In the center, tied to a post with her arms above her head, a woman stood naked to the waist. A large man stood a few feet away, cat 'o nine tails in his hand. As Julia watched, he laid on the vicious whip, provoking another loud scream of pain. Blood pooled at her feet. A few white men in waistcoats looked on, seemingly unconcerned. A small Negro girl rushed out and grabbed the legs of the man with the whip. Julia was too far away to hear, but from her face, it seemed obvious she was begging for mercy for her mother. The man shoved the little girl roughly away, threatening her with the whip. Julia turned away, sickened by the sight. She strode resolutely back into the dining room.

"Where's Mr. Johannsen?" she demanded.

"My dear," said Kirsten. "Calm yourself. You mustn't make a scene. Have a glass of claret, steady your nerves."

"I want to see Hiram!" Julia insisted. "I want him to make it stop!"

Kirsten quietly wiped her mouth with a white linen napkin. "He'll do no such thing, even if you find him. I expect it will stop on its own, soon enough. The point is to teach the slaves a lesson and prevent further trouble. I'm sure the owner doesn't want to damage her so much she can't be sold. That's why the other slaves must watch. You, however, have no place in such matters. It is not becoming to a lady to notice. The slaves belong to our customers. We may dislike how they are treated, but it is not our business. You'll grow used to it, in time, if you take many of these voyages."

Julia responded, "If I grow used to such displays of cruelty, then I am poor indeed. If you will excuse me...." She turned and left the room, lunch unfinished.

* * *

Will found a new job working as a hemp dresser in one of Morgan's factories. The nighttime hours spent separating the hemp fibers allowed him to work on the farm, keep up his studies, and drill with the Rifles. He advanced his riding skills now that his family had a horse, and spent less time walking. The weeks passed so quickly, he thought of little except the next task. He and Jenny met mostly at church, and he avoided the subject of the Rifles. In early February, he thought of Valentine's Day approaching. There would be a box social at church on Valentine's evening to benefit the town orphanage. Will focused on the idea of buying Jenny's box lunch and having time with her. Her uncle made sure there were no more buggy rides as long as Will was in the Rifles.

Will and Joe didn't meet much. Albinia seemed to blush when Joe's name came up. She told her father about Joe as a beau as promised, and she was home at night more often. Will decided she was just being silly about having a beau.

Valentine's Day came, and Will dressed his best after grooming and washing the Percheron and cleaning out the buggy. He heated bricks for their feet on the drive to town. He was hopeful that Dr. Simpson might relent and let Jenny ride with him. His parents also dressed in their best. Even Lydia shone, decked out in a new dress Albinia had found time to sew. Albinia said she had too much work for such an outing.

"Mrs. Crump, don't you dare let anyone bid on your box. I saw you pack my favorites in there, and I declare no one else is to have them."

"Then you just best have the highest bid, Mr. Crump," teased Sara. "This is for the orphanage, and it goes to the highest bidder. Along with my company for the evening, of course."

Robert turned to Will, scratching his head. "Will, how'd you horn-swoggle me into this, anyhow? I got to pay for my own wife's dinner and company? Highway robbery!"

Sara just laughed. "It'll do you good not to take me for granted for a change, Mr. Crump."

Lydia piped up, "I'll sit with you, Pa."

Both parents laughed and Robert scooped her up into the buggy.

Will drove, and his parents continued to banter back and forth on the drive. He had not seen them in such good spirits in a long time.

Once in the church, Will absently greeted a few of the other young people, scanning the crowd for Jenny. He spotted her near the front of the hall, chattering animatedly with some other girls. He recognized some in the group from his old school. They would be sixteen now, and no longer attending school, getting down to the serious business of husband hunting. A few titters broke out as he approached. It was widely known that he and Jenny were together, though not officially courting due to her uncle's disapproval.

Jenny broke off from the group and came over toward him. She wore the same gown as at the Christmas party, which made his chest ache strangely. In public, she was formal. "Mr. Crump! How nice to see you! You've been rather scarce, again."

Will responded in kind. "Yes, I'm sorry. Miss Morton, I wished to speak with you. I ... I wanted you to know I'll be bidding tonight. I got a new job, and...."

"Yes, I heard," she interrupted crisply. "With Captain Morgan, I understand. And still drilling with the Rifles."

"Yes, but I...."

"No need to explain. I think it's clear what your decision is. Certainly, in recent weeks you've allocated more time to the Rifles than to me. My uncle has also been clear," she said, removing the pin he'd given her and handing it to him. "If you feel you must bid, then you must. After all, it is a good cause. I wish I could say the same of your Rifles. Mr. Lincoln is correct, I believe—a house divided cannot stand. The country will become all slave or all free. I'm just a woman, but I cannot cast my lot with those who support the institution. My uncle has joined the Home Guard as a physician. At any rate, do not bid on my account. You will only waste Mr. Morgan's money." She turned and walked back to her group of friends, leaving him crestfallen and surprised.

Will walked to a table where his parents sat. Sara looked at him and excused herself.

"Will, what's wrong? You look like someone just hit you!"

"I think she did, Ma. Jenny just gave this back." He opened his hand to show her the pin. "She doesn't want me to buy her box. She says drilling with the Rifles and working for Captain Morgan makes me stand for slavery, and neither she nor her uncle will have it."

Sara looked at him compassionately. "Oh, Will! I'm so sorry. I know she means so much to you. You have to make your own decisions, just like your Pa said. But think, Will! Think! Isn't there some truth in what she says? There's still time. Go to Dr. Simpson. Talk with him. I believe even yet he would relent."

Will became stubborn. "No. I know you're trying to help, Ma. You know I don't stand for slavery. Why, even this Abraham Lincoln said just a while that he is not for equality of the white and black races, that he favors white superiority. Most folks, North and South, think that way. Even an Irishman thinks he's better than a Negro, not to mention an Indian. I am neither for slavery nor against it. It simply has nothing to do with me. Why will no one understand that? All I want is a peaceful life, to study law, and raise a family. Is that so wrong?"

"No, Will, it isn't," said Sara gently. "But in these times, people will assign you a side if you don't choose one. There is guilt by association. The Bible says bad company corrupts good morals. People assume your views are the same as Morgan's, because you are in the Rifles. Are your convictions worth losing Jenny? She loves you, Will. Your sister's husband, Hiram, is right on one thing: the time is coming when you'll have to take sides. I don't like your Pa being in the Guard. I don't like you being in the Rifles. Even worse, I can't stand the thought that you might face one another on opposite sides of a battlefield. What then, Will? What will your convictions mean then? Think on that." She turned away and went back to his father.

* * *

Julia felt lost and overwhelmed. She stood outside the Lutheran church in Cincinnati waiting for the processional for her wedding. The sky threatened rain. Had it not been for Albinia with her, she might have run to find the nearest train. Albinia said her sister was not going to get married with no one from the family present, if she had to spend six months wages to get there. For almost three months, Julia endured the prodding of her mother-in-law. Hiram was sweet and attentive when he was around. So often, he was enmeshed in the business or drilling with the blasted Guard. They did have some fun times. They rode in the sleigh. He took her to plays and the opera. They talked, and he actually listened to her, not treating her as a child.

It was March now. She'd heard the news about Will and Jenny. Why wouldn't this war leave them alone? It hadn't even started yet, and already was causing misery. Lincoln's recent speech at Cooper Union in New York had only deepened stubbornness on both sides. She hadn't slept last night, not a wink. Tossing and turning, she was afraid and excited about what the next day would bring. Her stomach felt nauseous, but she knew she had to eat the cake and delicacies at the reception. Mama Kirsten had been very specific about what she expected of her. There would be an interpreter present, to give the English translation of the ceremony for her. Everything would be in Latin and Swedish. She felt scatterbrained. How was she supposed to behave like a polished grand dame, when she felt like a frightened little girl? How she wished her own mother could be here! Even without training, her mother always seemed to know what to do, what to say, in any situation. Julia looked over gratefully at Albinia. She was ashamed for having snapped while Albinia helped her dress.

"Any time now," Albinia whispered, giving her arm a squeeze. Albinia had offered to sew her dress, but Hiram wouldn't hear of it, ordering from a designer in New York. Julia managed a weak smile.

"Promise you'll write to me. I … I know I've often been a bossy sister, not the best confidant. But I can't tell you how I've missed you these last months. It's like another world here. Mama Kirsten is always after me, and not the sweet little reminders like our mother. Oh, I've learned a lot. So often, though, I wish I were back home watching the chickens or Lydia. Then I see Hiram, and he reminds me that I've learned to love him. I really do! But I'm so glad you came!"

"Don't cry and make your eyes red. It's almost time. I will write whenever I can. I've missed you too, even your bossiness. Come to Lexington when you can."

They heard the organ playing the processional. The ushers swung the doors open wide. Julia felt Albinia following her, attending to her train. How she wished little Lydia could have been in front, scattering flower petals! Then she looked out through the veil and saw Hiram waiting at the altar, beaming. Suddenly, nothing else mattered.

LOST AND FOUND

March 1860

A lbinia felt nothing was the same. Her world was changing around her, unbidden. Spring beckoned, and should have been a time of joy. This year, it seemed as though in her world, things died before they bloomed. Julia was gone. David was gone. Her father and Will were seldom home, and increasingly distant from one another. She noticed Will morosely and mechanically going about his tasks, without his usual energy and drive. His break with Jenny seemed to make him a pale shadow. For the people in her life, it seemed like a spring where the plants did not come up and decided to remain in the ground. All the month of March, and into April, she felt as though an impending storm was about to break. It would come lashing and drowning all she held dear. The apprehension was wearing. Her secrets and constant dissembling erected unseen walls between her and her family, but she didn't know how to stop it. There had been no Underground Railroad activity for a few weeks now.

She walked out along the paths to the fields with Lydia running ahead. Only little Lydia, growing up but still blissfully unaware of tensions, provided a bright spot in each day. Albinia made a morning walk part of their routine, enjoying her sister's childish delight in a flower, or a bird, to relieve the void in her own heart. She pondered her situation, her reverie interrupted occasionally by some exclamation from Lydia or a tug at her hand.

During the early part of the year, she spent more time with Joe, but now, as spring came, she felt a choice pressing in upon her. She'd avoided the Valentine's box social. The previous social she'd attended with him felt awkward. Yet he persisted, showing up at the shop, leaving tokens and gifts, even inviting her to Sunday dinner at the parson's house. She wanted to be loyal to David, yet, in some ways, Joe did attract her. He was sweet, attentive, and handsome. His family was prominent. He was a Union sympathizer, staunchly against slavery. Her father approved of him. Many girls would love to have his attentions. Moreover, he was present, right here, not hundreds of miles away. So what was it that held her to David? Joe was … safe. And maybe … maybe that was the problem. All her girlhood, she had been the good little girl who followed the rules, worked for the family, tried to be proper, never stepping outside the boundaries. With David, a new exciting world opened. She was helping people, making a difference. It would be easy to settle down with Joe, follow convention and raise a family, rest in economic security. Yet Joe's father was a slave owner, and his brother drilled with the Rifles. She supposed she shouldn't hold that against him—after all, her own brother Will was in the Rifles, despite attempts from almost everyone to dissuade him. So was it David or the exciting life he represented that pulled her heart?

She and Lydia were nearing the cabin on their return walk, when they heard the rattle of buggy wheels approaching. Neither Will nor her father were at home. Sara emerged from the cabin with Will's rifle in her hands. Rustler barked loudly, dancing around the buggy as it came to a halt in front of the cabin in a cloud of dust. Her mother put the gun down and beckoned her.

"Come on, Lyddie. Looks like we're wanted. Better hurry!" In answer, Lydia began skipping along toward the cabin. Albinia picked up her skirts and walked faster. The Clay crest was on the buggy, and a familiar Negro slave talked to her mother. She recognized Jackson, from Ashland.

"Yes'm, Miz Crump. Miss Lucy she say bring Miss Albinia right away, if she can come. I'm to wait for her answer."

Albinia came up from behind. "What is it, Jackson? Is Lucy ill?"

"No'm. Not exakly. She fell, tryin' to come down de stairs by hersef. You know how she can be." Albinia laughed, then sobered.

"Is she badly hurt?"

"Jes a sprained ankle, I think. Makes it harder for her to walk, and she's more ornery. She upset that she ripped her dress, too. Auntie May, she offer to fix it. But Miss Lucy, she say only you can do it so it don't show."

"All right, Jackson. Mama, I'm sorry to leave you with Lyddie again. Let me get my things." She moved toward the cabin.

Lydia hopped from one foot to the other and said, "Could I come? I've never seen Ashland. Lucy likes me at church, maybe I could cheer her up."

"Well, I don't know…," said Albinia.

"Mebbe you could, at that," said Jackson, grinning.

Sara smiled. Albinia still wasn't sure. "I don't know how long I'll be. It's a longer drive than just to church. What if I have to stay overnight?"

"Oh, goody!" said Lydia. "I've never stayed with anyone! Please, Mama?"

Sara seemed to debate, and then said, "All right. If your sister doesn't mind. But you have to be on your best manners, and don't touch anything without permission. The Clays have many fine, breakable things."

Albinia knew when to give up. "You can come then. I don't want to hear you complain about the long ride. You mustn't pester Lucy with too many questions. If she seems too tired, you'll need to go find Sukie or her brothers to play with. Can you do that?"

"Oh, yes! And I'll bring my doll to show Sukie."

Albinia suppressed a grin, thinking of the fine china dolls and toys the Clay children had. "Sukie likes to draw, so maybe you can do that with her."

In a few minutes, they gathered Albinia's sewing things and overnight items, in case of need, and departed, Sara waving after them.

The ride was anything but boring, with Jackson entertaining Lydia with jokes, stories, and songs. Lydia fairly bounced in time to the bumps. Albinia marveled at how easily Jackson entertained her sister, kept the horses moving, and eyed their surroundings all at the same time. As they arrived at Ashland, Jackson stiffened and assumed a more formal attitude toward the ladies.

"You must settle down now, Lyddie. Put your lady manners on. Don't get Jackson into trouble," said Albinia.

"Why would he get in trouble?"

"No time to explain now. Just do as I say." They got down and went inside, going up the spiral stairs to a bedroom on the left, where Lucy lay in bed waiting for them.

"Good afternoon, Albinia! I can't tell you how glad I am to see you! You brought Lydia! How are you?"

"More to the point, how are you? Does your ankle hurt much?"

"Yes, like blazes! I'm trying to ignore it. Phoebe here has been keeping ice on it," referring to her maid who hovered near the foot of the bed. "I'm not sure which is worse: the pain or the annoyance of not being able to move!"

"Good afternoon, Miss Lucy!" said Lydia, remembering her "lady" manners for a moment. "I wanted to come and cheer you up! See?" She displayed a few straggly flowers she picked from the front of the house when Albinia wasn't looking.

"Lyddie! Those aren't ours—you shouldn't have picked them."

"Nonsense," said Lucy, smiling. "Our gardener may be vexed, but I am not. You cheer me up already, dear."

Encouraged, Lydia said, "But Miss Lucy, where's your mama? Why isn't she taking care of you? That's what my mama does when I'm sick."

Albinia was mortified. "Lyddie!"

"No, it's all right, Albinia. Lydia, my mother is a great lady. She has many servants and a whole household to manage. Especially with my father traveling so much. Phoebe is my maid, and taking care of me is her job."

Turning to Phoebe, Lydia said, "Do you like your job? Do you like being a slave for Miss Lucy? I like Jackson. And I like that other man, Luther."

Appalled, Albinia sternly reprimanded her, "Lydia Dorsey Crump! Didn't I tell you not to bother Miss Lucy with a lot of fool questions?"

Chastened, Lydia looked doleful. "I'm sorry, Miss Lucy."

"I do apologize, Lucy. She isn't used to...."

Just then, Lucy's mother, Susan Clay, came in. She took in the situation and turned to Phoebe. "That will be all, Phoebe. Take Miss Lydia to the nursery. I believe Sukie is playing there. I will call if you are needed."

Phoebe and Lydia left, Phoebe never raising her eyes or uttering a word.

"I was just saying I apologize for my sister. We did think she might cheer Lucy up. She doesn't really understand about slaves, especially Luther."

Susan looked angry. "I'll thank you not to mention his name in this house. Ungrateful wretch! We took him in, treated him well, gave him privileges. We trusted him with our daughter and you. And how did he reward us? Running away! Stealing slaves from Mr. Jameson! My husband gave him every consideration. We'll see what happens when he is caught!"

"You gave him everything ... except his freedom, his mother and sisters. Every consideration but that," said Albinia. Lucy looked shocked.

Susan's face turned scarlet. "If you're quite finished, Miss Crump, I intend to secure the services of Mr. George Alberti, a renowned slave catcher from Philadelphia. If anyone can find my property, it would be him. When you've completed the repairs to my daughter's gown, my butler will see you are paid and Jackson will drive you home. I trust the repairs will not take long."

Susan turned and swept out of the room.

"Whatever possessed you to speak to my mother so?" Lucy demanded. "She's never been anything but kind to you and your family."

"I ... I ... I don't know. I'm sorry, Lucy. I didn't mean to anger her. It's just ... well, I've learned to see slaves differently. As people."

"What do you mean, people? Of course, they're people. You've seen them for years—here, in town, everywhere. Why, a fifth of the population of Lexington are slaves!"

"I mean as individuals—people with feelings, hopes, and dreams. Take Phoebe, for example. What do you really know about her? What she thinks, what she feels, what she wants?"

"Why should I bother? She's a good maid, she does what she's told. I treat her fairly. My father provides for her. She's a great deal better off here than at Jameson's, from what I've heard."

Albinia turned away. There was truth in what Lucy said. She took the torn gown and her sewing bag, and began to work.

After a few minutes, she spoke again. "But you act like those are the only options. Being here or at Jameson's. What if she wanted to be somewhere else, be someone else?"

"She can't. I own her. Besides, you've seen her. Sometimes she can barely get my hair ribbons right. How could she manage at something else? She's lucky to be a house slave."

"That's just it. You own her. She has no choices. What if you had been born a slave?"

"Don't be ridiculous! I thought we were friends."

Albinia finished the stitching and tied it off. She came to the bed, took Lucy's hands, and looked her in the eye. "You are my dear friend, Lucy. I so enjoy the times we have together. Don't let's quarrel. I would be ever so sad. I just want to share the joy I've found with you, to open your eyes. Mr. Lincoln, he's from Kentucky, like us. He says, 'No man is good enough to govern another without his consent.' Not even you. We all mistreat each other at times. If someone is mean to me I can protest, or I can get away from him or her. I could even retaliate, though that's not right. Phoebe dares not say a word. Jesus wants us to treat everyone as we would like to be treated. How would you want to be treated if you were Phoebe? For our friendship, think on it. Now I'll fetch Lydia, and we can do something fun before I go home if you like." She hurried away to get Lydia from across the hall.

* * *

Luther's days passed swiftly. For the first time in his life, he knew contentment. He learned from Ned, and was well on his way to becoming a competent blacksmith. He learned to make tools, shoe horses, and sharpen knives. The work and good food built his muscles. He was at an age where he grew rapidly. When he made mistakes at the forge, there was no threat of whipping or days without food. Ned gently corrected and showed him how to do the task, again. Olivia blossomed, pitching in to help around the livery and the cabin. Clara ran and played, enjoying all the childish things denied her before. All three of the ladies were learning their letters. He heard Jemima exclaim, "Oh, to read de word of the Lawd!! Mah blessin' just done overflowed!"

He also studied at night, learning to read and write. Ned said that often orders came in on paper, and there were too many to remember anyway. Reading and writing were necessary skills for business. Luther could see the sense of needing these skills to stay free. The community here was friendly and accepting. No one asked about where he came from. They welcomed him as a new member of their community. From time to time, John Parker, who had sheltered them, came by. Occasionally he wondered what had become of Albinia, to whom he was now very grateful. He supposed he might never see her again.

He stretched, and thought he'd take a break from the forge. It was nearing noon, anyway. Most likely Katy would have lunch for all of them. As he emerged from the barn, Ruth came from behind the cabin, taking clothes down off the line. He walked over just as she was finishing, admiring her as she stooped and rose. She bent to pick up the basket of clothes.

"Here, let me," said Luther.

She smiled. "All right, Mr. Strong Man. But you watch out! Soon I'll be getting you to hang 'em on the line, too!"

Luther took her teasing in stride. "And I'll be getting you to shoe de horses!" He thought Ruth was one of the prettiest and smartest girls he'd ever met. She was another reason he was working on reading. It embarrassed him that she could read newspapers and books, while he struggled with simple sentences. He was determined to fix that. They walked toward the cabin, laughing and chatting. Luther concentrated on Ruth, not noticing Sam come up behind him, or that he stuck a foot out in front of him, under the laundry basket.

Luther tripped. Some of the clean clothes went flying into the mud from last night's rain.

Sam stood back and laughed, then picked up the basket from where Luther dropped it. "Looks like you folks might need some help," Sam guffawed. "Seems like Luther here ain't used to Ohio mud. Needs to get more friendly like wid it. How 'bout I help you with these, Ruth? I bet I can get to de cabin without falling over my own feet."

Ruth turned on him, eyes blazing, hands on her hips. "How 'bout you pick up all de clothes you just spoiled, and rewash them for me? You think you funny? You got less sense dan de dawg! Or would you rather I go talk to Pa?" She turned, offered Luther a hand up, then seized the basket from Sam. "I can handle these on my own. Luther, you go on get washed up for lunch. I'll tell Mama Sam ain't havin' lunch today, he too busy working." She walked off into the house.

Luther glared at Sam. "What you think you doin'? Ain't it enough you spoiled Mr. Jenkins' tools I was makin' last week?"

"I cain't help it if you burned them up," said Sam innocently. "You got de fire too hot, left 'em too long."

Luther boiled. "If I see you mess up one more order of mine...."

"What? How 'bout you stay away from Ruth and I stay away from your orders? You think you gonna do sumpin', come on!" said Sam, assuming fighting stance.

Luther knew Sam was too strong for him. In a direct assault he'd stand little chance, though now he's only about forty pounds lighter and two inches shorter. He also knew Ned did not tolerate fighting, and this position was too important to him to lose. Gritting his teeth and forcing his arms to his sides, he turned away.

Sam laughed and dropped his arms, slapping his knee. "I knew it! Just a plain ol' coward. Run home to Mama, boy!"

Luther was tempted to turn, but just kept walking to the pump.

* * *

A few days later, Luther saw Ned finish up with a customer. He hurried out of the barn to catch up with him. "Mr. Smith? Can I talk to you?"

"Sure, Luther. What's on your mind?"

"Are you happy with my work here, sir?"

Ned scratched his head, puzzled. "Yes, Luther. I've been very happy with it. I would've let you know otherwise. Why?"

"I just wanted to know if you think I have a future blacksmithing. Because … because I'd like to ask if I might keep company with Ruth. I wouldn't want you to think I had no way to support her," Luther said nervously.

Ned laughed. "That doesn't really come as a surprise. Have you talked to her about it?"

"No, sir. I wanted to ask you first."

"Well, I think you'll find she just wonders what took you so long. She and Olivia are becoming good friends, too." Then more seriously, he said, "I've no objection, except … except that you need to realize you are not secure in your life here. A slave catcher could come through any time and steal you and your whole family away. I've seen it happen, and I wouldn't want that heartbreak on my Ruth. I'm sure you can understand."

"Yes, sir," said Luther despondently. "But what can I do?"

"Well, for now, nothing. Let's keep this between ourselves and see how things develop. When John Parker came through, he said that someone might be able to ask some discreet questions, find out if they're still looking for you. He promised to pass back what he hears. Let's wait for that. Meanwhile, you may spend time with her—but just be careful," he said, his words laced with warning. "Be careful of my daughter's heart. I am not a man to be crossed."

"Yes, sir! Thank you, sir!" It was more than Luther hoped.

* * *

Albinia finished at the dress shop and locked up. It was late, near sunset, and summer humidity was beginning to creep into Lexington. She started toward the post office, to pick up the family mail from their box. She was distracted in thought, and almost walked out in front of a horse going down the street. She felt someone pull her arm back. Startled, she was about to grab a hatpin to stab the offender, when she recognized Joe.

"You should be careful, Albinia. Drivers can't always see well this time of day."

"Yes ... yes, thank you, Joe. I guess I was lost in thought, not watching as I should."

"What's so important? I was coming to ask you something, but it can wait."

"No, no. That's all right. What did you want to ask?"

"We've been going around together for a few months now. I ... I really want to formally ask to court you."

"Joe ... Joe, I can't."

"Why not? I mean, well, if you need more time, I can understand. But we have fun together."

Albinia felt strangely conflicted. She really did like Joe. It was flattering to have him ask. She strengthened her resolve.

"I know ... and I feel bad about refusing. But I simply can't. That business with Luther ... that hasn't been the only time, Joe. There have been others. I'm deeply involved. I can't ask you to...."

"If that's all it is, don't worry. I could help."

"There's more. I ... I'm committed to David."

Joe looked like she had struck him. "What? You mean all this time...?"

"I'm not proud of it. But yes. You are a dear sweet friend, and I do enjoy time with you. I ... I'm even attracted to you. But I love someone else. Don't you see? I could never settle into the safe, secure life with the Breckinridge family. I couldn't be the wife you want, that you deserve."

"So that's it then? You've just been using me?" he said angrily.

"Please, don't say that. It's not true, not really. Maybe in the beginning it was. As I've gotten to know you, I see what a fine decent man you are.

It's been a struggle for me, really. But it isn't fair to you to continue. My conscience has bothered me every time I've gotten a letter from David and responded. Please don't hate me. I've wanted to tell you the past few weeks. You asking about courting now, well, I just have to say what's in my heart. It won't do to hide it any longer. I hope we can be friends. Just not … courting."

"So you've been deceiving everyone? Your father? My parents? Maybe I was wrong … maybe you aren't the woman I thought you were. I guess I'm lucky to find out now." Joe turned and walked away, into the gloom of the evening.

Albinia went back into the shop, sat down, and wept.

* * *

The next morning, Albinia stopped at the post office. She'd spent a restless night praying, crying, and second-guessing herself, tossing and turning on the cot at the shop. She couldn't face Katy, or her mother, who would know something was wrong. She checked with the mail clerk—and there was a letter from David! Her heart soared, but she also wondered if anything was wrong. She hurried back to the shop, locked the front door, and sat down in the back to read.

March 19, 1860

Dearest Binia,

I apologize for not writing for so long—Mr. Garrison's schedule has been very demanding, and we have opposition at every turn. Twice we've almost been ambushed on the street. I don't wish to worry you, but please pray for our safety and for God to go before us with the message of freedom.

How I've missed you! I pray for your safety daily, and I wish
we could do a moonlit ride through the Boston Common, or out to
Concord, free of stress and danger.

I often think of you, and long for when we can be together.
I love your courage, your smile, and even your unpredictability. I
dream of a long happy future together. I will send for you as soon
as it is safe.

Love, David

* * *

They were gone. Just gone. Luther couldn't believe it. He came back to Ned's shop from getting supplies in Russellville and found the livery, the shop, the cabin deserted. No one seemed to be moving even on the streets of the village here. Where was everyone?

"Mama? Olivia? Anybody here?" called Luther, beginning to panic. And where was Ruth? And Ned? How could they all be gone? Luther quickly unhitched the horses and put them away. He began to run around the cabin and shop area, calling names. He climbed to the loft and called again.

"They gone."

He heard the flat tone in the voice. From under the hay, Sam rose up. "They all gone."

"What do you mean gone?"

"De slave catcher come. He surprised Ned, knock him out. He had de dogs, snarlin' and bitin'. He had guns, and chains, and whips. He and two other men, dey came and took 'em. Clara, she try to run."

"And where were you? Why didn't they take you?"

"I saw 'em hit Ned. Wasn't no use me fightin' three of dem wid guns. So I hid up here, real quiet. I don' know anymore. 'Cept I heard dem say dey come back for you."

"So you just hid? You just let them be taken? Ned, Katy, and Ruth, and the children? My family? Now who's a coward!" raged Luther.

"I tell you ain't no use! Dey woulda just got me, like Ned. Katy, she try to tell 'em we free. We not runaways. Dey jus laugh, hit her wid de butt of de whip."

"What about the rest of the village here?"

"Some, dey got. De rest, dey hide like me. We always hide when de slave catcher come. Free, runaway, don' make no difference. Some of dem slave catchers, dey kidnap free blacks, sell 'em into slavery just de same."

"How long ago?"

"I don' know. Dey come right about lunchtime. I gwine to wait for sunset, make sure dey gone. Stay hid till den. But I hear you, I figger dey must be gone, or dey have you squawkin' like a chased hen."

"Get up!" Luther grabbed Sam roughly. "Get up! We're going after them!"

"What! You crazy! You just get yo self caught. You best take one of de horses, ride for Canada, 'fore dey come back for you."

"I am not leaving my family in the hands of slave catchers. And not Ruth either. And you're going to help me or I swear I'll kill you." Luther grabbed a pitchfork in the loft, menacing Sam. "We're going to need help. Knock on doors, get as many men and guns as you can. These people owe Ned some favors. Time to collect. Tell 'em next time it could be them. We need to fight back, now! Before they've gone too far. Maybe they haven't crossed the river yet."

Sam stood, doubtfully, but seeing the pitchfork and Luther's determination, said, "All right. But dey gone." He backed away from Luther and scrambled down the ladder. Luther didn't know whether he would actually help or just run. He was determined to go after them, even risking capture or death.

He climbed down and began banging on doors, yelling for people to come out, that the slave catcher was gone. He looked everywhere, every possible hiding place he could think of. Soon he had a gathering of about ten men in front of the livery stable.

Luther stood on a hay bale and looked out at them. "Men, you been kind to me and my family. You know Ned Smith. You know how he has helped me. He's helped many of you as well. If you just stand by and see him sold into slavery, how can you call yourself men? Won't you just be saying the same as the white men, that we're just frightened children? I'm not gonna lie—I'm scared. Scared for myself, for what might happen. But I'm even more scared for my mama, for my sisters, for Ned, Ruth, and Katy. I'm goin' whether any of you come or not. Next time de slave catcher may come for you and your family. Who's with me?"

Several of the men looked doubtfully at each other, but a few stepped forward. Last of all, Sam moved to join them.

"All right. Now who has guns? We're gonna need 'em." Several hands raised.

"I got two shotguns, for squirrels," said one. "I got a rifle," said two others. "I got pistols," said another.

"Good, good. We ain't got much time. If dey make it across de river, we gonna have a lot more trouble. Meet back here in five minutes with guns, bullets, powder, and food. Jules, you take a horse from the livery, get word to John Parker."

The men all moved off. Suddenly the little village was bustling. One of the women took charge to lead the women and children into the woods, into better hiding, in case the slave catchers doubled back, thinking to catch them off guard. In half an hour, the men who volunteered were back. They started following the trail. It wasn't difficult, with all the people and dogs. The slave catchers did not attempt to hide their trail. They did not expect pursuit.

Fear and anger spurred Luther. About a hundred yards into the woods along the trail, the slave catchers had stopped. On the other side of the clearing, there was a trail of blood. There were marks showing someone being dragged. Cloth flapped in the breeze from a thorn bush. Luther looked at it—it was from Ruth's dress!

Now Luther trotted along. The trail was easy to follow. From the sign, it looked as though the slave catchers might be an hour ahead of them.

Moving so many was slower than the pace that Luther and the other men could manage in the light.

After about two miles, the blood trail seemed to stop. As he approached a clearing, Luther saw bright blue cloth at the edge. Another of the men pointed. Luther went over to it, heart pounding. Clara had worn a bright blue hair ribbon that morning. When he got closer, he screamed, "Noooo!" It was Clara's body, torn and mangled, ripped by the dogs. She was dead. Luther bent down and scooped up her lifeless form. Her sightless eyes stared at him, bite marks on her face, blood everywhere, her dress torn. Luther sat on a log, holding and rocking her, willing her to come back to life. "My baby, my sister, what dey done to you?" he moaned. Surely, any minute now she would wake.

Sam came over. He touched Luther's arm. "Luther. She's gone. If you don' want de others to be de same, we got to go. Now. I stay behind and bury her if you want, or cover her up wid rocks so we can bury her proper later. But we both know what dat slave catcher gonna do. You and de others, you got to go on. Luther?" he said shaking him gently.

Rising, Luther handed his sister's body to Sam. "Cover her good, den come. It gonna take all of us," he said grimly.

Sam gently took her. "I know we had some words. But I'll take care of her. Den I'll come. De others, dey need you to lead."

The men huddled in the clearing. Luther moved toward them. His voice shook with emotion, his slave dialect coming back in his strength of feeling.

"All right! You see? Dey killed my sister! My little eleben year old sister! Now if dey can do dat, dey ain't got no heart at all. Let's go!"

Without looking back, Luther plunged on along the trail.

* * *

Albinia read the telegram again, for the fiftieth time.

Albinia,

Miss you terribly. Cannot come. Needed here. Garrison attacked from all sides. Will you come? Answer soon. Will send bank draft. I love you. David

In twenty-five words, her world turned upside down. What should she do? She had broken with Joe. Her father was disappointed and confused at the breach. Her mother thought she must have lost her mind. They knew nothing of David. If she told them now, what would happen? If she eloped, how could she explain it? The crops were good this year, which was a blessing. Still, how would they manage without her income? What if this was all a mistake? She loved David, but she had compromised her values of honesty and integrity in so many ways since meeting him. If she refused him, their love would be at an end. She prayed. She thought. She wondered what he meant about Garrison being under attack from all sides. She went to Hobson's store and, under the disapproving eyes of the clerk, bought several newspapers. Some were local, some further away, including *The Liberator*. There were stories of riots and fiery speeches for and against slavery and secession. The presidential election was drawing closer, and the rhetoric became extreme. One article in the local paper caught her eye as she scanned, and she gasped. It was in the social pages, not normally a section she looked at much. It was an engagement announcement—between Joe Breckinridge and Jenny Morton. It pained her own heart, though she did not like to think on it. Moreover, she could not imagine what it would do to Will when he heard. She read the telegram again and made her decision. Leaving the shop, she locked up, and walked to the telegraph office. She sent a one-word answer.

* * *

It was near dark when Luther heard the screams. He wanted to charge into the camp, free the captives, and kill the slave catchers, but caution told him to wait. He must not fail. Sam had not caught up with them, and Luther wondered if he'd just gone back to the village. He felt a deep, soul-wrenching pain thinking of Clara. The screams centered his attention again, on what was ahead. He knew that voice. It could only be his mother. Warning the others to silence, he whispered that they should spread out, make a half circle around the camp. When he signaled with the call of a whippoorwill, everyone with a rifle was to fire on a white man target. The rest would charge the camp, to free as many as possible, and kill any opposition. Luther fingered his "good luck knife" that he had carried with him on the road to freedom; it was sharp enough to shave a beard.

Silently, the men did as he asked. He crept closer, to where he could see.

In the center, there was a main campfire. Ned and his family were in chains, along with Olivia. A downed tree held their chains fast. Jemima had an iron collar around her neck, attached to a chain thrown over a high branch. The chain suspended her in the air, her feet barely touching the ground. The chain could be raised and lowered to increase her pain, nearly hanging her if they chose. Above her head, a small fire burned in a pan, and over that, a grill sizzled with fat and meat. Whenever her torturer raised her from the ground, she choked, and burning grease and embers fell, scorching her naked body. Her hands were bound behind her in manacles. Luther saw a branding iron heating in the campfire, waiting.

"All right, you black wench! One more time. Who helped you escape? You are sure too stupid to have done it alone. Who helped?" snarled a fat bearded white man. A black felt hat covered his brow, and a pistol was stuck in his belt. He wore a light overcoat and baggy pants. He must be strong, for when Jemima did not answer, he jerked the chain and she rose in the air, off her toes, raining burning embers down on her bare skin.

She screamed again, "Lawd have mercy! Take me home! De Lawd, He help me escape, dat who! Don' burn me no mo'!" Her feet kicked wildly in the air, in pain.

"Maybe I'll just feed you to my dogs, like that little pickaninny of yours!" He let her feet touch the ground again. "Or maybe I'll let you go if you tell me. 'Course, I might get tired and switch to that other one," he said, gesturing at Olivia. "Jameson told me he don't much care about what condition she comes back in, gonna sell her south anyway, down to fever country. Might keep you for amusement, though. Or maybe sell you myself, to one of them black slave owners over in Carolina." The other white men laughed. "Now, let's try again. Where's your son Luther, and who helped you?"

The men were in position. Luther had seen enough. He made the sound of the whippoorwill several times. Shots rang out, but were mostly wild. The fat man jumped to the log where the other captives were, using them and the log as a shield. One of the slave catchers dropped, catching a shotgun blast full in the chest. Another looked toward his fallen companion as Luther rushed in, slicing the man's gun arm with his knife. He heard a pistol ball whistle near, and then the fat man called out. "I got my revolver on the head of a pretty girl here. If she means anything to you, drop your weapons. I can kill her and that woman hanging there before any of you get me." Luther had his arm raised to deliver a killing blow to the man underneath him. He hesitated, and the man fought back, knocking his hand against a rock, forcing him to drop the knife. "You have two seconds, and then she's dead."

A shot rang out from the forest, a scream of pain, and then a voice. "You'll be shootin' no one today, you slave catcher vermin!" John Parker, Sam, and five other men strode into the firelight, guns trained. "Drop your weapons, slave catchers, or we'll shoot the lot of ye. Stand up!"

Luther stood aside. The fat man stood, holding his shoulder wound. A dog tried to charge one of the men and was shot immediately. Sam came over, carrying a hammer. He handed it to Luther.

"I thought you might need dis," he said. Grabbing the hammer, he went to the fat man.

"Who are you? I want to know your name, you scum!"

"I'm George Alberti," the fat man said smugly.

"The key. Give me the key, before I bash your skull in," he said, his voice deadly with rage. He raised the hammer above Alberti's head, who quickly fished in a pocket and produced a key. Jemima's feet were on the ground, but the fire still burned above her. Luther put down the hammer and carefully unlocked her shackles, so as not to cause any embers to fall. Then he unlocked Ned and his family, and Olivia. Katy quickly moved to treat Jemima's burns and gather her discarded dress to cover her. John Parker used their shackles to chain Alberti and the other surviving slaver. Olivia and Ruth took turns embracing Luther. Lying on the ground, Jemima looked at him, her eyes shining in gratitude.

Alberti roared at them. "I'll see you all in court. You interfere with lawful recovery of property, chaining a white man. You'll all rot in jail!"

Luther snapped. He ran to the fire, picked out the waiting branding iron, and charged Alberti, yelling "You'll rot in hell, wid de debble!"

John Parker grabbed Luther just as he was about to brand Alberti's face.

"No, Luther. That's not the way. You want to hang or end up back in slavery? We can prosecute him for kidnapping free Negroes. His charges won't stand. But if you try to take revenge, you and your whole family will suffer."

Jemima spoke from her haze of pain. "You lissen, Mr. Parker, boy. Revenge is mine, I will repay, says de Lawd. Don' go tryin' to do His job."

Ned spoke, "Some things just cain't be forgiven."

Katy tried to calm him, but Ned shook her off. He picked up the discarded hammer, and his muscles rippled in the firelight. He advanced menacingly on Sam, who cowered.

"You! You de cause all dis. I saw you—two, three days ago—talkin' to a white man. You de one tol' dem dat Luther is here. You nearly get me an' my family sold down de river!" Ned raised the hammer as if to strike. Sam put his hands over his head.

"Please, Mr. Smith! I just want Luther out of de way. To court Ruth. I nebber thought the slave catcher hurt any free blacks. Please!"

Luther was stunned. Sam? He betrayed them?

John had loosened his grip on Luther but tightened it again, motioning to one of the other men, who restrained Ned's arm somewhat. The powerful blacksmith shook with fury.

"If I ever see you again, I'll kill you or give you to the slave catchers myself! Now—run! Before I change my mind and do something I'll regret."

Sam rose, and stumbled off, into the darkness.

* * *

The next day they held a brief service for Clara, burying her in the colored graveyard. Luther wept and cursed himself for the loss of Clara. How could he have been so stupid as to think anywhere, even in the North, was safe? Ned and family, as well as John Parker and the other rescuers, attended. Alberti and the other slaver were behind bars, for the moment, though Parker doubted they would stay there long. As the service concluded, Ruth came and took Luther aside.

"Say the word and I'll go with you," she said. "To Canada, or anywhere."

Another day, Luther would have jumped for joy. His grief and anger overshadowed him.

"I can't ask you that. Not now. I . . . I don't know what to think, how to feel. I have to see my ma and Olivia safe to Canada. Then I don't know where I'm going. I do know that I care for you. Very much. But there are things I have to do. I'm going to get Sam and my old master. I have to. Without them, none of this would have happened. Will you wait for me?" he asked pleadingly.

She looked deep into his eyes. "Luther, don't do this! I don't want to wait. When I see so much anger, it scares me. Whatever you feel you have to do, listen to your mother. Revenge won't help. If you feel you have to go, yes, I'll wait for you. If we move, as Papa says we might, I will leave word where with John Parker. Go with God, Luther." She reached up, encircled his neck with her arms, and kissed his cheek. She turned away, crying.

John packed Luther, Jemima, and Olivia back into the wagon, concealed under hay, the way they had come months before. They headed north, to Oberlin, a town distinctly unfriendly to slave catchers, a kind of sanctuary. Luther knew this was temporary. After talking with John Parker, they decided they would board a ferry steamer to Port Rowan, in Ontario, Canada, beyond the reach of the slave catchers. John said they might go on to Glen Morris. A woolen factory there often hired escaped slaves as lint pickers. It would mean starting over again. This time, though, they would truly be free.

THE STORM BREAKS

November 1860

The news electrified Lexington. Will was walking toward the livery to get the buggy when he heard it in the streets. Lincoln won! Lincoln was elected president. Will hurried to buy a newspaper from a passing newsboy. Will continued walking to the livery and sat down on a bench in front of it to read. Lincoln won only forty percent of the popular vote but won one hundred eighty electoral votes. Lincoln didn't carry a single Southern state. Kentucky's favorite son, John Breckinridge, came second, carrying most of the South, but not his own state. Astonishingly, after defeating Lincoln in the Illinois senate race, Stephen Douglas got only twelve electoral votes, carrying Missouri. There were cries of fraud, as Douglas got almost thirty percent of the popular vote. John Bell, of the new Constitutional Union party, split from the Democrats, carried Tennessee, Kentucky, and Virginia.

It was Wednesday, November 7, 1860. Will knew that the vote yesterday was tense. Breckinridge was so much for slavery that he alienated Kentucky's neutral and Union voters. Ultimately, Bell's neutral stance, though he himself was a slave owner, attracted Kentucky slave owners and those like Governor Magoffin, who held neutrality was the best course. Lincoln was not even on the ballot in the Southern states.

Sitting on a bench in front of the livery, Will scratched his head. He wondered what would happen now. Was there really going to be a war?

Already, states were talking about secession. Lincoln's statements were conciliatory, claiming no need for secession or war. He simply wanted to contain slavery to where it already existed, he said. The Southern press proclaimed him an embarrassment and a racist. There was a cartoon showing Lincoln dancing with a black woman, talk of forced marriage between black and white.

Will shook his head. He still didn't understand all the fuss. He folded the newspaper, hitched the horse to the buggy, and continued to think while driving. Lincoln didn't seem to want to change things that much, so why get excited? Why did Jenny think the slavery issue so important? He'd seen the announcement of her engagement to Joe. His heart ached, his mind felt confused. How could she, when so short a time ago she said she cared for him? His father was right: young girls are fickle, he supposed. At least it confirmed his mind—he would throw himself into the Rifles and do the best he could for Captain Morgan. Others in the Rifles, like his friend Archie, were excited about 'whippin' the Yanks."

* * *

December 1860

Albinia looked out the train window. She had taken time to wrap up her affairs, yet not given anyone warning of her elopement. She told her employer she was leaving for a long holiday with relatives. At the next station, she got off temporarily to mail a letter and use the necessary. The letter would inform Will and her parents that she was marrying David in Baltimore. Her heart was torn between not wanting to hurt her parents, and joy to see David again. She knew Will would never understand—he didn't see slavery as she did, and he'd chosen Morgan over his love. The miles went by quickly. In three days she alighted the platform at Baltimore's railway station, to find David waiting for her. It would soon be Christmas, but not like any she had ever known.

"David! David, I'm here!"

"I'm so glad, my love. Finally, I can share with you my life and my heart. I've been so worried, with all the troubles. Lincoln's election set off a powder keg. Did you hear? South Carolina seceded today! Oh, dear Albinia! I wish we had peace to enjoy our first days together. I wish I could give you a church wedding with friends and family. But I'm afraid we must be quickly married before a judge. Do you mind much?"

Albinia bit back her protest. She realized this is how it must be. They chose to elope. They could not expect all the conventional wedding trappings.

"No, David, I don't mind. As long as I can be with you!"

"Good! I'm sure you're tired. We'll stay tonight at the Barnum Hotel. You can rest and freshen up. Tomorrow we can buy you a new dress. Then we'll see the judge. I've a few days off, but we must be in Boston by the New Year. Georgia has announced a five thousand dollar reward for anyone who will kidnap Mr. Garrison and bring him there to stand trial. I cannot leave him for long. But oh how I've missed you!"

And right there, in the train station, he took her in his arms and kissed her. Albinia melted into his arms.

The next day they went on a mad round of shopping in downtown Baltimore, and found Albinia a dress that she liked. She actually would have liked to make her own, but there was no time. They appeared at the county courthouse before a magistrate. They filled out the necessary paperwork. Standing together with two witnesses from the court, they exchanged vows and were married.

Leaving the courthouse, David stopped, took both her hands, and said, "I have a surprise for you, my love. We only have a few days, but I have a friend, Horatio Ridout, who has offered us free use of his mansion and grounds, and Christmas with his family. It's Whitehall in Annapolis, on the bay. Of course, if you'd rather, we could just go straight to a hotel in Boston. What do you say?"

"How generous of your friend to offer. Yes, let's go there! It would be so much better to spend Christmas with a family than in a hotel. I enjoyed last night at the Barnum, but … I'll miss my family terribly, and watching Lydia open her stocking. It will be good, being around children.

"Good! It's settled then. I'll just send a telegram and we can be there by late tonight. We can walk in the snow, stroll on the beach, and...."

"Yes!" said Albinia, squeezing his hand and blushing.

* * *

Albinia and David arrived at the stately brick mansion. Albinia could barely imagine any place so grand, with the tall white Corinthian columns. A servant showed them to their rooms—everything was decked out for Christmas

As they entered their suite, Albinia saw that someone had put flowers everywhere, and a small table with two chairs was at the side of the room, complete with champagne and dinner. She was tired from traveling, from the disappointment of the civil ceremony, but now she wanted to make this first night as perfect as possible.

They talked, laughed, and finished the dinner slowly. Albinia was unused to champagne and only sipped a little of it. She felt awkward changing in front of David, but put on clothes more suitable and warm for walking. As the sun set, they walked hand in hand down to the beach.

"I wish we could stay forever," said Albinia. "Not the grandeur of the house, but just having time, when no one wants anything of us, just to be together. We've always been so busy helping slaves escape, working ... now for the first time, we have time alone."

"I wish it too ... but duty will call, and we must be in Boston soon. I ... I want you to meet my parents. I'm afraid I have another surprise for you ... hopefully not unpleasant. My father owns an iron works, making armaments for the military. I wanted you to love me for myself. I should have told you, now that I know you as well as I do, since I know you care little for money. However, we have a lot of it, and you'll never need to worry about being comfortable—you can use your needle for good purposes, but you needn't try to help support us. Does it matter very much?"

Albinia took this in a little nonplussed. Why hadn't he told her? It wasn't that she minded his being rich, just ... she supposed he meant what he said, that he wanted to be sure of her love not for his money but for himself. Still, he could have trusted her. She saw his hopeful look and decided it didn't matter.

"No, David, of course not—in fact, we can use it to advantage, to help the slaves. Tonight, though, let the rest of the world go on without us— let's concentrate on each other. After all, I've never had a husband before," she said shyly. "I do want to learn about you. I want to know everything."

He turned to her, took her hands, and slowly drew her into a kiss, his fingers unpinning her hair, and his arm circling her waist. The sensations made her excited, afraid, confused, and longing all at once.

* * *

Julia paced back and forth. Earlier that morning, Hiram's father had a stroke. The doctors were with him now. Hiram was in Pittsburgh, overseeing the purchase and launch of a new steamboat. Kirsten sat in a corner of the hospital waiting room, knitting.

"I wish you would sit down, child," said Kirsten peevishly. "You make me tired just watching you pace."

"I don't see how you can sit there and knit! Your husband could be dying in there!"

"Well, if he is, fretting won't stop it. Sit down! You'll wear a hole in the carpet."

Julia sat in the rather uncomfortable chair.

The doctor emerged, coming over to Kirsten.

"Well?" she demanded imperiously.

"I'm afraid … I'm sorry to inform you. Your husband has passed away. We tried to revive him, but it's simply no use. My sympathies, Mrs. Johannsen."

Kirsten folded her knitting into her bag and stood. "Well, that's it then. I'm officially a widow. I'm sure you'll see to all the necessary arrangements."

"Yes, madam. Do you want to see him?"

"No, no, I've seen quite enough death in my time to know what it looks like. Come, Julia, we may as well go home."

Julia could hardly believe her coldhearted attitude. "But we must tell Hiram! He'll be worried."

"All right, we can stop at the telegraph office on the way home."

"Mrs. Johannsen, didn't you love your husband? Doesn't his death mean anything to you?"

"Actually, my dear, I've been expecting it for years. He never did take care of himself. Love? I suppose, after a fashion. He was always kind to me, and a good provider. Ours was an arranged marriage, an agreement between our fathers. No one consulted me. I'm sorry to see anyone suffer. But if you expect me to be a grief-stricken widow, you'll be disappointed."

"But what will happen?"

"You mean to us? The business? Well, I suppose that all depends on what is in my late husband's will. We'll find out soon enough. Fortunately, due to the recent legal changes, women are able to manage their husband's business if he is away, falls ill, or dies. So I rather expect I will now run the company."

"I see," said Julia worriedly. If Kirsten were in charge, what would happen to her? She might be no better than a pauper. In her months in Cincinnati, relations between her and Kirsten had not improved. They stopped at the telegraph office, and Julia sent a short message to Hiram.

January 31, 1861

Hiram, Please come home soon. I'm sorry dearest. Your father had an apoplexy, and died.

Love, Julia

She would not rest until he returned.

* * *

February 1861, Canada

Luther was bone weary and freezing. He stretched, and shook Jemima and Olivia to waken them. The fire in the stove in their small flat had gone out. The February chill reached in from outside with bony fingers to strangle out the warmth. The sun got out of bed later than they did. They must be at the mill soon. Luther worried a little how his mother and Olivia would survive if he left, but they were safe now from slave catchers, here in Ontario. He must go back. He thought grimly of Sam, Jameson, and other scores to settle. He found one coal still alive in the stove and coaxed it to life with their meager supply of wood and coal.

"Nevah got dis cold in Kentucky, even when ol' Jameson didn' give us wood, or let us chop it," said Jemima, limping to the stove.

Olivia threw on her extra petticoats and woolen stockings, products of their hard work here at the German woolen mill.

"But we ain't got to worry 'bout Jameson no more," exulted Olivia. "I don' mind shivering some. I don' mind hard work. Here, what we get, we keep. We can feed ourselves."

Jemima coughed heavily. Luther came over to her.

"You all right, Mama? You ain't nevah seemed de same, since…."

"As all right as I'll ever be widout li'l Clara. Freedom has a mighty high price."

Luther paused and put an arm around her shoulders. "I know, Mama. And you paid, too. But not forever. Someone gonna make *them* pay!"

"Now you hush about that. Ain't nuthin we can do, or should do. De Lawd gonna take care of them. It ain't bad here. Mr. German, he say he give us a raise soon, 'cause we hard workers."

Luther replied angrily, "No, Mama! Sometimes, you got to help the Lord. We been learnin' a lot in school. Dat Ben Franklin, he say God helps them that help themselves. Well, I'm gonna help God and the Yankees. I'm goin' back. Already they got six states seceded, dropped out of the United States. Pretty soon, gonna be more, maybe even Kentucky. An dat

Lincoln, he gonna help the slaves get free—that's what everyone says. I'm gonna show them I can fire a gun just as good as any white man."

Olivia tugged on his arm, but he shook himself free. "Luther, you can't leave us. What if you get killed, like Clara? We're all alone here."

Luther smiled, but it wasn't a kind smile. "No white man gonna kill me. You all stay here. You got jobs. You got a better place to live than a slave cabin. I'm gonna find the ones that hurt Clara. I'll find Jameson too, and make dem pay."

Jemima spoke sharply, "You leave Jameson alone. Don't go huntin' that rattlesnake!" She grabbed him and made him look at her. "Besides— you can't hurt him. Don't you know yet, Son? He's your pa. You don't want his blood on your hands. Nuthin' he done to me be worth it."

* * *

Hiram and Julia stood before his father's grave. He had recently returned from Pittsburgh. The reading of the will occurred the day before.

"What will you do now?" asked Julia.

"I will do what I must. Mama is furious that Papa did not leave the control of the company to her but me instead. I will stay long enough to assure everything runs smoothly. But I will honor my pledge to the militia and fight for this country."

"But how will the company survive?"

Hiram smiled bleakly. "I don't know."

Julia said, "What if you change the registry of the ships? Make them Swedish. I've been reading the newspapers and listening to your managers. I don't think either side would attack a Swedish vessel."

Hiram brightened. "That is a brilliant idea. Maybe…."

"What?"

Hiram took her in his arms and lifted her off her feet, smiling. "Maybe Papa was very smart. Maybe he knew—you could run the company for me while I'm gone."

"Me? But I don't know anything about it."

"You just gave me better advice than all the clerks and accountants. I will teach you. In a few months when I leave, you will know how to keep things running."

"But what if something happens to you? And what about your mother?"

"She will be angry, of course. But she would be anyway. Try to be kind to her. And she knows many people, both here and in Sweden, that can help. Don't despise her counsel—but don't let her take over."

He set her down. Julia looked up at him. "Do you really think it is wise? Do you think I can do it?"

Hiram kissed her and then said, "Yes. Ohio Zephyr Steamship will be in good hands. It will ease my mind to know that you are looking after things. My boat captains will help you. Mama is wonderful, but she is spoiled. Papa never told her anything was too expensive, too outlandish. You come from a poor background. You know how it is to save, to scrimp. And you would grow bored just going to parties and gossiping."

"Oh, Hiram! I will surely try my best. I wish you didn't have to go. But we'll have time yet, won't we? And we can write." She hesitated, then spoke. "Hiram? If I'm to be in charge, I want to make one change immediately. We no longer transport slaves to market. For anyone."

He smiled and saw her earnestness. "All right. If it's important to you. Consider it done."

* * *

Spring was beginning to show. Tree buds and birds ventured out. Luther was still cold at night. He'd been walking for over a week, heading southwest. After crossing the border back into the United States, he only moved at night. He asked directions and questions each morning, and then walked south as the moon rose. He discovered from some farmers that there was an army camp under construction near Cincinnati. He thought of going to find Ruth, but finding her and then leaving again would be too hard on both of them. Instead, he penned a short letter and mailed it. He didn't know if the slave catchers were still looking for him, but he took no chances. He posted the letter at the end of the day, and then moved quickly so that he was thirty miles away by sunrise, even though he was moving through Ohio. He carried his knife from his old running days. He also carried a Navy six-shot revolver in a holster, with a full belt of ammunition. He did not intend to be captured, by anyone. Buying some food from a farmer on the outskirts of Findlay, he was told that a barber in town, David Adams, might provide him a haircut and a safe place to sleep. If he chose, he might even be able to earn some money shoeing a few horses.

Luther walked into town about twilight and saw a closed sign on Adams barbershop. The storefront had a window with a light in the second story, so he walked to the rear of the building, climbed the stairs, and knocked.

The door opened a crack, and a dark-faced woman looked through. "Who dere, and what you want?"

"I'm Luther. I come south from Canada, or north from Kentucky, take your pick. I'm looking for David Adams and a place to sleep."

The door opened wider. The woman stepped back, and a black man with a huge smile motioned him inside.

"I'm David Adams. We don't get too many like you comin' south! Come in and set a spell, tell us what you need."

* * *

Will walked up the long steps to the Morrison building, ready for class. He stopped and read a large sign.

April 13, 1861

Due to the commencement of hostilities, the university is closed.

He was amazed. What did it mean? Someone went racing by, yelling, "It's war! Finally time to whip the Yankees!"

"What's going on?"

"Didn't you hear? Beauregard fired cannons on Ft. Sumter in Carolina. The war has started."

Why would the university close because of something in Carolina? Kentucky was neutral, wasn't it? Bewildered, Will took his books back to the livery, got the buggy and his rifle, and drove to Morgan's house. He knocked at the door. Sid, Morgan's slave, answered the door.

"Yes, sir? May I help you?"

"I need to see Captain Morgan. Something terrible has happened."

Sid kept his eyes down and looked serious. "Sir, if you mean the war, Captain Morgan is aware. He is otherwise engaged, at present. His wife is extremely ill. I'm afraid he is not receiving visitors now."

"But you don't understand. I must...."

"Good day, sir. You may leave a card for Captain Morgan and he will return your call at his earliest convenience."

The door closed. Will slumped in dismay and confusion. What was he to do now? The university closed, the war begun. His studies were apparently at an end, and his dreams were crumbling. In a few short months, his life seemed turned upside down. Jenny was with Joe. Pa barely talked to him. Morgan was withdrawn, not giving much attention to the Rifles. Albinia and Julia were gone. South Carolina, Mississippi, Florida, Alabama, Louisiana, and Texas all seceded, forming the Confederate States of America. Will got into the buggy and drove slowly back to the farm. The farm was always there. He prayed as he drove, looking for answers.

* * *

April 1861, Baltimore

Albinia and David had a brief but sweet honeymoon in the previous months, and then they traveled north to Boston. They began following Garrison wherever he spoke. David saw to his security. To her surprise, Garrison occasionally asked Albinia to speak, as a Southern woman who had witnessed the evil of slavery. Uncomfortable at first, she grew increasingly satisfied with speaking to crowds in churches and at rallies. There were always those in the audience who were sarcastic, and even hinted that she was out of place. They would tell her that a woman should be at home. At these times, David would come from the audience to her side and speak to silence the critics. Together they told the stories of escaping slaves, and moved the hearts of the audience both to sympathy and to outrage at the inhumanity of the South's 'peculiar institution,' as Jefferson Davis called it.

In April, they found themselves traveling again to Baltimore. There was an abolitionist rally where Garrison was to speak. It was rumored that Frederick Douglass might appear as well, though Douglass and Garrison had split over some issues a few months past. David wanted to be in Baltimore in advance of the rally, since it was not a city friendly to their cause. Many were agitating for Maryland to secede and join the Confederacy.

David was relaxing in the dining car on the train, reading the newspaper. Albinia sat opposite him.

"Do you really expect trouble?" she asked.

"According to all I hear, yes. We must be clear. Maryland must not secede. With the battle at Sumter, and Virginia seceding yesterday, things are looking desperate. Lincoln has called for seventy-five thousand volunteers for the army to end the conflict. Militia from Massachusetts will be marching through Baltimore during the rally, and many in Maryland are not happy about that. We must be ready for anything. In fact, I wonder if it is really wise for you to speak at the church in the current climate."

She smiled. "Don't worry. Haven't we been through enough danger together for you to know that God takes care of me and I can handle myself?"

He put down the newspaper, reached over, and patted her hand. "Yes, I suppose we have, at that. But I still worry for you. This time I can't be there with you, since Garrison's rally is at the same time. I'll detail a carriage to wait for you, and a man from our group to drive as well as protect. Did you know that Baltimore has more free blacks than any other major city? Yet it is very divided, and there are plenty who would like to see trouble. Frederick Douglass comes from Baltimore area, you know. You've met him; you know how he is. He ruffles feathers. He doesn't fit people's idea of what a former slave should be like."

"Yes, I know. I often think that Luther could have been like him, given a chance. I wonder where Luther is now."

"Probably safe in Canada, like many others we've helped. However, this war troubles me. I wish the slavery problem could have been resolved without it, without splitting the country."

"It could have been, if people were willing to give up their comforts, turn to God, and treat others as they would like to be treated themselves. If we each help someone who needs it, then before long we're all doing better. What people mean when they say the slaves can't go free is that they personally are not willing to lend a hand and acknowledge black people equal to themselves. I've been shocked at the number in the North that think blacks inferior. It comes down to greed and pride."

"I fear you are right. The cost is likely to be tremendous, in blood and misery. Everyone seems to think the war will be short. Never believe any war will be smooth and easy, or that anyone who embarks on that strange voyage can measure the tides and hurricanes he will encounter. The statesman who yields to war fever must realize that once the signal is given, he is no longer the master of policy but the slave of unforeseeable and uncontrollable events. It is likely that we will lose friends and family on both sides."

Sadness seized Albinia. "I think of Will and my father. And Joe. It seems unreal to think of them fighting. Julia tells me Hiram is going to fight too. It's as if everyone has suddenly lost their minds."

The train soon pulled into Camden Station in Baltimore. David and Albinia collected their luggage, and found a carriage that David had hired. They went to a nearby hotel, dined, and David hurried off to arrange things for the following day. When he returned, it was nearing dark. Albinia was looking out the window as the lamplighter was going down the street, lighting the gas lamps. David let himself into their room and found Albinia seated at a small table, writing. As soon as he closed the door, Albinia was up and in his arms. The oil lamps were low, and the dark four-poster bed, rose petal wallpaper, and thick carpet created a sensually romantic atmosphere. She kissed him, at first shyly, even after these months together, then with growing passion.

As the morning light came through the window, Albinia stretched and yawned. The night had been glorious, but sleep was lacking. David was still peacefully snoring. Just like a man. She rose and put on a dressing gown. She attended to her hair, which had gone in all directions, with the help of the hotel mirror. Once that was done, she dressed carefully for the day and checked her derringer to make sure it was loaded. David seemed to think there might be trouble. It was likely unnecessary worry, but she had leaned after all her Underground Railroad experiences that the unexpected does happen.

David stirred, and she went over and kissed him playfully. He sleepily started to pull her into bed with him, but she resisted, saying, "No time for that. You need to wake up. We have work to do."

"Hmm. You *would* remind me." He got up. She left the room. He shaved and dressed, and just as he finished, she returned with coffee and breakfast on a tray. They read their Bible passage together while eating, their usual morning routine, and spent time in prayer. Then David looked at his watch.

"I'm lazy this morning. I'm due at the police station in fifteen minutes, to go over security." He rose and kissed her quickly. "Good bye, my love," he said. "Promise me you'll be careful."

"I will. I'll come to your rally as soon as I'm through speaking."

David hurried out the door. Albinia felt a sudden touch of dread, as though he might never return.

* * *

Albinia finished her speech to mild applause. She left the lectern in the church and found the man David appointed to wait for her. It was approaching noon. The church was near the President Street train station, and as she got into the waiting carriage, she was astonished to see thousands of people in the streets. She wondered what was going on. There were dozens of policemen about the station, as though expecting trouble. Perhaps this accounted for the small attendance at her speech, though she thought it more likely that it was due to no one having any idea who she was. The ladies group had listened politely and made some gestures of concern, but when she asked for volunteers, no one came forward. As she looked out the carriage window, the chaos in the street was becoming louder. Her driver was having difficulty keeping the horse moving and under control. They turned the corner onto Pratt Street, and the situation deteriorated. She shouted to the driver, but he could not hear her above the din. Then she heard someone shout, "There they are! The invaders! The Blue Bellies!" Someone threw a brick or a paving stone. Albinia remembered what David said about Massachusetts militia coming through. More shouting and curses, and the people around her carriage became a mob, intent on stopping the soldiers and wounding each other. Shop windows smashed. Fights broke out. Her driver urged the horse forward, trying to escape, to get to a side street. The air became dense with smoke. She could almost feel the hate, the anger, and the fear of the crowd. Albinia ducked as a brick came through the window of the carriage. She got on the floor and fingered her derringer, in case someone should open the carriage door, and prayed. Then shots rang out, and suddenly the carriage plunged ahead, as people scattered to avoid the gunfire. The horse, terrified, broke into a gallop, and the carriage careened crazily over bumps. Albinia wondered if they hit anyone. When they finally stopped, the driver scrambled down and opened her door.

"Get inside, ma'am. Get inside quick. No tellin' what those crazy folks will do!"

They were in front of her hotel. Down the street in the direction they had come from, the gunshots and fighting continued. There was an ambulance wagon, and people being carried on stretchers to it. Terror pierced her heart—was that David? She started to run.

"Ma'am, you can't go that way! Ma'am!"

She ignored the driver, and fear gave her strength. She pushed and shoved people aside. She stepped in mud and horse manure. Her dress was ruined. She didn't care. A heel broke off her shoe as she ran until she caught up with two orderlies carrying a familiar figure on a stretcher. It was David. His chest was bleeding, and his head had an ugly open wound, with part of the skull visible. He'd been beaten terribly. She told them to stop, to let her talk to him.

Her brain and her heart refused to process it. David! He couldn't be … she wouldn't let him....

The orderly looked at her sympathetically but said, "Ma'am, we have to move along. Others need our help. We're going to the morgue. He's dead."

* * *

June 1861, Camp Denison, Ohio

Luther rested, leaning on his shovel for a moment. He was sweating with exertion, and frustrated by his circumstances. After making enough money in Findlay to move forward, he came to Dennison, Ohio, where a new military and training camp was under construction. He found that the Union army would not take him as a soldier, despite the antislavery and equality talk of the North. Instead, he did manual labor digging latrines, breastworks, ditches. The soldiers were not there yet. The muster was set for eight weeks away. It was the Third Ohio cavalry. As he resumed work with his shovel, he looked over at the officer's tent and nearly dropped the shovel in anger and surprise. Talking to the officer who had sworn him in was none other than his old enemy Sam. It was all Luther could manage not to run over and use the shovel on his head. All the rage he held in after the slave catcher's torture of his mother threatened to break loose. In the back of his mind, he heard his mother's voice cautioning him, and instead, he dug harder and faster, channeling the fury into his work. He would wait. His time would come.

* * *

July 1861, Lexington

Will marched with new determination in the hot July sun. The Rifles were back in order and drilling in earnest, now that the war had begun. Basil Duke had returned to Lexington. Will attended the wedding between Basil and Henrietta in June. Captain Morgan's wife was dying and he still spent most of his time with her, delegating the Rifles to his new brother-in-law. Duke showed Will how to train his horse using Nolan's system. He told Will, "Of all bad tempers in horses, that which is occasioned by harsh treatment and ignorant riders is the worst." Will, with guidance, taught the Percheron to respond to legs and seat, and to stand firm when guns fired or flags waved.

Dismounting, Will saw Archie Moody approach. They had gotten to be better friends, spending more time together, now that Will and Joe barely spoke to each other.

"Hey, Archie! Good drill today. Thought I was going to drop in the heat!"

" Yes, it's good to be working again. Though we won't need much practice to beat them Yanks. One Rifle's worth ten of 'em. You're lookin' pretty good on that horse."

"Yeah, too bad I won't get to keep him. My pa would never allow it."

"Nice of your Yank brother-in-law to help us out, though," said Archie, grinning.

"It is at that. How 'bout your family? Any Yanks?"

"Oh, my ma has relations up North, but all my family here is Southern through and through. You should meet my sisters. They like men in uniform."

Will laughed. "No, sir. I'm staying clear of women. I've had enough of that for a while. Just fuddles up the brain."

"But worth thinkin' on and fightin' for. Sure hope Kentucky joins the CSA. Then them Yanks will think twice about botherin' our land."

"True. I just wish Captain Morgan…."

"Yes, I know. But only God can save his wife now. Mr. Duke, though, he's a good 'un. He and West will see us through. You know, Duke organized the Minute Men militia. Branch of the ones that gave those Massachusetts Yankees what for in Baltimore."

Will was stunned. "No, I didn't know. I mean, I knew he'd organized a militia in Missouri, but...." He thought about Albinia and wondered if she knew that Duke was partially responsible for David's death. He was to pick her up at the train station today, returning from the North.

"Yes, sir, those Yanks got more than they bargained for. Thought they could waltz right through Maryland, and no one the wiser. The Minute Men showed 'em! More fightin' in Virginia and Missouri. Some say the reason we lost in Missouri was Duke wasn't there. Well, see you tomorrow! I gotta get home and feed the livestock. My pa's feelin' poorly."

"Sorry about your pa. See you tomorrow." He watched Archie walk away in the direction of Broadway. Will unsaddled the horse and harnessed him to the buggy, giving him a nosebag of grain. After the animal had a long drink, Will drove him to the train station. They waited, flies buzzing, with the din of the station around them, until Will saw Albinia at the top of the platform, eyes searching everywhere for him.

* * *

Albinia was exhausted. In the two months since David's death, there had been little time to grieve. On the train trip back to Lexington, she finally had time to think, cry, and pray. After eloping, what would her family think of her? Would they be angry? She especially worried about her father.

"Binia! Over here!" Will waved and shouted. When he reached her, she gave him a big hug.

"Will! It's good to see you. I ... I'm sorry about everything." She smiled at him at first, then noticed the uniform and pulled away. "Still drilling with the Rifles, I see."

"Yes, I am. But I'm glad to see you home. I'm sorry about David. I didn't know him, but...."

"It's all right, you couldn't have known. We kept it secret from everyone. Now I wonder if we did the right thing. But he died defending what he believed: that slavery is wrong, that secession is wrong."

Will loaded her trunk. She accepted his help into the buggy. They rode in silence. A tear escaped Albinia's eyes and she turned quickly away, wiping her face with a handkerchief. When they arrived at the Crump's farm, Will helped her down, unloaded her trunk. He put the Springfield behind the door and disappeared to the back. He came out in farm clothes.

As soon as Albinia was down, Lydia ran from the house and jumped into her sister's arms. Albinia's heart melted at her sister's girlish enthusiasm for having her home. Soon Sara joined them. The women were laughing and crying at the same time. Will left, saying he would get Pa. When they returned, Robert gathered Albinia in his arms, like she was Lydia's age. They looked at one another for a long moment. She wondered if he would forgive her.

"Pa, I'm so sorry. I know I must have caused you great pain, but...."

"Shush, don't worry about that now. You are my precious daughter, and you are always welcome here. I know you were doing what you thought was right. I respect that."

Once the family was in the cabin and Sara served a noon meal, Albinia spoke again. "I need to tell you all I know. I'm tired of secrets. David and I worked together for months before I left helping slaves escape. Freedom for slaves and abolition of slavery was his life's work, and he was devoted to Mr. Garrison."

Her father bristled. "He sure put you in harm's way."

Albinia glared at him. "That's not true. I would have done it whether David helped or not. In fact, I mean to continue doing it. I discovered that David had quite a sum of money. With that, and his contacts in the abolition movement in Boston, I've purchased my own farm. In Trumble County, on the river. Liberty Road, near Milton. I'm going to start a school there for free blacks and help as many slaves as I can to freedom. So I won't be here long. I'm trusting you as my family to keep silent about what I'm doing. War has started. I cannot fight with guns, so I will fight with help and ideas."

Robert stood and paced. "You can't mean it, Binia. Why, you're just a girl! How would you ever manage a farm on your own?"

"I'm a widow. I'm not just your daughter anymore. I'm old enough to inherit, and I know this is what David would have wanted. Mr. Garrison gave me his blessing and helped me arrange the purchase. I hope to have your blessing as well, but I'm doing it whether I get it or not. I did want to see you all before I begin. I will probably go see Julia as well. After that, I cannot be sure of anything."

"We thought you'd be staying. Actually, Julia will visit here soon. But you'll be risking jail and ruin."

"I am quite aware. Jesus said, 'What does it profit a man to gain the whole world, if he loses his soul?' And also, 'But if anyone has the world's goods and sees his brother in need, yet closes his heart against him, how does God's love abide in him?' Aren't you risking everything, being in the Home Guard, now that the war has started?"

"But the state is still officially neutral, and so is the Guard. And I'm a man, the head of this family. I have responsibility. "

"We all have responsibility before God. Isn't that what you taught me?"

Robert threw up his hands, exasperated.

Albinia softened. "Let's don't spoil the visit with arguments. I came because I love you all, and I hoped you'd forgive me for the way I left."

"We do," said Sara, with a glance at Robert. "And we're ever so glad you came. Especially Lydia here. She's been hopping on one foot ever since we got your letter."

Lydia rushed to Albinia from the corner. "See my new dolly? Will got it for me. She has a face and everything."

Everyone laughed, breaking the tension.

Albinia looked down at the wharf in Cincinnati, scanning the crowd for Julia. At last she spotted her. She gave a coin to one of the stewards, having him take her luggage to her hotel as soon as the gangway was lowered. She rushed down to her sister. A few stared at her quick movements and her black dress.

"Julia! I'm so glad to see you."

"I'm so sorry about your husband ... I didn't know...."

"No one did. We wanted it that way. But the time for secrets is past. I'd love to just relax but I really don't have a lot of time, just a day or two. I'm starved—shall we get dinner at the hotel or your house?"

"Let's go to the hotel, but have them set up an area just for us. I want to catch up without Mama Kirsten interfering."

Albinia followed Julia to a waiting carriage. Julia gave the driver an address, and they laughed about helping each other into their seats for the short ride.

The hotel was a grand affair, with a crystal chandelier in the main lobby and a dining room off to the right, with musicians playing chamber music even in the late afternoon.

"Who would have thought we'd be in a place like this, after the way we grew up?" marveled Albinia. "How has it been adjusting to your new life?"

"Good and bad. The good is mostly Hiram. He's sweet and attentive, whenever he's here. The bad is how much he's gone, and the war. He'll be off in the army soon. Would you believe it? I am to run the company in his absence."

"That's amazing! But I know you'll do well—just put some of that natural bossiness to work!" Albinia teased, then grew serious. "Now that the war is started ... how do you and Hiram feel about slavery?"

"We both feel it is wrong, despicable. He used to see it as just business, but I've managed to influence him. We no longer take slave shipments on our boats."

"You know by now I've been working to free slaves, to help them escape."

"Yes. I confess it amazed me—my little sister. I never would have thought it of you. I know you have strong convictions, and you can be stubborn. But to take such risks...."

Albinia hesitated. Maybe it wasn't fair of her to ask Julia for help. The risks *were* great. Then she saw some of the faces of slaves she'd helped in her mind, both joyful and terror stricken. She had to ask.

"I know it's a big risk. I've dealt with patrols in the middle of the night. I know the penalties. But Julia ... if you could see the faces of the slaves when they reach freedom, when they really know that they're free. Knowing that no one will sell them, or their children, that no one will torture, starve, or whip them, ever again.... What I want to ask is: will you help me?"

"Help you? How could I possibly?"

"By hiding slaves on steamboats, when needed, and letting them off in Ohio and Indiana. I've bought a farm on the river, on the Kentucky side. It has a steamboat landing, a dock. If your boats stopped at times to pick up cargo, they could transport my slave 'packages' as well." Albinia tensely watched her sister's face, the furrowed brow. So much could depend on this decision.

"I'll have to consult Hiram. But yes, I think we can help. It will be risky, but I suppose if even one soul makes it to freedom, it is worth the risk."

Albinia was ecstatic. She almost knocked a glass of water out of the incoming waiter's hand as she stood and rushed around the table to hug her sister. She didn't care who saw. When the waiter withdrew, she sat down again.

"Thank you! Thank you, Julia. You have no idea how much this will mean to so many."

* * *

July 1861, Lexington

The news spread rapidly among the Rifles. Morgan's wife died. Will went to pay his respects, then to the funeral. As it ended, he walked over to Morgan and Duke.

"I just wanted to say, sir, how very sorry I am. I...I've never lost anyone like that, except my brother. But I know she must have been a wonderful woman. Please accept my prayers and sympathy. You've been ever so kind to me."

"Thank you, Will. It means a lot. I haven't given much time to the Rifles of late, and I never got back to you after you called. I'm sure you understand. It's been difficult for me. But now with God's help and my brother-in-law Duke here, we will fight for what is ours. I'm glad to have you with us."

"Thank you, sir!"

Morgan's approval made Will's heart soar, and he determined to be the best soldier he could manage.

* * *

August 1861

Will worked on harvest. He and his father worked out a system where Will did the morning chores and harvested corn in the north fields, while his father did evening chores and harvested in the south and west of the farm. They worked together only when one of them could not accomplish a task on his own.

Julia was due in town today, and Will planned to meet her at the depot. Albinia was gone to her farm on the river. Will thought she must be crazy to buy a farm after planting season. He knew she planned to hire workers, using her inheritance, but he wondered how long it would last. And what if her true purpose were discovered?

Commotion and excitement surrounded Will as he drove into town. Newsboys were running to and fro. "Federals invade Kentucky!" yelled one of them. Will tied the horse to a rail at the depot and bought a paper. He sat down to read, waiting for Julia. She came often now, acting for Hiram, who had joined the Third Ohio Cavalry at Camp Dennison. Julia hinted to Will that her company's steamboats sometimes landed at Albinia's farm, picking up runaway slaves. As he read, he discovered a

Federal Army camp was established in Kentucky, Camp Dick Robinson. When the governor protested neutrality, Lincoln just said that a bunch of fellow Kentuckians protecting their country was none of his concern.

He looked up as Julia waved from the platform. Just as he mounted the steps, he heard shouting and horses' hooves. He turned to look, and a large group of Federal cavalry approached the station. Will guessed there were hundreds of horses filling the street for blocks. Will felt shock and apprehension. What would so many Federals be doing in Lexington?

"Hello, Julia! Good to see you."

"Will, what's going on? Do you know?"

"No, I...."

"Hey, Blue belly! Did your mama forget to wash your uniform so it'd be gray this morning? Or did you just slither here through the mud?" yelled a man at the side of the station. Will watched in horror. One of the cavalry pointed his carbine at the citizen, threatening to shoot. Several women screamed. Just then, a bugle blew. Will knew that call—it was the signal for the Rifles to assemble, an emergency call.

"I'm sorry, Julia! I have to go!" Without taking further time for explanation, he ran back to the buggy, grabbed his rifle, and reported to the assembly point. Will heard the courthouse bell ringing, more scrambling, and the Home Guard, including Joe, faced off against the Rifles on the other side of the street, just to the rear of the Federal troops. Will was scared and nervous. What if the command came to fire? Could he fire on his friends and neighbors? His father? Will watched as Captain Morgan came at a gallop on his black mare, taking command of the Rifles.

"Rifles! Hold your fire. Do not fire unless fired upon," commanded Morgan.

Emerging from the Phoenix Hotel, Senator John Breckinridge, Joe's cousin, a Southern sympathizer, called for quiet.

"Gentlemen, gentlemen. Let us not be hasty, and so shed blood that we will all regret. Sir," he said, addressing the Federals commander, "what are your intentions? The state of Kentucky has no quarrel with you."

The commander answered, "My orders are to guard the cargo on that train and see that it does not fall into the wrong hands."

Morgan asked, "And what might that cargo be?"

"You know well enough," said the commander, "since it is you I was ordered to keep them from. Rifles, new ones."

"And to whom are they to be delivered?" asked the senator mildly.

"To the men at Camp Dick Robinson, so that they may adequately defend your fair state from an invasion by the Confederates."

Morgan said, "Indeed. And why should the Confederates invade a sister state? Unless to protect her from an invasion by Federals. In which case we should not allow these guns into enemy hands."

In answer, the Home Guard commander shouted, "Load! Shoulder arms! Aim!"

The Federal commander countered the order. "Stand down! We only want to peaceably take what is ours. Stand aside and do not interfere. We have no wish to make this a slaughter." Turning to Morgan, he said, "You are greatly outnumbered."

Morgan and Duke just smiled. Duke answered, "It's not the first time I've heard that. It likely won't be the last."

"Gentlemen!" pleaded the senator. "This is not the day. Captain Morgan, I appeal to you as a Southerner and a friend, let these men pass. If you do them no harm, then perhaps I can prevail upon the Federal commander to harm no one and contain any overeager Home Guards?"

"Agreed, sir," said the commander. The senator turned to Morgan. Will saw the conflicting emotions go across Morgan's face. He could tell that he hated to back down.

Finally, Morgan agreed. "Company, about face!" "Shoulder arms!" "Company, forward march!"

Will obeyed. After returning to the assembly point, he went back to the station and got Julia. He shook at the thought of what had nearly happened.

* * *

Julia visited her family for a few days and was about to go back to Cincinnati. She was in town at the freight office when a man named Lewis came to her with a sealed note. She recognized the writing as Albinia's and tore it open.

Dearest Julia,

I am coming to Lexington, but probably won't see you if you're there. I need your help. The man who gave you this note, Lewis, is a trusted friend. He will have a package for you in a barrel marked salt pork, delivered to my dock. Please take care of the package well and see it delivered to Cincinnati. My friend Franklin will have some other barrels for you to pick up as well, to ship north. He can help you load. Trust Franklin as you would me.

Your loving sister,
Binia

* * *

Julia paced up and down the dock. The boat landed half an hour ago at Albinia's dock. She could not delay much longer without arousing suspicion. Her boat captain was growing impatient.

Through the gloom she heard the jangle of harness, then saw a swaying lantern. She tensed, then relaxed.

"Franklin?"

"And you must be Mrs. Johannsen. I'm sorry to be delayed, but we had a little trouble. I'll help you get it on board."

"Yes, all right." Julia turned back to the boat. "Robinson! Come help this gentleman load the barrels. We must be off in twenty minutes. Have the one labeled salt pork taken to my cabin."

The men worked quickly. Waving to Franklin, Julia returned to her cabin and found a large fifty-gallon barrel labeled salt pork. She talked quietly, "I'm sorry, I can't let you out yet. You must be still and quiet until after the end of the first watch."

There was no acknowledgement. Julia wondered if the slave inside had died, or perhaps was asleep. Perhaps Albinia was just testing her and there was no one there at all.

She took dinner in her cabin, and the steward seemed surprised at the barrel, but made no mention of it.

After everyone had retired and it was nearing midnight, Julia took a walk down to the engine room. The fireman barely noticed her as he stoked the fires of the boiler with coal. But another man recognized her and snapped to attention.

"At ease, Mr. Penn. Do you know where I might find a crowbar? I've a mouse in my stateroom."

"But surely the steward...."

"I wouldn't bother him for such a trivial matter. I grew up on a farm; I'm quite capable of dealing with mice, given a suitable weapon."

"Yes, Mrs. Johannsen. I believe Paddy keeps one over by the coal pile for that purpose."

Julia retrieved the crowbar and soon pried open the barrel in her stateroom after locking the door. She sighed, looking down. Just salt pork, after all, she thought.

Then the salt pork on top began to move, and a full grown man, medium height but powerfully built, stood up from the midst of the barrel, a piece of salt pork still entangled in his black curls. He looked rather comical.

Julia suppressed a laugh, then wondered if she should be afraid.

"Well, I almost decided you weren't there! Let's get you out then."

"My knees and my ears got pretty friendly in there, ma'am."

"I imagine so," she said, pouring him a glass of water. "Thirsty and hungry too, I expect. Sorry I can't do better," she said, handing him a few biscuits. "We don't have long. I have to re-hide you. I'm afraid you'll be in the boiler room. It's going to be hot. Shifts change in about fifteen minutes—you must be in place before the new man takes over. You'll have to follow me down there, pretend to be my slave, in case someone sees you—but try not to be seen! Once we're landed in Cincinnati, I'll come and get you. You must pick up this barrel and carry it off the ship, to a green wagon at dockside. Once you're in the wagon, the man who owns it will take over and take you to the next stop. If you're discovered in the boiler room, I've never seen you—you're on your own. You must follow all my instructions exactly if you're to get away. Clear?"

The big man stretched—Julia moved back, frightened he might grab the crowbar and do her harm. Instead, he just said, "Yes, ma'am. And I'm mighty grateful."

A few minutes later Julia left the room and, seeing no one, came back to lead the man down below. She purposely avoided the crew stairways, where someone was more likely to recognize her. The black man shuffled behind, playing the part of an obedient slave.

She saw an officer emerging from the salon ahead and stopped, motioning the slave into a hallway. He responded quickly. Julia tensed, unconsciously holding her breath as the officer tipped his hat and walked by, to the staircase up to the pilothouse. Julia quickly got the slave down to the boiler room. She checked ahead and found the room briefly unattended—they must be using the privy or gone for a smoke, she thought. Motioning to her charge, she showed him an area behind and above the third boiler where he could fit, barely, without being burned.

She returned to her stateroom. As promised, when they docked in Cincinnati, she was able to get him to the barrel. He picked it up easily, waved, and vanished down the gangplank, out of sight—into freedom.

* * *

Albinia disguised herself well. It wouldn't do to be recognized. She drove the farm wagon to the outskirts of the Ashland Plantation. She was far from her home, but this was special, and she knew the area. The hemp grew in the fields, and some of the slaves were working down a row, tending it. Further down there was a grove of ash trees, in a hollow near a pond, at the north end of the farm. The hollow hid her and the wagon from anyone in the fields. If anyone questioned her, she simply would claim to be visiting Lucy, though they had seen little of each other since her return from the North. She waited quietly a few moments, annoyed with the heat and the mosquitos. Far away, she heard the field hands singing. When she was satisfied that no one was near, she set the brake and got down from the wagon, careful not to tear her petticoats or dress. She walked off the path, down further in the grove of trees, and began to sing. "*Steal away! Steal away! Steal away to Jesus.*" She continued singing the song but walked back up the path, further away from the wagon, until she could not even see it was there. It was afternoon, and the early September sun was blazing down. When she felt she had waited long enough, she returned to the wagon, mounted, and drove slowly away, confident that her cargo was secure in the back of the wagon, under the tarp and vegetables. She had not let anyone know she was coming to Lexington except Julia. When she received word through the underground that this package was to go north, she volunteered. Though it was bright daylight, she felt somehow that David was with her. They had helped other slaves together. Now she must do it alone—but not alone, really. God was with her, and she felt David smiling at her.

Once she got out in the country, she put the horses to a smart trot. The wagon held extra feed for the horses. She supposed she would have to overnight somewhere north of Frankfort. Albinia had never taken a slave this far before. It was almost a hundred miles from Ashland to her new home on the river. On her last visit to Lucy, she managed to keep things pleasant and obtain stationery from Ashland, stamped with the Clays' seal. She wrote a bill of sale for one Negro male, Jackson Clay. She felt that was her best protection, though of course she carried her derringer. When it was near dark, she would have Jackson come out and drive for her. Her story would be going to visit relatives in Cincinnati, with Jackson as her slave. After hearing from Luther what Jackson had done for him, she always felt she owed Jackson a debt. If he ever wanted to run, she would make sure that he could. She wouldn't trust him to the Railroad. She would risk herself. She told herself that now that David was gone, what happened to her didn't matter anyway. In a way she felt scandalous, so soon after his death shedding her widow's garb. However, she knew that David would have wanted her to carry on leading slaves to freedom, and black dresses were not helpful for that. It would attract too much attention.

The drive to Frankfort was peaceful, if hot and dusty. Albinia wondered if she dared stop at a hotel restaurant, as the wagon came into town on the Leestown Road. There was less risk than stopping outside of town, where a passerby might ask her business. She found one near the state capitol on Main St., and after refreshment, drove on, passing near the state prison. Albinia wondered briefly about those inside its walls, and then turned her attention back to the waning afternoon. She would have to find a safe place to overnight soon. Sometimes, the safest place was in plain sight, as though you had nothing to hide. Since she was traveling as a slave owner, and curfew was coming in a couple of hours, she decided to just camp near the road, with Jackson in the open, near Stoney Creek. The horse crossed the covered bridge. With no one nearby, they stopped. Albinia called to Jackson. He emerged from under the tarp and joined her on the wagon seat.

"Miss Albinia, you sure dis is safe?"

"Never sure about anything in this business. But safe enough I think. We'll camp off the road, by a creek for water. I've been this direction before—a friend told me it was a good place. Then in the morning, as soon as it's light, we'll head for my place. You may have to stay there a few days, until we can make a safe river crossing. I have my own boat now, and I've made the crossing a few times."

"How do I ever thank you?"

She laughed. "Simple. Don't get caught."

They drove on quietly, stopping at the appointed spot. It was heavily wooded, but a small path led off the road, and then along the creek. They set up camp. Jackson soon had some salt pork sizzling and coffee brewing. Albinia extracted the coach gun she had hidden under the wagon seat, verifying that both barrels were loaded with ten-gauge shot. After supper, they extinguished the fire. Jackson set up two pup tents and Albinia took first watch, agreeing to wake him in a few hours. She watched the stars and prayed, missing David, wondering about her family. She woke with a start, having dozed off. Some distance away, she heard hoofbeats and voices. Waking Jackson, she made sure she could grab the derringer and the coach gun.

"Remember, don't run, and no fighting unless absolutely necessary. We're going to visit my relatives in Cincinnati, the Johannsens. I have your papers, if they want to see them. If it does come to a fight, you take the coach gun. I have a derringer, and I'm better with that anyway."

They waited tensely as the horses approached on the road. It was a moonless night, with only the light of the stars. One of the riders carried a torch, as usual. It seemed to take forever, but finally the horses passed. Albinia let out the breath she didn't know she'd been holding. The night passed without further incident, and soon after sunrise, they hitched up and drove at a trot to Albinia's farm, arriving about noon.

Her friends Franklin and his wife Mabel greeted Albinia, along with a large bullmastiff.

"Heard the wagon coming; guarded the road with the rifle just like you said, Mrs. Horner," said Franklin, helping her down from the wagon. The dog bounded over, rolling on the ground at Albinia's feet. She patted him playfully.

"Good dog, Rex." Then turning to her hand, "Thanks, Franklin. Please get Jackson into hiding, and see that he's comfortable. Tomorrow I'll go over to Madison and see what arrangements can be made for him."

"Yes'm. Come this way," he motioned to Jackson. Jackson followed him and Albinia into the house, a two-story affair with front and back porches, a parlor and dining room, and a rear kitchen. Once in the kitchen, Franklin moved a rug aside to reveal a trap door, which he raised.

"There's not much light down there, but don't be burnin' candles unless it's night—there's a window at the end of the passage. If you hear commotion up here, stay put, put out any candles. If you hear this door raised, run out the back and try to get across the river, with the boat down at the landing. Otherwise, we'll knock three times and come down singing, "*Steal away*" if everything's all right." Albinia watched as the door closed over Jackson, leaving him in darkness.

* * *

Albinia heard shouting and the noise of many horses. She rose from bed quickly in the darkness, put on a dressing gown, lit a lamp, and grabbed her derringer from a nightstand drawer.

"Franklin! Mabel!" she shouted. She went down the stairs and opened the front door. Outside was a mob of men, torches, and dogs, trampling her dooryard. Men opened the barn.

"What is the meaning of this?" she shouted angrily.

A fat older man on a tired-looking chestnut horse rode forward. "What we're doing is searching. For a runaway slave. We have a tip says he came here. And this," he said, handing a paper to Albinia, "is a search warrant, signed by the district judge. We don't want trouble, ma'am. You can go back in the house. We'll call you when you're wanted."

Albinia trembled and turned to go back in the house. Franklin was downstairs by now, with Mabel.

"What's the trouble?" asked Mabel.

"They're looking for runaway slaves. They have a warrant. We can't stop them. It's legal. We need to pray."

The three of them were standing in the parlor, still praying, when the sheriff's men burst into the house and began searching everywhere. They were very thorough, room-by-room, even moving furniture, testing bookcases, looking in every possible location that might conceal a human. When they went to the kitchen, Albinia heard loud growling and she hurried into the room. Rex was lying on the rug that covered the trap door, in a crouch, growling threateningly at the men. One of them nervously pointed a pistol at the dog.

"Put that away!" Albinia said sharply. "Unless you want to lose your hand!"

"Call off your dog! Or he's dead!"

"Rex! Heel!"

The big dog obediently moved toward Albinia, sitting at her feet just at the edge of the rug, but still growling low in his throat. The men searched the room, never taking their eyes off him, and they did not move the rug. As they were leaving, Albinia told the one who had pulled the pistol, "You're lucky you didn't try. Rex would have taken your arm off before you could shoot. I'm a woman alone, and he's very protective."

The man sneered and left. Albinia sighed in relief and went out to where Franklin and Mabel were still praying. They turned and thanked God aloud when they heard a loud knock.

Albinia, puzzled, went to the front door and opened it. Three things struck terror in her heart. The sheriff was there, holding Jackson, and behind them, James Clay, Lucy's father.

The sheriff said, "Ma'am, you are under arrest."

* * *

The next morning, Albinia stretched sore muscles unaccustomed to sleeping on a concrete floor. The holding cell stank of feces and body odor. It was crammed with other women, all black. Each barely had enough room to lie down. The jailer came and escorted Albinia to a courtroom. She had an opportunity to speak with a court-appointed attorney, who advised her that the evidence was incontrovertible. She should plead guilty.

The judge entered the court.

"All rise for the Honorable Judge Davis! The case of the people of Kentucky against Mrs. Albinia Horner. All draw near who wish to be heard."

The judge entered, sat, rapped the gavel, and intoned, "The court will come to order."

"Your honor," said Albinia's attorney. "May we address the court?"

"Certainly, sir. But bear in mind, we have no time to waste here."

"Yes, sir. They arrested my client only last night, sir. She has attempted to send messages to her father, to Mr. Cassius Clay, and others who might aid her defense, but the court has denied these attempts. I would like to request a delay, your Honor, in order to prepare an adequate defense and investigate the circumstances of the case."

"Denied," said the judge. "I believe the circumstances are fairly clear. The state accuses your client of stealing a slave and abetting his escape. The property is valued at two thousand dollars, a very serious crime. Mr. Lodge, call your first witness."

The prosecutor, Mr. Lodge, called in turn the sheriff, the man who caught Jackson running out the back of her house to the river, James Clay, and Susan Clay. Susan testified that she suspected Albinia in the theft of one of their other slaves, Luther. She also said Albinia knew the plantation well, and knew Jackson. She positively identified Jackson as their slave and denied selling him to Albinia.

"She betrayed our trust, sir. We had taken her into our family as a friend. My husband will tell you he was a benefactor to her, though she is of a lower class. She repaid my daughter's friendship with theft and lies."

"Thank you, madam." Turning to the judge, the prosecutor said, "The state rests, your honor."

"Defense?"

"Your honor, in light of the refusal of more time to prepare, the defense rests, and my client throws herself on the mercy of the court."

The judge turned to Albinia, who looked helpless. "Is that what you wish to do, my dear? Are you sure?"

Albinia straightened. "As God is my witness, sir, I never intended anyone harm. I have acted in friendship many years towards the Clays. If their cousin Cassius were here, he could vouch for me in this regard. However, I cannot and will not pretend that I honor the law that says one man can own another, or that a slave must be returned to an owner. I believe slavery, whether benign or cruel, is a sin against God. If I can fight it, I will, and that to my last breath. I believe Jackson and countless others of his oppressed brothers are equal in every respect to you, or me. I am only a young woman, recently widowed, but I must answer to God. My late husband gave his life for the cause of freedom. Many other lives may be lost in this cause. If you feel this is a crime, then by all means punish me. But one day we will all stand before God, and He is my true judge. I believe, with Mr. Garrison, that even the Constitution itself cannot stand higher than the Word of God. And on Him, I throw myself for mercy."

"Very nice speech, dear. However, the law is clear, and has been upheld by the highest court in the land. This court finds you guilty under the provisions of the Fugitive Slave law and the laws of the state of Kentucky. In view of your youth, and your fair gender, I wish I could be more lenient. I find you guilty of forgery, larceny, and conspiracy. Sentence is two years hard labor at the state penitentiary. Accused is remanded to custody. The slave Jackson is returned to his owners, after one hundred lashes, administered in the courthouse square in Lexington. Court adjourned."

The judge banged the gavel, and the jailer led Albinia away, to the prison wagon. As the wagon went down the road, Albinia beseeched God, wondering how she could have been betrayed.

* * *

September 20, 1861, Lexington

Will felt like a thief. He got the summons from Captain Morgan that morning. Now, he snuck out of his parents' cabin at night, walked the miles to town as he used to, carrying his rifle, his Bible, and some hastily assembled provisions, not knowing when or if he would return. Morgan's message emphasized the need for secrecy. Will told his parents nothing. He did not know which other Rifles would be coming, except that Basil Duke had returned to Missouri and would not be with them tonight. When he arrived at the assembly point, a few of the other Rifles were already loading wagons with crates of weapons. There was an arrest warrant out for Captain Morgan. The Federals were coming to confiscate all weapons belonging to the Rifles. Morgan was determined that would not happen, so the Rifles were disguising crates of weapons under hay bales and leaving under cover of night, secretly. Will felt torn between pride that Morgan trusted him, wanting him to come, and guilt at taking food and causing his parents pain. He was aware that Morgan probably knew the route as well as he, having an uncanny knack for keeping a map of terrain in his head, yet Morgan asked for him specifically, as they would go out the Versailles Road. The Rifles worked quietly, but there were some whispers.

"Won't those Federals be surprised in the morning!" whispered Archie. "They find the bird has flown, they're gonna look like pretty dumb foxes."

"Yes, but the question is will they chase us?" wondered Will. "And what if we run into scouts tonight?"

"Word is if that happens, we fight," said Tom Logwood.

Morgan came over. "Good work, men. But once we leave this barn, we need to be silent as a churchyard, until we're well out of town. Even then, keep it down and stay alert."

Will saw to tying rags around the wagon wheels and making sure the leather straps of the suspension wouldn't creak too loudly, greasing them with pork fat. The moon would not rise until after sunrise, so darkness worked in their favor. There were three wagons. The first two were filled with weapons and hay, the last with the other Rifles coming on the journey. Any patrols that were out would be Southern sympathizers, so unless they ran into Federal scouts, they should have no problem. Finally, all the gun crates were loaded, some confiscated from the Home Guard, as an enterprising Rifle member picked the lock on the unguarded arsenal.

"Will, you drive the lead wagon with me. James, take the second wagon. Tom and Archie, you drive the third. If trouble comes, do not fire unless I fire first," said Morgan, checking the chambers of his revolver.

They mounted the wagons and drove out, Archie closing the barn doors behind them. They were on the road to war.

* * *

Will was exhausted, wet, and hungry. Rain drenched them on the way. They had driven the wagons of weapons to Woodsonville. There, Captain John Cripps Wickliffe joined them with a group of infantry volunteers. Wickliffe brought with him rifles and horses "liberated" from his nearby Home Guard. They agreed that Morgan would take command of the entire group. Others came trickling into the Woodsonville camp, hearing about Captain Morgan's escapade. They marched for two days, hardly stopping, from Woodsonville to Greenville. They named the place Camp Charity. The pro-Union Home Guards stayed out of their way, deeming them too strong to attack. Morgan's cousin, Thomas Hunt Morgan, was there with two hundred men, and an old friend of Morgan's, Roger Hanson, "Old Flintlock," had six hundred men. The original group of seventeen from the Rifles swelled to a force of almost one thousand. Many things were in short supply—horses, guns, and food. The days were spent nonstop drilling. The nights were beginning to be cold, and as October came in, Basil Duke arrived to help his brother-in-law.

For Will, Camp Charity was not like anything he'd ever experienced. He and Archie shared a pup tent, about ten square feet of ground. There were endless inspections, as the officers tried to bring the men to some level of military competence and efficiency. Many of the officers had served in the Mexican-American war, like Captain Morgan. The food was scarce and indifferent. Before an officer told him not to waste ammunition, Will used his marksmanship to bring in squirrels, rabbits, and once, a deer. The men in his company grew to respect his skills with a rifle. Even Ben Drake came by with grudging congratulations when Will shared the deer with the whole company. On Sundays there was a preacher, and Will often joined the men going to the camp church.

Finally, Will heard of someone going to Lexington, and sat down to write a letter.

October 6, 1861

Dear Ma and Pa,

I miss you. I hope you are not angry with me. From the beginning,
I've felt that God wanted me to keep my word to Captain Morgan,
and so I have done. We've joined the Confederate Army. I know
how you feel about that, so I will say no more. The enlistment is
short, only one year. Since school is not possible, after that, I will
deem my debt to Captain Morgan paid, and come home. I will send
my pay to you as I get it, to make up for my absence. Give my love
to Lyddie, and to Julia and Albinia when you see them. Please pray
for me often. My prayers are with you.

Your loving son,
Will

FIGHTING RIFLES

October 1861

B asil Duke came to Will's tent. Duke was the newly elected first lieutenant of the second Kentucky Cavalry, CSA. James West was now
second lieutenant, and Morgan was captain. They were regular army now,
not a militia.

"Yes, sir! What is it, sir?"

"We've found some horses. The captain hopes to persuade the command to give us more. It's driving him crazy to have a cavalry unit without
enough horses for each man. Some of the commanders think cavalry is
only good for picket duty. We intend to show them otherwise. The captain
ordered me to pick a few men that can ride and shoot. We know that there
are Federal messengers and scouts in the area. We want to teach them that
this is Kentucky land, not for Federals. What do you say? It's night duty,
using surprise. You'll still have to drill tomorrow."

"Yes, sir!"

"Good, then report to the quartermaster and draw your mount. We
leave in half an hour."

Will checked his ammunition and his bayonet. Mounted, he didn't
expect to use it, but he thought being prepared was best. He went and got
saddled up. His mount was a dapple gray mare, probably some Arabian
in it, with the small head. The large hindquarters promised speed. Will
saw Captain Morgan and the others. He mounted and joined the group.

Morgan briefed them. "I've gotten permission to scout, to try and find Federals, especially messengers, and intercept dispatches along with anything else we can get them to tell us. Duke and I will lead. Will, I want you in the rear. The rest of you spread out in a single line behind Duke and me, about ten feet apart. Go quiet. If you have to shoot, aim to wound or unhorse them. Remember, the goal is information, and dead Federals don't talk. Of course, don't let them shoot you—if you must kill them, so be it. I aim to show what a cavalry unit can do. Any questions?"

"No, sir!" they all said in unison.

The group set out in the growing darkness, traveling as quietly as horsemen can through woods and rough country, occasionally breaking the line to dodge fallen trees. They used hand signals to communicate whenever possible, rather than talking. Duke called a halt, and everyone stopped to listen. They were all tense, fingering their weapons.

Will heard the sound of horses approaching on their right, from the rear. He signaled those ahead, and the troop turned to face the oncoming horsemen. Duke signaled their right and left flankers to move slowly ahead, so that the horsemen would walk into a trap.

Will quietly dismounted and tied his horse. He was now near the front of his company, since they reversed. He intended to have a clear shot and make sure the horsemen did not escape. He was nervous. He'd never pointed a gun at a human being before. But he was determined to justify Morgan's faith in him.

The moon came out from behind a cloud. Will could see the blue uniform and brass buttons of the horsemen. At the same instant, they saw their peril.

"It's a trap!" yelled one, pulling a revolver from a holster.

Will fired quickly, striking the one with the revolver in the leg, and sent his horse rearing skyward. The revolver shot went wild, and the man fell backward off the horse, hitting the ground heavily. The rest of the Rifles encircled the remaining horsemen, revolvers, swords, and bayonets at the ready. He dropped his reins and quickly surrendered.

Will began to shake—he'd just fired on another man and wounded him.

Other ones of the company dismounted and surrounded the wounded man. Morgan spoke gently to him.

"You've done your duty, son. No one can call you a coward. We mean you no further harm. We just want your dispatches and whatever you can tell us about the Federals around here." Turning to one of the other men, Morgan ordered, "Adams, see to his leg. Patch him up. Then check his horse. If the horse is ridable, take him back with us. Otherwise, put him down."

They gave him water, and talked quietly with those they had captured. John Adams found the dispatches on each of the horses and gave them to Morgan. Soon all mounted again, prisoners riding in front. Will saw that the Federal soldier just had a flesh wound. By great good fortune, the ball struck first a saddle skirt, then a rib of the horse after wounding the soldier. Even the horse would recover.

When they arrived back at camp, Will accepted congratulations, but felt both elated and troubled by the night's events. The intelligence they recovered about troop movements was valuable. Will tumbled into his tent and caught two or three hours sleep before reveille wakened him for drill. Archie was shaking him.

"Better get up! No tolerance for sluggards in the regular army," Archie said, hurrying off toward the makeshift parade ground.

Will groaned and wished for coffee.

This pattern repeated for several nights. Others made captures. Two of their company were wounded. Then one evening, Morgan came to Will's tent.

"Will, you've been doing a great job. I want to let you know—headquarters has decided our unit is making a difference. Tonight, I want you to rest and get some well-deserved sleep. We'll rotate and give some of the other men experience. Tomorrow, see Duke—he'll have a surprise for you."

"Yes, sir!" Will grinned. "Could you take Archie out tonight, sir? He snores somethin' fierce!"

Morgan grinned back. "Don't see why not."

Will wondered what surprise the morning would bring.

* * *

Will felt heat and smelled smoke. His eyes flew open to see flames traveling down a length of paper toward him, threatening to catch his tent on fire. He jumped up, knocking the pole loose that supported the tent. It crashed down around him. There was loud laughter, and then water drenched everything.

Will emerged spluttering and ready to fight.

"What's going on?" he demanded angrily. "Can't a fella get some sleep?"

It was full daylight, past time for normal reveille.

"Aww, mama's baby needs his beauty sleep! Here that, Jesse?" said Ben Drake. "We just thought we'd warm up the morning for you."

To one side, Will saw Archie standing with a bucket, which had doused the fire. He took in the situation, quickly deciding he could be angry and make things worse, or he could join in the joke.

"Guess you did, at that, Ben. Since you made the fire, where's the breakfast? It's the least they can do, eh, Archie?"

The tension broke and they all laughed together.

"Eggs and bacon comin' up, Crump. We, uh, helped a farmer that had too much last night."

Tom Logwood came over and helped Will pick up the tent and his belongings. "We decided to let you sleep, wake up the rest of the company quietly. As soon as you've had breakfast, you're to report to Duke."

Will soon felt better with some coffee, eggs, salt pork and bacon inside him. He dressed carefully and reported to headquarters.

"Private Crump, reporting as ordered." He stood stiffly at attention.

"At ease, Private. I have some news I think you'll like. First, the regiment has been allotted new horses. The commanders think our little nightly forays have yielded worthwhile results and want to encourage our activity as cavalry. The horses are ones judged too small, old, or tired for hauling wagons and artillery. Still, there are some strong, fast ones in the group. I've seen to it that you'll get a Morgan gelding, Toby, about fifteen hands. He's yours, so take care of him. You won't have to draw random mounts for assignments anymore."

"Thank you, sir!"

"You've earned it—but you'll probably get more assignments because of it. Second, I'd like you to test a new type of rifle we're trying out. If it works well for you, you can keep it as well. But it will change your assignments, so that you do more escort and long range shooting. In future engagements, we'll be up against artillery. The Whitworth rifle, in the right hands, can shoot up to two thousand yards. Your job would be to take out the Federal artillery soldiers. Do you think you can do that? It's very important, and will save lives in our company."

Will felt troubled about shooting men who were no direct threat to himself, but answered with only slight hesitation, "Yes, sir!"

"Good man. Last, the men have decided to vote you Corporal. You'll learn from Tom about your extra duties. That's all."

"Yes, sir!" Will was elated with his promotion. The other men must feel he was doing well.

* * *

December 1861

A few days later, just after reveille, Will received a summons from James West, the second lieutenant.

"Corporal Crump, reporting as ordered, sir." Will stood at attention and waited.

"Congratulations on your promotion, Crump. We're doing a daytime scout. Captain Morgan requested you for the mission—but it's completely volunteer. If you'd rather not go, you don't have to."

"Sir, with respect, I should go."

"Excellent. There will be a few volunteers from the Tennessee cavalry as well. Be ready in half an hour."

Will went to tend his horse and inspect his gear. A few minutes later, he saddled up and joined the group of about fifty who were heading out on patrol. For the first hour, they saw and heard little. Under other circumstances, Will would have thought they were just a group of friends out for a ride in the crisp November morning. Will stayed near the rear of the group, as he usually did on these scouting expeditions. The scabbards on his saddle held the old Springfield on one side, and his new Whitworth rifle and scope on the other side. Morgan and Duke were at the front.

Suddenly the command was whispered down the line to halt. Someone spotted Federals on the road. Everyone dismounted and moved into the thickets at the side of the road. A few men in the front gathered the horses. Will went with them further to the rear, and then mounted a small rise where he had cover, but a good view of the road near the Nolin River.

Morgan, alone, moved forward about one hundred yards in front of his troops, to a little house at the side of the road, and went inside. The Federals kept coming down the road, their bayonets reflecting the sun. Morgan slipped out of the house and back to the main body. Will put his scope on the mounted Federal officer, but just as he was about to fire, Morgan stepped out into the road in full view and shot the officer with his pistol.

The Federals were greatly confused and surprised. Morgan was able to get back to cover, and the Federals likewise retreated. Taking Morgan's volley as permission to open fire, Will and the eight or so others with him opened fire on the Federal troops. A few dropped, but most made it to the safety of the little house Morgan had come from, or a knoll with downed trees. There was no coordination, no plan of attack. For the next ten to fifteen minutes, both sides fired spontaneously, each man following his own orders. Morgan and one or two others crept closer to the Federal lines and killed several men. Will saw through his scope a Federal rise and take aim at Morgan, so he quickly guessed the range and fired. The Federal dropped, shot in the chest. In another few minutes, the rest of the company retreated to Will's position. They heard from scouts that Federal reinforcements were coming, and others were attempting to encircle them. Morgan ordered everyone to horse, and they escaped.

* * *

Will had bad dreams that night. He woke in a cold sweat. The temperature outside the tent was freezing. He and Archie had a small fire pot that kept a few coals burning without producing much smoke. They kept that inside the tent, with a bucket of water just outside. It wasn't much, but with the tent flaps tied together, blankets, and heat from their bodies, it kept them from freezing. In his dream, the Federal soldier fell repeatedly. Before morning, the dream changed and it was Morgan falling, as Will failed to shoot in time. He wondered if the Federal soldier had family, maybe a wife and children. He shoved the thought aside, thinking how the company would suffer if Morgan were not there to rally them.

Christmas was around the corner. Will had heard nothing from his family. He wondered what was happening to them. He wondered if his father and Joe might be in a Union tent on some hillside, perhaps not that far away. He resolved to attend church the next day and confess. He rationalized, thinking that King David from the Bible was a man of war who killed hundreds in battle—yet didn't the Bible also say that David was a man after God's own heart, a friend of God? Hadn't he gotten on this course by following God's command to take vows seriously, and not to lie?

In the next few days, a new group from Shelbyville and another from Louisville joined Morgan's command. With so many now reporting to him, Will saw him less frequently, though he always seemed to retain a particular affection for those who were original members of the Rifles. Will worked with some of the newer men on shooting and riding.

The next morning at assembly, Duke addressed the command.

"Men, the Federals have occupied Green River, where we were a few weeks back. We are ordered to Bell's Tavern, to support a group of Texans that got themselves in trouble. Also, the Federals are rebuilding the Bacon

Creek railroad bridge to move supplies to their troops. Captain Morgan is looking for a few volunteers to help blow the bridge. Anyone interested, step forward."

Will and about ten others stepped forward.

"Volunteers, report to Captain Morgan with your horses in two hours. Draw four days rations from the quartermaster. The rest of you we leave in three hours for Bell's Tavern. We want to be ready to attack tomorrow morning. Whoever has a horse can ride it; the rest of you will have to march or ride one of the wagons if there's room. We'll be traveling all night. Dismissed."

In gathering twilight, Will and the others followed Morgan to Bacon Creek. Reports said there was a large camp of Federals nearby, so surprise and secrecy were paramount. They split the group, with two riding in the front, two riding in the rear, and the rest of them bunched in two columns of fours. Whenever the front riders thought it safe, they proceeded at a trot. Will was glad that he had the Morgan horse, whose stamina at a trot made it possible for him to go for miles at a time. Will's rear end was not faring as well as the horse, and he had a feeling he'd be quite sore the next day. From Bowling Green, it took them nearly fifteen hours riding to get near the bridge, with a few hours stop for rest and food. Morgan cautioned them against fires and needless chatter. They found a ravine about a mile from the bridge and rested there until dark. Some of the men played cards; others gathered black walnuts and persimmons. Will sat at a distance from the rest, reading his Bible by the failing light. He thought of the coming fight and read Psalm 144, "Blessed *be* the LORD my strength, which teacheth my hands to war, *and* my fingers to fight: My goodness, and my fortress; my high tower, and my deliverer; my shield, and *he* in whom I trust; who subdueth my people under me."

As the moon rose, the men mounted and rode closer to the bridge. They dismounted again about a hundred yards away. Making their way down to the edge of the creek, they gathered dry wood and kindling. Will and one other sharpshooter stationed themselves in trees back from the creek, with orders to pick off any Federals who ventured from the guardhouse near the bridge in an attempt to stop the burning. Soon the men had a roaring blaze going. They relaxed on the creek bank roasting food, playing cards, and generally being unconcerned about a possible Federal attack. Two men came out of the guardhouse. Will fired, purposely hitting the ground just in front of the first man. He quickly reloaded, keeping his already loaded Springfield nearby in case the man tried to run. The dirt kicked up behind the other man as his comrade fired. Two other Confederates rushed to the entrance to the bridge, rifles aimed, urging the men to surrender. The men laid down, hands behind their heads. Ben Drake and Jesse quickly took them prisoner and hustled them to Captain Morgan. Will came down from his tree and walked close to where Morgan was questioning the men.

"How many Federals in your camp?"

"About two hundred in the stockade. Another brigade to the north," answered the man, obviously scared.

"Which units?" queried Morgan, testing him.

"Ninety-first Illinois. Please, sir, I got a wife just had a baby. I want to live to see my son."

Morgan patted the prisoner's shoulder. "Don't fear. You will see him, as far as it depends upon me. Tell the truth, answer my questions, and you'll be set free."

Will listened as Morgan questioned him further, then appearing to be satisfied, he said, "Go back to your commander. Tell him not to bother rebuilding this bridge. As many times as he builds it, I will torch it. Tell him further that within a week, I will burn him out of Woodsonville."

Morgan then dispatched men to burn the stockade a half mile from the bridge, and others to set fires and bend the rails all along the line. Will went with the stockade group, to discourage Federal resistance with his long gun.

* * *

Two weeks later, as they sat in camp at Bell's Tavern, two things happened to raise Will's spirits. First, Archie came into camp with a copy of *Frank Leslie's Illustrated Newspaper*, which showed a woodcut of the Bacon Bridge, charred and in ruins, with one Federal soldier looking on.

"Will! Look! We're famous!" said Archie. "This here picture been printed in all the newspapers up North. They've heard of Morgan now!"

Will grinned. "We did a lot of good, with hardly anyone hurt. Maybe the Yankees will give up and go home!"

"By the way, this came for you," said Archie, handing him a weather-stained letter.

Will opened it and found a letter from his parents, mostly in his mother's handwriting. His hopes soared.

December 10, 1861

Dear Will,

I do not know if this will reach you. I've given it to a neighbor who says he has contacts among the Confederate troops. Your father is leaving soon to join his unit at Camp Hobson, a unit formed by your old boss, the storekeeper. I understand Dr. Simpson, Jenny's uncle, will be in the same unit. May God keep you from each other, so that you do not face one another across a battlefield. Hiram, we hear, has joined the Third Ohio cavalry. All the men here are joining one side or the other. I'm not a very good farmer, so it will be a lean winter I'm afraid, while I learn. Only Lydia will be here with me, soon.

Albinia has gotten into trouble. She was arrested and imprisoned for two years for helping escaped slaves. I do not know what will become of her. The slave she was helping belonged to the Clays, so we cannot depend on them for any influence.

With Hiram off fighting, Julia has assumed much of the responsibility for their shipping company, trying to keep it out of war. I fear like many others, she will soon be forced to take sides.

Son, I know you are trying to follow God. I beg you, please come home as soon as ever you can. We need you. I love you, and nothing will change that.

Will recognized another few lines in his father's hand.

Will, I know we don't see eye to eye. But I forgive you for leaving, and you are always welcome back home. Remember, God is the only one worth following—not a man, a state, or a country. God uses men to accomplish His aims. Make sure to follow Him, and somehow, we'll all come out well. Pray for us all. Christmas won't be the same without you.

Love, Ma and Pa

Will folded the letter, putting it inside his Bible, and wept, filled with both relief and sorrow. Relief came from knowing his parents forgave him. Sorrow filled him when he thought of Albinia's arrest, his father in the Federal army, and the home he had left.

FLY AWAY

December 1861

J ulia sat through yet another ladies' tea, hosted by her mother-in-law.
She smiled, but inwardly gazed around at the group of gossiping rich
older women, wanting nothing more than to escape. What use was all of
this? Kirsten told her that these women had power, that they were the
key to contracts for shipping, bending of tariffs, and other advantages
mixing social and business connections. Julia thought they were terrible bores, and all much older than she. More than once she was tempted
to say something controversial, just to bring life to the conversation.
Unfortunately, she had to admit, these women did hold influence with
their husbands, who in turn provided the bulk of the business. She gazed
around the room, seeing the wife of John Gurley, Ohio congressman,
Lucy Hayes, wife of Rutherford Hayes, the city attorney and Union general, as well as other luminaries. Kirsten gave her access to such people.
Often she needed to remember that, and held her tongue. Joining a group,
she heard them discussing the war. Almost everyone had a relative in the
war, so the usual prohibition on women taking notice of the news had
almost disappeared. Everyone wanted to know what was happening.

"My husband says that Lincoln will order a general advance soon,
working up the Virginia peninsula to Richmond. Those rebels won't last
long," said one woman.

"Don't be too sure," said another. "My husband is in the Navy Department, and he heard Stanton say that the rebels have taken over ships that were being built in the Norfolk naval yard, even one made of iron! They might just sail right up the Potomac and attack Washington!"

"And no one thought they'd win Bull Run—but they did!"

"Balderdash! My husband says the New York bankers are building new foundries, and the Union will have as many cannon as the South does cotton balls. The war won't last another year."

"What about England?" Julia ventured. "There were those Confederate diplomats—what if they convinced England to enter on their side? England might regain the South that way."

Kirsten joined the group and said patronizingly, "My dear, of course that won't happen. The prime minister, Henry Temple, is no fool. He knows that the South can't last, and has no wish for another war with the victor. Now that the Trent affair is over, he'll simply watch North and South destroy each other and consolidate the Empire's position around the globe. Look at what they're doing in Mexico and China."

Irritated at being spoken to like a child, Julia excused herself. "I must see to the refreshments." As she walked away, a germ of an idea took hold in her mind. She engineered the steamship company being neutral. What if she could gain access to similar social circles in Lexington, or even Richmond? The military information these women dropped so casually might be of great value in the right hands. Women in Richmond or Lexington would be no different. If she pretended some sympathy for the South, maybe she could help Hiram and the Union with information. Maybe there was some use to these ladies' teas after all. First, she needed to use influence on the Federal side. Ever since Albinia's arrest, she wracked her brain looking for a way to help. Could she gain some influence that would help her sister? She visited Lexington, Louisville, and Frankfort representing the steamship company, anyway. Kentucky was not part of the Confederate States of America; it was still part of the Union. She smiled and thought of people to call on.

* * *

Luther was frustrated. His plans for revenge had so far yielded nothing but sweat and a return to near slavery. The whites of the Ohio regiment treated him little better than the Clays had, except that he was free to leave. The regiment moved to Indiana, near Louisville, then to Tennessee. He'd dug latrines, hauled freight, and done any other dirty work the whites didn't want to do. As they wintered near Jeffersonville, Luther was nervous that any of the whites might decide to claim a reward and send him back to Ashland and punishment. He was less than a hundred miles from his old home.

He bent over the horse's foot he was shoeing. The commander, Lew Zahm, had recently discovered Luther's talent for horses and blacksmithing, and put him to work at the forge. He was to draw wages from this skilled work, and he hoped to send some regularly back to Jemima.

One of the new officers, Lieutenant Colonel Doug Murray, came in, watching Luther work.

"That's fine craftsmanship. What's your name?"

"Luther," he replied, surprised at the compliment.

"Well, Luther, I've a cannon wheel that broke a tire, and I need a pair of tongs. After you finish with that horse, do you think you could make those for me?"

"Sure. Just take a couple of days."

"All right. I'll send my orderly for them. He's a big Swedish fellow, Corporal Johannsen. You've probably seen him. He's hard to miss."

Luther nodded. Perhaps doing this job might get him on friendly terms with the officer and lead to better work.

"Yes, sir. Just give me the wheel and I'll have it for you Thursday."

As John turned to leave, Luther noticed Sam quietly sneaking out of the barn. So far, they'd managed to ignore each other. He hoped it would last, until his opportunity came.

The wheel came, and Luther saw the iron tire was nearly worn through, besides having pits in the tire. He made a new one and riveted the ends together after heating the tire to expand it, and fit it around the wheel. He left it to cool until morning.

Luther looked up to see a huge Swede entering the shop.

"Luther?" the Swede said tentatively. "I'm Corporal Johannsen. I've come to pick up the tire and the tongs that were ordered."

"Yes, sir. I'll roll the tire over to the cannon, if you show me where."

Hiram motioned and Luther followed, rolling the big wheel. When they arrived at the cannon, the axle was lopsided, resting on the ground. Luther sighed in disgust—he hadn't brought a wagon jack.

"Now what? Guess I'll go back to the stable, get the jack."

"No need," said Hiram. He looked around and saw a sturdy log next a tree. "Help me." Hiram rolled the log over next to the axle, standing it upright. Hiram took off his uniform jacket, laying it over the cannon barrel. He motioned Luther to grab the axle.

Luther shook his head. This white man was crazy. Nobody was going to lift that axle. He bent over and grabbed it, prepared to jump back when it dropped on him, to avoid breaking a foot. Hiram squatted and wrapped his arms around the axle, leaving Luther to grip at the tip. "Now!" said Hiram. Hiram's face showed the strain, but the cannon lifted from the ground. Luther put his back into it, and was able to slide the log over under the axle. In another few minutes, they had the wheel on. Slapping Luther on the back, Hiram grinned. "Good job! Thanks for your help."

Luther grinned. "You crazy! I couldn't have lifted that."

Waking the next morning, Luther heard the trumpet blowing assembly and men running hurriedly. This didn't feel like a drill. He quickly dressed and headed for the barn. Men were already mounted, moving south toward the river. An officer saw him and motioned him over. "Hitch these horses to the cannon. They'll be needed!"

Luther hurried to obey. Soon all the cannon were moving toward the river, including the one he and Hiram had repaired the day before.

Luther followed the brigade on foot, arriving in time to take many of the horses to a corral area away from the river. Men were spread out all along the riverbank, behind cover. Shells from a Confederate gunboat in the river whistled overhead. Occasionally a canister shot burst and the cries of those hit were heard everywhere. The Federals fired at the gunners on the boat, but mostly with little effect. Then the Union cannon were brought to bear, and the boat started taking hits. The Federals cheered, but were soon occupied by a flanking force of Confederate cavalry trying to come in behind them on the riverbank. The gunnery officer gave a sharp order. A cannon turned on this new threat, and it was the one recently repaired. Just as it turned, the wheel struck a rock and a root sticking up out of the riverbank. When the gun fired, the wheel came off, and the iron tire split at the seam. The shot went wild, ricocheting and nearly hitting their own troops. The officer cursed, and brought another cannon to bear, leaving only one on the gunboat. In the chaos, the Confederate cavalry advanced, nearly gaining the area where the crippled gun lay useless.

In the end, the Federals prevailed. Luther lay in his bunk that night, after a visit from the officer who had ordered the wheel, berating him for his careless work, which had cost lives. He seethed. He knew he had fixed the wheel correctly. What could have happened? He thought … then he remembered. He'd left the wheel in the shop overnight. He hadn't checked it the next morning. Sam!

* * *

Albinia sat in the cell, crying softly so that her jailers would not hear. She prayed, but felt like God had abandoned her. Had her sins caught up to her, her lies and deceptions, and now He too had left her? David was gone. With her arrest, her dreams of helping slaves seemed shattered. Bitterly, she thought of the "help" she'd given Jackson—arrested, branded, given one hundred lashes, sent to the fields, and locked in shackles each night. That was his reward for helping Luther, for dreaming of a future in the North.

For now, the warden had taken pity on her, giving her a private cell. She knew that would not last. She also wondered at his motives. Could it be that the purpose was to break her will, to torture her more effectively?

She'd been here what seemed like forever. There was a hard wooden bunk chained to the thick stone wall, just a platform on hinges. There was a stove in the corner, but no coal or wood to burn in it. Winter was here and nights were cold. So far, the mosquitoes and other insects still found their way in through the bars. There were no blankets or pillows. The high window, far above her reach, had bars spaced about four inches apart. As a woman alone, she would be at the mercy of male guards, should they decide to take liberties. There was a bucket in the corner to relieve herself. The only furniture other than the bed was a single wooden stool. The cell had two doors, one solid steel, the other with open bars. During the day the solid door was open, affording no privacy. There was the occasional rustle of rats or mice running across the cell, especially at night. A guard came twice a day to give some poor gruel and stale bread, and collect her bowl from the previous meal. The bowl and spoon were wooden, to afford no chance of making a weapon or tool to gain freedom. For their own protection, no women prisoners could join the exercise time. The cell was about six feet by four feet. The window faced north, getting minimal sunlight.

Occasionally, even in the middle of the night, she would hear keys in the lock, and the creaking of the door opening. A prison official or sheriff came to question her. They came in and sat on the stool, probing to see if she was now willing to tell more of her connections and association with the Underground Railroad, routes, or safe houses. Albinia was glad at these times that she had memorized as much of the Bible as she had, for this was the only answer she gave them. She repeatedly asked the guards for a Bible or a minister, but they just laughed and asked what a hussy like her would do with it.

She almost lost track of days. She got lice, and her clothes were dirty. Once they allowed her to go to a prison washtub, where she had to take off her garments in front of male guards, to wash them. Her hair went uncombed, and she gnawed her nails to keep them short. She often thought about who might have betrayed her. Then she would push the thought away, determined not to let revenge get a foothold.

One morning when the sun had barely begun to come through the windows, she heard the rattle of keys in the door. She shook herself awake, and futilely combed at her hair with her fingers, expecting another prison official.

Instead, a guard came in. It was early for breakfast. He set the food dish on the floor as usual, as if she were a dog. He was tall, with a scraggly black beard and eyebrows that seemed scrunched together. He was wearing a nasty smile with yellow teeth. He carefully locked both doors behind him.

"Thought you might like a little company, you bein' alone in here so long," he said, moving toward her.

She jumped up and moved toward the end of the bed where the stool stood. She tried to stay calm.

"No, thank you. Just leave the food and go."

"Now, now, no need to be afraid. I was just thinkin' we could be more friendly like. Maybe I could get you that Bible you been wantin', or some other books, educated lady like yourself. Or maybe a little better food. Might be able to find a cat to help keep the mice down some." As he spoke, he eased toward her. He was close enough now she could smell the alcohol on his breath, above the other stenches.

She was almost cornered. He started to reach for her. Quickly, she grabbed the stool and brought it down hard on his skull.

He raised his arm to block her blow, but was too slow. He looked first angry and lustful, then surprised, and fell backward in a heap.

Albinia looked around, scared. What should she do? If he came to, she would again be at his mercy. The keys were on his belt. Escape? Perhaps, but she was so weak she wouldn't get two miles before they caught her. And where could she go? They would hunt her like an escaped slave. Get help? But what if the other guards simply took his part? Who would believe her?

"Lord, help me! I don't know what to do." In that moment, she thought of Paul in prison in Phillipi, how even when the jail was opened and he could have escaped, he and Silas stayed.

She knew she didn't have much time. He could come out of his drunken stupor any moment. Deciding, she unhooked the keys from his belt and opened the cell doors.

"Help!" she shouted, as loudly as she was able, standing in the doorway. "Help! Someone help!"

After a few minutes, two other guards came.

"He just collapsed. I didn't know what to do," she said, assuming her best helpless female role. "He brought the food in and just fell over."

One of the guards bent as if to pick him up and pulled back at the smell. "Drunk, is he? Well, the warden will want to be hearin' about that. But say, it looks like he has a fair sized lump on the back of his head." The other guard looked at her suspiciously.

"He hit the floor hard," Albinia said helpfully.

The two guards conferred in whispers for a moment. "All right. I'll be takin' those keys, missy. I expect the warden will want to speak with you. Eat your breakfast before the mice do."

They dragged him out, locking the door, and left her to her breakfast.

* * *

The day dragged for Albinia. She expected at any moment to be taken out of her cell and punished. Yet the sun rose high in the sky and no one came. Finally, in what was late afternoon, she judged, she again heard the keys in the lock. The steel door had been shut all day. She could not see who was coming, and dreaded that it might be the same guard, now enraged and prepared. She stood with her back to the wall and grabbed the stool again. It was a forlorn hope that she could overcome the man, if he knew she would fight, but she would go down trying.

The door opened, and relief washed over her. It was one of the other guards, and behind him, the warden. The warden stepped into the cell.

"Come with us, please, Mrs. Horner."

Albinia moved to comply, a hundred questions buzzing in her head, and no small amount of dread. The warden walked in front, the guard behind. She followed them to the warden's office. He sat at a large oaken desk and opened a file.

"Please be seated, Mrs. Horner. Jacobs, you can wait just outside the door."

The guard left, closing the office door with frosted glass in the top behind him.

Albinia sat in the horsehair chair with arms intended for guests.

"Mrs. Horner, you've been with us for some weeks now, following the unfortunate incident with one of James Clay's slaves. I understand you've declined to provide additional information regarding your accomplices. The slave has likewise been less than forthcoming, despite, shall we say, significant persuasions. However, in view of your race, and your gender, as well as lack of previous recorded offenses, I've been inclined to extend some leniency. We don't get many white women here that are not prostitutes, if you'll forgive the reference."

He stood and paced a moment.

"My guard tells me that you assaulted him. I understand that at the time of your arrest, you had a derringer on your person. You are familiar with violence. However, I find it difficult to believe that a woman as slight as yourself could overcome my guard without some extenuating circumstance. Then there is the fact that you had the keys, and opportunity to escape, but you did not attempt it. The guard was undeniably intoxicated on duty, making his claims less credible. This leaves me a dilemma—what to do with you, Mrs. Horner? Discipline is extremely important in this institution. Some of our inmates are quite dangerous, and without it, we would all be at risk. Do you understand?"

"Yes, sir," said Albinia respectfully. She was now hopeful that she would not be punished, but still afraid.

"So here is what we will do: I'm moving you today. You will be placed in a cell with other women. They will all be black, I'm afraid, but given your slave-liberating tendencies, that shouldn't trouble you, I imagine."

"No, sir."

"Good. In addition, I suppose I should find you some labor, since that was a part of your sentence. I don't imagine a small woman like yourself, unaccustomed to manual labor, would be of much use on a railway gang, nor do I wish to referee the problems with male prisoners that might occur. You are not an unattractive young woman. Do bear in mind that this is an option for you, however, should there be future incidents with my guards." He paused, waiting for a response.

"Yes, sir."

"There have been some letters across my desk in your favor, indicating you have some powerful political friends in the Union. Since Kentucky is still a Union state, though under siege, I am inclined to give those some weight. I understand you have some talent with a needle. Therefore, on a trial basis, you will report to my house, just beyond the prison walls, each day except the Sabbath. You will sew uniforms for the Union armies and give lessons to my children, since you seem to be decently educated. Is this agreeable to you, Mrs. Horner?"

"Yes, sir!" Albinia replied excitedly. It was more than she had hoped.

"Your father is in the Union army now, I understand, though your brother is regrettably with the rebels. Your father has been asking after you, and your sister as well, I believe. It is possible that a visit from one of them may happen around the holidays, if you maintain good behavior. Let me caution you that any trouble on your part and you can expect the same treatment as the worst slave offender among us. Is that clear, Mrs. Horner?"

"Yes, sir."

"Very well." He turned to the door. "Jacobs!"

The guard came in immediately. "Yes, sir?"

"Take this prisoner to cell block thirteen. Tomorrow, and each day after, you will escort her to my house in the morning and bring her back just before sunset."

"Yes, sir." The guard motioned Albinia, and he followed her. "All the way to the end of the corridor, down the stairs two flights, and left. No funny business."

* * *

December 1861

Julia knew that before she tried to gain information from Confederates, she must not alienate those she knew on the Union side, if she was to help her sister. Accordingly, she wrote to the governor and prison officials in her husband's name, showing his unit of service, and citing their company's service to the Union. Now that Magoffin resigned as governor, she felt she had a better chance with Robinson, who opposed the Fugitive Slave Law and the war. She hoped to affect Albinia's release, but barring that, she was working on a plan to help her escape. Since her company no longer carried slaves, and attempted to be neutral, Julia felt she might legitimately appeal to government authorities to let her sister go. If it didn't work, she was prepared to take action.

On December 23, she journeyed to Frankfort, to the prison, to see Albinia. The prison told her to go to a small frame house near the prison where Albinia was teaching, as this would be more suitable for a visitor. She found her sister surrounded by three laughing children.

"Well, this is surprise! I expected to see you in much more miserable conditions than this."

Albinia looked up with surprise and joy. She dropped the books she was holding and rushed over to hug Julia. When she recovered, she turned back to the children.

"Annie, why don't you take the other children to the back room and draw for a while, so I can talk to my sister?"

"Yes, Mrs. Horner."

After the children departed, Albinia seated herself in the parlor with Julia.

"I suppose it is a surprise. I can't quite believe it myself. Still, you should see the cell where I spend the night." She shivered, as if thinking of it. "Every morning they bring me over here, though I don't suppose they will for Christmas. Every evening I go back. Mornings I teach, afternoons I sew. It could be much worse. What's the family news, and Hiram?"

Perfect, thought Julia. "Hiram is doing well, learning about soldiering with his company. They are actually in Kentucky now, Elizabethtown, for the winter. And you'll never guess who's with him—Luther!"

Albinia was startled. "Luther? But how? I thought he'd escaped."

"He did—to Canada, even. But he's come back to fight the rebels. Hiram says he's mad that they won't let him be a soldier. But he's learned blacksmithing, and makes himself very useful to Hiram's regiment. They've seen a few battles, but nothing very major."

"What else?"

"Pa has joined the 19th Kentucky infantry, formed by Will's old boss, Hobson the storekeeper. He says he'll come if he can. I'm expecting him anytime, as long as he gets leave."

"Who's keeping the farm?"

"Ma, as best she can. Lyddie is big enough to follow behind and stick seeds in the ground now. I've asked Ma to leave it, come to Cincinnati, but so far she won't. Says she'll be there when Pa comes home. Everyone thinks the war will be over soon."

"Maybe. But I've heard that for months."

Julia leaned toward her sister and whispered, "Is it safe to talk here?"

Albinia raised her eyebrows in surprise. "Yes, I suppose so. Why?"

"Pa and I—we want to get you out of here. I've been writing everyone I can think of. Hiram's family has a lot of influence. And I hear Garrison is championing your cause as well, pointing to you as another victim of slavery. But in case that doesn't work, we want to help you escape."

Albinia looked shocked. "You can't! What if you were caught?"

Julia shrugged. "A chance we may have to take. But I don't think so. You must know some places to hide. We could get you to a steamboat, land in Illinois or Ohio. With the war on, they'd never bother to look for you up north. We can't just leave you in jail."

Albinia considered. "I'll admit I'd like to be free. But it's too dangerous, too much risk. God is with me. I'll survive this place. Let it go."

"At least promise me you'll think about it. We have a plan. If the governor doesn't pardon you by Christmas, be ready."

* * *

Back in her cell in the evening, Albinia tried unsuccessfully to get comfortable. This cell was about twelve feet square, with three beds that folded up to the wall, a chamber pot, and a stove. It was dark and damp in the basement, and had three other women in the cell. The stove did have coal, producing enough warmth to take the chill and dampness out of the air. The prison allocated them one scoop of coal per day—if it ran out, they froze. By its feeble light, she could barely make out the face and form of the others. One, called May, was about fifteen, slender, tall, and quiet. She seemed lost and discouraged. Another, called Polly, was short and plump, seemed about forty, and told endless stories of "her boys" who were "sold down south." The third, just called Old Molly, was a huge woman, about six inches taller than Albinia, and looked over two hundred pounds. On her first night in the cell, Polly advised Albinia to "steer clear" of Old Molly, that she could be mean.

As the newcomer, Albinia had no bed, and her "place" was the corner near the cold outside wall—where the rats came from. She managed to take some scrap cloth from her sewing and cobble together a rough wool blanket. She lay on the floor, trying to rest until supper came.

The jailer opened the door and put four wooden bowls inside on the floor, carefully watching Old Molly all the time, then locking the door and retreating hurriedly. Albinia roused herself, going over to retrieve her porridge with weevils in it. As she stooped to lift the bowl, Molly put a big foot on her arm, pinning it to the floor.

"I'm a little extra hungry tonight, white lady. I 'spec you had good meals all your life. Not me. My Massa eat off china and silver, but we hardly got the slop from the hogs. Think I'll just make up for it, eat your bowl too." She quickly grabbed Albinia's other arm and twisted it behind her back, wrenching her shoulder. "You ain't gonna object none, are ya honey? 'Cause

I'd hate to break this pretty arm, like Massa broke mine when I was eight." She released Albinia's arm and stepped back with two bowls in her hands.

"C'mon, leave her be," said Polly. "She ain't done you no wrong. I hear she got in here for helpin' slaves like us."

Molly set the bowls on her bed and turned toward Polly threateningly. "So, you ain't hungry neither, huh? And maybe you need some teeth knocked out, to learn not to interfere with your betters." Molly took a step toward her and Polly cringed, arms protecting her face. Molly just laughed.

Albinia, recovered by this time, started to get up, saying, "No one means you harm, Molly. Not in here. Leave her alone."

For answer, Molly turned and kicked Albinia's ribs as she was attempting to get up. The kick slammed her head against the stone wall, and she had no breath. Her ribs instantly ached, and she wondered if one was broken. Blood trickled down her temple.

"High and mighty white woman. In here, you don't tell nobody what to do, you hear? You just stay in your corner, keep your white mouth shut, and your eyes down, like y'all tell us slaves to do. If you do that, I might let you live, and not hit you more than once a week."

Albinia stood, determined not to show fear. Molly moved toward her, ripping her blanket from her grasp.

"I think I'll stay warm tonight. You can cuddle with the rats. Ol' Ferdinand, the big plump black one, he's my favorite. You can have him tonight."

Molly laughed again, and sat down to eat both bowls of food.

Albinia painfully crept to her corner, lay down, and prayed, crying softly. She regretted her easy confidence of the afternoon. Would she survive this? Where was God when she needed Him?

* * *

Christmas 1861

Christmas did not seem real for Will. It was extremely cold, and he was far from home. No stockings hung over a fireplace. He had no family around him. He and Archie had worked hard the last two days to build log base and wooden platform into a small hill, covering it with their canvas tent and making a small stone fireplace surrounded by earth. Since they were unlikely to move camp for some weeks yet, it seemed worth the effort. Camp life settled into a dull routine of drill, eating, and trying to stay healthy and warm. Many in camp were sick. They all had lice, and stank. Some played cards and gambled. There was a Christmas service early in the day, but rather than giving a message on the hope for mankind represented in the birth of Christ, the minister, a colonel, went on about how God would give them victory over the Federals in the days to come.

"What do you think your family's doing about now?" asked Will.

"Aw, same as usual," opined Archie. "My pa ain't very religious. He'll prob'ly go to Mass, but he'll still feed the hogs and work like a reg'lar day. No money to spend on fool gifts, he says. What about yours?"

"I don't know what Ma and Lyddie will do. There's never been a Christmas like this. Pa's off in some Federal camp, just like us. My sister Albinia's in prison, the letter said, for helping slaves escape, and mourning her lost husband. Maybe Ma and Lyddie will go to her brother's, but with the war on, she probably wouldn't think that was safe. Hiram's off in a Federal camp too. Julia will probably be with Hiram's family, in a fancy house with lots of presents—but from what she says, not much love in the family there. How is your pa not in the fighting?"

"He got kicked by a steer a few years back, gave him problems with his leg, and dizzy spells. Don't think any army would want him when he might suddenly go all dizzy and shoot the wrong side. He still farms well enough, just rests when one of the spells comes."

"Tom's all sick. I'm gonna make him some dogwood bark tea, like a doctor did for me a while back. Don't seem like the doctors in this bunch know much about how to fix the quickstep.'"

"That so? I'll have to remember that. 'Course ain't always a dogwood tree handy."

"There's some about camp here I saw. As good a way to celebrate Christmas as any, I expect, helping a friend."

* * *

December 26, 1861

Robert and Julia hid behind bushes and trees along the path from the prison to the warden's house. Robert got furlough to visit his daughter in prison, with orders to return in two weeks. Colonel Hobson remembered Albinia and was sympathetic to her plight.

"Pa, why hasn't she come out yet? Do you suppose something's wrong? Maybe I should just go and see the warden again," fretted Julia.

"Just be still. If we're going to do this, break her out, we got to be patient. You know I don't like this. I'm not sure yet how you talked me into it. We could get in prison ourselves for this. She didn't come out on Christmas, but I expect she'll be along today. Let's just hope we can do this with no worse than a sore head for the guard," said Robert. He checked his Union-issued revolver to be sure it was loaded.

"Why don't you go down to the buggy and give the horse his nose bag? Looks like we may be here a while," said Robert.

Julia did as he asked, all the time imagining a thousand things that might go wrong with their plan, yet determined to rescue her sister. Just as she hadn't hesitated when Albinia asked her to use the steamships to help escaping slaves, she now risked everything to help her sister escape. On a previous trip, she watched the prison and discovered her sister's visits to the warden's house, and formed a plan. She knew she couldn't do it alone, so she begged Robert to help, and influenced Hobson to allow her father's leave. She trudged back up the slope to where her father was waiting.

The hours passed slowly in the cold. Julia rubbed her hands together and stomped her feet. She wore woolen petticoats, but the chill still crept up her legs.

Robert turned to Julia. "Are you all right, Jule? Do you think we'd better go back to the hotel, try again tomorrow?"

"No, no, we have to keep trying. What if we miss it? Or what if she's sick, or hurt?" said Julia. She scanned the prison walls, trying to imagine where her sister was. "Look! There!" she said, the cold forgotten.

The prison gate opened. A wagon came out, with two people on the front seat. One was the figure of a woman. They couldn't see well enough to identify her, but she was definitely white, not Negro.

"What do we do? She isn't usually in a wagon," panicked Julia. "If it's Albinia, and we let her go, she may be transferred somewhere, and we have to start over. If it's not, and we go up there, we could end up releasing a criminal for nothing."

"Calm down," said her father. "Take the buggy. Drive fast. Get in front of them. Pretend you have trouble and wave them down. Do anything to make them stop. I'll come up behind, take out the guard. If it's not Albinia, climb back into your buggy and I'll know to hold off. Go quickly!"

Julia turned and ran down the hill again, as quickly as her skirts would allow, using one hand to hold them almost to her knees, the other to balance against trees and rocks on the steep slope to where the buggy waited below. Her feet were so cold they tingled with the exercise, as the blood flowed faster through them. She almost fell twice, but finally came to the buggy, quickly removed the nosebag from the horse, and mounted the driver's box. She took the brake off, and then urged the horse forward as fast as she dared, not knowing the road well. She only knew this path came into the main road less than a mile ahead.

The buggy rattled and the harness strained as she urged the horse to canter, still pulling. As she rounded a curve, she could see the main road ahead, and pulled back on the reins to a walk. The horse's sides were heaving, and he showed some lather. She looked carefully to the right. She could not see the prison wagon approaching. Julia pulled onto the main road, then off on the right hand side, setting the brake letting the horse breathe. She climbed down. Her hair had flown in all directions, and she did her best to look like the victim of a runaway. After two or three minutes, she heard the rattle of a wagon and the footfalls of a horse. The black wagon rounded the curve and approached. Julia went to the middle of the roadway, waving her arms wildly.

"Help! Help! Excuse me, sir! Can you help me?"

The driver of the wagon pulled back on the reins, and the wagon lumbered to a halt. Julia looked carefully. It *was* Albinia. She murmured a silent prayer that her sister wouldn't give her away. "Sir, my horse ran away from me, and I think something is wrong with the wheel. Struck a rock or something."

The driver started to get down, and Julia saw Robert sneaking up from behind the wagon, his Enfield rifle raised as a club, when Albinia, startled, spoke up. "Julia! Whatever are you doing here? I've been freed. The governor pardoned me."

There was no time to clamber back into the buggy. Julia waved her arms wildly again, and yelled, "Stop!"

Robert redirected his swing, before clobbering the unknowing guard. The butt of the rifle hit the ground harmlessly. The guard turned, drawing a pistol.

"What is the meaning of this?!" the guard shouted.

"I ... I ... meant no harm," ended Robert lamely.

Julia recovered herself and interrupted. "The woman you are transporting is my sister. This is my father. My sister was unjustly imprisoned. We came to rescue her, but I see that is no longer necessary."

Albinia climbed down and ran to her father, embracing him. "Pa! Pa! You shouldn't have come, but I'm glad you're here."

"Well, I'll have to tell the warden about all this. He'll be wanting to see all of you, I reckon, to see if charges are warranted."

Julia commanded, "Put that pistol away. And you'll tell the warden nothing if you value your job. The governor has pardoned her because of my letters and those of my friends. Or would you like *us* to tell the warden how you were so derelict in your duty as to allow yourself to be surprised and nearly lost a prisoner?"

"Well, now ... I guess if you put it that way. And seeing as the lady was set free and all, I suppose no harm done."

"Exactly. Thank you, sir. I suggest you let us take my sister to town, and you can go about your duties."

The guard turned, muttering about high-minded women, and climbed back into the wagon. In moments, he had turned and headed back to the prison. Robert, Julia, and Albinia all embraced, laughing and crying.

* * *

The next day, at a hotel in Frankfort, Robert, Albinia, and Julia sat together, enjoying breakfast. Albinia felt like she'd been raised from death, to a new world. Her months in prison gave her a vibrant new appreciation for simple creature comforts, like good food and no one threatening her.

"What will you do, now, Binia?" Robert wanted to know. "Your ma could sure use your help at the farm, you know."

Albinia was surprised. "Why? Why aren't you helping her? Why do you need to fight?"

Robert said, "Most all able-bodied men have enlisted. There's talk of a draft, so I figure to defend our home, and do it while I have some choice in the matter. I have to get back to my regiment as soon as possible. I'm in the 19th Kentucky Infantry. When my time is up, I'll go back home. Hopefully, Will can come home too."

Julia said, "I've asked Ma to move to Cincinnati with me, but she won't hear of it. However, with Hiram in the army now, I may decide to visit the farm more frequently. If you're willing, Binia, I think we could work together to hire someone to help Ma while Pa is in the army. Everyone says the war won't last."

Albinia thought and carefully wiped her lips with her napkin. "Yes, I can help with hiring someone for Ma. However, I intend to go back to my own farm and continue doing exactly as I was."

Robert almost jumped up and exclaimed, "You can't mean it! You just got out of jail. Don't think they'll pardon you a second time."

"Binia, dear, you just can't," said Julia. "They'll be watching you."

"And so will God. I cannot sit by and watch people suffer because I am fearful for my own safety."

Julia reached over and touched the bruises on Albinia's face that she had tried to cover with makeup. "But next time, they may not just bruise you."

"It is a chance I will have to take."

* * *

February 1862

Albinia was getting settled into life on the farm again. Mabel and Franklin had kept it for her while she was in prison. She was determined to continue helping slaves, but knew she would need to be more cautious and find new hiding places, or simply put runaways directly on a steamboat, with as little time at her place as possible. She tired more easily after her long time in prison, and hadn't yet fully regained her strength. It was often full dark by seven, so she decided to retire early and get some sleep.

Albinia woke to the smell of smoke. She heard shouting and flames crackling. Her house was on fire! She quickly threw on a dressing gown and ran to the hallway, and down the stairs. Rex was barking furiously. She almost ran into Mabel coming out of her room.

"What's happening?"

"Some night raiders! They set the whole place on fire!"

"Where's Franklin?"

"I don't know. He heard a noise. I think he went outside to see. Took his shotgun."

"Let's get out of here!" Albinia grabbed Mabel's arm, propelling her outside. The two women watched as horses wheeled around. The men on horses wore masks and fired shots in the air. The fire cast an eerie glow in the darkness.

"Burn it down, boys! Every stick!" yelled one. One of the men set a torch to the haystack. Another threw coal oil on the barn and lit it. Soon the entire farmyard was engulfed in flame. Horses screamed in the barn.

Albinia moved toward it and was blocked by a man on a black stallion. Rex jumped to defend her, and the man shot him from horseback as his teeth sunk into the man's boot.

"You listen real good! 'Cause what happens to those horses and that dog is what's gonna happen to you! You got two days to get out of this county, out of the state. If you don't, we'll be back and kill you and everyone here! Two days! We're done with you stealin' slaves. If the state won't fix you, we will." He turned his horse and encouraged the men again. "Make sure it all burns, then head out. If the women try to stop it, shoot'em!"

Albinia then saw Franklin, stretched out on the ground, shotgun in hand. In the glow of the firelight, a red stain blotched his shoulder. He appeared to be dead. Mabel ran to him as soon as the men left. Albinia went over to Franklin, feeling helpless, and then cradled Rex's lifeless head, sobbing.

MORGAN'S RAIDERS

January 1862

Sickness had spread through the camp. Will and Archie were among the lucky ones who were not ill. The doctors and medics in the camp had little medicine or supplies to work with, and did the best they could. Fortunately, food was abundant, so they were able to prescribe diets that helped some of the ill soldiers to recover. Some got better, some got worse, and some men died. No one really knew why. Tom Logwood recovered, but four others in the company grew steadily worse. Will and Archie attended the first of many funerals due to illness in January.

Though not much fighting had really happened yet, Will counted himself fortunate to have the Springfield musket. Less than half of the men had good rifles. Many had shotguns, revolvers, and Bowie knives. Will hoped he could find a revolver soon. At times, he wondered if he should give his personal Springfield to a companion and rely on the Whitworth, feeling guilty that he had two long guns while others had none. Duke encouraged him to keep both, since rapid fire might be of use, and ammunition for the Whitworth was uncommon. He gave Will an extra rifle scabbard for his horse to carry the guns.

By mid-February 1862, the regiment prepared to move from winter quarters. The winter guerrilla actions they carried out continued to gain the attention of newspapers, which referred to them as "Morgan's

Raiders." Morgan liked it so much he began printing and distributing his own regimental newspaper, "*The Vidette*."

The weather was intensely cold, with sheets of rain and sleet. Movement along the muddy roads and paths was slow. Word was the Federals were advancing, and the Raiders were falling back south to Nashville. Some of the sick rode in wagons.

Will's mood was by turns impatient and bored. The few missions he'd been on were exciting enough, but there were long periods when he wished for the family farm in Lexington. He had no real desire for more killing, but if they were going to fight, why couldn't they get to it?

He rode behind one of the supply wagons, watching on all sides for ambush, but only seeing squirrels. His gray hat dripped a steady stream. Lately, he'd begun to sprout a beard. Rather than shave, he decided to let it grow, to look older. Now, however, the scraggly strands of it collected water that dripped on the pommel of his saddle. That night after they made camp, in spite of the weather, the order came that no fires were allowed.

Archie grumbled to Will, "How do they expect us to march or ride all day and not even have a fire to dry out with at night? We'll all be icicles by morning."

"You're right about that." He helped Archie pound in the stakes for the tent lines. "After little cabins all winter, now we just have this canvas. Reckon it'll snow tonight?"

Will looked up at the sky. "Maybe. I hope not, though. Just make tomorrow tougher."

"Well, if it does—do me a favor. Just cover me up and leave me here," joked Archie. "That way I'll see home before summer."

They crawled into their tent and huddled under blankets.

* * *

February 1862

In two more days, they were in LaVergne. Morale was at an all-time low. No one was calling the march a retreat, yet here they were in Tennessee rather than Kentucky.

Lieutenant West approached Will and Archie's tent.

"Crump, Moody! On the double—guard duty! Some men in the regiment think Christmas didn't include them enough. They're breaking into stores, helping themselves, and getting drunk with whiskey. Captain Morgan is not pleased. Try not to shoot anyone, but round them up and bring them back to camp," he ordered.

"Yes, sir!" They both snapped to attention and gathered their gear for the short march to town. They joined a group of ten to fifteen others who tapped for the same duty. Will checked his ammunition for the Springfield. They were near a railroad junction, so ammunition was more plentiful at present. He hoped he wouldn't have to use it. The marching activity actually felt good in the cold. The news of the fall of Fort Donelson and Fort Henry at the critical junction of the Cumberland River had not helped morale. He understood the reaction of some of the soldiers after the long winter months. Some had died without ever firing a shot.

Arriving in town, they saw a mob forming. Their fellow soldiers gathered around a whiskey keg in the street, taking turns getting a glass. A few fired into the air with their revolvers. Some actually broke a store window and grabbed cheeses and other food items. The town citizens were becoming angry. One man drew a revolver, only to have a soldier bash his arm with the butt of his shotgun, and then point both barrels at him.

West took command. "You soldiers! Stop and come to attention at once! Anyone who disobeys can look forward to stockade and cleaning latrines. Company, present arms! Company, take aim!" he bellowed.

Will and those with him aimed at their fellow soldiers. Will was shaking. He didn't want to shoot.

West's commands had the desired effect. The town people and the soldiers froze for a second, then the soldiers dropped whatever articles they had and formed up in lines of fours, at attention, although some rather unsteadily.

West did not hesitate. "Company, shoulder arms! Company, right face! You who were in the town, shoulder arms! Right face! March!"

Will followed orders. He glanced at Archie, and could see relief similar to his own. Violence was avoided.

❋ ❋ ❋

The next night, as evening fell, Will and Archie were cooking dinner. They'd caught some fish from the Stones River nearby.

"Too bad about Tom. He was a real good guy," said Will.

"Yeah, but when we joined the regular army, we knew discipline would change."

"At least he's just demoted to private. Getting drunk in uniform could have been a lot worse."

They both jumped to attention as they saw Captain Morgan come striding up.

"At ease, Will, Archie. I'm planning a little outing tonight, wondered if you might like to come along. We're just taking fifteen or so, a night raid. Interested?"

"Yes, sir!" they both replied instantly.

"Good, good," said Morgan. "Meet on the north side of camp in an hour. You have time to finish your dinner. Looks like good fishing today," he said, grinning.

"Yes, sir. Tennessee bass tastes mighty good after hard tack on the march," said Archie. "Not that we're complaining," he added hastily.

"See you in an hour." Morgan walked off, seeking his other volunteers.

❋ ❋ ❋

In the deepening twilight, Will followed the others on his horse, moving toward Nashville. The wind howled, and sleet hit his face like ice daggers. They moved out on the main road. Even after an hour, they saw no one moving. He could barely hear the clinking of spurs in the occasional breaks in the gusts. No one talked after Morgan said that their objective was to set fire to a steamboat, cast it loose on the river, and thereby possibly set Federal gunboats on fire downstream. Federals had moved into Nashville. By the time Will reached the city it was dark, but with a full moon that went in and out of cloudbanks. They communicated with hand signals. Will was at his usual position for such sorties, in the rear, Morgan at the front. Looking down a slope into the town, they saw a group of twenty or so Federal cavalry making the rounds on the streets. After a few minutes, Morgan moved out, giving the signal to follow. Everyone followed quietly, Morgan and his men about one hundred yards behind the Federals. Morgan communicated that five or six were to follow him, the rest to move into the thickets at the edge of the city near the river, to serve as a rear guard. There were a large number of tall brick and frame buildings next to the Nashville Wharf, and some smaller buildings back a couple of blocks. Will signaled Archie, and together they went to the smaller buildings. They went behind them, and Archie secured the horses while Will climbed a back stairway to the roof, where he had a clear view of the steamboat tied to the wharf. He primed and loaded the Whitworth, putting in a new cap, and a sight adjustment ring good for about five hundred yards. Will's intent was to protect Morgan and the others from any Federals who might come and interrupt them. At this distance, they wouldn't know where the shots were coming from.

Three men climbed into a canoe left by the bank and made their way out into the river. They almost tipped over, but were successful in setting fire to the boat. Will wasn't sure why the boat wasn't set adrift according to plan, but within a few minutes, the Federals on the shore saw the fire, and the cavalry troop came charging.

Will again felt that tug in his chest that came when he was required to kill to save his friends. He aimed more for the horses than the men, and managed to get off about five shots, each hitting its mark, before Morgan and the others came galloping back toward them. Just as he rose to run down the stairs, one of those with Morgan fell back out of his saddle.

Will jumped on Toby, ramming the Whitworth into its scabbard, and again took the rear as the Raiders galloped back toward camp. The Federals were in hot pursuit. Will heard the whine and whiz of bullets passing by, but he bent low over his horse to offer less of a target. Ahead, Morgan signaled for the group to split, some following a straight south path, others going southwest, to confuse the Federals and reduce their number, perhaps decreasing the intensity of fire. Galloping in the dark was hazardous enough without angry minie balls whizzing around him. Will began to pray, asking God's protection. Just when he was wondering whether he should dismount and shoot to protect the rest, Will heard the hoofbeats in pursuit fade. The Federals were giving up the chase.

Morgan signaled a walk, to rest the horses. Everyone breathed a collective sigh of relief. They walked for perhaps two miles, gaining the Murfreesboro Pike. Just as they turned onto the Pike, a Federal patrol came out of nowhere. Morgan signaled a charge. The Raiders gave a rebel yell and charged the surprised Federals like gray banshees in the moonlight, firing and screaming. It was over in seconds, with the Federals in full retreat, though they outnumbered Morgan's men. Will's heart hammered his ribs, but he joined his fellows in exulting on their victory as they road back to camp, arriving about midnight. Will and Archie fell into their bunks, exhausted from the emotion and exertion of the raid. Tomorrow, they would hold a brief service for Peter Atherton, the one of their company lost in the attack. He felt some guilt, wondering if he had stayed on the roof just another couple of minutes—might he have been able to prevent Peter's death? Will feared Peter might be the first of many. Tonight had been close. The whine of bullets around him was something new. Their previous night excursions had little resistance.

* * *

March 1862

The next day, the entire command packed up and marched to Murfreesboro. Will happened to see Morgan passing by.

"Sir? Why the retreat, sir?"

"Oh, I wouldn't call it a retreat, Will. Just a strategic relocation. I believe there will be some significant fighting in the days ahead. We are to be under Breckinridge's command. Besides protecting the rear, Murfreesboro has some other, shall we say, attractions? You should use your free time to find them," said Morgan, smiling.

"Sir?"

"I've found a young lady there. Perhaps you might as well."

"No, sir. Thanks, but I've already had my heart broken once. I don't care to venture it again, when life is so uncertain."

Morgan looked serious. "Ah, yes—I remember. And you were very kind when my wife died. Will, life is always uncertain. That's what I've learned. You think you know what will happen, but none of us really do. You have to take things as they come, grab life by the throat, and shake it till it gives you what you want. If you can't adapt to what life throws at you, you'll always fail. Good shooting last night, by the way."

Patting Will on the shoulder, he moved on through the camp.

Over the next few days, Will alternately spent time drilling and waiting for something to happen. As if by design to encourage him to follow Morgan's idea of relaxation, Will was not chosen to go out on the missions waylaying Federal messengers and supply wagons. Archie related how they surrounded messengers, interrogated them, and sent them back to their camp on foot, in their underwear.

Some of the other fellows tried to interest Will in trying the pleasures of the camp followers, women who acted as laundresses, prostitutes, or both, following the army from camp to camp.

"C'mon, Crump! Gotta have a little fun. You 'fraid of a girl?"

"No. I just don't want to do something I'll regret."

"Oh, I forgot—you one of them Bible guys. I'll introduce you to Bessie—she'll keep you a lot warmer tonight, and you'll forget all about that Bible."

Will just shook his head. "I'll remember just fine, especially when you're getting treated for the clap. No, I'll just read my Bible, thanks."

The next morning, after drill, Duke came to see Will.

"We're gonna have fun with some Federals. Morgan wants you to come. Bring some rope."

* * *

Will joined the group of about forty riding north. Scouts told them that the Federals were camped around the old Tennessee Lunatic Asylum. Will split off with Archie and Tom, lying in wait off one of the trails. Archie and he crouched behind a log, Tom standing behind a tree. After what seemed hours, but really only a few minutes, they heard footsteps, then saw a blue uniform moving down the path, as though just out for a Sunday stroll. Waiting until he passed, Tom came out from behind the tree and lassoed him, while Archie and Will jumped on him.

"Don't move," said Archie, leveling his revolver at the man's head.

Seeing his terror, Will said, "Do as you're told, no one will hurt you. Make a wrong move, you can tell it to St. Peter."

Tom pointed a rifle with a fixed bayonet at him. "Now, roll on your stomach, real slow. Keep your hands where I can see 'em or I'll use you for target practice."

"What you Johnny Rebs doin' here?" said the man, rolling over.

"We ask the questions. Put your hands behind your back," said Archie.

Will took a short length of rope from his pocket and tied the man's hands together securely, testing the knots.

"All right," Archie said. "Stay in front of us, march down to your left and down the hill path."

They arrived at a holding area at the bottom of the hill, where some Federal wagons had been captured, and about thirty other prisoners were being guarded, having been captured by other Morgan men in the thickets around the asylum.

Will and the others dropped off their prisoner and returned to their station, repeating the process three more times. In the end, they had about eighty prisoners. Most of the company started off toward Murfreesboro, with the prisoners in the wagons.

Morgan rode up beside Will. "Come with me," he said. Will followed him a distance off the main road, curious as to what Morgan had in mind.

"Here, take this. Put it on," Morgan said, handing him a Federal officer's overcoat, hat, and pistol. "We're going to have some fun."

Following beside Morgan, Will rode hesitantly. They rode down the main road, right toward the Federal camp. They dismounted, moved off the road, and, tying the horses, scouted ahead. Will could see a Federal guard station with about ten Federals lounging about, guns stacked about fifty feet from the guard tent. Some were drinking coffee at a little fire, some were playing cards. They seemed completely unaware of any enemy nearby.

"Follow my lead," Morgan said. "We'll circle through the woods and come from behind them. Move quickly between them and their weapons. We're Federal officers, not Confederates. Get as close to that sergeant as you can, and on my signal, put the pistol to his head. After he surrenders, we'll take them all prisoner. Don't let on anything. Understand?"

"Yes, sir!" Will grinned at the daring plan.

They dismounted and quietly moved in a wide circle into a ravine. They mounted and came trotting quickly into the guard station. Morgan placed himself in front of the stacked rifles. Will moved toward the sergeant.

"You there! Soldier! Just what are you men doing? Are you on guard duty or at a party? Attention, every last one of you. I'll have you under arrest! I'm Colonel Byington, Fourth Ohio. I've never seen such sloppy soldiering! Arrest that man, Lieutenant!" Morgan shouted at them.

Will quickly moved forward and cocked the revolver at the sergeant's head. "Give me your weapon, slowly," said Will. The sergeant grasped his revolver with two fingers and handed it to Will, grip first.

"Haven't you men been told there are Confederates not twenty miles from here? Slipshod guards like this allow that Morgan fellow to get away with his tricks. You should be ashamed of yourselves!" Morgan berated them. "Mount up!" he said, seeing their horses tethered a small distance away. The soldiers hurried to comply.

"Column of twos, we're in the rear. I'll take you to your commanding officer. Move out!" ordered Morgan. "Lieutenant, keep that pistol ready for any that try to run!"

Will rode just behind the sergeant, praying that no one would notice their gray trousers under the overcoats. Even though weaponless, ten of the federals would be hard to manage for just the two of them.

After ten to fifteen minutes riding, the sergeant turned and spoke to Morgan. Will drew the pistol from its holster, keeping it ready. "Beggin' your pardon sir, but aren't we going the wrong way?"

Will noticed smoke rising off to the east. Morgan drew his own pistol and cast aside the overcoat, showing his Confederate uniform.

"No," he replied coolly. "You are my prisoner. However, I shall not hesitate to shoot you dead, should you offer any sign of resistance. I am Captain Morgan."

The sergeant could not have looked more surprised had Morgan announced himself to be Jeff Davis.

"Let's move, gentlemen! I believe we might soon have company," said Morgan. He was behind the Federals on the left side of the road. Will dropped back on the right, so the Federals were ahead and between them. They increased speed to an extended trot, then a canter. It was difficult to control his horse one handed, bounce up and down, and keep his pistol trained on the Federals. Fortunately, they didn't seem to notice.

From behind and left, they heard the sound of a large number of horses coming fast. Bullets filled the air. One of the Federals tried to dodge off the road, but a shot from Morgan at his ear convinced him to stay with the group. Over fences and gulches, through fields and thickets, as hard as their horses could go, fled the one party and followed the other for ten miles. Morgan and Will never looked back, trusting to their evasive movement on the horses to avoid gunfire. They caught up to the main body of Morgan's men and passed them.

Will's horse took a fence, sailing over with a foot to spare. One of the

Federals on his side was trying to escape and turn back to those behind. As soon as he landed, Will aimed and fired. His aim was not precise. The Federal's hat flew off, and he looked over at Will in white-faced terror. He jerked his horse to the left, back in the direction of his fellows, unwilling to risk another shot.

In another few minutes, they reached the outer pickets of Morgan's camp. The Federals had fallen back, and now receiving volleys from the Confederate guards, abandoned the chase altogether. The prisoners dismounted, and guards marched them away. Will learned that in the main body of Morgan's troops with the wagons, most of the prisoners of the morning escaped due to the Federal pursuit. One of the Raiders died. Will dismounted and tended his horse, lathered and exhausted from the long frantic ride. Will himself was shaking, but Morgan clapped his back and congratulated him, seeming exhilarated by the day's events.

* * *

March 15, 1862

March had indeed come in like a lion, but was softening. The middle of the month found Will riding northeast with two companies, Duke and Morgan at their head. They skirted the main body of Federals to the west, going to Gallatin to disrupt the Federal supply line via the railroad. They stopped a short distance from town. Duke and Morgan went into town alone, using some of their borrowed Federal uniforms. When they returned, Will saw them laughing and learned that they had tricked the telegraph operator into getting them the latest news of Federal positions. The whole command then mounted and moved into the town, which was unguarded.

"Tear up the rails," ordered Morgan. "When the train comes through, warn them with some shots. Will, get up on the roof at the hotel. If you see Federals coming, warn us and pick them off—though the telegraph says there aren't any within ten miles. Still, be alert."

"Yes, sir!" Will took up his position and watched as the others set fire to boxcars of supplies on a side rail, burned the depot, and destroyed the wood sawing machinery.

No Federal opposition came. The men were in high spirits, singing and joking on the leisurely thirty-mile ride back to the Murfreesboro camp, arriving about noon of the following day. The joy was short-lived. Within four days, Will got orders to pack everything. They were moving to Mississippi. With the success they'd been having, he wondered at again moving further south. Would they ever get back to Kentucky?

* * *

Albinia surveyed the damage to the farm. Essentially, there was nothing left. Mabel walked to town earlier in the day and, with some difficulty, hired a horse and wagon, bringing the doctor back with her. He tended Franklin, weak from loss of blood, and left instructions for tending his wound, heading back to town as quickly as he could.

The farm was a charred assortment of half-burned boards. She managed to find a trunk that somehow escaped the flames, covered by sheet metal falling from the roof. The trunk contained one or two gowns, now all the material possessions she had. The horsemen had dragged burning branches through her fields, destroying any crops. The windmill lay in ruins. All her horses were dead. Her dog was gone.

"At least the hooligans didn't kill Franklin," huffed Mabel. "Though I expect they meant to. What will you do now, Miss Albinia?"

"What can I do? It's obvious that they'll be back. At least packing won't be hard," she observed with a wry smile.

"Where will you go? Back to your parents?"

"No. I'll never go back there. I'll try again to get Ma to come and live with me, and bring Lyddie. I'll go north, sell this farm for what I can get for it. I'll pay Franklin's expenses with doctors. You're welcome to come with me, though I can't offer much. I'll understand if you've had enough and want to go elsewhere."

Mabel brushed aside her graying chestnut hair, tucking it under her scarf. She didn't answer for a moment, her stout frame bent over Franklin, who was too drunk from the whiskey the doctor had given him to do anything. He just lay in the wagon, moaning occasionally. She straightened and turned to face Albinia.

"Thanks just the same. I'll go where you go. I'll not let these ruffians frighten me away from doing what's right. Besides, Franklin and I, we have nowhere else to go. He'll need tending. But I know he'd feel the same."

Albinia let the relief show on her face. "Thank you, Mabel! I was hoping you'd feel that way. Let's get over to Madison, in Indiana, and see what can be done.

* * *

April 1, 1862

The rain came in sheets. The Third Ohio was on the move, Luther and Hiram moving in the ranks. Hiram marched with the private soldiers, slogging through the mud. Luther was cold, and soaked to the skin. So far, there was little opportunity for his plans for revenge. He was becoming discouraged. He'd gotten to know Hiram, now about twenty yards ahead, and found him one of the more likeable whites. Moreover, Hiram seemed to treat him as a person, not a tool. They were moving south from Nashville, chasing the Confederates.

"Halt!" called one of the officers. Luther turned to see what was wrong. Just behind him, one of the cannons stuck in the thick mud. The horse was straining its traces trying to pull it loose, with no success.

"You there!" said the officer, pointing at Luther. "Grab the wheel, see what you can do to help."

Luther simmered with anger. What did they think he was, an ox? Nevertheless, he went and took hold of the wheel of the cannon carriage. He pushed with all his might as they urged the horse on, but it only moved slightly. As he fell back, sweating and breathing hard, he was astonished that Hiram appeared at the other wheel of the cannon carriage. He had two boards in hand, and put one in front of each wheel.

"Let's try it again," he said, motioning to Luther and the driver.

Together, they exerted their full strength on the cannon. This time, it broke free of the mud, rolling up onto the boards. Hiram made it look easy. He came over to Luther with a smile and stuck out a hand, then clapped Luther on the back.

"There's no telling what we can do together," he said. Luther smiled back, wondering at this white man.

* * *

As the regiment halted for the night, Luther moved along the line, taking horses, bedding them down for the night with hay and water. It had been a long muddy march, and he wanted nothing more than to go to sleep. The sky had been cloudy and threatening all afternoon. Now there were peals of thunder. As Luther led three horses to their picket line for the night, a flash of lightning hit a tree ten feet away, causing it to burst into flame. The horses reared, tearing the reins out of his grasp. He dodged the hooves and grabbed for the reins, trying to regain control, but the horses spun around, knocking him into the mud, and then bolted south for the woods.

As Luther picked himself up, cursing, an officer came over, hands on his hips, as the rain cut loose.

"You there! What are you waiting for? After those horses! You lost them—I can't have three men dismounted tomorrow because you can't do your job. Take a lantern and bring them back!"

Luther wanted to tell the officer what he thought of the idea and ask him if *he* could hold three terrified horses, but he swallowed it. They were in enemy territory. Being left here to make his own way would be suicide. Yet wasn't this officer ordering him to do just that?

"Sir, with respect, if I go out there by myself, a black man in Tennessee, I might just get scooped up and you'd never get your horses back."

"Oh, all right! Sergeant!" the officer yelled. "Get two men and accompany this black to find those escaped horses."

Luther barely heard the sergeant mutter under his breath as the officer strode away. But soon he and two others, Hiram and a private, brought lanterns and guns, using their rubber blankets as hoods to shelter from the rain.

"Move out!" said the surly sergeant. Luther took the lead, since he was held responsible. The tracks were evident in the mud, though the dark and the rain made following them through the brush more difficult.

Luther stopped to listen, but just heard the rain and more thunder. The horses had moved at a gallop. How far would they have to go in this mess, and would they find them at all? Again, Luther privately cursed the stupidity of the officer. They were just as likely to all get lost as well as the horses. Luther guessed they had gone about a mile, following the tracks. The impressions weren't as deep now, indicating the horses were moving slower.

They came to the banks of a small stream, and in a distant flash of lightning, saw the horses standing on the bank. Luther turned back and motioned to the others. The sergeant signaled to spread out, to keep the horses from escaping. They focused intently on the horses ahead. As they started to comply, a voice came out of the gloom.

"One more step, Yank, and it'll be your last. Drop the rifles and the lanterns, real slow."

Luther looked back and found about twenty men in gray surrounded them, rifles leveled at them. His heart jumped in terror. He looked for escape—there was none possible. Luther thought Hiram looked like he might try to fight, but seeing the rifles aimed at them, his shoulders slumped, defeated.

Out of the dark he heard a familiar voice.

"Hey, boys, looky what we got here! A black! You blue bellies so dumb you have to have a slave to lead you?" Jameson said, approaching Luther. "I know this one—I hear he's escaped. Doesn't know how to respect his betters." Jameson punched Luther hard in the stomach, causing him to double over.

"That's enough of that!" said a Confederate officer. "Bind their hands, take their weapons. We'll take them to Captain Morgan."

* * *

Luther, Hiram, and the other two soldiers in blue marched into the rebel camp. There were tents in rows, with one or two small fires. The rain abated. Men were sitting in front of their tents, cleaning weapons, talking, and looking at the new arrivals curiously. The soldiers brought the escaped horses with them, jeering that they'd learn to whistle Dixie.

Luther's mind was in a whirl. Was this the end? All his work to be free, and here he was, back in Jameson's clutches. He raged at himself, the officer that sent him, even God. How could God abandon him to slavery again?

"Captain Morgan, sir! These men were found sneaking up on our position. We surrounded and surprised them. We thought you might want to speak with them," said the lieutenant.

Jameson piped up, "Or shoot them. I'd take care of that for you, if you like, especially the black."

Luther couldn't stand it any longer. "You no excuse for a man, Jameson! You want to beat on the weak and the women, anyone who can't fight back. My momma tell me that you're my pa, but you just a devil. You untie any one of us, we'll teach you about respect!"

Morgan looked mildly surprised. "That true, Corporal Jameson? You this boy's pa? And you want to shoot him?"

Jameson laughed. "He's nothing to me. He's the whelp of some slut on my plantation. But I don't keep track of my dog's pedigrees."

Luther's eyes bulged, and he shouted, "I kill you! I kill you if it's the last thing I do!"

Morgan looked amused. "Well, it seems you are not popular. We do not have accommodations for prisoners, and are moving fast at present."

Jameson interrupted. "Let me have them, Captain. I'll see they don't cause trouble."

Now Morgan was annoyed. "Attention, Corporal! These prisoners are no longer your concern. You will speak when spoken to. Return to your tent! Lieutenant, bind the prisoners to trees until morning. I'll decide what to do with them then. You may question them, without violence, to see what you can learn of their unit and movements. Dismissed!"

Morgan turned back to his tent.

"All right, you. Turn and march that way," he said, indicating some trees. "You, Private, escort them. Tickle them with your bayonet if they get frisky. Tie them to the trees like Captain Morgan said. I'll be along to question them."

They tied all of them to the trees. Luther was tied to a medium pine tree, so tightly that sap got stuck in his hair. The ropes went around his arms and chest, in addition to those binding his hands. He was in a sitting position, and they did not bother with his feet, so sure were they that he couldn't move.

He heard Hiram being questioned—Hiram gave away little beyond their unit number. He tried his ropes, nothing moved. When he thought it safe, he whispered to Hiram, on the other side of the tree.

"Can you move at all?"

"No. I've tried. I think they use extra big rope on me because I am big."

Luther thought their situation looked hopeless. He could already see himself loaded on a wagon, chained, headed back to Ashland.

Suddenly, he remembered. His freedom knife! They'd taken the guns, but hadn't bothered to search him. Probably thinking who would let a black man have a weapon? The knife was in his boot. If he could get his boot off and kick the knife up near his hands....

Using his other foot, after a few minutes the boot came off. He was careful not to push too hard, lest the knife be out of reach of his foot. He pulled the knife along the ground with his foot. He prayed, "God, if you can hear me, help me now." He gave the handle of the knife a backward kick, toward the tree. He strained, and the ropes burned his skin. He shut his eyes tight against the pain. He tried again, craning his neck and trying to move his hands closer to the point of the knife blade. He got the tip between two fingers, and pulled it closer. Painstakingly, a little at a time, he moved the knife nearer to the tree, until he could just grasp the hilt. Then he began sawing with it, and in minutes his hands were free. Moving his arms to his sides with his hands apart created enough slack in the ropes around his arms and chest, and then he cut those ropes. He was free! He looked about, and was about to stand up, when he heard voices from the other side of the tree.

"Hey, blue belly! Those look like some nice boots! Mine got some holes. S'pos'n we trade, huh?" The soldier in gray set his rifle against the tree. Luther could see it just out of reach.

"Not my boots!" Hiram protested.

Luther figured the Confederate was busy, and wouldn't expect opposition. He quietly rolled to the right, crawling on his belly in the darkness. Now he could see the soldier, foolishly with Hiram's leg between his own, facing away from Hiram, trying to tug off a boot. Luther touched Hiram's arm and put his finger to his lips. All at once, Hiram kicked up with his massive leg, sending the soldier toppling backward. Before he could yell or make a sound, Luther brought the stock of the rifle down on the Confederate's skull, and the gray soldier went limp.

He quickly cut Hiram's bonds and moved to the other men, freeing them, leaving Hiram with the rifle. The Confederates appeared to be sleeping, all the other guards on the other side of the camp, toward the stream they had come from. Once free, the sergeant took charge. He pointed at the guards and shook his head. They couldn't make it out that way. He beckoned and they followed, moving at a crouch, around the outside of the camp, as quietly as cats. The sergeant pointed at Luther, and motioned him toward where the horses were tied. Luther nodded. If anyone could get the horses free without making noise, it would be him. The Union horses were used to him. They were still saddled.

Luther quietly crept forward to where the horses were tethered on a line. He untied one, led it to a companion, then another and another. The three soldiers mounted. Just then a shout rang out, "Hey! Them prisoners escaping!" Luther had meant to untie another horse and ride without a saddle—but bullets pinged around them and there was no time. At first, he thought they might leave him—but Hiram reached down with a big arm and lifted him up behind him. They turned and ran at a gallop, with havoc breaking out in the camp. Branches whipped them, and any moment they expected to stumble and go flying over the horses' heads. They headed south, away from the camp, then turned west, and finally north, crossing the stream they had earlier found at a lower point.

After they were across the stream, the sergeant held up a hand to signal a halt. The horses were breathing hard, and lathered. They listened—but there were no sounds of pursuit. Morgan evidently didn't think they were worth the trouble. They proceeded at a walk, rejoining their regiment the next morning.

SHILOH

March 1862

After leaving Albinia on her release from prison, Julia shocked everyone by declaring herself a Confederate sympathizer. She told no one of her true designs. She backed up her declaration by offering discounted shipping to Confederates.

"You'll ruin us!" declared Kristin. "I thought the whole idea was to remain neutral. What about your father, Hiram, and your sister? What about your fine notions about the slaves?"

"The South is winning the war," Julia said practically. "Most major battles have gone in their favor. The business at Donelson is just a temporary setback. We need to be realistic. Besides, my family is from Kentucky. My brother is with Morgan. You cultivate the Union people, you're good at that. Someone has to get business from the South, and I intend to do it."

She traveled to Richmond, intent on securing some Confederate shipping contracts. The rich Confederates did not yet entirely accept her. However, attending this dinner party enabled her to listen to conversations without seeming to hear.

"My brother is with Johnston in Mississippi," said one. "They're moving north soon."

"Yes, my son is on his way there from Georgia," said another. "He tells me he has a new sweetheart there."

"I've heard Morgan is moving south," said Julia innocently. "I wonder what's to happen."

"The Thunderbolt of the Confederacy? He'll show the Yankees something! It seems like they're going to get together and push the Yankees back to Maine, if you ask me!" said another. "And none too soon! My darkies are getting restless, talking about freedom."

A tall man with a dark beard in gray uniform with gold braid joined the group. "That's the spirit! What we need is field coordination, and one big push. It will be like felling a tree. You saw on one side more than the other, and with persistence and patience, it falls. McClellan and Halleck are all bark and no fight. We'll smash them, along with this upstart Illinois storekeeper, Grant, by Christmas. Wait and see. Spring is when armies move. Lincoln will be suing for peace. Why, when Johnston gets Bragg, Beauregard and Polk together with his own men in Corinth, Mississippi, we'll see something!"

Julia quietly excused herself from the group and slipped out, telling the servant she had a headache. He called for her carriage, and she went directly to a train station.

* * *

Arriving in Louisville three days later, she immediately telegraphed Kirsten.

March 4, 1862

Mama Kirsten,

I desperately need to see someone in authority in the Union army here in Louisville. Please use your contacts, and let me know.

Julia

She went to a hotel restaurant and sat to wait for a reply. Three hours later, a messenger came in.

"Paging Mrs. Johannsen—Mrs. Johannsen!" cried the messenger.

Julia waved him down. "I'm Mrs. Johannsen."

"Sign here," said the messenger, handing her the telegram.

She tore it open impatiently, and read

Julia,

I cannot imagine you have anything important to say. It is difficult to think any Union officer would see you at all. However, go to General George Thomas tomorrow and mention our name. He was friendly with Hiram's father. I urge you to come home soon, where you belong, and mend fences.

Kirsten Johannsen

Julia sighed in frustration. Her mother-in-law would never understand what she was doing, even if she knew. At least she had a starting point. She fretted at the delay, not knowing how much time she had before her information would be useless.

Accordingly she inquired where to go, and appeared at General Thomas's headquarters early the next morning.

An orderly greeted her, "Yes, ma'am? May I help you?"

"I need to see the general as soon as possible."

"Ma'am, if you'll just explain your business, I'm sure I can help you. The general is a very busy man. If it concerns one of the soldiers in his command...."

"No, it does not. Please tell the general that Mrs. Johannsen is here to see him. He and my father-in-law were friends. My husband owns the Ohio Zephyr steamship company, and I am representing his interests while he serves with the Union army. It is very urgent."

The orderly looked at her thoughtfully. "I must admit I am dubious. However, I shall inform the general of your visit. Please wait here."

Julia seated herself, drumming her fingers on the arm of the chair. In a few moments the orderly emerged, his manner changed to obsequious politeness.

"If you'll come this way, Mrs. Johannsen, the general will see you immediately. Would you care for refreshment, perhaps?"

"No, thank you. I must travel on as soon as my business is concluded."

The general's makeshift office was small and in disarray, as though being packed to travel. General Thomas was a large stout man, with a salt-and-pepper beard and wavy black hair, with a slight receding hairline. He stood as she entered.

"Mrs. Johannsen. I was grieved to hear of Gunner's death. Please accept my condolences."

"Thank you, sir."

"Please be seated. And now, I've no wish to be abrupt, but I understand you have some business to discuss. My time is limited at the present."

"Then I shall come directly to the point. Three days ago, I was in Richmond."

The general's eyebrows rose in surprise.

"A woman may travel more freely across borders than many men, and since I'm from Kentucky and have family on both sides of the war, I can do many things without raising suspicions. I attended a party with many high-ranking Confederates. My husband is serving in the Third Ohio cavalry, and my father in the 19th Kentucky infantry. Regardless what you may hear, rest assured that my loyalties are with the United States. I despise slavery. My sister was in prison for helping escaped slaves. You may verify all this."

The general nodded, motioning her to continue.

"I heard intelligence that may be of value to you, so I hurried to give it in person. The Confederates are massing a force near Corinth, Mississippi, to thrust north. They hope to surprise the Union troops, outnumber them, and push them far north. My information says the attack will come during the first days of April. I believe many lives could be saved if you move to counter this."

The general looked slightly amused. "Mrs. Johannsen, I appreciate your desire to help. However, you can hardly expect that I can commit the lives of thousands of men and valuable military equipment based on a party rumor. I should be a laughingstock."

Julia protested, "But it's true! I've asked other women whose husbands and brothers are serving the Confederates. You'd be surprised how much information women let slip when they think it can do no harm."

"I'm sure. But whether the women actually know what they're talking about may be another question, if you'll forgive me. And while I treasure Gunner's memory, for all I know, you could be purposely feeding me misinformation. Or the women at the party may have been deceiving you. As you say, you have family on both sides. Meaning no disrespect, of course."

Julia rose. "As you wish, sir. I have done my duty as a patriot." She withdrew a card from her reticule and laid it on the desk. "In future times, I may have more information. When time has proved my information reliable, you may wish to make use of it. I can be contacted at the address on the card."

General Thompson was apologetic. "I'm very sorry, but I'm sure you can understand my position. I shall mention your visit to General Buell. More than that, I cannot promise. Meanwhile, I urge you to be cautious. Passing information is a dangerous game, and not one often suited to ladies. My orderly will see you out."

* * *

April 3, 1862, Mississippi

Will and Archie were tired. They'd been traveling for a week, moving one hundred sixty miles southwest, to Burnsville, Mississippi. The weather was rainy often, slowing their progress. They'd just arrived today. Word passed down said they were moving north again soon, to attack. The camp was bustling with activity and preparations. Will sat outside his tent, not caring about the rain, only for the opportunity to relax a few moments. He made sure Toby got a nosebag of grain and checked the horse's feet for stones. Then the order came to move out again. They headed north, back into Tennessee, to a place called Pittsburgh Landing on the Tennessee River.

Will and the others of his company rode, with no time for fires and hot meals.

"You horse boys let the animals and us foot soldiers do all the work! Y'all afraid to get your feet muddy?"

"Naw, we just move ahead of you to the battle. Somebody's gotta make it easier for you boot sloggers," said Archie, laughing. "But we'll leave some Yankees for you if you want."

"You do that. I don't want to march all this way just to have a picnic," replied the infantry man.

Archie's horse spattered mud on the man, and he cursed.

The whole army seemed to move with an intense, grim sort of joy. They were moving to attack, not retreat. There was promise of a major battle, not just the skirmishes they had been in thus far. News spread through the camp that Morgan was promoted to colonel, which all the Raiders took as recognition of their work. The rain let up that night. Will and Archie pitched their tent. They could have a small fire after dark, as they were not yet close enough to the Federals to spoil the surprise. Using his new pistol, Will was able to bring down a swamp rabbit, which he and Archie stewed, supplemented with hardtack. Their tent pitched over a rubber blanket to keep out the wet, they settled in front of their fire.

Will felt jumpy. He'd been in fighting before, but somehow this felt different.

"Archie, how many Federals you reckon there'll be?"

"Don't know, Will. Thousands, I expect, judging from the number on our side."

"You nervous? I mean, about somethin' happening?"

"I'd be lyin' if I said I wasn't. But somehow, we'll come through. We been in some scrapes, like back in Nashville. We come out all right."

"Yeah, but we never took on a whole army before. It's like we been playing tag with the Federals."

"You think you'll be scared?"

"Only a fool ain't scared. I jes figger I'll be too busy. You just focus on not gettin' killed, on getting the guy that's trying to get you."

They were sitting on stumps by the fire, other tents and little fires around them like fireflies in the dark. The night had cleared. The incessant rain stopped, and they saw stars above. After a few minutes silence, each in his own thoughts, Will said, "Archie? I don't think I ever asked you. Why'd you join the Rifles to start?"

Archie chuckled. "Oh, glory, I guess. I never had nothin' my whole life. My pa ain't rich, we only had the farm. I'm no good at books like you. And in case you ain't noticed, I'm no beauty. Nuthin' to make the girls hearts flutter. I figgered with Captain Morgan—guess I should say Colonel—I had a chance to be something. The girls sure liked the uniform mighty fine. It made me feel important. Later, when everybody was signin' up, I could say I'd been there since the beginning."

"What about the killing? I never will forget the first Federal I shot. Does it bother you?"

"Well, of course. Nobody human can't be bothered by it some. But here in the South, even if we aren't in Kentucky, it's part of our home. The woods and fields here look like home. There's farmer's tryin' to raise crops and families. If'n the Federal didn't want to risk being shot, he shoulda stayed home. It's like someone bustin' through the door of your cabin, pointin' a gun at you, and sayin' he's gonna take what's yours or kill you. Nobody invited him. We could try askin' nice for him to go home, but somehow I don't think he'd listen. It's like he don't understand, unless I add a little lead from the Enfield here, to my argument." Archie stood and kicked dirt on the fire.

"We better turn in. Another long march tomorrow, I'm thinkin.'"

They were up before dawn, and moving out again, thousands of horses, men and equipment trudging through Tennessee farm land and woods. By about three o'clock in the afternoon, that Saturday, April 5, they reached their encampment. Men and horses were tired, and eager to set aside their burdens. They set up camp in a field just southeast of Little Creek, to be near a source of water. Will saw commanders down to the company level, like James West, go off to strategy meetings and return with orders on where to camp and sleep. They were to sleep in the order they would attack in the morning. No fires allowed. Morgan's troops deployed on the far left of Breckinridge's main force, near the rear.

"What do you suppose they're thinking?" Will asked Archie. "It's like being invited to the dance, then told to stay outside the hall."

"There's West. Ask him."

Will went over to the no-nonsense lieutenant. "Sir. I'm wondering why we're in the rear, sir, if we're being situated in the order we attack."

West gave him a half smile. "Corporal, because someone thinks we're just horse boys, and with the thick woods, they think cavalry won't be of a lot of use. Colonel Morgan is just as frustrated as you. Return to your post, get some rest. See to your horse. Tomorrow could be a long day, with surprises."

"Yes, sir."

They spent a somewhat restless but quiet night. At least it wasn't raining, though the temperatures were chilly. Will slept fitfully, dreaming again of the first Federal he had shot. In his dream, his mother Sara begged him to come home. All too soon the sound of reveille broke the stillness, and everyone began to move at once. Everyone was excited, jubilant as if going to a party. No one thought about death, the uninvited guest. Lieutenant West came and gave them a short pep talk, telling them the fighting had already begun. Will and Archie grabbed quick breakfast of biscuits and cold bacon. Will saw smoke above the trees with the dawn, and a dull roar and rattle of muskets that grew louder as time passed. Will's company brought up the rear, but they had orders to be ready to move out at a moment's notice. Will checked his revolver and his cartridge belt for the Springfield. With the dense woods, he doubted the Whitworth would see much use, but brought a few of the hexagonal cartridges in an extra box anyway. There would be no time to return after them.

They marched in the bright sunshine for about two hours. Will thought about Sundays at home, listening to Breckinridge in church, wondering what would be for dinner. It seemed a great day for a picnic. Instead, General Breckinridge, cousin to Will's pastor, was about to preach an entirely different sermon, made up of musket and cannonballs. Rebel yells would accompany the message rather than songs of praise.

The noise of battle drifted back to them—booms and thunder, screams, and the buzz and rattle of a thousand gigantic bees as musket balls filled the air ahead of them. Finally they came to the first Federal camp, just north of Fraley field, where the fighting started. Here Will nearly lost his breakfast at the effects of those bees. The Federal tents were riddled with holes. Someone's half-eaten breakfast sat on a rock. All manner of guns and equipment lay discarded, as though they were toys emptied out of a trash bin by a giant, scattered everywhere. The Federals evidently retreated in haste, with great surprise. As Will stepped forward, the mud oozed with blood, and it was difficult not to step on dead bodies, which lay everywhere. Most were in blue uniforms, gazing sightlessly at the morning sun. Many were horribly mutiliated—arms blown off, guts hanging out, parts of heads or faces missing. Here and there were piteous loud moans, from those not yet dead but too injured to fight. The Raiders hesitated, sickened by the sight, but then moved on. Will was on foot, leading his horse. Some men stopped to rob the dead or gather food from the tents. Will saw a pistol similar to his own in the hand of a dead Federal and stuffed it in his belt.

Will looked over at Archie, who looked as though he might throw up. "Some glory, huh?" was all Archie said.

"Order, men, form a line!" shouted Duke. Those who were foraging broke it off and formed ranks of fours. "We're to support Hardee," shouted Duke. "Our time has come."

Everyone stepped lively, marching faster. Someone started singing the regimental song that the Raiders loved, "*Cheer Boys, Cheer!*" The music lifted Will's spirits, helping him to forget the carnage. He sang loudly with the rest.

As they advanced, the thunder grew louder, drowning out their song. Soon shells burst in the air above them, and minie balls flew over their heads. To Will's left, a horse and man screamed in pain, as shrapnel from an exploding shell lay open the man's shoulder to the bone. Will watched in fascinated horror as the horse went down, the man's forearm and shoulder lacerated and bleeding. Looking ahead, when the puffs of smoke moved enough for him to see, was a line of trees, and then a field, clear to the road, with woods on the other side. From those woods erupted a wall of smoke and flame, followed seconds later by cannonballs dropping and shrapnel scattering in their midst. Will took cover behind a tree, but was worried for his horse, Toby, who had nowhere to hide, and occasionally whinnied in terror. Training held them both fast, and they did not panic or run. The gray line appeared stalled. No one moved forward into the hail of death from the batteries across the field. No one appeared to give direction. The sky grew increasingly dark as the sunshine of the morning gave way to an incoming storm. Will glanced back and saw Morgan and Duke rallying some laggards to move forward. Duke stopped near him, seeming to confer with a Tennessee recruit, then move on.

Will watched as a line of infantry formed and bravely stepped out onto the field. The Federal batteries roared with canister shot, and most in the front of the line fell. Those behind did not run but marched forward, resolutely, into the mouths of those yawning beasts. They gave the rebel yell and moved to a trot, forward. Again the cannons roared, and thirty or forty fell. The field fogged over in smoke. When it cleared, the gray line, or those who remained, was within thirty yards, Will guessed, of the firing cannon. He was afraid in the chaos and confusion, yet he hated to just stand watching soldiers slaughtered. If he must be here, why could they not help them? Still, he waited for orders. He suddenly realized that with the movement and smoke, any attempt to fire might hit their own men. The men in the field dropped to one knee and fired their rifles. Those behind them did as well, as the front line fixed bayonets. They charged, screaming their yell like demons possessed. Seeing that line coming, the Federals took to their heels and fled, leaving the cannon.

"Mount up! Push 'em to the river, boys!" commanded Morgan. Another battalion of cavalry on their left, the Eighth Texas, or "Terry's Rangers," heeded the call as well, and moved out with the Raiders across the field. They moved cautiously at a walk. Toby seemed calmed by the other horses moving, surrounding him. They moved in a line of threes, spread out across the field. Archie was next to Will. A few horses ahead on the right, Will saw the Lieutenant, James West. Duke was on the left and slightly forward. Behind them, a Confederate battery was moving up, hauled by horses.

Suddenly from the left, bullets whistled around them once more. They seemed to be aiming at the men with the battery. The blue uniforms were about one hundred yards distant.

"Threes left wheel! Charge!" he heard Morgan yell. Will drew his pistol, touched his heels to Toby's sides, and leaned forward as the horse quickly leaped to a gallop. He swerved slightly to avoid a boulder sticking up in the field, and a bullet whizzed past his right ear. In seconds, they were on the Federals. In the blur, Will aimed and fired his revolver over and over, switching to the second one. Archie went down, knocked off his horse. Wheeling left, Will saw a Federal aiming at West, so he fired—but too late. The Federal's weapon discharged, and West fell. Will fired again, and the Federal toppled over backward. Toby jumped over him as the Raiders continued the charge. Duke's horse moved in front of him just as another Federal fired. Duke cringed in the saddle as a ball hit him in the shoulder. Duke switched hands with his sabre, holding the reins in the wounded arm, then slowly fell out of the saddle, onto the field. Up ahead, Will saw Morgan's horse go into the trees, chasing a running Federal. He soon returned, and ordered the men to tend the wounded and round up the prisoners. Will rushed back to where he'd seen Archie fall. He was face down, a large pool of blood surrounding him. Will rolled him over, and saw the gaping chest wound from the fifty-caliber bullet. It was no use. Archie was dead.

* * *

Night of April 6

Late in the afternoon, the order came to fall back. They bivouacked just south of the Hamburg-Purdy Road. They made what simple camp they could. Darkness fell, and with the ebony of night, sheets of rain fell. Lightning and thunder boomed, as though heaven or hell joined in the battle. In the distance, Will could see the flash as the Federal gunboats fired their cannon. Whenever there was a break in the storm, Will heard the cries and pleas of the wounded left on the field. Occasionally a winking torch marked a group of brave soldiers going out to retrieve wounded. Will huddled in his pup tent, alone in the midst of the tents of the other Raiders. No one knew why the order to halt was given. The horrors of the day passed in his mind, including the cold dead eyes of his friend, Archie. Was it worth all this? Why was he here, really? Where was God in the midst of this hell? Suddenly it was too much, and he broke down sobbing, wishing for home. What if his father lay dead on some field, perhaps even this one? He thought about the fact that each of the Federals he'd seen dead today, and the companions in gray, had parents, siblings, sweethearts—people who loved them. This was nothing like doing drills in front of Morrison, or even the skirmishes they'd seen in the war up to this point. What compelled men to don clothes of different colors, like skins, march out on a field, and kill without thinking, based on the color of that woolen skin? Will prayed, asking God to make Himself real in this, and if Will survived, he made up his mind to go home as soon as his enlistment was over. He'd fight to defend his home, but only his own home, and no other. Will slept poorly, reliving the battle in his dreams.

* * *

April 7, 1862, Shiloh

The next morning, they were up before dawn. Will learned that Duke survived but West did not. Morgan's own brother died in the battle as well. They had barely eaten breakfast when the battle began. They mounted, and word passed down the line—their commanding general, Johnston, was dead. Beauregard was in command. More Federals landed in the night—General Buell had come with fresh troops. The Federals were coming. Morgan passed up and down the line, encouraging the men who were weary from battle and little sleep.

The Federals came in waves. It seemed to Will that every dead man in blue from the day before had become two live Federals, relentlessly marching and intent on revenge. Miraculously, few of the Raiders fell. Their job became holding the line, occasionally charging advancing infantry, as their own infantry fell back, then joining the retreat. Will lost count of the times he reloaded and fired, sometimes from the cover of woods, sometimes from horseback with the revolvers. He was running short of ammunition. As he moved to the rear to get more, Morgan approached.

"Will! Come, I need you!"

Will hurried over at a trot on Toby. "Yes, sir?"

"I want you to carry a message to General Breckenridge—you know who he is, you'll recognize him. Wait for a response, but don't assume we'll be in the same place you left us. Move cautiously coming back or you could find yourself surrounded. This day is not going well," he observed grimly. "Just go past a peach orchard and up the Hamburg Road," he said, showing Will on a map. "You should find Breckenridge there. Don't stop for anything—and hurry!"

"Yes, sir!" said Will, tucking the message into his shirt, behind his Bible.

Will grabbed ammunition for his revolvers and set off at a gallop.

* * *

The mud, rain, scattered bodies, and equipment were all hazards for riding quickly, leaving out the threat of rounding a bend and finding a group of Federals ready to kill or capture him. He whizzed past the peach orchard, coming to the fork in the road. Will focused on riding, occasionally slowing to a trot, both to get his bearings and to let Toby breathe, but for no more than a few seconds. Then they were again galloping along. Will heard sounds of battle all around but saw few troops, all of them gray. He rounded a curve and topped a small hill. There was rifle fire ahead, with gray to the south and blue to the north of the road. He slowed pace, looking for a way to get off the road. A Federal sprinted from the woods toward him, grabbing Toby's bridle. Panicked, he drew his pistol and fired point-blank at the face beside him, and again twice more into the woods where he could see rifles pointed at him. Then he kicked Toby hard, and the horse took off as though shot from a cannon. Will crouched low over his neck, giving the horse his head, and hung on. They raced through the crossfire of bullets. He felt something hit the rear of his saddle but kept riding. In a few minutes they were clear, and Will slowed Toby to give him a rest and regain control. After a minute or two, not wanting to risk being caught in a vulnerable position, he resumed at a canter along the road, ready to spur ahead at any sign of trouble. He soon came upon a line of Confederate troops, who seemed to be firing and falling back, but not yet south of the road. Seeing an officer, he asked for General Breckenridge and found him.

"Corporal Crump! Good to see you again, sir. Give this message to your colonel, if you can." Will related his encounter with the Federals on the road.

"Bad news, and no mistake," said Breckenridge. "All right then," changing his mind. "I see you have one of the Whitworths. That says something about your shooting. Perhaps I can put you to better use. I'll find someone else to carry the message back. Go on up the road to Shiloh Church. Find a good position and put that Whitworth to use covering the retreat. Make the Federal who wants to go to church meet his Maker before he gets there."

"But sir, Colonel Morgan...."

"No buts, soldier. That's an order. You're not the only one that can ride."

"Yes, sir."

Will followed orders and set up the Whitworth on a rise near the church. In an hour or so, lines of Federals came. A few other Confederate sharpshooters joined him. They picked off the troops as they advanced, sometimes aiming at officers, other times at those manning batteries, when they could see through the smoke. Then the order came to retreat.

On the Underground
Railroad

April 1862

Albinia looked the farm over. It lacked the good soil of her previous farm. However, it was near the river. She was on free soil, and would not have to worry much about the fugitive slave law here, she figured.

"What do you think, Mabel? Can we make this work?"

Mabel looked around, scratching the dirt with her toe. "Well . . . it doesn't look like much, Mrs. Horner. Franklin's still recovering some. How will we live? It's planting time now."

Franklin limped over to them. "Woman, ye worry too much. I'll be fine. I wouldn't mind another hand, mind ye, if you're aiming to grow anything beyond a garden. At least until I'm totally well. But getting a crop planted and a house built in a month or two could be a tough proposition."

Albinia hoped for better, but it matched her own views of the prospects. "Well, we lost a lot in Kentucky. About nine thousand dollars. I have about twenty-five thousand left, from David. Because of the Homestead Act, people want to move west and escape the war. We can get this place very reasonably, though riverfront property is harder to come by—we need a dock if we're to help the slaves crossing the river or coming by steamboat. This place seems to be what's available on the river.

The problem is finding men to help—they're all off fighting. However, the Negroes aren't. Suppose we ask the African Methodist church for help and pay Negroes the same as we would white people? Do you think we'd find enough?"

Franklin scratched the gray stubble of a beard and chuckled. "Mrs. Horner, I think you'd be turning men away—you'd have so many that wanted to work."

"Good! Then let's get started!"

Over the next few weeks, into the beginning of summer, Albinia watched as the farm transformed. Word in the community spread about her imprisonment in Kentucky, and many in the Georgetown black neighborhood of Madison responded with help. She stayed at nearby Bachman House, with Franklin and Mabel, until they constructed a house of their own. They bought horses, mules, oxen, wagons, and farming tools.

The house took shape, and they were soon able to move, reducing their expenses.

One morning, Albinia awoke early. Going out into the farmyard, she saw Franklin feeding chickens. "Franklin! I'm going into town. Can you supervise for a few hours? I may be gone until evening."

"Sure, Mrs. Horner—but shouldn't I send someone with you?"

"No, it's all right. I have a lantern and my old friends," she said, raising a double barrel derringer and a short shotgun for him to see. "Don't worry unless I'm not back by morning."

She drove the two miles into town, going to the Presbyterian Church on Broadway. She tipped a young Negro boy to watch her horse and wagon, going inside the church. She looked around hesitantly, and then spotted what appeared to be the minister coming into the sanctuary from the rear.

"Excuse me, sir. I'm new in the community. I'm trying to help with the plight of slaves and the Negro population here. I wonder...."

The cleric looked annoyed. "Yes, yes, I think I've heard of you. You're the one who bought a farm to the east, from Kentucky."

"Yes, sir, and I was wondering if your church might be willing to help."

After several days she arrived in Memphis, and discovered that Will was likely in Mississippi, along with General Bragg. She caught a train to Tupelo, figuring Bragg's headquarters would be the most likely place to look for information, both about the Confederate's movements and Morgan's location with Will. She disembarked the train, entered a hotel, and addressed the desk clerk.

"Excuse me, sir, but can you direct me to General Bragg's headquarters? I need to speak with one of the officers concerning my brother."

"Bless you miss, I expect the general is rather busy. Half of his troops moved out in the last few days, on the train. I hear they're goin' to Mobile, Atlanta, and Chattanooga. Prob'ly all be gone by tomorrow."

"Really? Well, perhaps you know of Colonel Morgan? My brother serves under him."

"Too late for them too. They are gone north, and I hear the Federals are chasing them. If your brother's with Morgan, I wouldn't stick around here. Federals may come in from the south, Alabama, any time."

"I see. Well, thank you, sir. I suppose I must make my way north, then. But General Bragg's headquarters…?"

"Well, down the main street and left on Spring Street. You'll see the activity."

Julia approached the headquarters, but hesitated about going in. Instead, she turned to a line of tents nearby.

The young guard stopped her. "Halt! I'm sorry, but you need a pass to go further, ma'am."

Julia thought a moment and assumed her most piteous look. "But my brother! I need to see him! My mother died, and I want to tell him in person. It's been months since we've seen him. I've traveled all this way from Kentucky. Can't you at least let me look for him?"

"What's your brother's name and unit?"

"Will Crump. First Mississippi," she said, taking a chance.

"Hmm, well, there is still some of them here, I reckon. I s'pose it can't do any harm, you bein' a woman and all, lookin' for him. But you gotta be quick. An officer catches me lettin' you in, ol' Bragg is apt to shoot me."

The minister sighed. "Young woman, you'll find not everyone around here is sympathetic with your views. Our community has had much trouble over slaves in the past two decades. This church has split over the issue. We want no more trouble. I do not believe I can be of help to you. You might try the African Methodist Episcopal group. Mostly black, I'm afraid, but more inclined toward your views."

"They are already helping. I thought surely some of the white folk, in a free state, might…."

"Not here," he cut her off. "You might try up in Lancaster. Oh, there are those in the white community with your views, but you'll have to seek them out. I believe there's a group in Lancaster called the Neil's Creek Antislavery Baptist Church. Now if you'll excuse me, I have work to do."

Albinia knew she was dismissed. She drove back to her new home, discouraged. This is supposed to be a free state, she thought. How many like that minister were there?

Her new house was a small affair—one story and four rooms, with a center chimney of local stone. The white clapboard sides and black shutters gave a clean but austere appearance. She decided not to waste money on luxuries except for glass windows. The wood still smelled new. There was a front porch, with rocking chairs. The kitchen and a small parlor were at the front of the house, with two bedrooms separated by a small hallway at the back. The house was about a hundred yards from the riverbank, enough to be safe in most floods, given the slope down to the river.

She woke the next morning and found that Mabel had already made coffee. She took a cup and wandered out to one of the rockers on the porch. No workers had arrived yet. After sitting for a moment, she noticed what appeared to be a piece of paper nailed to the railing of the porch. Curious, she walked over and pulled it loose, seeing writing on it.

GO HOME!—The Knights of the Golden Circle

Albinia's face turned white, then red with anger. How could they! She wondered if her visit to the minister had anything to do with this.

She hurried and dressed. "Franklin, this time I do want you to come.

Please have Mabel tell the workers not to come today. There may be trouble."

"Yes, ma'am," Franklin said. "But where are we going?"

"Lancaster."

* * *

May 1862

Julia felt heartsick after she read the casualty list from Shiloh. So many young men, some whose names she recognized. At least Will's name was not on the list, or Hiram's. From the account of the battle, her information had been correct. If only General Thomas had listened. She didn't know where Will was, or if he had been in the battle—she hoped not. She was determined that the Federals should win the war, and quickly. Many lives might be saved, and the demon slavery defeated. The Johannsens' shipping company could legitimately claim to be in no position to help the Confederates, since New Orleans had fallen. The Union mostly controlled the Ohio and Mississippi rivers. Shipping for the Federals and normal business along the rivers was now the only option.

For a few months, she returned to Cincinnati. There seemed little else she could do. Then she received a letter from Will, telling of the battle of Shiloh, and his desire to come home. However, Will told her that shortly after the battle, the Confederate Conscription act passed. It meant that all able-bodied men between seventeen and seventy in the Confederate army must serve the duration of the war or risk execution as a deserter, unless the soldier owned twenty or more slaves. Will told of seeing General Bragg order to shoot those young men who attempted to return home. There would be no escape for him. Will did not say where he was.

She cried for him. Oh, the evil of this war! Why could the South not see that slavery had to end? Why could the North not see that fighting was not the answer—though in truth, she acknowledged, the South fired the first shots. Mostly, why could people not see that hate, bitterness, and

selfishness were the real issues? What could she do? Perhaps she h given up too easily. Perhaps she could yet provide information that wou be instrumental in hastening the conclusion of the war.

It was July now, and the heat had begun in earnest. A servant enter and gave her an envelope on a tray. Tearing it open, she found a let from General Thomas, telling her he regretted not taking advantage her information in March, and to please contact him should she ha anything further. Julia exulted—now she could make a difference. If o she could discover something worthwhile of the rebel battle plans. must travel to where the Confederate commanders were, or at least th wives. She could use the excuse of looking for Will.

Kirsten disapproved of her traveling again. "Really, my dear, you t altogether too many risks! If you're going to run the company, stay h and run it. There's a war on! Telegraph communication to run a busin is not enough. Of course, I could do it for you, if you'd like."

"No thank you, Mama Kirsten. I know you are far too busy with y charity events. Besides, that is what I have managers for, to attend to day to day, and a good accounting firm to watch them. In spite of the we've been profitable. Hiram will be home as soon as it is over, please may it be soon! When it does end, the South will need to rebuild. That take a great deal of money and materials. Keeping contacts in the So will pay off later. And that is what I intend to do. I understand Gen Bragg is somewhere in Mississippi, and the rail lines there are ope intend to go there and see what news I can find of my brother."

"Stuff and nonsense! You'll get yourself killed."

"Perhaps—but that wouldn't bother you much, would it? I'm you'd pick out another wife for Hiram more to your liking. But accor to my last letter, Hiram is in the South also—I may be able to see o news of both. A wife has a right to visit her husband." She turned and with Kirsten spluttering behind her.

* * *

"Bless you," Julia moved forward and gave the boy a quick peck on the cheek. She moved quickly past before another guard challenged her, or the boy changed his mind.

A woman moving through the camp did attract some attention, but Julia walked quickly with purpose, as though she knew where she was going, to avoid questions. A regimental flag flew in front of a larger tent, with no one seemingly about. She hesitated, then approached, figuring she could always play dumb and lost if asked.

No one was in the command tent. The flaps were open wide. A table and chairs were just inside, with what looked like a map of Kentucky spread out on it. A quick glance showed troop movements. Impulsively, she took the paperweights off the map and folded it up. There was no time for real concealment, so she took off a shoe and stuck it inside. She moved quickly away, heading for the opposite side of the camp. *No one will stop me leaving*, she reasoned. *And if I leave by another way, the boy won't get in trouble ... or ask me questions*, she thought.

She moved quickly, not looking right or left. Ahead, a group of soldiers lounged around a fire. Not wanting to arouse suspicion, she kept walking straight ahead.

"Hey, pretty lady! Us soldiers ain't seen a belle for a while. Can't you stop and talk with us?" called out a private.

Julia's throat went dry. She knew she had to respond in some fashion. Her mother always told her 'You catch more flies with honey than vinegar,' so she put on a sweet face and turned toward them.

"You are too kind, sir. However, I am seeking my brother, with a message of some importance, and I must find him. I fear he may have left north already. I must hurry in case he is still here."

"Well, most of company D is off drillin'. Do you know which company your brother's in?"

"No, I'm afraid not," she lied. "I'm mostly ignorant of military things, just a poor woman, you know. Now if you'll excuse me...."

Another of the men got up and came toward her. "Hold on, there missy. Your brother might be in that drillin' group, and if you go, you'll plumb miss him. Anyway, I'd like to see your pass—ain't likely ol' Bragg or his officers would let you prowl through here without one."

"I already showed my pass to the guard. Now, really, I've tried to be nice, but I must insist on leaving."

"You mean this guard?" said an officer coming up behind her. Julia whirled and saw the guard who had admitted her to the camp. The officer had a pistol pointed at the guard.

"Private, arrest this woman! Take her to General Bragg—my authority."

"Yes, sir, Colonel!"

Julia's heart sank. They caught her. What would happen to her now? She must think quickly, and pray.

* * *

June 1862

Albinia arrived in Lancaster, and Franklin pulled the wagon up to the church. They heard hammering noises and saw a young man, sleeves rolled up, in denim trousers, working on the roof of the church.

"Hello! Sir? Can you tell me where to find the minister?"

The young man paused hammering and smiled politely, wiping his brow with a handkerchief, moving back a shock of curly brown hair. "I'm the minister. How can I help you?"

"Well, I, ah … could we talk for a few minutes? Down here?"

The minister's smile grew broader, and he climbed down a ladder. "All right, now we're on the same level."

"Thank you, sir. I am Mrs. Albinia Horner, and this is my hired hand Franklin. I've recently moved to the area from Kentucky. I have a farm down at Lonesome Hollow, on the river."

"Welcome to Indiana. Are you planning to attend church here?" His piercing green eyes lit with curiosity.

"Well, no. A pastor in Madison told me about your church. You are an antislavery congregation?"

"Yes, we are very opposed to slavery. What's your interest?"

"You see, I've been involved with the Underground Railroad in the past. You could ask John Rankin about me. I went to prison for a short while in Kentucky for helping slaves. I decided to relocate to Indiana. I'm trying to get the support of churches for helping escaped slaves make a new life."

"I'm Peter Jenkins. Nice to make your acquaintance. Our church has been quite involved in doing just the sort of thing you propose, Mrs. Horner." He shook hands with Franklin, and Albinia noticed muscles rippling. He really was quite handsome—she pushed the thought away.

"I've helped slaves over the border and on to stations in the past. My farm was burned down in Kentucky. I've started to receive threats here. Who are the Knights of the Golden Circle?"

Peter's brow creased. "If you've already run into them, you'd better brace for trouble. It's a group that supports slavery and keeping blacks in their place. They dislike the work we do with educating blacks and helping slaves."

"If I bring escaping slaves to you, can I trust you to help them?"

"Yes, we'll do the best we can. With the war on, slave catchers aren't coming as much. We help free and slave to either make a life here or get to Canada, as they wish. But what does your husband think of all this?"

"Oh. I'm a widow. My husband died in the Baltimore riots. He was a friend of Mr. Garrison."

"I see. My condolences on your loss. Well, if you'll forgive me, I will verify what you've told me. I'll be in touch. It was nice to have met you, Mrs. Horner."

"Thank you! I appreciate it. I'll look forward to hearing from you. My contacts in Kentucky may be of some use."

Albinia mounted the wagon. As Franklin drove home, she couldn't get the young minister out of her mind.

You Can't Go Home Again

July 1862

W ill rode onto the grounds of Cumberland University in Lebanon, Tennessee, discouraged and disheartened. It was the mid-July. He began to doubt the point of fighting. The dark and the sheets of rain reflected his mood. He wasn't the only one who thought of quitting after Shiloh, but within days, the Confederate conscription law eliminated that possibility. He was stuck for the next two years at least. Their enlistment time extended to three years.

His only cause for hope was the letter he'd received. He had no idea how it could have found him—the Raiders had been on the move almost constantly. The letter was from Jenny.

April 20, 1862

Dear Will,

I hope you may forgive me, and receive this letter. Joe and I have broken off our arrangement. I've realized how much I care for you. My uncle lost an arm. He is no longer in the army. He's told me some of the terrible things you must have endured. I know now that you were never fighting for slavery, only for honor. This terrible war is ruining so many lives. When I heard that you were at Shiloh, I

read the casualty lists and realized how devastated I would have
been if you'd died.

I know you are committed now until the end of the war. I pray
it may come soon. If ever you are near, please come and see me, if
you will forgive me.

With great affection,
Jenny Morton

Will remembered his father's words about the fickleness of young women and wondered whether to be encouraged. He'd just about closed that wound, but the memories of the carnage at Shiloh, the stacks of feet, arms, and legs outside the hospital when he'd visited Duke left him needing hope. Archie was gone. How many more friends would die? He'd heard that over one thousand seven hundred had died in the battle.

He dismounted, tied his horse, and spread his rubber mat on the wet ground, getting his small tent up quickly to avoid being drenched. He tended his horse. Exhausted, too tired to consider Jenny's letter, he fell into a deep dreamless sleep.

* * *

He woke to shouting, followed by gunfire. All around him, men were hastily mounting up, leaving everything but weapons behind. It was still dark and raining hard.

"Federals! We're under attack!"

Fear gave Will speed, and he quickly mounted. A minie ball whizzed through the tent where he had just been sleeping. Others in his company fell back to a stone fence, dismounted, and prepared to return fire. Will joined them.

Crouching behind the stones for cover, he loaded the Springfield and fired just below the muzzle flashes of the Federals. Another company of Raiders on their right joined the fight, but there was no order. Will wondered how long it would be before the Federals surrounded them. A few brave ones decided to mount a running charge, but fell before a volley.

Suddenly Morgan rode up on his black mare and rallied the troops. Everyone took heart at seeing their commander. Morgan ordered them to hold their fire and let the Federals approach. After a minute or so of quiet, the Federals grew confident and surged forward. At about forty yards, Morgan ordered "Fire!" The Federals fell, and those still alive retreated. A few on horseback couldn't stop and rode in among the Raiders. The Raiders took these prisoners, including a parson and the colonel of the regiment.

"Please, sirs, let me return to my regiment," pled the parson. "I must pray for them."

Another of Will's company spoke up, "The hell you say! Don't Morgan's men need prayin' for just as much?"

The Federals regrouped and tried again. They surrounded other Confederate companies. Morgan, seeing the trap closing, yelled, "Follow me!" and took off up the Carthage Road. Will wondered at his not staying to reform the men and continued firing, until only a few of his company remained and the Federals were about twenty yards away. Mounted Federals came from the rear, sabers drawn, approaching Ben Drake, still firing. Will shouted a warning, "Come on, Ben! No sense getting caught!" Will spurred away after Morgan. Glancing back, Will saw Ben barely mounted in time, and then they were riding together at the rear of Morgan's column. It was not an orderly retreat. Will didn't have time to wonder how they had been surprised. He watched the path in the early dawn breaking now, and zigged and zagged to throw off the aim of the hotly pursuing Federals. Toby gave his best dodging boulders, jumping logs, avoiding mud holes, galloping. Will had no idea how many were chasing them, but the hail of bullets gave testimony that it was more than a few. They gained some space, now more than two hundred yards ahead of the Federals, and the bullets ceased. They could hear yelling behind them. They came upon Tom Quirkey, one of their company, dismounted. He'd been riding a captured Federal horse that threw a shoe. Tom ran sideways, into the woods. Later he passed them, on another horse, from one of their company who'd been hit. Both Ben's horse and Toby began to show the strain—they'd been galloping for miles. They passed Morgan, discovering that his bridle had broken, but he urged them on. Will and Ben turned north onto side roads. The sound of the Federals was approaching again. Morgan came dashing up from behind, passing them. They pounded on, and came to the ferry at the Cumberland River, about twenty miles from Lebanon. Their horses were totally spent. The ferry was on their side of the river. It pained Will to leave Toby, but seeing Morgan leave his famous Black Bess, he felt there was no choice. They escaped—but only about twenty men. It seemed to Will the rest were gone, probably captured.

* * *

The next day, men from Morgan's command straggled in by ones and twos, all through the day.

"What happened, sir?" Will asked Morgan.

Morgan sighed. "Apparently our picket guards all retreated to a house for the night to be comfortable. One of them saw the Federals and rode to me as hard as he could, but they shot him just as he reached me. We had no warning beyond that. Now we shall have to scout for horses and supplies. I heard you saved the Whitworth—good man. Many have no guns at all now."

They camped at Sparta, provisioning and recouping. They recruited new men. Will got a new tent mate, Thomas Hines. Another man, said to be a wizard with a telegraph, joined them, "Lightning" Ellsworth. To the delight of all the old hands, Duke joined them, recovered from his shoulder wound. Soon they had a force of one hundred fifty. Morgan promoted Will to brevet second lieutenant. By May 9, they moved north toward Glasgow, Kentucky. Will felt his new responsibilities, leading ahead and to the side, rather than his usual place in the rear.

The Home Guard thought them too strong to risk an attack, but heralded their coming by blowing conch shells heard for great distances. They had to take to side roads to avoid them.

They moved quickly, hoping to catch up to the train carrying their men captured in the Lebanon disaster. However, that was not to be, as Morgan discovered the men were shipped north by boat. Instead, they marched overnight to the area around Cave City. Scouting ahead, they found a stretch of the Louisville and Nashville railroad that was undefended. A long train full of Federal troops with horses and supplies was coming.

"Will, Duke, Hamilton—I want you to cut off any retreat the train might make. Bedsloe, you take the front—tear up the track, make them stop. We'll seize supplies, horses, and prisoners. The Federals think us destroyed, that the Raiders are no more," said Morgan.

"They'll soon learn differently!" said Duke.

Will and the others waited in ambush until the train went by. Then he and others in his company threw logs, boulders, and any large object they could find onto the tracks. The train seemed unaware of its danger, even increasing speed.

Suddenly they heard the squeal of wheels on the rails, sparks flying. Will and the others came out of hiding, ready for anything. A Federal officer stepped out onto the platform, firing his pistols, but one of the new men, Ben Bigstaff, fired at him with a rifle, narrowly missing him. The officer then saw twenty or so rifles pointed at him, and dropped his pistols. There was no further resistance.

Will supervised unloading the supplies and horses. Now most of Morgan's command would again be mounted. Will chose a long limbed Friesian, liberated from a Federal officer, and named him Shadow. They captured two hundred prisoners, along with food, ammunition, tents, and most of the things left behind in Lebanon. Will saw one of the women on the train beg Morgan to let her husband go, which he did. Morgan did not burn the train, for the sake of the ladies. After confiscating weapons,

Morgan promised to parole most of the prisoners, to enable the Raiders to move quickly.

Will searched the train, to see what the men might have missed. He found a strong box in the coal car and brought it to Morgan.

"Good work, Will! Get a crowbar and open it!"

"Yes, sir!" Will and a private soon had the box open, and saw thousands of dollars in greenbacks, United States money, staring back at them.

Morgan laughed. "I think this calls for a celebration! Go over to the hotel and order a banquet for all the men and our Federal guests. We'll pay the bill with the Federal's own money!"

A few hours later, Will and all the Raiders sat down to dinner with crystal and china, across from the Federal soldiers. Had they met under different circumstances, they might have been shooting one another. Will escorted some of the wives back to the train, making sure they had every reasonable comfort. The engineer backed the train onto a siding and turned it back to Louisville.

They marched north, going northwest of Lexington. Will would have loved to go home and see his mother. He also wanted to see Jenny. The command was moving quickly, however, and they were not in friendly territory. He contented himself with posting letters to Jenny, his mother, and Julia at Versailles. The next morning, Will saw Morgan and Duke in high spirits and wondered what could have happened.

"What's the good news, sir?" Will asked Duke.

"Oh, nothing, nothing. It's just that our dear Colonel Morgan rode into Lexington last night, under the very noses of the Federals. Someone saw him and sounded the alarm, so he rode his horse through the door of his mother's house on Mill St., gave her a kiss, then rode out again with twenty Federals giving chase. Gave'em the slip, though." Will shook his head in wonder.

Morgan and the Raiders skirmished and burned, causing chaos for the Federals. Then Will heard that Morgan had received orders to go to Chattanooga. After ten days forced march, they rested for two or three weeks in Chattanooga. More recruits joined, and with all the new men, drills were intensified. Few of the original group from the Rifles remained. Will could barely keep track of the changes in rank, company, and function. A group of three hundred arrived from Virginia to join. The command received two howitzers and swelled to nearly nine hundred men. Duke was now lieutenant colonel. From disaster in Lebanon, they had grown again into a large fighting force. Will rarely saw Morgan now, tending instead to his own group of twenty new recruits. It felt good to rest. It even felt good to drill, a change from actual fighting. Everyone talked of a new northern push, to free Kentucky from the Federals and end the war. Soon they were on the move again, marching from Chattanooga to Knoxville, then on to Sparta, where they found their camp of two months before overgrown with weeds, but otherwise little changed. The roads were rough, and traveling two hundred miles in a few weeks was exhausting. Their recent success revived Will's spirits some. Most important, they were on their way home!

* * *

September 1862

The Confederates had them surrounded. Luther looked over the earthworks he was digging, trying to see the severity of the danger. It was mid-September and still hot. As long as he was in the midst of Union troops, he was safe. Yesterday, here at Munfordville, the Confederates had suddenly come out in force, but were not yet attacking. He didn't know why. He was frightened—if the Confederates captured him, he'd be put in chains.

He resumed digging for another hour, concluding that the earthwork was tall enough to block rifle fire and broad enough to withstand a cannonball. There were perhaps twenty other men similarly engaged. They called their earthwork creation Fort Craig. He was wiping the sweat from his forehead when over near the bridge on the Green River about forty yards away, a group of Confederates advanced with a flag of truce. He decided to move toward the headquarters tent, since no one would likely trouble to tell him what was happening.

He pretended to be busy, no one paying him any attention.

"We come to offer y'all a chance to surrender," the Confederate officer was saying. "You're outnumbered, and surrounded. No sense in y'all dying when you haven't got a chance."

Colonel Wilder, the Union commander, responded, "Mighty generous. If it's all the same to you, we'll fight a while. Might be the tables will turn."

"Not unless the Almighty Himself comes to fight for you. One last chance."

"Not today," said Colonel Wilder.

"Suit yourselves. May God have mercy on you, for Bragg will not."

Within an hour, the shelling began. The air seemed to rain iron and shot. Men pressed against the earthworks, returning fire, but the Union forces had only six guns in their battery. Luther, not allowed to fight, manned bucket brigades putting out fires and saddled horses. One of their officers was determined to mount a sortie, to drive back the rebels, and perhaps break through.

The fort was in the shape of a five-pointed star. Anyone poking their head up on the southeast side of the fort got their head blown off almost immediately. It could only mean one thing—Confederate sharpshooters. Luther saw a private's brains spatter the man next to him, who immediately ducked. Thinking quickly, Luther went and dragged the dead man away from the wall, and took his pistol with its ammunition belt, thus arming himself. He moved quickly back to the horses. The sortie was mounting up. Luther saw little chance of survival for the surrounded Union troops. He didn't want to be caught there. He grabbed an extra horse for himself and followed. If there was a chance of getting out of here, this was it. A desperate chance, he thought. The prospect of a hundred lashes in a public square spurred him on.

He followed at the back of the group, staying a few yards behind. Everyone seemed intent on staying alive and didn't pay him any heed.

Hiram was near the front of the group. Luther worried that his friend would make too big a target. They rode northwest, toward the railroad bridge. An occasional shell from the Confederate cannon whistled their way, making them accelerate for the river. Just as their officer reached the river, preparing to swim his horse across, Luther saw them.

A group of four or five Confederates stood from their hiding places near the riverbank and took aim. The first one seemed to have their officer in his sights. Luther decided in that split second, kicking his horse to a gallop. He shot the lead Confederate and ran his horse over two more, knocking them aside, then wheeled and shot another. By this time, the Federals recovered and shot the other two. It was all over in ten seconds. The Union soldiers, even Hiram, looked astonished, wondering where he'd come from, but this was no place for a parley. A canister hit the beach and splattered death about one hundred yards away, and shrapnel embedded in the tree near Luther's leg. They all pushed on rapidly across the river, reaching the streets of the town. Luther wondered where they were going, but as long as it was away from the Confederates, that was good enough for him. He heard firing off to the left and ahead. In a few moments, a picket challenged them—one in blue. It turned out they'd found Konkle's battery and the 68th Indiana infantry. This brought the welcome news that reinforcements were on the way, from Dunham and Buell. There was no need to ride further north. Reinforcements were already coming as fast as possible. Luther saw the officer from their sortie conferring with Hiram, and Hiram pointing at him. The officer came over to him.

"Sir, I am Captain Horace Howland. I believe I owe you a debt. In spite of the fact that you were not supposed to be part of our expedition, which I'm inclined to ignore, you fought well. You were brave, and your interference was very timely."

Luther was astonished to have such courtesy by a white man. "You're welcome, sir. I just don't want to go back to those graybacks and what they'd do to me. I wish I had the chance to fight as a regular soldier."

Captain Howland seemed amused. "Well, you've certainly shown some ability in that area. To show my gratitude, and since we are short-handed, I'll see that you're issued a rifle. I cannot make you an official part of the company. But I may turn a blind eye to you accompanying us in a fight from time to time. You've shown that you know how to ride a horse as well as shoe one. If things go poorly for us, I personally guarantee you will have a way to escape before the end."

"Thank you, sir!" said Luther, smiling with disbelief. The captain wheeled his horse and turned toward the battery. Hiram trotted over.

"Luther, you do very brave today. I am honored to call you a friend," he said, sticking out a hand. Luther was dumbfounded—a white man wanted to shake hands? Luther shook his hand, but even his blacksmith muscles rebelled at the crushing from Hiram. "Oh, sorry," said Hiram. "Sometimes I forget. Are you all right?"

"Yes, I'm all right."

"Stay close to me in the battle."

"Mr. Johannsen, right?"

"Just Hiram."

"Don't I recognize you from somewhere? Like before the army, I mean?"

"Perhaps. I'm from Cincinnati, and Sweden before that, but I spent a good deal of time in Lexington. My wife Julia is from there. Julia Crump, before we married."

"She wouldn't have a sister named Albinia by any chance?"

"Yes, yes, she does. But I heard Albinia was put in prison for helping slaves. I haven't gotten a letter from my wife for some time now."

"Albinia the one that set me free. I'm proud to know you."

They both returned their attention to the battle, seeing a wall of gray across the river, headed for the fort. There was no way to rejoin their command, as a swarm of Confederates charged up the hill to the fort.

As evening fell, Luther saw nothing but Confederates around them. His mind raced—how would he get free? He'd never thought about being in a situation where he risked being in chains again.

Hiram approached as he knelt by the campfire. Out of habit, he stood.

"Luther, the captain he says come now. It doesn't look good for the troops. Part of our army broke out to the south. He wants me to go find them, take them a message, and you come with me. It's a risk, but he think tomorrow might be too late. He says he promised you a way out. But you have to come now."

Luther looked around. "All right then. Let me grab my knapsack and bedroll. Any food for us? And what about that rifle I was promised?" Luther still had the pistol under his jacket that he used for a pillow.

"Already in the boat," said Hiram. "We have to be quick, before the moon comes up. We're floating right past the Confederate batteries."

Luther didn't argue. He grabbed his bag and followed Hiram to the river.

* * *

Albinia used her contacts in the Negro community to inquire about Pastor Peter Jenkins. The reports were universally favorable. She figured if he was going to check up on her, she might as well do the same regarding him. Following this, she sent messages south on the Underground Railroad, to let people know she was taking in slaves again. With the Federal occupation of Kentucky, the trickle of slaves became a small stream. Most nights, she or Franklin lay awake, looking for lantern signals from the other side of the river. Occasionally a wagon came in during the day, crossing the bridge.

One bright full moon Saturday night, there were lanterns waving, and Albinia went down to the small landing they constructed for the arrival of boats. Within a few minutes a boat arrived, containing one white man at the oars and a young black family with three children, two boys and a girl. She helped them out of the boat and led them to her barn. Most times now, with less fear of slave catchers, she let them walk north from her place, giving them food and directions. This time, on impulse, she decided she would drive them north in the morning.

"I'm Moses Jones, and this here my wife, Patty. Our young'uns Joe, Katy, and the baby is Ben. The Confederates, they say I got to serve in their army. I ain't goin' to fight to keep my family in chains. So we run north all the way from Alabama."

"Rest easy here till morning. I'll drive you north to a pastor friend. I'll see you have food and he'll help you decide what to do next. You're free!" said Albinia, smiling.

The next morning they loaded a wagon, and Albinia drove north to Lancaster with the family.

"Why so early, Mrs. Horner?" asked Franklin.

"Oh, I just love the early morning. And not so many people on the roads to ask questions."

Mabel snorted. "Couldn't have anything to do with that young minister up there and getting there in time for church now, could it?"

Albinia blushed but said, "Why, of course not. I hardly know Pastor Jenkins. He seems a very … proper man of God."

Mabel smiled and kept kneading the bread dough. "Ye needn't play innocent with me, dearie. I've noticed him making a trip or two here when there was scant need, just to check on you. It's all right—I've prayed for ye to find an honorable man. It's been more than a year since ye lost Mr. Horner. It's time."

"Nonsense," protested Albinia. "He's just a good man, dedicated to God and helping the slaves. I'm a widow. I'm sure he could have his pick of young unmarried ladies. Besides, how could I be a pastor's wife?"

"Quite easily," said Franklin, "if my opinion is of any worth. If you're going to hear him preach, you'd best start."

"You two are impossible with your matchmaking," said Albinia. Once on the road north with her charges, she had to admit the thought was not unpleasant. Mabel was too close to the truth.

* * *

Julia wanted to pace in her dark prison cell, but her shackles would not allow it. Since she was captured at Tupelo, she'd been dragged along with the army from one camp to the next, ostensibly because the general officers did not have time to consider her case. Privately, she thought they simply didn't know what to do with a rich female spy. After days on end on the train, chained to a seat, and more days rolling in a prison wagon, she arrived at this barn converted to a prison. Since there were no other women prisoners, she was forced to be in with the men, most of them Confederate soldiers who violated Bragg's niggling rules.

She would be tried the next day.

* * *

Luther and Hiram made good their escape, joining other elements of the Army of Ohio. They heard that Wilder surrendered all four thousand men of their unit, but they were free a few days later. That meant their unit couldn't fight for a time, under terms of their parole. Hiram and Luther were gladly received into the other battalion of the Third Ohio. Luther carrying a rifle met with some consternation, but Hiram vouched for his story, and he won grudging admiration. He learned to shoot quickly, soon accurately picking off targets at fifty to one hundred yards. In view of the recent Emancipation Proclamation, the commander was inclined to allow Luther to fight. Luther could hardly believe the Proclamation. He felt at once joyful and bitter. That Lincoln fellow said the slaves were free, in the Confederate states, at the start of the New Year. It was September, and if the Confederates didn't rejoin the Union by January 1863, Lincoln declared all their slaves free, and negated the Fugitive Slave Act. However, it didn't really apply to him—Kentucky was a slaveholding state but had not seceded. Luther was still technically the Clays' property. The war changed things, however. He'd been in Kentucky a while now, and no one made a move to reenslave him. He couldn't trust all the white men, but he didn't think most of the men in the Ohio regiment would allow him to be put back into slavery, even if they did still think him inferior to themselves. The Proclamation would clear the way for Negroes to fight in the Union army.

Though they started south of Munfordville, their new battalion moved west and north, retreating toward Lexington.

* * *

Will took position on a high hill in his old role of sharpshooter. That morning, they had marched north over a bridge near Gallatin and found the body of one of their men, a scout Morgan sent north. The townsfolk said that the Federals abused the body after killing him, and propped him up to be a warning to Morgan. Enraged, the whole 2nd Kentucky, now about one thousand men, set off after the Federals.

From his position, Will could see through a glass the Federals behind stout stockades, shooting out at the line of his comrades, forcing them to take cover at the side of the road. Three men fell, wounded or killed, Will couldn't tell. He loaded the Whitworth and set it on a log for support as he lay hidden. Every time a Federal head popped out above the stockade, the Whitworth barked. Soon the fire from the Federals decreased greatly. Will reloaded and paused, looking through the glass. He saw his old nemesis, Ben Drake, recently promoted to lieutenant, lead a charge up the hill toward the stockade. Two Federal heads popped up and took aim. Will didn't hesitate—he took up the Whitworth and began firing as rapidly as he could, reloading, firing. The first two Federals toppled backward. Ben and the others ran forward. Other Federals tried to fire. The line with Ben knelt and fired a volley of their own, reloading quickly, fixing bayonets, and charging again. Will kept such a steady rate of fire he thought he might exhaust his cartridge box. The barrel of the Whitworth was hot. Then Ben and the others gained the stockade, and it was over in seconds. The Federals were defeated.

Later in camp that night, as Will sat in front of the fire, he was surprised to see Ben approach with Jesse. They were equal in rank, so no ceremony was needed. Ben seemed a little awkward.

"Will? I ... I ... just wanted you to know—I heard what you did today. It was you shooting up on that hill. I know we haven't been the best of friends, but I want you to know I appreciate what you did. You could have held off, you could have been just a little slower to load—no one would have known, and I wouldn't be standing here now. I could have been like Niles and Smith when they attacked that last stockade. I just want to say thanks—and I wonder if we could bury the hatchet?" he said, sticking out a hand.

Will rose and went forward, taking the proffered hand and shaking vigorously. "Nothing I'd like better, Ben. I just did my duty, same as you. That was incredibly brave, charging that stockade and ordering that volley. You're a good officer, and I hope we can be friends. There's not many of us left from the Rifles. You too, Jesse," said Will, extending a hand again. Jesse smiled, shook it, and he and Ben left. As Will settled back by his fire, he reflected: some days are just better than others.

* * *

September 1862

Will marched as in a parade, right down the streets of Lexington. The Federals retreated and today, the Raiders were coming home. He and many others petitioned their officers for time off to see family and friends. Will saw Morgan riding proudly at the front of the group.

As soon as the parade was over and they made camp, Will got his horse and rode for home. Home—he hadn't seen the little farm in a year. He still carried his guns, as caution dictated—the Federals might not be that far away—but he didn't wear his uniform. Today he was just a civilian, a son returning home for a visit. He turned off the main Versailles road, imagining Rustler coming out to meet him, and his mother maybe baking a pie. How tall would Lydia be now? Will himself had just turned eighteen—Lydia was six now. How might she have changed?

As Will turned toward the cabin, his anticipation turned to dread. What had happened? The cabin, or what was left of it, was a burned out shell. The barn, too, had been burned. The place was deserted. There were no animals, no people, no crops growing. He just couldn't believe it. Where was his family?

* * *

Julia rose. Two soldiers came to her cell. It must be time. She prayed and mustered her courage. She must not let them see her fear. Everything depended on it.

"Mrs. Johannsen? If you'll come with us please," they requested. Moving behind her, one of the soldiers apologized, "I'm sorry, but we must bind your hands behind you. General Bragg's rules."

"Of course, you must do your duty. Though I'm surprised the general would be concerned about a mere woman like me."

"From what I hear, one of the reasons the general has held off so long with you is because you're a woman. We're taking you to see General Forrest first."

Julia walked quietly, composing herself. She had heard rumors and stories of Nathan Bedford Forrest, none of them good, except his genius as a commander. He had a reputation for harsh treatment of enemies, which she supposed he would consider her.

Entering the command tent, the soldiers stood at attention on either side of her, while at a table, eight or so officers with General Forrest in the center sat waiting on her.

"Sir! Bringing the prisoner as ordered, sir!" saluted the soldier to her right.

"Very good, gentlemen. Please stand guard outside the tent," he said, turning his attention to Julia. "Now, Mrs. Johannsen. What am I to do with you?" He glanced down at his notes. "You are accused of treason and espionage against the Confederate States of America. Your husband and your father serve in the Federal army. But you have a brother on our side, is that correct?"

"Yes, sir. My brother Will is with Colonel Morgan, the last I knew."

"And you came to General Bragg's headquarters looking for him, you say?"

"Yes, sir. I hadn't heard from my brother for two months. I was concerned he might have fallen in battle and not been reported."

"Admirable, I'm sure. Such sisterly devotion. But wouldn't a letter or a telegram have served just as well? Surely you are not stupid, madam. You know there is a war on. Why would a lady like yourself, currently in charge of a shipping company, risk such a dangerous trip alone? Could you have had, perhaps, other motives as well?"

"Why, no sir. I simply wanted to assure myself of my brother's well being, and to see him—he left suddenly when Morgan smuggled, ah, took, the rifles out of Lexington. I was in Cincinnati at the time. I haven't seen him since. You can't do that with a telegram."

"True, true. And I note here that your company, the Ohio Zephyr, has been of some service in the past to the CSA, in spite of being headquartered in the North. You're a Kentuckian by birth, I believe, a sister of the South. Your family has a farm near Lexington. But then we come to the crux of the problem. After sneaking into a Confederate camp, ostensibly looking for your brother, you gave conflicting information to the hotel clerk and the unfortunate camp guard concerning your brother's regiment. The guard has since been shot, I must say. If you knew the camp was for the First Mississippi, why would you even look there? Clearly you knew your brother was with Morgan, the 2nd Kentucky. After your arrest, when the female matron searched you, maps and battle plans were found in your shoe. Can you explain that to me, Mrs. Johannsen?"

Julia racked her brain for the right answer but could think of none. What would appease this man? "I can only think they were placed there after my arrest, to cast doubt on my story. Possibly someone has a grudge against my company or my husband."

Forrest closed the file with a sigh. "Mrs. Johannsen, in spite of your acting skills, which you have ably displayed, and your courage, I don't believe it any more than you do. Are you aware that the penalty for your crimes is death by hanging? It's not a pretty sight. Come, Mrs. Johannsen.

Confess and tell us to whom you would have passed the plans. Or if not for yourself, think of your brother, your family, and the vengeance that may fall on them for your treachery. What would your brother think of you exposing him and his comrades to ambush and death?"

One of the other officers spoke, "General, the facts seem clear. This woman is a traitor, both to our cause and to her fair sex. Women have no business mixing in war—however, it seems clear that she knew what she was about and the possible consequences. Therefore, I don't see how we can extend mercy. She's just as apt to do it again. And who knows how many times she may have affected a battle before now?" There were noises of agreement from the others.

"Very well," said Forrest. "It is General Bragg's decision as commanding officer, but I think the verdict of this tribunal is clear. Guard! Take the prisoner to General Bragg, along with this message." He hastily scrawled the results of their investigation and handed it to a soldier.

"This way, ma'am," said the soldier. They soon arrived at the farmhouse Bragg was using as a temporary headquarters.

Bragg looked up at her with fierce bushy eyebrows. He was gruff, and looked like a lion about to pounce. "Yes, yes what is it? Oh, yes, the spy," he perused the note from Forrest. "Well, everything seems in order here. Do you have anything to say for yourself?"

"Only that I want this war to end. I want my husband, my father, and my brother back. A woman can't take up a rifle and fight. I want to save thousands of lives by bringing a swift conclusion to the killing."

"Admirable—but not at the expense of the Confederacy, madam. We shall yet drive the Federals off our land," Bragg said. He sighed, dropping the paper. "In the meantime, it is regrettable, since you are a noncombatant and a woman, but the evidence leaves me little choice. It is clear you are guilty. You've as much as admitted it, not that it mattered. I sentence you to death by hanging. May God have mercy on your soul. Guard! Remove the prisoner." Bragg turned back to his paperwork, dismissing her as an errant child.

* * *

October 1862

After seeing his home in ruins, Will wondered what other tragedies had happened. He turned his horse back toward town, hoping someone among his acquaintances might give him news of his family. He decided to go see Jenny—surely she and her aunt could give him some news of what had happened.

He arrived at the Simpsons' house, tied his horse, and knocked at the door. There was no answer for several minutes. The house looked dark. Desperate, he tried again. After a few more minutes, the door opened. Jenny's aunt, Mary Simpson, stood there, but didn't seem to recognize him.

"Yes? What is it you want?"

"It's Will Crump, ma'am. I got a letter from Jenny, and I've come to see her. I wonder too if you can tell me what happened to my family—I went to the farm, and no one is there."

Mrs. Simpson seemed to be speaking from far away, not really looking at him. "Crump? Oh, yes. Jenny's not here."

"Not here? Do you expect her back soon?"

Mrs. Simpson seemed to come to herself and now answered angrily. "No. She's not here. Go away! She and my husband have gone to Philadelphia to seek help. After ... after what happened. She may never return. I ... I've lost them both!" she said, sobbing now. "Go away!" She turned and started to close the door. Will reached out a hand in desperation and blocked her.

"Mrs. Simpson, I'm sorry. Truly I am. But please! I must know— what's happened to them?"

"Your family? I have no idea. The Federals were here for months, now it's the Confederates! I wish all soldiers would rot in hell. Nothing but misery since this war started. My Tim lost an arm—and he lost himself, his mind. One of the Federals came and raped Jenny, if you must know. She sits and stares all day, then screams and cries, and has nightmares when she does sleep. She'll never be the same. Satisfied? I'm selling the house—we're getting away from this war. Now go away or I shall be forced to use this," she said, producing a pistol from the table by the door, and leveling it at Will.

Will turned and left, the feeling of joyful victory turned to hopelessness and dread. Where now was all that he had been fighting for?

* * *

Will made a few more inquiries, visiting families of those he had known in the Rifles. He discovered that a group of Southern sympathizers had gone about trying to terrorize those perceived to be in sympathy with the Federals. They thought that might have been how the farm was burned, but no one in town knew anything specific about his family. There was no mail for him. He decided to write to Albinia and Julia again, to see if he could discover what happened to his parents and Lydia.

There were more here wanting to fight for the Confederacy than he would have imagined—he talked to Duke and found new companies, battalions, and even regiments had been raised in the past few days. Will recognized one familiar face from his boyhood—a planter named Jameson, now in Company H. Morgan took part of their regiment east toward Louisville. Will was soon kept busy, moving with Duke's command, north toward Covington, and engaging in some sharp battles.

Then on October 6, 1862, his hopes of rescuing his home from the war disappeared completely. Orders came—they were withdrawing from Lexington. A large federal force was on its way south from Cincinnati. They said Bragg hadn't beaten Buell in the east, and was now threatened from behind. Morgan's Raiders were to withdraw. Will briefly saw Morgan, and he seemed as dispirited as the rest of the men, unusual for him.

* * *

Luther never expected to see this place again. The Third and Fourth Ohio Cavalry camped on the grounds of Ashland. His tent was only a few yards from where he had hidden that black night to escape. Conflicting emotions warred within him—hate for the life of slavery, longing for his mother and sister, fear at possibly being recognized. What would the Clays do if they saw him? The overseer, Flanagan, was gone, as were many of the slaves he had known when he was here. After a day or two, he risked going down to the field slaves' quarters, to see whom he might find after dark.

As if he'd never left, there sat Auntie May at her fire, softly singing.

"Auntie? Auntie May?"

She turned in surprise, "Who dere?"

"It's Luther."

"Luther! What you doin' here, boy? Are you clean outta yore mind? Dey catch you...."

"They won't catch me. I'm with the Union army. They wouldn't dare. And you won't tell my secret."

Recovering from her shock, she embraced him. "My, my, my! You done growed to be a man. What happened to you?"

Luther briefly related all that had happened since he escaped the plantation, leaving out the names of Albinia and those on the Underground Railroad. Sorrowfully, Auntie May told him about Jackson, how he'd been caught, whipped and branded, and sold south. She also told him about the massa.

"He done fled north, to Canada. They was gonna arrest him again. Mrs. Clay, she run de place now, but it's fallin' apart. Every time de Union comes, lots o' darkies run off. Ain't no patrols hardly to stop'em any more."

"What about you, auntie? Why don't you leave?"

"And go where? Raisin' hemp all I know how to do. I'm too old to run. Got no family to live for—my chillin all sold long ago. Bill, my husband, he been dead twenty years. But you ... you made it free! Why you come back?"

"I got some scores to settle," said Luther grimly.

"Mmm mm. Nothin' but trouble gonna come of dat."

"You sound like my mother."

"Wise woman! Someone got to knock sense into yo haid! You get on outta here, go back up north. This old woman sleep better, knowin' you free."

"We'll all be free, some day. That Lincoln gonna see to it."

"War ain't no answer. Mebbe I'll see it, mebbe I won't. Go on now, let an old woman get some sleep."

Luther embraced her and went back to the Union camp by Richmond Road. He was careful to stay clear of the big house. His one fear was being reenslaved. So far, it looked like the only one here besides the Clays who might know he was an escaped slave was Auntie May. And Sam. Luther hadn't forgotten. Sam could be a threat. He'd waited long enough. Something had to be done. It was time for revenge.

* * *

Hiram walked the grounds of Ashland, looking at the large trees and the parklike atmosphere. It seemed surreal to him that war could touch this place. He prayed he might come back here someday, in time of peace. He knew Albinia had once been friendly with the Clays—Julia talked of Lucy inviting her here. He wondered where Julia was now. He hoped she was safe at home in Cincinnati, but he knew her headstrong nature— it was part of why he loved her. If anyone could tame Mama Kirsten, it would be her.

As he wandered by the windows of the big house in the dark, he heard the sound of a pianoforte. Seized by curiosity, he mounted the back steps and tapped on the window of the dining room. Phoebe opened the door for him, and he entered. Phoebe trembled at the huge white man in a blue uniform.

"No need to be afraid, miss. I ... I just heard the music. It made me think of home, of my mama. Who is playing?"

Phoebe, still seeming frightened, kept her eyes down and answered in a voice just above a whisper. "Miss Lucy, she playin'. She often does that, of an evenin'."

"Might I go in and listen? She plays very well. Some of the other men might like to as well."

"I ... I don' know, sir. I ask Miss Lucy."

Turning, she moved away toward the drawing room. Impulsively, Hiram followed her toward the sound of the music.

As he entered the room, Lucy was seated at the pianoforte, with her mother Susan in a rocking chair knitting, her sister Sukie on the floor drawing, and her five-year-old brother engaged in playing with wooden carved horses.

Lucy sensed Phoebe coming in and started to turn in irritation, then started at seeing Hiram. Another door opened, and a man in a Confederate uniform entered, saw Hiram, and stopped, drawing a pistol.

"Not in my house!" Susan commanded. Turning to Hiram, she said coolly, "What is the meaning of this, sir? Why have you invaded my home?"

"I meant no harm," said Hiram. "I just heard the music. So beautiful. I think of home, and wonder if I might listen. I'm sorry. I didn't mean to cause trouble. I had no idea.... Please forgive me. I'll tell no one."

Lucy and the other children seemed frozen, tense, waiting what would happen. Susan seemed unperturbed.

"Well, since it seems you are not entirely devoid of manners, and my cousin was just leaving," Susan motioned at the man in gray to be gone. "I suppose we might entertain a few of you, in Christian charity. Poor homesick boys."

Hiram returned shortly with a few others, and they listened to Lucy play Bach and Mendelssohn until the moon rose.

* * *

Julia sat in her cell crying, praying, and despairing. What a mess she'd made of things! She hadn't helped Hiram at all, and now she would die. In the cell with her were two Negro men, and two boys, about fourteen and sixteen. At dawn, the guards came. She thought it early for breakfast, and it filled her with foreboding. She lay down as best she could, feigning illness.

The guards ignored her and commanded the two boys to follow them. Seeing that no one cared about her, Julia moved to the door, to see what would happen.

The boys were marched roughly up steps to a platform. In horror, Julia watched as they were handcuffed behind their backs. Ropes slid over their necks. The younger boy began sobbing loudly, pleading and begging. His brother told him to be quiet, to show these rebels how a Union man could die. In a loud voice, a lieutenant read the charges—espionage and spying against the Confederate States of America. Julia heard the command given and turned away heartsick. This was what awaited her?

After that, each day, she pretended fever and illness, too weak to stand. The guards reported her condition, and Bragg delayed her execution three times. She wracked her brain for a method of escape—they were in Kentucky. If she could get out, she might find help, people she knew— maybe her aunt and uncle near Nicholasville. No method suggested itself, however. She was not strong enough to overcome two guards, let alone the whole camp. She had nothing but promises with which to bribe anyone. Who would believe her and risk death? How much longer could she hold out?

* * *

Will rode hard all night. After attacking a Union wagon train and burning tons of supplies, the Raiders rode north again. Will knew this territory, as they galloped hard up the Tates Creek Pike, heading for troops near Lexington. After the Confederates evacuated Lexington two weeks before, Morgan obtained permission for some lightning raids north, to disrupt Union supply lines.

"Will, you know this country better than I, and Morgan is off to the east. Pick some of the other Lexington men you know and ride point. Our intelligence is that there are Union troops camped at the Clay mansion, Ashland. You've been there, I believe. We will come from the south and west, Breckenridge and Gano from the north and east," Duke said, filling him in on the plans. "We want total surprise."

They got close to Ashland and formed up, resting the horses for half an hour or so. It was completely dark, though dawn would come soon. At about five o'clock, Will heard the signal, and drawing his pistols, charged with the rest into the midst of the sleeping Federals.

* * *

Luther heard gunfire, shouting, and horses. He grabbed his pistol, hastily loaded his rifle, and made sure his knife was in his belt. What could be happening? He stayed low, crawling outside the tent to the familiar ash tree. There were soldiers everywhere—it was too dark to see uniforms. Some of the men came out of their tents in their long johns, attempted to return fire, and were shot immediately. Luther took aim at the men on horses, firing repeatedly. Suddenly one broke off, riding straight for him saber raised. He rolled, and coming up on one knee, fired the revolver at the rider. The man pitched backward in the saddle and fell. Luther started to turn away, and the man jumped to his feet, rushing Luther and grabbing him from behind around the neck. He tried, but even his black-smith's hands could not pry the man's grip loose. He was losing air, and consciousness. He jabbed backward quickly with an elbow, as hard as he could, knocking the wind out of the man. The grip loosened, and Luther twisted free, throwing the man to the ground and stabbing him through the throat. In the pale dawn, the surprised eyes looked up at Luther, and Luther recognized him. It was Jameson.

* * *

Will had no time to think, just fire, wheel, twist, and fire again. He was aware of some horses going around without a rider. Anytime there was a flash of steel from the ground, or movement, he fired. It seemed like some of the Confederates were firing at him. Exhausting his revolvers, he began using the bayonet on the end of his carbine like a spear. As the battle went on, the light improved, so he thought it worth riding away from the fight long enough to reload the revolvers. Then he charged back, seeking targets. To his surprise, a tall black man picked up a revolver and aimed at him. Without time to consider why, Will pulled his horse hard to the right, leaning at the same time. The shot went wild, and Will righted himself, urging Shadow down on top of the man. As the black man raised the pistol again, Will fired, catching the man full in the chest. His arm fell and moved no more.

* * *

Luther quickly jumped up, found his pistol, reloaded his rifle, and scanned the field. In the improving light, he recognized a black man—Sam! He was about thirty yards away, taking aim at a mounted soldier. Before Luther could aim, the soldier avoided Sam and ran his horse over him, firing. Luther could have shot the soldier. Instead, he watched as the soldier killed Sam. He did not feel the joy he might have expected. Perhaps later—now there were Confederates everywhere, and he must escape. The battle was not going well for his Union friends. Seeing a riderless horse, Luther grabbed the bridle, quickly stuffing his rifle in the scabbard on the saddle. He swung up and headed north, in the direction of the Paris Pike. His knowledge of the area driving for the Clays might help keep him safe.

* * *

Will saw a horse escaping north, but there was no time to worry about that. Nearer to the house, a woman and a child poked out of the upstairs window, as though the woman was trying to draw the child back in. Near the rear porch of the house, a large man was using his rifle as a club, moving quickly. He knocked three men over, then flipped it to use the bayonet, when four more gray uniforms surrounded him. Will rode over. "Stop! Unless you want to go to heaven now! Surrender!" Will yelled. His men had their rifles leveled at the giant, who looked Will in the eye. Will, astonished, recognized Hiram.

* * *

A few days later, Hiram found himself paroled, exchanged for a Confederate prisoner. He found his way back to his regiment, along with the others released. After a few days rest, about October 19th, his company advanced again. Fortunately, he was able to find a horse large enough to carry him. The army had to issue him new weapons, his old ones having been taken by the Confederates. He'd talked to Will, but could furnish him no news of his family. He'd told Will he didn't know for sure where Julia was, and was concerned for her.

Now the third and fourth Ohio moved southeast, in pursuit of Bragg's army. The orders were to move quickly, lest Bragg escape.

They marched through the frost and cold. They marched in the rain. The army moved about twenty miles each day, on short rations. Finally, word passed down—the Confederates were just ahead.

* * *

Pandemonium descended on the Confederate camp. Julia didn't know what was going on, but something was happening. She dared not appear too lively, lest someone see and report. She could see tents being struck and wagons being loaded. It looked like they were preparing to move out.

Then the guards approached and unlock the cell. An older man, steel gray hair and spectacles, with the jowls of one used to being well fed, was with them. He wore a curious instrument with tubes about his neck.

"Madam, this army is about to move. General Bragg has extended you hospitality long enough. He has sent me to determine whether you are well enough to walk to your execution, though personally I don't see what difference it makes. I am a doctor, and I am to examine you. I apologize for not being able to observe the niceties, but I am ordered to examine you, with or without your cooperation. These gentlemen here," he said, gesturing to the guards, "will hold you down if you resist. May I have your cooperation, madam?"

Julia saw no alternative. "Of course," she snapped stiffly. "If you think it necessary. Anyone can see that I am ill."

The doctor approached and opened his bag. He felt Julia's forehead and used his stethoscope to listen to her heart and breathing. Her heart beat rapidly as she was beginning to panic.

After a few minutes, the doctor closed his bag and straightened.

"Madam, I am sorry to report for your sake that you are no more ill than I am. I shall tell General Bragg. Good day to you."

The doctor left, the soldiers locked the cell. In a few minutes, a soldier came and, through the bars, asked her, "Madam, the general has extended you the courtesy of a last meal, given your gender. Is there anything you would like?"

Stalling, Julia thought wildly. "Have you any duck? I am partial to it. Also, of course, I would appreciate mercy even more than a meal, if the general is inclined to extend it."

"I'll see what I can do about the duck—there's a pond nearby, and many have shotguns. But you may have to do with ham and hardtack. As for mercy, the general has been most generous toward you. Had you been a soldier, he would have killed you months ago."

In an hour, he returned apologetically with the hard tack and ham. Julia ate a small amount, not really tasting it. She prayed and thought of Hiram, her parents, her sisters, and Will.

At last they came. The soldiers entered her cell and bid her walk ahead of them. She determined not to blubber—it seemed no use. She climbed the stairs of the platform. They tied her hands behind her back. A minister appeared and read the twenty-third Psalm.

"Would you like a hood, ma'am?" said one of the soldiers.

"No, thank you."

They bid her step up on the box, and then slipped the noose around her neck. Frightened, sick to her stomach, she clenched her teeth and closed her eyes. Nothing happened for a few seconds, which seemed like hours.

A shot rang out, then another, and another. The soldiers on the platform scattered, looking for their guns. Julia was left standing there, a rope around her neck. She dared not move as the bullets whizzed around her. Turning her head, a line of blue uniforms advanced. The Confederates were mounting up, retreating pell-mell as though totally surprised. Cannon shells landed in the camp—a piece of shrapnel caught her in the knee, threatening to make her fall to her death. Ridiculously, she thought about her dress being ruined. The battle raged on, passing her.

Then suddenly he was there. Hiram came running up the stairs, a knife in his hand. First he cut the rope around her neck, then the one around her hands. He pulled the noose off, and she was in his arms.

ON THE RIVER

November 1862

Albinia made the trip to Lancaster so often that she barely had to guide the horse. She took the four-hour drive at a trot, scarcely resting. She began teaching at the mixed race school, working with the little ones to learn to read and sew two days a week. Other times she took new escaped slaves as they ran to freedom or to flee the war. She heard tales of both plantation houses and cabins burned by both sides. Here in Madison, she felt safe. No battles.

Sometimes she took the trip to Lancaster on the excuse of looking in on the slaves she'd helped. Mabel just smiled and packed her a lunch.

Today she enjoyed the early afternoon sunshine and was grateful for little wind, as the temperature hovered about forty degrees, rather agreeable for mid-November. She'd gotten a late start, wanting her new gown to be perfect when Peter saw it. It was a royal blue, with white lace around the scooped neck and at the end of the puffed sleeves. She had a hot brick for her feet in the floorboard, a woolen shawl around her, and extra flannel petticoats. She had bathed, having Franklin heat several tubs of water, and washed her hair. She even applied lavender water to her skin. Today, she was making the trip for no other reason than to spend time with Peter. In two weeks, it would be her birthday. Peter said he had something special planned. She looked forward with anticipation now. After all, twenty-one wasn't so old. Peter didn't seem to mind about her being a widow—in fact, he'd been very sympathetic, understanding when memories made her melancholy.

It was almost sunset when she arrived. She had stayed with his housekeeper a time or two, but tried not to make a habit of being there overnight. She didn't want any gossip to hurt him with his parishioners. The moon would be full tonight—she'd just go home after their time together.

She pulled up in front of the parsonage, and Peter was there before she could get down, helping her.

"I was getting worried you wouldn't come, or had an accident," he said.

Albinia smiled at him warmly. He was always so protective. "No, I just was silly and got started late. I wanted everything to be perfect."

He set her down and stepped back, whistling. "Well, you certainly did a good job on that! You look absolutely gorgeous. Come, I think dinner is just about ready. Let's get you warm."

Albinia started to say that just seeing him made her warm from head to toe, but thought better of it.

They entered the small parsonage, where a fire crackled in the fireplace, and Melinda, the housekeeper, was bustling making the final changes for the meal. She was short, stout, and looked about fifty years old, with black curly hair and chocolate-brown skin. There was a sofa, three benches, and the cast-iron wood-fired stove in the corner, a small dining table set for five with pewter dishes. To her delight, Joe and Katy Jones, children of the slave family she'd helped a few weeks before, were there playing on the floor.

They ran over and hugged her. "Look, Mrs. Horner! See my giraffe?" Katy said, holding up a wooden toy. "He's eating all the leaves off the trees—that's why there aren't any there anymore!"

Peter knelt beside the children and laughed. He clowned when Joe wanted to ride him like a horse. Albinia watched the spectacle, laughing and making appreciative remarks when the children wanted to show her something. She read stories to them, and told them the story of David and Goliath from the Bible, which Peter acted out, making grimacing faces as he mimicked Goliath. Albinia thought to herself, he would make such a good father—then blushed and turned her attention back to the story.

Then the meal was ready. Albinia listened appreciatively while Peter returned grace. The children, still not quite used to getting enough to eat, gave lavish thanks to Melinda for her cooking, which made a broad smile. After the meal, Moses and Patty arrived. Melinda made room for them, serving dessert and coffee. They shared more of their journey up from Alabama, including some close escapes. When they left with the children and Melinda was cleaning up, Peter proposed a walk.

"Are you sure? It's bound to be freezing out there," said Albinia.

"Well, if you'd rather not…."

"No, no, it's all right."

"Outdoors, I just feel closer to God when I see the stars. It's good for me. Sometimes I start focusing on how my world is instead of how big God is. Keeps me in my place. And thankful for my fire," he smiled.

"Yes, somehow, the world seems more at peace at night," she agreed.

"Peter? Can I ask you something?"

"Delving into my deep dark secrets, eh? Sure."

"Why did you choose the ministry? And why aren't you in the war fighting?"

"Well, I chose the ministry because I can't imagine living a single day without God's help. I see Him as my creator and father. I started down the wrong path as a boy, but I started seeing bad results—lying, stealing, eventually drinking. I knew then I didn't want to go that way, and I needed Jesus as my savior. I still get excited about introducing Him to other people. But I don't want my faith to be some lofty thing that's not practical. I think Jesus was more radical about love than most people imagine, and wants us to live it out, regardless of the cost. As to the war, I come from Pennsylvania, and Quaker roots. I'm not as against violence as some of them are—I think you should be able to defend yourself or another person from a direct threat. I won't go along with shooting someone because a general gave orders. I'm glad there are those that want to defend our country—but I'm more inclined to let them and let God work it out. I believe it when the Bible says, 'So far as it depends upon you, live at peace with all men.' I try to love people no matter how they treat me. There are usually other ways to solve problems than violence. But at the same time, I won't tolerate someone abusing or hurting people. Does that make any sense?"

Albinia absorbed this thoughtfully. "Yes, I think so. It's mostly what I've done."

"How about you? What got you into the Underground Railroad?"

"I just woke up and saw how slaves are really treated. I heard Mr. Garrison talk and show how the Bible said slavery was evil. People thought I was crazy, once they knew, especially after prison. My parents weren't thrilled. They never would have approved of David. But like you, I don't think faith is just for Sundays—if it doesn't change what you do, it isn't real faith."

They reached a pond on the path. A willow tree waved in the slight breeze, and Albinia had to acknowledge she was getting cold. The full moon filled the night with bright soft light. They stopped, turned to face each other, and it seemed natural to take his hands in hers. She looked up at him, and the smile was in his eyes as well as on his lips. She could see the question in his eyes, and she tilted her head back, closing her eyes. He kissed her, at first tentatively, but when she responded, he took her in his arms and kissed her again with more passion, leaving her breathless. A hundred feelings and thoughts went through her brain, her body responding and tingling. She felt slightly guilty, both for kissing a man not her husband, and for David. She also felt deliciously alive, not wanting the moment to end. They moved apart, and she laughed to break the tension. "I'd better get home or I'm going to have some more confessing to do," she said, smiling. "I don't want to harm the reputation of my favorite minister."

Peter laughed, but then his brow furrowed with worry. "But Albinia, it's nearly midnight. Can't you just stay with Melinda? I'd worry about you going home this late."

They started walking back up the path to the parsonage. "Peter, you know that's not good for you. It was one thing when I was new here. As many times as I've been to church, stayed for dinner, and spent time at your house, people will start to talk if they see me come in the evening and leave in the morning. The Bible says to avoid even the appearance of evil—I don't have to tell you that."

"But it's freezing. What if you hit a rock and broke a tire? No one would find you until morning."

Albinia smiled, "Really, I appreciate your concern. I know how to drive a horse—there's a full moon and I have a lantern. I've been building fires since I was six. I have extra blankets in the wagon, and I have my 'friends' with me. I've driven hundreds of miles in the dark for the Railroad. Besides, my horse would walk home even if I fell asleep—Chester's done it that many times. So quit worrying and get some sleep. It's been a lovely evening."

Peter stopped her and held her hands again, looking serious, "I've enjoyed it more than I can say. I hope it's the first of many."

* * *

Albinia found that Melinda had reheated her bricks for her feet and made a jar of hot tea with honey as well. She mounted the wagon and began her drive, her mind wandering agreeably over the day. She pushed away too many thoughts of what the future might hold. She wanted to hold onto the moments—watching Peter preach, watching how he handled opposition integrating the school with the races, playing with the children, and that exquisite kiss. She had loved David, but she had to admit she was tired of being alone, and had no wish for people to pity her as a widow and a spinster. David wasn't coming back, and filling herself with those memories and grief wouldn't help. Maybe Mabel was right—it was time.

She kept looking at the moon, woolgathering and imagining the most contented sort of thoughts. She looked up ahead, nearing her home, and saw something bright. The slight breeze brought a new smell—smoke! Chester pranced a little nervously, and then settled back into pulling the wagon. Albinia slapped the reins to hurry him on, and they increased to a fast trot. Now she could see flames dancing in the night. Fear gripped her heart—what could have happened? Mabel wasn't one to be careless with fire.

As she pulled into the barnyard, Mabel jumped up and waved her back. "Go back! It's a trap!"

She heard the warning as a shot rang out, hitting the earth at Chester's feet, causing him to rear. Albinia grabbed the short shotgun and scrambled over the wagon seat into the back of the wagon, hearing her dress rip. A petticoat snagged on the seat, and while she tried to free it, another shot hit the seat where she had been seconds before. From the sound, the shots were coming from off to the right, up the road toward Madison. She couldn't see an assailant, and only had short-range weapons. Just as she freed the petticoat, another shot came, this time hitting the side of the wagon. Chester had enough, and bolted toward the barn, causing her to lose her balance and fall flat into the wagon bed. The shotgun flew out of her grasp onto the ground behind the moving wagon. Another bullet passed overhead, which probably would have hit her if she had remained standing. She felt helpless. She peered out a knothole in the side of the wagon and saw horsemen approaching, probably to see if she was dead. She prayed, "God help me!" She let them approach, remembering her derringer. If she played dead, they'd have to get close enough for her to use it. Chester was standing at the barn door, neighing and pawing. No telling what he might do as the other horses approached.

As the horsemen drew nearer, she heard galloping hoofbeats from the road north, back toward Lancaster. She didn't dare look over the edge of the wagon, but supposed someone else had arrived, friend or foe, she did not know. Now she could see her assailants wore black hoods. They were surprised at the new arrival, pausing. She moved closer to her knothole and saw one of them raise a pistol, aimed at—Peter! Peter quickly drew a revolver and began firing. One of the hooded men pitched backward as a shot hit him in the stomach, and another hit one of the hooded men's horses. The other two horses were frightened, wheeling around, causing the shots from the hooded men to go wild as Peter quickly dismounted and took cover behind a rain barrel. Albinia took courage, looked over the edge of the wagon, and fired one of the horsemen. She didn't think she hit anyone, but the men turned wildly and fled, leaving their fallen comrade. His black hood covered his face, with eyeholes cut out to see. She stood and jumped from the rear of the wagon, ignoring the damage to her dress. From behind the rain barrel Peter stood, and she rushed to him. He gathered her in his arms, quieting her. Then they turned, Peter to the man on the ground, and Albinia to Mabel. Mabel sat on the ground, next to a fallen Franklin, sobbing soundlessly. The house continued to burn. She turned and looked up at Albinia.

"They've killed him this time. My poor brave Franklin. They've killed him."

* * *

In the gray light of dawn, Peter and Albinia assessed the damage. The house was about half standing, but would require extensive repair to be livable. She had unharnessed Chester and let him loose in the corral. The barn and corral were undamaged.

Mabel was inconsolable. They helped her to the inn nearby, where Albinia had stayed when she first came to Madison. Peter promised to take care of Franklin's body and the body of the hooded man. Peter said little but looked grim. He insisted that Albinia come with him to the sheriff—he didn't want to leave her alone.

"I'm glad you were here," said Albinia. "But why?"

"I was worried about you coming back at that hour alone. You told me about the note from the Golden Circle. Since you were being stubborn, I thought I'd follow behind, just out of sight. Albinia, this has to stop. I want you to seriously consider whether to rebuild here or just move up to Lancaster, where you have some protection."

"I'll pray about it. I must admit, having this happen again and losing Franklin scares me. The sheriff didn't know the man—no one seems to.

I've certainly never seen him before. Why would someone do this to a person who has never wronged them?"

Peter pursed his mouth then replied, "You haven't seen the levels of hate that some people have. They don't need a reason beyond that you are different. Your skin, your religion, the fact that you challenge their beliefs and way of life. Sometimes, there isn't even that much reason—they just have hate eating them because of things that have happened in their lives. You and I, helping the Negroes, makes us a target. I'll regret having to shoot that man to my last day—but when hate overflows and threatens life, you meet it with force. In any case, I don't think it's safe for you to stay here. They hit you on the other side of the river before they came here—they'll be back if you try again. They've shown willingness to kill—what happens if I'm not here the next time? They certainly would have killed you."

They held the funeral for Franklin a few days later. Albinia decided Peter was right and looked for a place she could rent in Lancaster. She would have to give up most of her Underground Railroad activities, but she could still teach the children. It would eliminate the long, dangerous drives, and be closer to Peter—that was a happy prospect. Mabel decided to go to her sister's in Connecticut for the time being, until she determined what else to do.

"You take care of yourself, Mrs. Horner. Don't go messin' with those Golden Circle people!"

"I won't. I think I've learned my lesson. There are other ways to help the Negroes. Besides, with the Emancipation, I think most of the Negroes will be free soon. And here's something to help out until you settle," said Albinia, pushing a small bag of money into her hand.

"Bless you, Mrs. Horner!"

They hugged and parted.

Albinia spent the next two weeks cleaning up at the farm. She figured whether she kept the farm or not, it needed work, even if just to sell it. Peter got help from the Georgetown community to watch over her.

A new arrival in the community surprised Albinia—Ned Smith and his family, the blacksmith who trained Luther. Albinia knew of them through John Parker and her connections in the Underground Railroad. They had no news of Luther, however. Albinia liked Ruth immediately. Ruth began helping her with teaching children to read.

* * *

Soon it was the end of November. Albinia was worn out from the last two weeks, but filled with excitement. Peter told her to come to Lancaster for her birthday, December 1. What was the surprise Peter had planned?

She woke up in her boarding house, and dressed carefully with one of the few good dresses she salvaged from the house. She would have to sew more soon. Peter told her to come after breakfast.

Arriving at the parsonage she opened the door, and nearly dropped her reticule in surprise—Lydia came rushing to her and jumped into her arms! Her mother and father sat in chairs by the fireplace—and another person Albinia did not know stood nearby—a tall beautiful blonde woman, plainly dressed, but with a perfect figure and exquisite features.

She carried Lydia to a chair, listening to her sister babble on, but wondering who the stranger was. Peter came from the kitchen, where he'd been helping Melinda prepare coffee and rolls for the guests.

After everyone exchanged hugs, Sara exclaimed, "It's so good to see you! Tell us everything."

Albinia related a short version of her story, but then said, "Pa, your foot—tell me what happened."

Robert looked at the stump that used to be his foot and said, "Let's talk about happier things. Miss King here was just telling us about her journey from Pennsylvania when you came in."

Peter said, "Where are my manners? Albinia, this is Miss Mary King from Gettysburg, Pennsylvania, an old friend. Mary, this is Mrs. Albinia Horner, a good friend and neighbor—and you've met her parents, Robert and Sara Crump, and her sister Lydia. Mary has come west with her family, getting away from the war. They are Quakers, members of the Society of Friends."

Mary looked to be about twenty. The part about being an old friend bothered Albinia. She didn't want to be jealous, but couldn't help wondering what kind of friend, given her easy manner with Peter. Surely, Peter wouldn't trifle with her in that way. However, how could he have known that Mary would show up? Albinia decided to relax and enjoy time with her family, obviously the surprise Peter intended.

"I'm delighted to see you all, but what brings you here?"

"Well, we had our own trouble down in Kentucky. Similar to yours. Because I was in the Union army, slaveholders came and burned the farm while I was away. We decided it wasn't safe with your ma being alone on the farm so much, so we're looking to move north. Guess we might have to hire some hands for help and security here too. Or we might keep going further west, now that the land is open out there," said her father.

"What about your foot? Pa, please!" Albinia wanted to know.

"Not much to tell. At the Battle of Cumberland Gap back in June, took a minie ball in the foot. Bone shattered, not much for it but to cut it off. I won't run, but I get around all right."

"I'm glad Pa is home!" piped up Lydia.

Robert gathered her up, smiling. "So am I, Lyddie, so am I. So what do you say, Binia? You got room for us for a while till we decide what to do?"

"Well . . . I was sort of planning to sell the farm and move up here due to safety concerns. They killed Franklin—I certainly wouldn't want that to happen to you. And the house isn't in good shape."

"I understand—but I think if we bring some more people out to Lonesome Hollow, maybe get the beginnings of a little village, we could make a stand. They can't fight all of us. I'm hoping to open a general store, become more of a storekeeper now that farming is harder. What if we got some of the folks from Georgetown to come out, let 'em garden a few acres, make another little town?"

"Well, I know one family just arrived—they might come. But Pa, they're all black. Wouldn't that just make us more of a target?"

"Folks got to get used to black folks bein' like anyone else. If we have enough guns and try to find out who's behind the trouble, get 'em to realize we mean no harm if left alone, I think we could do it. Maybe white and black livin' side by side. You game to try?"

"All right, Pa. I'll talk to people. Maybe I could open my own dress shop and still work with the children here."

"Some of the men here might be willing to come down," said Peter. "We're mostly a way station for them heading somewhere else. But you'll need to set nightly guards—some of the Knights mean business."

"We could do that. I know how to train men for military duty now. Got one piece of bad news for you. The Clays. Seems folks thought James Clay was gonna betray the Union, and they wanted to arrest him again—so he ran off to Canada. They actually had a battle at Ashland I heard. Then just this month, three of the children died—one was your friend Lucy. Some kind of sickness. I'm sorry; I know you two were good friends."

Albinia gasped, then recovered. "We were. I came to realize that our different classes and views on slavery were more of a division than I had thought. I helped her slave Luther to freedom, and they never forgave me for that. Now I suppose it's too late to heal that breach."

Mary said, "I'm sorry to hear you lost a friend. Perhaps … we can be friends. Though I don't know yet what Father will decide about staying here."

Albinia turned to her, surprised. "Yes, that would be nice. Perhaps you can tell me some stories about Peter that I don't know," she teased, glancing at him.

"That shouldn't be hard," Mary said, smiling. "We grew up together. He's like a brother."

Albinia felt immense relief.

* * *

Luther rode north, traveling at night. He was armed and not the same scared youth who had escaped to freedom on this road. If anyone tried to stop him, he would fight. He dodged some Federal patrols, but wasn't concerned about them. If Federals questioned him, he could simply reference the Third Ohio and Howland would vouch for him. He wasn't deserting, since he'd never officially been part of the Third Ohio. He was more cautious about the prospect of running into Confederates—no telling what they would do to a black man out on the roads.

In the end he reached John Parker's house without difficulty, and he asked for news of Ned and Ruth Jones.

"Luther, they left. After what happened, Ned just didn't feel safe anymore. I heard they tried up in Oberlin, but Ned couldn't find enough work. Just recently, I hear they turned up in Georgetown, over by Madison, Indiana. I think someone else you know is over there too—Albinia Horner, used to be Crump."

"Ruth and Albinia are in Indiana?"

"That's what I hear."

"Thank you kindly, Mister Parker."

With that, Luther rode through Ohio and on to Indiana. He would find Ruth. If it was safe, he'd send for Jemima and Olivia.

* * *

Julia required several days of rest and good food to begin to recover. Her knee was bandaged. She walked with a limp. She had come very close to death and it scared her thoroughly. Hiram had to follow his regiment. She found her way north through the Union lines, to the river. Now she was on one of Hiram's steamboats, headed back to Cincinnati. He'd extracted a promise from her—no more spying. She would go home and wait for him. She barely had the presence of mind but asked him about an idea she had before she was taken prisoner, that of expanding the company into railroads. He had approved, so she had a new, safer mission to perform.

She reflected back over the past few months and thanked God for His protection. Her spying had little effect in the end, except to make her realize how much she truly loved Hiram and how dependent she was on God for everything. After the dangers she had endured, even the prospect of dealing with Mama Kirsten seemed tame.

MORGAN'S RAID

December 1862

The winter of 1862 had its triumphs and disasters for the Raiders. Morgan spent less time with the troops, Will observed, and more time with his new wife, Mattie. This changed somewhat when the shocking news came that Mattie's sister was arrested as a Union spy, along with a man carrying letters between Morgan and Mattie. In another instance, when Morgan was preoccupied, there was almost a repeat of the Lebanon disaster, with Morgan barely escaping capture.

Will was greatly troubled and discouraged. He'd seen Hiram, but still knew nothing about his parents. And after raising hopes, Jenny seemed lost to him forever. The war seemed to drag on. In early December, the Raiders fought at the Battle of Hartsville, but Will spent the time in the hospital tent, ill with fever. The running battle continued intermittently for a few weeks, with the Confederates winning initially. For Will, it was a bleak Christmas in the hospital at the rear. Will wanted nothing more than to go home—except that home no longer existed for him. He heard that Morgan was promoted to general, and Duke to colonel. Morgan's command swelled to seven regiments. In the end, however, at Stones River, the last day of the year, the Federals routed them. Will found himself stumbling to a hospital wagon to be evacuated. As part of the Second Kentucky, Will was under Duke's command, with Lieutenant Colonel Gano in between.

When Will recovered and returned to duty, his unit had retreated as far as McMinnville, Tennessee. It was now mid-January, and bitter cold. There was little to eat. Will requested and received extra blankets, obtained in the last raid. His tent mate, Thomas Hines, was away on a scouting mission. Will wanted to stay well, and built a large fire in front of his tent. He foraged for food, and occasionally brought the camp a deer or an "escaped" pig.

Throughout January, February, and March, the entire command was constantly moving. Expeditions of all kinds, dashes at the enemy, and fights between reconnoitering parties were almost a daily occurrence. When Colonel Gano and General Breckinridge were not harassing the enemy, they were recipients of enemy attack. Will could barely keep track of it all. In all his time with Morgan's cavalry, they'd never been busier than the last few months.

Sitting one night with Duke around the campfire, Duke said, "If all the events of this winter could be told, it would form a book by itself of daring personal adventures, of patient endurance, of great and continued hardship, and heroic resistance against fearful odds. We've done so much. So many faces of good men lost pass my memory."

Will looked up at him, "Where will it end, sir?"

"I don't know, Will. But we must try and never stop trying for victory."

After the Confederate defeat at Stones River and retreating out of Kentucky, Will again began questioning whether this war was worth the cost. As he sat around the campfire, others expressed the same doubts.

"There ain't no glory in starvin," said one.

"For sure, and no matter how many Federals we kill, seems ten more pop up. Early days we didn't hardly lose anybody till Shiloh. Stones River, I heard we lost eleven thousand. That's more'n in my whole hometown. We ain't defendin' our homes—the Federals got 'em already. Then there's all the ones died of the brain fever and the quickstep."

"But ol' Bragg, he'll shoot us sure, do the Federals' job for 'em if we light out for home."

"I hear they takin' blacks into the Federals now, to fight! And any of us they capture, no prisoner exchange."

Will said gloomily, "I wonder sometimes if capture might be better. I can't count the friends I've lost anymore. Sometimes I even wonder where is God in all of this—can't He stop the slaughter?"

"Only problem with that is if it stops, it spares the Federals, too."

"My shoes got holes the size of 'Bama. I ain't seen nothin but Lincoln coffee, that chicory stuff, since Christmas."

They heard a bugle, and scrambled for their horses.

* * *

The end of May arrived and the news spread through camp. They were between the towns of Liberty and Alexandria, Tennessee. A private called Will to an officer's meeting. Duke was presiding.

"Men, it's time to do some damage. We're going to hurt the Federals and make them chase us. Morgan has permission to go north. We're going to be raiding in Kentucky. Confidentially, we intend to go north to Ohio, against orders. Anyone who doesn't want to go, I'll see he gets a transfer. We'll either come back victorious or we won't come back at all. The idea is to disrupt the Federals and cause so many of them to chase us that Lee and Bragg have a clear field. I won't lie to you—going on this raid is going to be different from the ones we've done in the past. There's a good chance we'll all be killed or captured—but it's the chance for our cause to win. If you want to transfer, apply by tomorrow. Then we move north."

Will hadn't been reading his Bible. He hadn't even really prayed in weeks. Now he had a decision to make and little time to consider. He drew out the Bible from the bottom of his knapsack. Leafing through, he stopped at Luke 9:62, "*And Jesus said unto him, No man, having put his hand to the plough, and looking back, is fit for the kingdom of God.*" It was talking about following Jesus, but he thought it applied equally to his situation. He'd followed Morgan into this war—now was not the time to turn aside. Many did take the transfer though, and Morgan's force diminished as units were detached to other commands.

Will wondered and second-guessed his decision when they encountered bad roads and worse weather. However, just before the beginning of the raid, a large quantity of supplies came in by rail, so that the men now had food, blankets, and clothing. Will rarely saw Morgan himself now, interacting mostly with Duke.

In Lebanon, they ran into Federal resistance but managed to cross the Cumberland by early July. Will guided Shadow, swimming across at a shallow part near Burkesville, though the river flooded and ran swiftly.

"The Federals will never expect this," said Duke. "We'll surprise them."

Will hoped this was true—he figured some amount of supplies would be lost in the crossing. They moved toward Tebb's Bend, just north of the Green River. On July 4, Will moved with his company to attack a bridge and a force of Federals defending it. The mud was like glue, and the horses moved slowly through it and the thick timber. Finally the company dismounted, owing to the steep terrain and thick underbrush. Will heard firing below as they descended to help another company pinned down. They came to a clearing with a rifle pit holding fifty Federals. Duke sent a flag of truce, asking for the Federals' surrender, but they refused. There was no high point to climb and gain advantage. Will held his ears and hugged the ground as artillery raked the rifle pit and the Federals retreated to higher ground, behind fortifications already prepared.

There was no way to use artillery on the area the Federals now occupied. The ground was all open, with no cover, until reaching a group of felled trees stacked haphazardly in front of the Federal earth works. The trees effectively prevented a cavalry charge, since the horses could not jump over them. Will saw that all they could do was an infantry charge, right across the open field. Colonel Johnson ordered his company to advance and Will relayed the order, much against his better judgement. He charged, running with his men, and heard the screams as they fell around him. The Federals were not laying down a barrage of fire, but selectively picking them off from covered positions. Will and about fifty others dropped to a prone position and fired. It was difficult to tell with the smoke and the upward slope whether the shots through the felled trees had any effect. Will heard Colonel Johnson call retreat, and as some men bravely returned covering fire, they retreated again to the woods, regrouped, and charged again. Will felt a ball hit the ground next to his boot, but otherwise was unscathed. The fire from the Federals became heavier. Will knelt and fired, knelt and fired. He heard the bugle sound retreat, and fell back, still firing occasionally to cover for others. Back in the woods, he was breathing hard and sweating—he hadn't realized how afraid he was until it was over. Word came that Morgan decided to bypass the Federals rather than lose more men in another vain attempt. Will mounted Shadow, and they were soon moving north again, to Lebanon, Kentucky, on the Danville Highway.

The morning broke bright and clear. A large group of Federals held the town congregating at the train depot. Here Will was able to station himself above the depot and used the Whitworth with some effect. Then Duke ordered Will's regiment to take the depot, and they charged. Will gained the walls of the depot and fired pistols in through the windows. Will flinched with horror as General Morgan's brother, Thomas, a friend, rushed to the middle of the field in front of the depot, fired into the windows. Thomas made no attempt at cover. Another brother, Calvin, caught Thomas as he fell, shot through the heart. Will had no time to stop and grieve, but knew he had lost yet another friend. Blast this stupid war anyway! His rage led him to empty both pistols into the depot, and was at the front of the charge when his men stormed inside, capturing it. He and some others were angry enough to have shot the surrendering Federals. Arm shaking, Will ordered his men to stand down and take them prisoner.

Within two days, they reached the Ohio River. An Ohio militia on the other side attempted to fire at them, but Will watched as one of the Confederate artillery fired, and the Federals soon retreated. The river at this point was too broad for effective sharpshooting. Thomas Hines, Will's tent mate, rejoined them, now promoted to captain. Hines had secured two large steamers. Will and the rest of the Second Kentucky left their horses on the Kentucky bank and crossed to Indiana to challenge the Federals. Just as they disembarked and formed a skirmish line, shells began to fall among them. Will heard the roar, then the whistling sound, followed by cries. A Federal gunboat steamed down the river, threatening their rear.

"Take cover!" Will yelled. With the militia ahead and the gunboat behind, no horses, and Morgan's command divided, the situation was tense. Will looked about for an advantage, but with shot landing everywhere, the best he could do was the cover of a fallen tree near the shore. The Federal militia tried advancing, but Will ordered a volley and they retreated. Will felt immense relief when Morgan's artillery repositioned and fired from a hill above the river. Will watched as the Confederate shots landed all around the boat, not seeming to harm it, but slackening its rate of fire in his direction. Around him, Will could almost smell the fear.

"Here they come!" yelled someone to his right. The Federal militia was again venturing out, this time being very unmilitary, not coming in a line but dashing from one point of cover to another, as if trying to reach a position of advantage. Will stopped worrying about the gunboat and turned, jumping to the other side of the log, to meet this new threat. The Federals were now about one hundred yards away, behind some houses and fences, slowly advancing. A ball hit the log, another kicking up dust and stones in front of his position. Will had only his Enfield carbine issued by the CSA and his pistols. The Whitworth was on the other side of the river. He concentrated on whoever was closest, taking careful aim. Spray from a shot fired by the gunboat drenched his legs, but he ignored it. He fired, and the running Federal fell. He rolled signaling one of the men to cover for him, then reloaded while still lying down. If the Federals could be unmilitary, so could he. He rolled back quickly and took aim again. Before he could fire, another of his company brought down the advancing Federal, and Will transferred his aim to the next. They hit more than they missed, and over the next twenty minutes, which seemed like hours, the Federals were discouraged and fell back. Turning, Will and his men cheered as they saw the gunboat steaming up river, away from them.

Will looked to the other side of the river, waving an all clear, while stationing three pickets in case the militia advanced again. His joy surged as a boat bearing their horses set out from the other side. He was never so glad to see Shadow. Apparently the Federals were discouraged, as they got no further challenge from them. Within three hours, using the two boats Hines got for them, the entire command was in Indiana, just east of Maukport.

Encouraged by their success and escape from danger, Morgan ordered them to press forward, until they reached Corydon, about twenty-six miles west of Louisville. Will saw a house ahead, with smoke coming through the chimney. He dismounted, gave Shadow to a private, and choosing two others, pushed forward cautiously. When they arrived at the house, they found it empty, but evidently the occupants had recently fled in the middle of preparing supper. Numerous chickens were scattering around the yard, and there was one fat hog. Will sent a message to Duke by one of the men, who returned with a favorable reply for camping and spending the night.

An hour later, Will sat comfortably in front of the fireplace, listening to the hiss of chickens turning on the spit, while his men tended the horses and posted lookouts. Two others were butchering the hog. He sighed with weariness and satisfaction—they would be well fed and rested tonight.

* * *

Albinia didn't know whether to be joyful or frightened. The news rippled through the small Indiana town of Madison. Morgan's men were at hand. Albinia wondered if Will was with them. Regardless, it couldn't mean good things for her people. But maybe it meant that Will was alive. She hurried over to a general store and bought a copy of the *Louisville Daily Democrat* for July 11, 1863. The paper recorded Morgan entering Corydon, pillaging and burning, with a force of at least four thousand men. Other people whispered that it was eleven thousand, with women and children fired upon.

She mounted her wagon and hurried back to the farm.

"Pa! We have more to worry about than Knights of the Golden Circle!" she shouted. Climbing down, she showed her father the newspaper.

"What if they come here, Pa? I don't know whether to hope Will is with them or whether to be ashamed that he might be a part of such crimes."

Robert took her shoulder and looked her in the eye. "It's war. Union troops did the same, some even worse. The Confederates are desperate now. We have to prepare—even if Will was with a group that came here, it's doubtful he could stop them. We just need to work faster." He turned and went to talk to the workers, including Ned Smith. In the last several months they built a brick kiln, and were now making their own bricks. Using these, and Ned's skill at the forge, they built a brick wall topped by wrought iron spikes around the farmyard, with loopholes to shoot rifles from. The Georgetown community was grateful to Albinia, and they mounted a round-the-clock watch, taking turns until the wall was nearly completed. Now they only had one section near the east road left unfinished. Robert formed a company of Negro militia and trained them in what he had learned of war.

Peter came down from Lancaster regularly, but insisted that Albinia stick close to the farm, teaching the children in Georgetown rather than making the longer trek to Lancaster. Occasionally, Mary King came with him. Albinia watched them together, and had trouble pushing away twinges of jealousy. Was it her safety or Mary that made him not want her in Lancaster?

At night, the iron gate closed and locked. Just as the gate was about to close for the night, a lone horseman approached. Albinia watched as her father took his rifle and hobbled over to the gate, loading and taking aim in case of trouble. The horseman drew closer.

"Miss Albinia! Miss Albinia! I'm looking for Albinia Horner," shouted the horseman, seeing the rifle.

"Who wants her?" responded Robert, not lowering the gun but hesitating, seeing a black man on horseback with no hood or arms in sight.

"It's Luther. Luther Clay."

"It's Luther, Pa! Put the gun away!" Albinia ran to meet him.

He dismounted, and she took his hand warmly. "You're welcome here! We're glad to see you."

"Greetings later," he said. "There's a force of Confederates making for Madison right now. I've just outrun them."

* * *

Will was exhausted, and Shadow stumbled occasionally. They were riding twenty-one hours a day. There was no time to make camp, barely time to eat and catch an hour or two of sleep. In the July heat and humidity it would have been hard to sleep, except that he was just so completely tired. Each morning he woke with new mosquito bites. Each day filled with skirmishing, bridge burning, dodging bullets, and patrolling. He rode over eighty miles in four days, fighting and tense all the way.

"Where are we headed?" Will asked Duke.

"Where Morgan leads. I don't know what he'll decide. Some say he'll attack Indianapolis. Others that we're headed back to Kentucky through Ohio. He hasn't shared his mind with me. Only God and Morgan know," Duke said. "But that's good enough for me."

Towards afternoon, Colonel Johnson came with orders to send a battalion toward Madison, not to attack but to discourage Federals from following Morgan's forces. Will's company was detached to go with the group. He and Shadow rested two hours, then the battalion rode out. They approached the town from the northwest. Will and two privates rode in front, cautiously feeling for pickets or any other sign of Federals. The town seemed peaceful as they crossed Crooked Creek and moved into town on Jefferson St. Will saw several townspeople and a few Negroes. They began running at the sight of the gray uniforms. A bell tolled at a church, and the command passed down the line to be ready.

They encountered no regular Federal troops, but as they turned down the road paralleling the river to the east, they saw a small force of militia in front of the depot, deployed behind barrels, boxes, and wagons. Johnson gave the order to spread out, sending one company to the north, another to the south, planning to converge on the depot from three sides, flanking the militia. Will moved south toward the river, then turned back north.

Johnson sent an envoy under flag of truce to ask the militia to stand down, since they were badly outnumbered. That offer being refused, he positioned a Parrot rifle where it could easily hit the depot. Shots rang out from the militia and the Parrot opened fire, hurling ten-pound shells. Will saw rather than heard the signal to charge, and ordered his men forward. He approached the depot at a controlled canter. To his surprise, the faces that looked out at him were mostly black, and there wasn't a blue uniform to be seen except at the center, where a tall fellow with a limp seemed to be directing the defense, wearing a Union coat, but not a full uniform. He registered all this in a second, and then just saw targets—men pointing guns at him, so he fired his pistols automatically, turning from one target to the next. Bullets whizzed around him, but the shots went wild— these were clearly green troops. As he reached the barrel barricade, he felt Shadow gather himself and leaned forward for the jump. Two or three blacks scattered as the big Friesian flew through the air toward them, but the blue-coated figure stood firm. As Will landed, the stock of a musket swung toward him, and he ducked even lower, so it hit him a glancing blow. He lost his seat and fell out of the saddle. His shoulder crunched against the hard ground, but he sprang up and lowered his head, running into the blue coat and knocking him over on his side. Will drew a pistol. The man on the ground twisted, knocked the pistol wide, and was about to land a fist in Will's face when they both stopped. Will was looking into the face of his father.

* * *

The fight was quickly over. Johnson's troops burned the railroad depot and water tower. The militia were taken prisoner and the wounded tended.

Will sat next to his father, shaken by what had almost happened.

"What happened, Pa? How did we get here? I went to the farm, and no one was there."

"Some secesh from town came out one night and burned it. I had just come home and was too ill to fight. Your ma was barely getting by, so we decided to come up to Albinia's. She has a farm east of here. She got burned out too, had to move out of Kentucky. She's even had trouble here in Indiana. We just don't want to lose our home again."

"You won't. I'll speak to Colonel Johnson. We don't have much use for prisoners, so it's likely you'll all be paroled in exchange for a promise not to fight. Even the blacks—some officers would kill them, but Johnson's not that kind. I ... I'm sorry, Pa. I never wanted it to get to this point. I ... I could have killed you."

"Or I you. We both know on a battlefield it becomes just what color uniform and survival."

"So where does that leave us?"

"I don't know, Will," Robert said honestly. "I know that you're my son and I still love you. Nothing's going to change that. I also know it may take some time to heal, both for us, and for the country. I can see that you haven't let hate take over, and I'm glad."

"No, but it's been hard losing so many friends."

"A lot of good men have died in this crazy war. Seems like there has to be another way."

"There is, Pa. Let it start with us." Will extended a hand. Robert shook it, and then drew him into a bear hug.

Will got permission to take a few hours leave and go see his family. He got his father a horse and recovered Shadow. They rode up to the farm, Robert giving the password to the gate guard. Will admired the fortifications, hearing the stories about the Golden Circle. It angered him that men would prey on his sister. She introduced him to Luther, Peter, Mary,

Ned, and Ruth. Luther looked at him coolly, being polite for Albinia's sake, Will thought. The gray uniform did not endear him to any of the Negroes. He wondered at the relationship between Peter, Mary, and his sister, but this was not the time to ask. Peter and Mary seemed ... close. But wasn't there an understanding between Albinia and Peter?

Sara rushed to Will and hugged him, crying. Lydia looked wide-eyed at her big brother, not sure what to make of him, then ran to him and hopped onto his lap. For Will, it was as if the world had suddenly righted itself, yet here he was about to leave all that was sane and dear to him again.

"Where will you go, Will?" Albinia asked.

"No choice. I go with my regiment." He noticed a disapproving gaze from Mary and most of the company.

Peter spoke, "You don't have to, Will. You could surrender. You could change sides. You're in the North—we could hide you, you'd never be caught."

"And how will I then sleep at night? I swore an oath to the Confederate States and to Morgan. You're a minister, you should know. 'When thou vowest a vow unto God, defer not to pay it; for *he hath* no pleasure in fools: pay that which thou hast vowed.'"

Seeing his mind made up, they turned to other topics. After a meal and a few hours, Will rejoined his troop and they rode north to Vernon. His heart was torn between leaving his family behind and his loyalty to his oath. He shook it off—he couldn't put his hand to the plow and look back.

* * *

Luther wasn't sure what made him more nervous, seeing Albinia's brother in a Confederate uniform or seeing Ruth again. They were initially shy of each other, unsure what the passage of time and events meant for their relationship. Finally, Luther couldn't stand it any longer.

"Ruth, will you come for a walk with me?"

"All right, Luther. Just let me tell my daddy."

She returned quickly and said, "It's all right—but if we're gone more than an hour he's gonna come after us with a shotgun" she said, smiling mischievously.

They walked out east of the farm compound. Luther went round and round in his mind about how to say what he wanted.

"Ruth, I know you didn't want me to go. And I know that you aren't happy about my killing Jameson. My ma ain't going to be happy, either. I'm sorry about Sam, but I had nuthin' to do with that. Fact is, once those were over, my mind and heart cleared—but not as much as I might have thought. I killed Jameson in battle, not just revenge, but it still troubles me in spite of all he did. I don't know what to feel."

Ruth listened but made little response.

Luther rushed on nervously. "You said you would wait for me. I came here lookin' for you. No other reason." He turned and took her hands. "Please. I still love you. Will you marry me?"

Ruth looked down as if thinking, then broke out in a wide smile. "Yes, Luther, I will marry you. I will be with you forever."

Luther kissed her and then yelled, "Whooeee! I'm the happiest man on earth!"

Ruth laughed and hugged him, laying her head on his shoulder. They walked back to the farm, hand in hand.

* * *

July 1863

Will heard that there was a large Federal force chasing them, led by Hobson, his old boss at the general store. After a night's rest, they rode all the next day and the following night. Some of his men were so tired they slept in the saddle, still moving forward. They moved into Ohio, reaching a point about thirty miles from Cincinnati. Morgan no longer seemed to care what his troops did as they moved east. Will watched as some of his fellows looted and stole food, horses, silver, and anything else they fancied. He limited his own foraging to obtaining a ham from a meat packing plant.

He was bone weary, but the Raiders kept moving. Will was continually thankful for his Kentucky-bred Shadow. Many of the men had to change mounts four or even five times a day to keep up. Finally, they reached a point near Buffington Island, where the Ohio bordered Virginia, on July 18.

Will was riding near the front of the column. It was about eight o'clock at night, and the darkness surrounded them like thick ebony velvet. They had to be near the river, and Will knew the plan was to cross it.

"Column, halt!"

"Private Lappin, Private Lane! Go forward carefully, see what's ahead. Don't engage anyone. If you find pickets or resistance, get back here quickly," Will ordered.

"Yes, sir!"

The two privates went off in the night, walking their horses. Will waited impatiently. If they could only get across the river, the thick forests and hills he'd heard about might provide them a chance to rest. He thought he heard gunfire, and the two privates returned at a gallop.

"There's Federals! They've got the ford at the river, got earthworks dug in. We didn't stick around to ask them to supper, but I saw at least one field piece poking over the edge."

"Good work! Lane, go report it to Duke and Morgan, wait for orders."

Private Lane left and returned again in an hour.

"Sir! General Morgan commands that we are to make camp here tonight and attack in the morning."

"All right, men! Dismount, make camp, but don't get too comfortable. We're going to have company early, I think." Will saw to setting guards out, tended Shadow, and then gratefully sank onto his bedroll, not bothering with a tent.

Dawn came, and he got his men up and moving. Duke came to lead the attack. He conferred with Will and the other officers, where Will learned that two full brigades would advance. They set up a Parrot gun on a slight rise, but more for effect than anything—they only had three cartridges left for it. When all was ready, they moved forward cautiously, expecting any moment that the earthworks would spit bullets and death. All was strangely quiet. Will was tense—why were the Federals not attacking? Was it some sort of trick? They were within fifty yards now. Will saw Duke motion, and sent his troop to the south side, flanking the earthworks. Still no resistance. Then they were beyond them and could see the river. There was no one there. The Federals had vanished. Will was bewildered. If they had known, they could have gotten across safely in the night.

Will began to make preparations to cross. Duke said they were taking all the wagons and wounded—no one was to be left behind. By about noon, they were ready. The first horses were starting to enter the river when it happened.

Artillery shells came screaming in among them, and cavalry from the northwest. The attack caught them off guard. They had supposed they had at least a day's march between them and the Federals chasing them. Will's company turned and met the charge in their rear. Chaos was everywhere. Men and animals were screaming, the air was full of bullets. Two Federals charged at Will, and he jerked Shadow hard to the left, causing them to run into one another. Will drew his pistol and fired, hitting a horse. The men with the Parrot gun were captured. Then more artillery shells, this time from the river. Two Federal gunboats arrived, steaming up the river and shelling them with impunity.

Will dodged, swerved, and fired. His pistols were empty, and no time to load. He fired the Enfield carbine at an approaching Federal.

"Form a line, men! Form a line!" yelled Will. It was no use. Terrified horses plunged about in the midst of the melee. Wagons and supplies rolled over the edge, down the sloping ravine to the river. Federal infantry arrived on the southwest, pushing them toward the river.

"Retreat! Sound retreat!" yelled Duke. Through personal courage, he managed to restore a semblance of order, and the cavalry formed a column of fours, moving north along the river to escape the gunboats.

"Cover for me!" yelled Will at a private. Within a minute, he reloaded his pistols and the Enfield.

Many of their fellows were left behind, but Will took up his old position in the rear, guarding the retreat.

The Federals pressed from behind, but Will and four or five others made them pay if they got too close. They were moving at a quick trot. Will knew from maps that there were other fords to the north. If they could gain that, they might still escape.

The road bent west, away from the river. On the eastern side was a steep ravine, with bluffs on the east rising again before plunging to the riverbank. Suddenly a new force appeared, Federal cavalry from the northwest, charging, firing, and swinging sabers. Caught between the force behind and the new attackers, there was nowhere to go but into the ravine. Shadow stumbled down the steep side, losing his balance. Will was thrown, his head hitting the ground hard. Blackness descended, and he knew no more.

* * *

When Will woke, he was lying at the bottom of the ravine. He tried to sit up, thinking the fight was still going on, but saw that Duke and others were standing around, with Federals guarding them. It was over. Seeing him move, a medical orderly came over to look at him.

"How are you feeling?"

"Like I wish I had a different head. Don't think anything is broken, though."

"Can you march?"

"I can manage," replied Will. His head felt like his horse had stepped on it. The pain throbbed, but he managed to stand. He joined a line of gray uniforms, and the guards, ever cautious, moved them out of the ravine by a sloping path to the north. Someone had carefully taken all his weapons. He briefly wondered what happened to the Whitfield. When his head protested, he stuck to worrying about just putting one foot in front of another. If he stumbled, a bayonet prodded him. He felt exhausted from weeks in the saddle. His head wound throbbed. He had no urge to fight.

They huddled in a group in a field about five hundred yards from the river. Here the bank sloped gently, but there were vigilant guards to prevent any escape. The Federals allowed no fires.

"What you s'pose they'll do with us?" said one.

"I don't know," said Will. "All I know is that I failed. If I'd kept watch on the Federals, scouted in the night, known when they withdrew, maybe none of us would be sitting here."

Will slept fitfully. All sorts of images haunted his dreams. The first Federal he killed. Archie dying at Shiloh. He dreamed Morgan was shot. Albinia came in his dream, scolding him for following Morgan. Toby looked at him as though betrayed when he had to leave him at the river.

When he woke, he heard among the men that officers and private soldiers were to be separated. News of the Confederate defeat at Gettysburg reached them. It was thought that with so many Confederate prisoners, officers would be less likely to be set free, if indeed any were set free at all. Will determined then to hide his rank, stripping his uniform of insignia and assuming the role of a private. He asked the others not to give him away.

"All right you Johnny Rebs! You gonna get some Northern hospitality. Form ranks of twos, and march!"

Will's head felt slightly improved. He marched with the line down onto a small steamboat. Since they thought him a private, he remained on deck. He watched as two or three managed to jump overboard in the night and escape. He felt that if he tried, he would just drown. He lay on a blanket on the deck, looking up at the stars. He wondered if Morgan had escaped. He wondered about Tom Logwood and Ben Drake. They were not in his group. He wondered if his fellow soldiers blamed him for their predicament. The boat was crowded, barely room to lie down. So far the Federals were courteous, accommodating, supplying little niceties like his blanket. It was stifling hot, but a breeze stirred over the water. What would happen to them?

BEHIND BARS

July 1863

For three days, the steamer wound its way down the Ohio, taking Will and the rest of Morgan's command to an uncertain future in Cincinnati. Will's head grew worse, and he felt as though he had a fever.

"You Yanks got a doctor on board this tub?" he asked.

"Reb, no use getting healthy where you're going. But I'll ask," said the guard. He returned an hour later with balding bespectacled man in a dark suit coat, who examined Will.

"Anything unusual in how you feel?"

Will thought he must be an idiot. "Of course it's unusual. I got thrown off a horse. My head hit the ground, maybe a rock. It hurts something fierce most of the time. One minute I wish they'd shot me. The next minute I feel like we'll still win the war. Can you at least stop the pain?"

The doctor rummaged about and then said, "I'll have someone bring you a willow bark tea. I have no laudanum to give you; it's for soldiers at the front. I'm afraid you'll just have to cope with the pain. Of course, if you try to escape, one of the soldiers here may grant your wish to be shot."

When the tea came, Will drank it gratefully, and then tried to sleep. Twice a day someone came by with a bucket of alleged soup and hard tack. Will swayed and struggled to get down to the privy in the stern, and then back. He passed in and out of consciousness.

Finally, they docked in Cincinnati. The officers were unloaded. Will watched Duke disembark and wondered if he would ever see him again. Should he have stayed with the officers? It was too late to change his mind. The private soldiers spent the night on the boat. Early the next morning, a few wagons were at the docks. Will saw that prisoners who could walk were herded off and made to stand in the heat. He was helped off the boat and allowed into one of the wagons. He sat listlessly. He scratched his scruffy week-old beard. He was filthy and sweaty. It was hard to think, hard to concentrate. In some ways, he didn't want to. After all, what was the point? This is where his devotion to honor and to Morgan led him. The wagons began to move.

* * *

Julia sat in the kitchen reading the newspaper. Mama Kirsten rarely entered the kitchen, declaring it the domain of servants, not a true lady. Julia rejoiced in that, and used it as an escape.

"More coffee, Mrs. Johannsen?" offered one of the kitchen maids.

"Yes please, Laura," said Julia, looking up and then returning to the article. The headlines proclaimed General Morgan and his command captured. Some sources disbelieved it, but others said the prisoners would arrive in Cincinnati in a few days. Could Will be among them?

"Laura, bring me some writing paper and ink. I need to send a note to my family."

Julia had recently returned from visiting Albinia and her parents on the river. She quickly penned a note advising them that Will might be among the prisoners. Then her eye caught another article. It said that portions of the Third Ohio Cavalry were captured, and on their way to Libby Prison in Richmond. Hiram!

* * *

Julia and her family crowded in with the rest, lining the dock, held back by a rope line and soldiers. Most of the crowd was hostile, jeering and yelling at Morgan's men coming off the boat. Some actually threw stones or bottles at the men. Julia and Albinia craned their necks to see, but were too short to see over everyone's head. Little Lydia climbed up on her father's shoulders. More than once Robert nearly dropped her, as his uneven legs struggled to retain his balance, jostled by the crowd.

"There he is, Pa!" Lydia shouted. She wiggled and got down. She wanted to run to her brother.

Sara held her. "You can't, Lyddie. You can't."

"But it's Will. I want to go see him!"

Albinia knelt down, pushing someone aside, to be at her sister's level. "I know, sweetheart. But you can't. Will is going to have to go away for a while. Maybe they'll let us see him. Remember what I told you about being in prison? That's what's going to happen to Will."

Julia thought Lydia appeared confused. "But Will isn't bad. What did he do wrong?" Lydia said.

"I wasn't bad, either," Albinia said. "Prisons have bad people in them, but they also have people who just didn't make the right choices."

"Well, I'm going to do something!" said Julia.

Julia pushed forward to speak to the officer in charge of the prison detail.

"Sir, my brother is in this group. I'm Mrs. Johannsen, of the Ohio Zephyr steamship company. If I could speak to him, even for a moment...."

"I'm sorry, ma'am. The governor says these men and their officers are common criminals, looters and thieves. The officers are going to the penitentiary. The men are going to Camp Morton."

"I helped the governor get elected! Please, just for a moment. I can promise you won't get in any trouble."

The captain made a face. "Ma'am, I have my orders. Once they arrive at Camp Morton, you can speak to the commandant there. Meanwhile, you best clear the way. Go home, ma'am. These rebels aren't worth your trouble. Mrs. Lincoln has brothers with the rebels too. She ignores them. You should do the same. Go home."

She tried to shout and wave to get Will's attention, but it was hard to hear over the noise of the crowd. She could see Will just sitting, as though made out of wood.

Disheartened, they watched as the men marched and the wagons rolled out. They went back to the Johannsens for lunch. The Crumps and Albinia boarded an Ohio Zephyr steamer, courtesy of Julia. Julia waved them off at the dock, returning home to write to Hiram.

* * *

Albinia couldn't wait to get home. She wished she could have talked to Will, to comfort him, to let him know prison wasn't forever—but also to warn him, based on her own experiences. Prisons did sometimes have bad people in them, or at least, people with pain who wanted to take it out on you.

Since that hadn't been possible, she offered prayers for him and turned her mind to Peter. Since her parents' coming, the year had been so busy she barely had time to think. Her school for young Negro children in Georgetown was going well. She and Peter had a few Mondays together, when he would come down after church on Sunday and stay in town for the night. There had been no repeat of their intimate evening together. Could it have been eight months? Had something changed? In all that time she had seen him regularly, but there had been friendship, not intimacy. Increasingly, Mary was always around. Mary was unfailingly friendly toward her, but Albinia saw the glances between them, the laughter when they thought no one was looking. It was hard not to be jealous.

When they arrived at the compound, Albinia peered ahead and saw Peter's wagon in the yard. As Robert helped her down from the wagon, she thanked him and rushed inside.

As she entered, Mary turned from the stove in Albinia's kitchen and stumbled over an iron left by the fireplace. Peter caught her, and Albinia gasped a little. They were in an awkward embrace. Peter quickly disengaged himself, seeing Albinia. The image hit her like a knife. She turned and went back out the door, running down the path to the north along the river, toward the inn. She ran past her parents, not yet in the house, even ignoring a question from Lydia as she went by. She couldn't believe it. Peter must be in love with her, his childhood friend. She was angry, and hot tears streamed down her cheeks as she ran. How could he? She had been a fool to trust him, to dishonor David's memory! Vaguely behind her, she heard someone calling, but she was determined not to listen. She would stay at the inn tonight. Tomorrow she would figure out what to do. Her parents could have the farm. Ruth could take the school. She wasn't needed here.

Her eyes were red and swollen, her face blotched with tears, and her hair flying in a hundred directions. She reached the fence that marked the entrance to the yard around the inn, and slowed. This would never do—she couldn't let herself be seen like this. She stopped to repair the damage as best she could. She heard footsteps pounding up behind her and looked for somewhere to hide, suddenly frightened, checking for her derringer.

She turned and saw Peter running toward her. Her anger and hurt returned. She did not want to see him!

"Albinia! Wait!" Peter gasped, galloping up to her. "I need to talk to you!"

"We have nothing to talk about, apparently," said Albinia icily. "It's Mrs. Horner to you."

Peter reached out for her elbow, but she pulled free and glared at him. "How dare you!"

"Albinia, please! It's not what you think. Really. Mary and I are just good friends. We've known each other since childhood."

"I've heard that story," said Albinia drily. "Now if you'll excuse me, I'm not stupid. I'm hot and tired. I've come from a long journey, seeing my brother put in jail. Go away!"

"Please, just hear me out. Just give me a few minutes," Peter said, holding his hands out palms toward her and backing off a step or two. "Then if you want, I'll leave you alone," he said bitterly.

Albinia turned to go, then turned back. "All right. You have two minutes."

"I know I haven't been the suitor I should have been these past months. But before you condemn me, at least know that Mary is leaving. Tomorrow. I'm sorry that I've let work and friendship steal time from you. I could give you a hundred excuses, but you deserve better than that. I could say I've been out here on the Railroad for so long, with no family, that having Mary and her family around has been like a visit to home. But mostly, I just want to ask you to forgive me. I love you, no one else. Not that way. Mary is like a sister. Please. If you won't forgive me, I'll regret it until I die."

Albinia softened a little and was about to reply, when Mary came up the path. She stopped a few feet away. Albinia's anger flared again and she was about to leave, when Mary spoke, "Please. Mrs. Horner. Wait. I haven't heard all that Peter has told you, but I can imagine. It's true. I have no claim on Peter except long friendship. He loves you—he's told me that. I am not interested in him romantically at all. Peter's a fine man. He's just slow at times about how women think." She flashed an impish grin at him. "I hope you'll listen to him. I would ask you to forgive us both. I meant it when I said I'd like your friendship. However, I am leaving for Texas tomorrow." She walked closer and took each of their hands, placing Albinia's in Peter's. "But I'm also going to leave now. I think you two have things to discuss." She turned and walked back down the path.

"Will you forgive me?" Peter pleaded.

She burst into tears and threw her arms around his neck. "Yes, Peter. Yes. With all my heart."

* * *

Will looked around the derelict camp. It looked like a place abandoned, stomped on, and then reinhabited. Will guessed that over a thousand of Morgan's men were in the wagon train to Camp Morton, on the north side of Indianapolis. The march in the summer heat, with little water and rest, covered over one hundred miles, and they arrived on July 23, 1863. Will supposed he might have been lucky to have the head wound, after all, since he got to ride in a wagon with other wounded, in spite of the putrid smell of gangrene.

The camp gate arched, rising from two sides to a point. There was a high white board fence around the outside. Inside were long low-slung barracks and rows of tents. There were trees around the interior, and grass. One of the barracks had a hole in the roof, and a door flapped lazily on its hinges in the wind. Everywhere Will looked, men were sitting, playing cards or checkers, looking bored.

A sergeant from the Massachusetts artillery checked them in and assigned them a bunk. Will walked into the barracks, hundreds of feet long, lined with tiers of bunks stacked four high. Down the center was a long thin table, apparently for eating purposes. Mosquitoes and gnats buzzed around his head, and he felt a wave of dizziness. The stench was overpowering. A rat skittered across the floor in front of them. The bunks were just wooden platforms with straw tick mattresses. Will was assigned to one of the bottom bunks, as the sergeant doubted his ability to climb.

The sergeant looked Will over and said, "You one sorry excuse for a soldier, Reb. I reckon they'll be plantin' you with the smallpox group before the week is out."

Will sank onto the bunk, despairing, and began to pray.

* * *

August 1863

Camp routine was dull. There was an attempt to make the prisoners drill, without weapons, but after a week or so, the Union soldiers gave up. There was fresh bread, baked daily, but little else besides occasional beans. Still the rest did Will good, and after two weeks he began to feel more normal. It was now three weeks since the battle.

"Hey, you Johnny Reb! You hear the good news? They got that scoundrel Morgan. He's goin' to jail worse than here. Who knows? If you're good and kiss Lincoln's boots, they might let you outta here by Christmas. Course most of you leave in the natural way, greetin' Saint Peter." The guard walked off laughing nastily.

Most of the guards were former prisoners of the Confederates, given parole, but for whom the Federals had not yet exchanged prisoners South. Under the terms of their parole, they were not supposed to fight, but could do guard duty for the army, freeing other troops for combat.

There were two men on each bunk level. Will's bunkmate was a Scot, Jamie McPherson. Will thought him a good companion, a God-fearing Presbyterian with a mischievous streak. He stood about five feet six inches, with brown hair, wide set eyes, dimpled chin, and prominent nose. He had a wiry strength, and was from the Third Kentucky Cavalry, where he served Morgan as a gunner manning the howitzers and Parrot rifles.

One evening around the stove, Jamie took Will aside.

"What d'ye say we liven up that guard's life? I'd do it meself, but I need a lookout. Are ye game?"

Will thought and shrugged. He felt all right, just cold and hungry. Some fun to pass the time couldn't hurt. "Sure. When and where?"

"Tomorra mornin', early like, before the guards are awake."

Accordingly, Jamie poked Will the next morning before dawn, and they quietly rose and put their boots on. They cracked open the door and looked around—no one was moving in the camp. It was dark, and any guard on the wall wouldn't see them. They moved quietly from one barracks building to another, until they reached the guard's building.

Will stood lookout at the door, though most of the guards were inside, sleeping. He shook his head at Jamie's daring. Jamie found a bucket and went to one of the few water outlets in the camp. He returned with it nearly full of cold water. Removing his own boots, he crept into the guard's quarters. He was out again in five minutes with his bucket nearly empty. No one made a sound, no one approached. Jamie stowed the bucket beside the rain barrel, and they both ran back to the barracks.

When they were safely back in their bunk, Will saw that Jamie was having trouble not exploding in laughter.

"Jes wait until that Federal tries to put his boots on this morning! I filled each boot with water and smeared a bit o' butter from their mess on the floor around them, just to make it slippery like."

Will quietly chuckled and agreed that it would be a good joke.

After dawn, roll call came. The guard who had insulted Morgan the previous day looked angry and sported a black eye.

"You Johnny Rebs think this is some kinda circus, don't you? Think you're funny! When I find out who rigged my boots, you're gonna wish you'd died instead of bein' a prisoner."

A few days later, however, the prisoners turned out for an announcement.

Colonel Rose, the commandant, addressed them. "You Kentucky men that came in from Morgan's command—you're all being transferred. This here's a paradise compared to where you're going. You're all going to Camp Douglas in Chicago. May God have mercy on your souls."

True to his word, the next day Will, Jamie, and all the other Morgan men were loaded into freight cars on the train and shipped like cattle to the slaughter, north to Chicago. They arrived at Camp Douglas August 18, 1863. Morgan's men arrived on successive trains over the next five days, until Camp Douglas had over three thousand new arrivals.

The barracks here were smaller. Will talked with one of the guards and learned they were intended to house about eighty men—they were now crammed with about one hundred per building. Will and Jamie managed to stay together. Will listened and found the sentiment among the men much changed—they were determined to escape and rejoin the fighting. He learned also that mail was easy to get in and out of the camp, and promptly sat down to write letters to his family.

The barracks were pine board construction, raised on stilts off the ground about three feet, to make tunneling more difficult. The camp was laid out in streets and sections, with names like White Oak and Garrison. It was right up against the city, with the University of Chicago across the street. When Will arrived, there were streetcars of gawkers come to see the new prisoners. He learned that the camp was intended for Federal troops, but was converted to a prison. The high walls made it look difficult to escape, but Will soon learned that security was lax and corruption among the guards rampant.

Once he and Jamie settled, they strolled about the camp. Jamie got a favorable reception from the guards, many of them Irishmen, who thought a Scot close kindred. Will saw a post office, barbershop, photographer's studio, two sutler stores, a commissary house, and a chapel. He smelled sewage, rotting food, and the stench of several thousand unwashed bodies.

There was only one water hydrant for the entire camp, and it wasn't working. Prisoners were not obliged to work, but Will saw it as a way to pass the time and improve conditions for everyone.

At assembly, the guards took roll. Then DeLand, the commandant, addressed them:

"I'll not tolerate trouble here. Any man that causes trouble will be confined to the dungeon. I do not have enough troops to work on the camp, only enough to guard you sorry Rebs and keep you from mischief. Should any of you desire to improve your circumstances, see the sergeant of the guard in your section and he will assign you work to help your fellows. Anyone volunteering to work on the walls will receive one dollar and fifty cents Federal per day. Other work will not be paid, but may result in less sickness and better living. That is all."

Will sought out his sergeant and volunteered to work on digging new sewer and water pipes.

Two weeks later, a ragged gray-clad soldier wandered over to where Will was digging.

"Say, soldier, suppose you take a rest a while and let me borrow your shovel."

"You want to dig pipes?" Will asked.

The man guffawed. "No, siree, not interested in doin' the Federal's work for them. But some of your fellows could use that shovel for the cause," he said slyly.

Will looked him over.

"No, sir. If you want a shovel, go and ask the sergeant. I'm sure he would let you dig pipes, but not for another purpose."

"Don't you want to get out of here?"

"Yes, but not to fight. I'm done with it. I'm tired of killing men and having them try to kill me because of the color cloth we wear."

"Suit yourself," the man shrugged. "Some of us are going to find our way back to the captain, or General Morgan, should I say."

A few days later, Will heard about some of the men sneaking out, only to be caught in the dens of gambling and prostitution that were near the camp. They were marched into the White Oak Dungeon. The dungeon was a hole in the ground accessed by a trap door, lined with white oak logs more than a foot in diameter. Will meant to stay clear of it, only to find that Jamie was in the group. He learned that those in the dungeon would be given only bread and water, and no exercise. It was not quite eighteen square feet, and had twenty-four prisoners at a time in it. Just walking into the square where the dungeon was could make Will gag, so much worse was the stench than the rest of the camp. He went anyway, to see if he could help his friend. The guards went away for a few minutes, and he raced over to the wooden grate.

"Jamie! Jamie Mac! Are you in there? Can you hear me?"

"Aye," came a weak reply.

"Is there anything I can do for you?"

"Aweel, ye could pass in that shovel ye dig with. And keep yer mouth shut."

Will felt conflicted—if he gave them the shovel and was found out, he'd likely be in the dungeon himself. If he became ill, it could be a death sentence. In the weeks he'd been here, dozens died of disease.

He had only moments to decide—he ran and got the shovel, passing it through the narrow opening. He'd barely gotten it in the dungeon and turned away whistling when the guards returned.

Up to this point, prisoners who were private soldiers were allowed to take an oath of allegiance to the United States and be released to fight in the Federal army. Now, in October, the Federals announced no more applications for allegiance would be processed. No prisoner exchanges were to happen. They were stuck for the duration of the war. Will began to wish he had done more to help the stranger who wanted to break out.

A few days later, on October 26, a furious Commandant DeLand lined up the prisoners in the yard.

"Last night, some of you Kentucky men decided to make a mockery of this camp by escaping the dungeon. Somehow, the prisoners obtained a shovel. They dug through the plank floor, into a garbage pit, and out under the wall. They must have had help. I demand to know who helped them. If that man will step forward, he alone will be punished. If not, you will all stand at attention without food or water, all night if necessary."

Will did not step forward. He waited. The night grew colder. The wind howled. The men shuffled and grumbled, getting poked with bayonets when they became too restless. DeLand retired to his quarters to wait. Whispering began.

"Musta been someone diggin' for the Federals."

"Good for him, I say! We'll show these Federals what we're made of."

"Easy for you to say. Rations is short enough already. And then we got to stand here in the cold and starve? Ought to give himself up."

There were many murmurs of agreement. Finally around midnight, as the temperature dropped toward freezing and a light rain began, Will could stand it no longer. He couldn't let his fellow soldiers suffer because he'd helped a friend.

Will stepped forward and in a loud voice declared, "Sir! It was I who helped the prisoners."

Will was astonished when twenty more men stepped forward, making the same declaration. The commandant was summoned.

"You clearly cannot all have been responsible. However, since you wish to suffer with your fellow conspirator, your wish is granted. Sergeant! Take these men to the dungeon. Make them repair the floor and fill in any holes. Any who hesitate or lag, shoot them! You prisoners will then stay in the dungeon for three days. We'll see if you are then ready to tell me who actually helped."

After the dungeon was repaired, Will stood for three days, because there was no room to lie down in the dungeon. There was only a single slice of bread each day, and two cups of water. There was one bucket in the corner as a privy for twenty-one men, and no way to empty it. A guard, sometimes retching, entered every two hours, day or night, to check the security of the dungeon. Two other guards stood by, with pistols and rifles ready, in case of a revolt.

At the end of three days, three prisoners were chosen at random, James Allen, John Sweeney, and William Wason. Will watched as the men who stood up for him were strung up with their thumbs supporting the entire weight of their bodies. After a few hours, they began to groan, but none recanted their confession. Will again protested that it was he alone, but others would not let him take all the blame. John Sweeney and William Wason died of exposure. Finally, the sergeant sent the other men back to their barracks and threw Will back in the dungeon for an additional three days. When he emerged, he felt he'd lost twenty pounds and was hot with fever.

For the following two weeks Will lay on his bunk, mostly unable to move except to eat and go to the privy. A private named Curtis Burke came and helped him.

"Will, what you did was brave. Morgan would have been proud. I'm gonna see you get better. Maybe we can break out of this hellhole together."

Will looked up gratefully. "Thanks, Curt. But all I want to do is survive." Will took the cup of water Curt offered and then sank back. He went into delirium. He had no idea how long he was out.

When he became conscious again, he felt weak but the fever had broken. He discovered it was almost Christmas.

"Hey, Crump! You got a package here!"

Will's fingers shook as he untied the string from the large parcel. Inside, he found a veritable treasure trove. There was a warm winter coat, willow bark and dogwood bark, quinine, new socks knit by Albinia, a flannel shirt, new breeches from his mother Sara, hard tack, dried oranges, and eighty dollars in Federal money from Julia. Just as important to Will, there were letters from everyone. Even Lydia scrawled a note and drew a picture of her big brother Will and herself. Albinia also sent a new Bible.

In the letters, Will learned that Luther and Ruth would be married soon. The real surprise was that Peter and Albinia would also be married. Not all of the news was happy. Julia wrote that Hiram was a prisoner, and was in Libby Prison in Richmond. Will felt truly sorry for him, imagining the trials facing that gentle giant. Julia also stated that Morgan had escaped prison and was on the loose again.

With the gifts provided, Will's recovery accelerated. He began reading the Bible Albinia sent, again turning to God as his strength. He thought about Joseph in prison in Egypt. He didn't think he was anyone that important, but maybe, somehow, God had a purpose for this difficult time. He began attending the chapel and heard Dwight Moody speak, offering challenges and encouragement. Some others of Morgan's men listened. Others scoffed at him, said the punishment made him go soft, turned him to a coward. Will ignored the naysayers, except to pray for them.

Day followed weary day. One morning the camp buzzed with news— most of the escaped prisoners were returning, captured. Will stood at the gate as they came in. A much thinner and bedraggled Jamie MacPherson was among them.

DeLand grew furious—prisoners were shot, winter coats from home confiscated as the temperature dropped to zero. The men were living on frozen mud. As the winter dragged on, sickness and death from disease mounted—twenty in Will's barracks alone died. He carefully measured out and shared the medicine sent from home, but some died anyway. Packages from home were now forbidden and confiscated.

In late February 1864, Will rejoiced at the news—DeLand was out. A new commandant was coming. A letter from Julia had the welcome news that Hiram had escaped from Libby, with many others, and was expected home soon.

News of Federal defeats made the guards surly, victories made them exultant and jeering toward the prisoners. The new Federal commander, Strong, seemed uncertain how to handle the prisoners. His superior, General Orme, had his own ideas.

"What the Federals doing now, Will?" asked Jamie, looking at the wall.

"I dunno, Jamie. Looks like they're stringing lanterns."

That night, the walls suddenly lit up, with dozens of oil lamps. A new rail was put up ten feet from the wall, with a notice that any prisoner found between the rail and the wall would be shot.

Will got up to use the privy and check out the new lights. Suddenly he felt a bayonet in his back.

"Halt! You there, out of quarters at night! Stand at attention!"

Will halted and did as he was told.

"What's your name?"

"Will Crump, sir."

"We'll deal with you in the morning, Crump. Back inside."

The next morning, Will had to report and received a ball and chain shackled to his ankle. The ball weighed about twenty pounds, and he was forced to drag or carry it wherever he went for the next week.

As spring came, yet another commander took over, Colonel Benjamin Sweet. Sweet thought prisoners should not be idle, so in spite of having few guards in proportion to the number of prisoners, he forced the prisoners to work improving the camp. Sweet also restored the prisoners' ability to receive packages from home. Will wrote to Julia, and soon a weekly stream of goods came his way. The guards pilfered some, but because the packages were regular, he was able to have enough for his needs and some to share with grateful companions like Jamie and Curt. It was largely due to this lifeline from home that Will stayed well and survived when so many died. Rations were cut, and work increased.

By June, food was scarce. Will saw men eating rats and chasing a poor dog, which rumor said turned up in the prisoners' kitchen and on their table. The prisoners could no longer buy vegetables.

The prison administration again banned packages from the outside, so that Will's promised birthday presents in August did not arrive. On his twentieth birthday, August 21, 1864, Will was digging trenches for another new sewer at the camp. His birthday breakfast was a single slice of bread and two cups of water. Coffee was now not allowed for prisoners. He heard that the Federal generals wanted to retaliate, and would not allow prisoners to eat better than the Confederate soldiers in the field. On Sunday, boiled beef and hominy was added to the bill of fare.

Curt and some others formerly in Morgan's command protested the reduced rations vigorously.

"Will ye not join us, this time?" Jamie asked Will. "A few of us are going to try escaping again. These new Pennsylvania boys I don't think could hit a squirrel with cannon at twenty yards."

Will just laughed, but then sobered. "You shouldn't try again, Jamie. It's not worth your life. I know it's bad here, but if we band together, share, and trust God, we can make it. You heard the news—Atlanta has fallen. It's only a matter of time now. The war will end."

Jamie shook his head. "I'll never stop trying. It would be like admitting that these blue bellies are right and all we fought for is wrong. There's always a chance. Never count out Bobby Lee."

The guards paraded a newspaper in front of the Kentucky men. The headlines told of General Morgan's death, shot while evading capture, on September 4. Will was sorrowful. Whatever else Morgan may have been, he was consistently good to Will.

Will kept his silence, and on the night of September 7, Curt, Jamie, and about forty others from Morgan's command rushed the fence, in spite of the dead zone and the lights. Will clanked a bucket noisily near a water hydrant, trying to help distract the guards. He watched as the men successfully broke a plank in the fence as bullets whizzed around them. About ten men made it through the fence before the guards came running to corral the prisoners with bayonets, Jamie among them. Curt however was not successful, and remained in the camp.

"Jamie was right—those Pennsylvania men can't shoot," Curt said. "But I guess with Morgan gone and Atlanta fallen, it may not be worth trying again."

Will nodded. "It can't be long now. Ol' Sweet just made it a shooting offense to walk between the outer barracks and the wall."

Over the next few weeks, Will fell ill again with dysentery. Typhoid was also sweeping through the camp. The weather turned colder. He was shivering in his bunk on the morning of Sept 28 as he woke, when he noticed many of the men missing. He rose to go to the privy and found a guard stationed at the entrance to the barracks. Apparently there was another attempt at mass escape. Thirty prisoners were involved, and two were wounded—the Pennsylvania boys could shoot after all.

Curt fell ill with smallpox. The guards carried him to the hospital wagon, and Will wondered if he'd ever see his friend again.

Will knew that many felt their chances of survival in the camp were worse than if they were fighting. His illness made him wonder, but he didn't agree. He asked others not to tell him about planned escapes, so he could not be considered guilty, whether they succeeded or failed. He had no medicine left from home.

He gradually regained some strength, but then fell back into a fever. The wind howled, the temperature dropped. Christmas was bleak, with no word from home.

Just after Christmas, a huge storm hit the camp. A late Christmas present arrived from home, with new medicine, food, and dried oranges. This time, Will had to guard his treasure, else it would have been stolen. The storm brought feet of snow, and temperatures about twenty below zero. Pipes froze, and clean water became scarce. Men melted snow on the boilers for drinking water. Will gave a few of the oranges to those most afflicted with scurvy. Many had teeth fall out, and their lips gave way to the disease. Will just stayed in his bunk, attempting to be warm, but shivered and teeth chattered, particularly after the commandant deprived the prisoners of all extra blankets in retaliation for an escape attempt.

When the snow abated and the trains were able to run, more prisoners flooded the camp. They were four to a bunk now, good for warmth but bad for the spread of disease. Will could barely walk. No one bothered with funerals anymore—too many were dying, and the coffins were just carted off in wheelbarrows to a common grave. To combat the problem, those able to walk formed vigilante juries—any man who failed to keep himself clean was liable to be carried to the bathhouse, stripped, and scrubbed, regardless of the outside temperature. Will's fever grew worse, and only the solicitude of his bunkmates kept him alive. Around him, some got frostbite. Men used to sing hymns after the eight o'clock curfew, but now even talking was forbidden. News of the fall of Fort Fisher, a main Confederate supply depot, spread through the camp, lending credence that the war was almost over.

Will regained some strength. Curt emerged from the smallpox hospital shaky but walking. Curt didn't live in the same barracks, but came by to see that Will was cared for. Guards were beating and whipping prisoners now for any small or sometimes imagined offense. The camp designed for four thousand now had over thirteen thousand prisoners.

As the weather warmed, news of the war continued to look worse for the Confederates. In late February, word came down that some of Morgan's men were going to be transferred out of Camp Douglas. Will and Joe Dunavan from Company D, Second Kentucky, were among the group.

They boarded a train on March 2 bound for Maryland, a camp called Point Lookout. Joe was a Mason, and managed through talking to the engineer to get himself and Will a better spot in the train, with more ventilation and privileges to be near the stove.

They arrived at the camp on the ocean and saw a sea of tents. There were few buildings. The wind blew off the ocean and made the coming spring cold. There were eighteen to a tent meant for ten. Will and Joe were separated. Sanitation was nonexistent, and Will fell back into fever.

A week later, he was placed on a train headed south. By March 15, he checked into a hospital at Farmville, Virginia. The male nurses there were kind to him, and the conditions better than any of the camps he'd been in. Will felt he knew very little of what went on. After two weeks, he was able to stand and walk. At the end of the third week, the news came—Lee had surrendered. The war was over. Will was free.

THE SUN BREAKS THROUGH

April 1865

W ill had a uniform coat with holes in it, a boot with a sole flap-
ping, no money, no horse, and no weapons when he tottered
out of the hospital in Farmville. Nights were still cold. One of the nurses
took pity on him and gave him a loaf of bread, a blanket, and a flint and
steel to make a fire. He still felt ill, but the hospital was turning out all
Confederate soldiers. The war was over—they were on their own. He'd
never been in this country before. He walked west, stopping often, con-
serving his bread. He camped at night under whatever tree was available.
After four days walking, he came upon a gray-bearded farmer mending
fence near Appomattox.

Will approached him. "Sir, I'm a stranger here. Can you tell me the
nearest town with a good telegraph?"

"Lynchburg, about twenty miles west. You don't look in much shape
to walk it, though. You a soldier?"

"Was. Just got out of the Federals prison. I need to make it to family
in Indiana."

The farmer looked at him kindly. "You look about the age of my son.
Lost him at Chickamauga. Wounded myself at Cold Harbor. Come on up
to the house. I 'spect my wife can find you food and a bed. Tomorrow I'll
drive you to Lynchburg, get a telegram sent for you. I don't imagine you
have any money."

"No, sir, but I'll fix that fence for you. I can work."

The farmer waved it off. "You're in no condition, boy. If my son were wandering home, I'd want someone to show him kindness. But he'll never come," ended the farmer sadly, turning away.

Will accepted gratefully. The next day, he sent a short telegram to Julia.

Julia Johannsen,

I want to see you all. In Virginia. Send cash to Lynchburg bank.

Your brother,
Will

* * *

Julia heard a knock at the door. The servants were busy elsewhere, and Hiram was at the office, so she answered the door herself.

"Telegram, ma'am. Is there a reply?"

Julia read the short note and began crying. She hadn't heard from Will for months and wondered if he was alive. Despite all her attempts, the authorities wouldn't let her visit him—and since the last commandant took charge of Douglas, she couldn't even get a confirmation as to whether he was alive or dead.

"Yes—take this down. Will, funds on their way to First National Bank in Lynchburg stop. Go to Huntington, steamboat arranged, stop. Love Julia stop."

She signed for the telegram, and the messenger hurried away.

Kirsten entered the room. "What's all the fuss?"

"It's Will! He's alive. He's coming home."

"Is that all? That no account Confederate brother of yours would have done better to die in the war. Why, he could have killed Hiram."

"And I'm just happy they both survived. My brother would have quit years ago if he could have. Now if you'll excuse me, I need to see he gets home," observed Julia with some asperity. She grabbed a bonnet and headed for the stable.

* * *

Albinia heard the news of Will's impending arrival and sank to her knees, thanking God. Then she hurried to the barn, where Sara was feeding chickens and Robert mending a harness.

"Ma! Pa! It's Will! He's coming home!"

"Praise God," said Sara. "When?"

"Probably a week or so—he's in Virginia. I don't know how he got there or why. Julia is arranging passage for him. Pa, could we make him a room, or build a little cabin or something? I want him to know he's welcome here. It won't be like coming home to Lexington, but...."

"Sure we can. I'll get Ned and some others; I'll bet they'll help."

Albinia hesitated. "Maybe. But Pa, remember, he's a Confederate, or was. Not all of our black friends are likely to be charitable toward him. Some of our white friends suffered under Morgan's raid. You know that better than anyone does. Look what almost happened with you and Will. They know you and me, but the gray uniform represents something that tried to put them in chains. They don't know Will. And after Lincoln's assassination...."

Robert shook his head. "You're right, of course. It's more just than people despising them because of the color of their skin—it's what's in a person's heart that counts. But they don't know Will. I'll hire some help from town, not tell them what it's for."

"I'll help," said Olivia, coming up behind Albinia. She and Jemima arrived from Canada the week before. "And Luther will too, if he wants to eat. Any brother of yours is family to me. I can lift logs and chop wood."

"Thank you, Olivia! Bless you!" cried Albinia, hugging her.

Luther walked in from the forge. "Miss Albinia, I remember your brother. He was always kind to me. I admit when I saw him here in that uniform, it fired somethin' in me. But I thought about it, and what you and the parson talked about—livin' at peace. My mama been on me about it somethin' fierce. Guess my sister now too," he said, grinning at Olivia. "I want to give it a try. I figger we can't change how everyone thinks. Some folks just gonna hate. But I tried that and it don't work. I still hope the slave catchers rot in hell. But Mama's workin' on me to pray for them. If she can do it, I guess I can. She say we got to love people one at a time, even those that hate us. And Ruth, she say the same."

"Thank you, Luther. That means a lot, knowing all you and your family have gone through. Let's get the wagon and go tell Peter. Maybe Ruth would want to come? I think Peter has some things to talk to you two about the wedding. It would be like old times, you driving me. I don't think we'd have trouble, but...."

"You can count on me, Miss Albinia. I'm pretty good with a revolver these days."

* * *

The roads and byways were full of Confederates trying to make their way home. Will saw many of them pass. He got Julia's telegram and stayed with the farmer for a week waiting for funds, which Julia sent by courier. When the funds arrived, he paid the farmer handsomely and bought a new suit of clothes, throwing away his uniform. He traveled by stagecoach to Staunton, and then by rail to Huntington. Once there, he had to wait two days for an Ohio Zephyr steamboat. When he boarded, the captain showed him to the most luxurious stateroom on the boat. There was feast at every meal. Will could hardly grasp the difference from Point Lookout only a month earlier.

He tried not to think about the future, just living in the moment enjoying his surroundings. From freezing and sweating, hunger and rags, guards wanting to torture or shoot him, to a soft bed with silk sheets, roast beef and pudding, and a steward who jumped at his every wish. It felt like a different world. Will learned from the steward that Ohio Zephyr extended free passage to every soldier trying to reach home regardless of uniform—though not the luxury he experienced. After three days on board, Will felt physically recovered. Mentally, scenes haunted his dreams from battle, and from the camps. He woke more than once in a cold sweat that had nothing to do with fever. He purchased a Colt revolver and a Spencer rifle from the money Julia sent, and he kept them near.

Arriving in Cincinnati, he found Julia and Hiram at the dock waiting for him. There was a throng, many looking anxiously at the boat in hopes of catching a glimpse of a loved one returning from war or prison.

"Will! Over here!" Julia shouted.

Will waved and went to hug his sister. "Thanks, Julia, for bringing me. I owe you." He looked over at Hiram—still gaunt, with a haunted look in the once friendly eyes. They shared a look of understanding, and then looked away. No words were needed.

Will stayed with Julia a few days, and then made the journey to Madison to see the rest of his family. Julia gave him a big buckskin quarter horse named Dusty, with dark legs, mane, and tail, and all of the tack needed for him. Will rode in and saw that guards still manned the gates at the farm. He gave his name and business, and they let him pass. Before he could make it to the barn, his family surrounded him, laughing and crying. Lydia ran to meet him, but seemed shy and a little reserved. Will couldn't believe how tall she was at ten.

"Look at you!" he said. "You're practically a lady!"

"Will—you look thin. And different, somehow. Are you home for good?" Lydia asked him.

"I ... I don't know, Lyddie—seems funny to call you that—you seem so grown up." He dismounted.

Sara came and hugged him a long time. "I'm so glad to have you home, Son. So glad."

Robert extended a hand that ended in a bear hug. "I'm glad we made it, Son. Can you forgive me?"

"Sir, there's nothing to forgive. I'm the one that stands in need of your forgiveness, for my bull headed pride."

"It's over, Son. It's over. Lincoln said it best—'With Malice toward none, with charity for all, with firmness in the right, as God gives us to see the right, let us strive on to finish the work we are in, to bind up the nation's wounds.' We need to bind up each other, and others. Welcome."

"Thanks, Pa."

Finally Albinia, Peter, Luther, Ruth, and Ned came over.

"We waited for you, Will," said Albinia after a hug.

"Waited?"

She beamed at Peter. "We have a double wedding—me and Peter, and Luther and Ruth. Next week. We wanted to wait for you to be home. I . . . I've never had a wedding with all my family. You will stay, won't you? Come and see!"

She led all of them over to a modest log cabin, much like the one the family used to have in Kentucky, except it had a real bed in it and three glass windows.

"It's yours, Will. We want you to know you're welcome here."

Will shook his head in disbelief. "That. . . . That's kind of you, Binia. I appreciate it. I can't say I know my plans just yet."

Luther attempted to take his horse, but Will said he'd care for him.

"I'm sorry for the way I behaved when you came through before," Luther said. "I know you never meant us harm. Miss Albinia, she's the reason we're free. I'd do anything for her."

Will smiled sadly and offered a hand, which Luther hesitated and then shook vigorously. "You're a good man, Luther. I hope you find happiness."

"Well, we want to do the ceremony with Miss Albinia and Pastor Peter—but we'll likely have to do it again next year. Pastor Peter say the government might recognize Negro marriages next year."

"Just a reason to celebrate twice," said Will, grinning.

"You right about that!" said Luther, slapping his thigh.

* * *

The day of the wedding was bright and clear. They all traveled north to Lancaster, to Peter's church. A pastor friend from Cincinnati came to marry Peter and Albinia, now Mr. and Mrs. Jenkins. Peter officiated for Luther and Ruth's marriage—no other white minister would do it.

Ruth insisted that Peter read Galatians 3:28: "There is neither Jew nor Greek, there is neither bond nor free, there is neither male nor female: for ye are all one in Christ Jesus." Jemima and Sara took one another's hands, cried together, and hugged everyone.

At the reception, Will sat apart, under a tree. After a time, Robert came looking for him.

"Anything wrong, Son?" he asked.

"What will you do with the farm in Kentucky, Pa?"

"Sell it most likely, unless you want it."

"No, you and Ma should get for it what you can."

"But what about you, Son?"

"I don't know, Pa. You asked if anything is wrong. It's me. I'm wrong. It's like I'm broken inside and I don't know how to fix it. Maybe I'll never be right again. But I know I don't fit here. I can't go back. Sometimes I wake and I'm in the middle of a battle, reaching for a gun that isn't there. Sometimes I'm back in prison, listening to the men dying."

"I know about part of that, but I can't say I know how you feel. I do know that God provides healing, in time. Keep looking to Him, Son."

"I've been thinking about that, Pa. I keep thinking about the verse that says 'I lift my eyes up to the mountains, where does my help come from?' I wish I knew the answer, Pa. The war took almost everything—it could have taken it all. I almost killed you. Ma and the girls never would have forgiven me. I could have killed Hiram that night at Ashland, though I didn't know he was there. Or Luther. I lost Jenny. And I did kill so many. How many wives, mothers, sisters and brothers are looking today for one that will never come home, who died by my hand? I don't know where my help comes from. I don't know how to heal my wounds, or the nation's wounds. I think all I can do is take a stand, to love and be a friend, to never again kill because someone orders me to. But I need some time. I'm thinking of going west, to the mountains. I want to find peace, if it exists. Somewhere it must."

* * *

The next day, everyone turned out. To Will's surprise, even some of Albinia's Negro friends from Georgetown came.

Lydia and Sara were crying. "Will, you don't have to go. There's a place for you here."

Will smiled and started to tousle Lydia's hair as he used to, then thought better of it.

"I know you don't understand. I'm not sure I do myself. But I do know I have to go. I promise to write. I'll come back if I can, someday. Will you write to me?"

"Oh, yes, Will!" she said, hugging him fiercely.

He watched as the three couples—his parents, Peter and Albinia, Luther and Ruth—stood with arms around one another. Then he mounted Dusty and pointed him west along the river. It was time to look for home.

AUTHOR'S NOTES

William Dorsey Crump is an historical person, as are the members of his family, the Clay family, and many others in the story. In the case of Robert Breckinridge and William Lloyd Garrison, I have quoted them directly from their own speeches and writings. I have relied extensively on Basil Duke's first-person account, *Morgan's Cavalry*, for much of the detail about Morgan's movements and battles, as well as insights into Morgan's thinking and character. Thanks to the National Park Service staff at Shiloh National Battlefield for their assistance in charting Morgan's movements during the battle. Many other first-person sources are cited. However, in most cases the speech of historical individuals in the story is my own invention, and not intended to reflect the character or speech of the actual persons, which is largely unknown.

Luther and his slave family, along with Jenny Morton, Hiram Johannsen, and the events and staff at Kentucky Penitentiary are my own invention, though based on accounts of others.

Luther's story is a composite of many first-person slave diaries and accounts. There is little accurate information on the treatment of slaves at Ashland, the Clay plantation, nor any extant record of a roster of their slaves. Many thanks to Eric Brooks, curator at Ashland, for his kind assistance on the plantation, the battle, and information on the Clay family.

Will had other brothers and sisters who were left out of the story. Julia and Albinia actually did none of the things in the story, but their characters are based on real women, Pauline Cushman and Delia Webster, who did carry out most of those actions.

Pvt. William D. Crump served in Co. C, 3rd (later designated the 7th) Kentucky Cavalry under Morgan. He enlisted in Central Kentucky (possibly Taylor County) on September 10, 1862. He was captured on July 19, 1863 Meigs County, Ohio, near Buffington Island. He was imprisoned at Camp Morton on July 23, 1863 where he is listed as age eighteen, 5'8" tall, light complexion, brown hair, and gray eyes. His residence is listed as Louisville and his occupation as farmer. He was transferred to Camp Douglas and arrived there on August 22, 1863. He was transferred to Pt. Lookout on March 2, 1865 and exchanged at James River, Vancouver, March 10, 1865. He appears on a list of patients at the Confederate Wayside Hospital in Farmville, VA, on March 15, 1865. Sources: *Morgan's Light Brigade by Dr. Dwight Watkins, Compiled Service Record for William D. Crump under 3rd Kentucky Cavalry.*

William D. Crump later became a judge and founder of Lubbock and Shallowater, Texas. Will's involvement in the earlier Lexington Rifles is fictional. He has no known living descendants.

His father Robert Crump was a farmer and merchant in Louisville. The real Albinia died in Cincinnati; no one knows the date. Julia, in the story, was a sister named Sara in real life—her name was changed to avoid confusion with Will's mother. Sara and Albinia moved in with Lydia in Cincinnati after the war and faded from records. Albinia married a butcher.

Ben Drake, Jesse Davis, Tom Logwood, Archie Moodie and James West were all actual members of the Lexington Rifles, and served courageously under Morgan.

For all my African American readers, please note that the scenes and descriptions of mistreatment of slaves in the book are in the interests of historical accuracy, and in no way reflect an intent to disrespect African Americans. These incidents are based on biographies, letters, and notes concerning events that actually happened in the time period, though the characters are fictional. I believe we can rejoice in how far we have come from those days, yet look forward to how much more there is to do, as the divided races and groups in our country come together to reach "Across the Great Divide".

The Civil War killed more Americans than World War II, World War 1, Vietnam War, and the Korean War combined—620,000 men. Some estimates are even higher—750,000 men. The Battle of Gettysburg alone killed more men than the Revolutionary War, War of 1812, and the Mexican War combined. In 1860, the population of the United States was 27,489,561 free and 3,953,760 slaves. Twelve-and-a-half percent of the population were slaves. Approximately one in five adult white males in the United States at the start of the war died in the war. More men died of disease than bullets. Fifty-six thousand men died in captivity, many no better off than concentration camp survivors of World War Two.

Let us strive together never to repeat it.

CPSIA information can be obtained
at www.ICGtesting.com
Printed in the USA
BVHW081841150221
600155BV00007B/26